A WOMAN'S AFFLICTIONS

CHELLE RAMSEY

OTHER WORKS BY CHELLE RAMSEY/C. MICHELLE RAMSEY

Available on Amazon.com:

@ bit.ly/ChellesAmazon

REFLECTIONS OF PROMISES

REAL SECRETS

IS THE GRASS REALLY GREENER?

BEJEWELED: THE FLIGHT OF AN ANGEL

BEJEWELED: WHAT A TANGLED WEB WE WEAVE

BEJEWELED: A BEAUTIFUL BLEND

BEJEWELED: STANDING STRONG

This eBook is a work of fiction. Names, characters, places, and situations are complete creative works of the author's imagination.

Resemblance to actual events or persons is entirely coincidental.

Copyright © 2015 Chelle Ramsey

All Rights Reserved

Cover design by: The Killion Group

Edited by: Pink Cashmere Pub Co

Any unauthorized reprint or use of this book or any portion thereof is prohibited. No part of this book may be reproduced or transmitted in any form or by any means, electronic or mechanical, including photocopying, recording, or by any information storage and retrieval system without express written permission from the author / publisher.

Contact Me:

www.chelleramsey.com

ISBN-10: 1547137487

ISBN-13: 978-1547137480

Printed in the United States of America

ACKNOWLEDGEMENTS:

All praises to Jesus Christ, my Lord and Savior, for the blessings You have bestowed upon my life. Father, thank You for the opportunity to continue to pursue my dreams to Your glory. Thank You for Your wisdom, compassion, and grace that You show me daily. May all the praise be given unto You and Your Name always be glorified.

Marvelous, you rock, babe! Thank you for diligently working with me on these projects, keeping me balanced when I struggle, and pushing me to strive for excellence all the time. Thank you for your unselfish love and tireless devotion. I am everything I am because you are you.

Corey, Bianca, and Marcus, you are my hope, my drive, my inspiration and my dreams come true. God has blessed me with three beautiful and wonderful souls to love, cherish, and protect, and I thank Him for you every day. Your dad and I are so proud of you. Continue to walk in your gifts and anointing. Mommy and Daddy love you to infinity!

To my family and friends, I am blessed to be surrounded with such beautiful people. I love you all.

Adrienne Thompson, thank you for your professionalism, critical eye, and attention to detail. I pray that God will continue to bless you.

Special thanks to my Beta Readers: Glynnis Simmons, Sharon Blount, Sherry Blum-Pretty, Tiffany Miller, and Tina Young. Your invaluable input helps keep me on my toes and taking it to another level. I always anticipate handing off another project to you ladies.

To everyone else, if I did not call your name, charge it to my head and not my heart. I love you.

DEDICATION:

Marvelous, the love of my life. You have taught me so much and molded and shaped my life on so many things: friendship, loyalty, commitment, love, sacrifice and the beauty of life itself. You've taught me the freedom that comes with not judging others and living life according to our own terms. You have helped me to pursue the journey called inner reflection, getting to know myself…not an easily-traveled road, but definitely a well-traveled one with you as my companion.

Everything that I'm not, you are…to create that synergy we need to keep our lives flowing in harmony. I may be the most hard-headed, stubborn person you've ever met. But thank you for putting up with me, never giving up on me, and always loving me through it all.

I love you beyond the highest heights and the deepest depths. You are my strength and my truth. You are the realest shit!

TABLE OF CONTENTS

1_AMBIANCE_NOTHING LIKE A FRIENDSHIP 9
2_NAOMI_MR. KNIGHT 5
3_PAIGE_USE OR BE USED 15
4_AMBIANCE_VANILLA ROSE 20
5_NAOMI_HAVANA'S COCINA 30
6_PAIGE_GETTING MY LIFE 40
7_AMBIANCE_ANOTHER LONELY NIGHT 51
8_NAOMI_MEETING JAIME 68
9_PAIGE_A RUN AWAY 78
10_AMBIANCE_LUNCH DATE 88
11_NAOMI_BONES & STIX 98
12_PAIGE_BOOTY CALL 112
13_AMBIANCE_MY HUSBAND & MY FRIEND 128
14_NAOMI_MENDING FENCES 153
15_PAIGE_JUST ONE NIGHT 162
16_AMBIANCE_MRS. CALDWELL 174
17_NAOMI_FAMILY EMERGENCY 187
18_PAIGE_POT-A-LET 198
19_AMBIANCE_MY FRIEND & HIS MISTRESS 205
20_NAOMI_BENEFIT OF THE DOUBT 216
21_PAIGE_SEX AS A WEAPON 226
22_AMBIANCE_A CUP OF COFFEE 235
23_NAOMI_HELENA ROSE 249
24_PAIGE_BREAKING NEWS 260

Denise,

Thanks for all of your support and love for my art. You are a blessing to myself & others like me as we pursue our dreams. May God continue to bless, keep & protect you.

Love,
Chelley R

A WOMAN'S DESIGN: AFFLICTIONS

"But if a wicked person turns away from the wickedness they have committed and does what is just and right, they will save their life. Because they consider all the offenses they have committed and turn away from them, that person will surely live; they will not die."

Ezekiel 18:27-28

"As we reflect on yesterday, as we glide through the gift of today, and our minds wander about the future, every moment of your life, life shows you, teaches you, and prepares you for what's to come. That's if you pay attention to who you are."

MARVIN RAMSEY, SR.

1_AMBIANCE_NOTHING LIKE A FRIENDSHIP

Married, mother of none. Diva of the fashion consulting world! Personal shopper at Vanilla Rose Boutique and owner of Bleu Diamante Fashions, guaranteed to put your style on top. One hundred seventy pounds of mocha chocolate rolled into five feet and eight inches of woman. Wife of Eric Caldwell, daughter to Alexis (my step-mom) and my father, Jerry Richardson, best friend of Naomi Blankenship and Paige Dougherty. Those were the words most people would use to describe me.

But if I were to take out a personal ad, the description would sound more like: emotional, lonely, unloved, desperate thirty-two-year-old woman seeking, no, scratch that…maybe not seeking, but craving, yeah, that was more like it, craving personal attention. Yep, that's me, Ambiance Lorraine Caldwell. And this is my story…

****

I stepped out of Naomi's car and went to the trunk to remove my bags. While waiting for our friends, Jon and Sharon, to return to the vehicle, I decided to show Naomi what I had purchased in the market earlier. It was taking Jon and Sharon a while to come back with their lunch. Naomi was sitting in her new, navy blue Mustang trying out the Pandora radio feature. She was proud of the features and the horses it sported underneath the engine.

We were parked close to a nice, charcoal sports car. Just as I tried to open the back door and swing my big behind in, I accidentally bumped Naomi's car door against the sports car. *Oops.* I looked to make sure I hadn't dented either one. Assured that I hadn't, I closed the door back and decided to get into the front seat instead. When we first arrived, Naomi had pulled in forward. The car next to us was parked in reverse. The sports car's passenger side mirror and Naomi's car door were making it complicated for me to squeeze my booty in.

Just as I prepared to slip inside the front passenger door, the driver's side door of the other car opened and a gentleman stepped out. *Uh-oh.* My heart began thudding, I knew he was coming to check the damage to his car. I was ready with attitude to check him and let him know there was nothing scratched on his precious vehicle. One day I would have a new, beautiful car to be protective over the way Naomi was about hers and the way I was sure this gentleman was about to be. Not that I shouldn't have had a newer model car to be proud of, but finances didn't allow it at the moment. But that was another story.

"Excuse me, ma'am."

"Yes?" I questioned, turning around. He was dark-skinned and appeared to be six-foot-three. He smiled a crooked, beautiful white smile at me. I looked at the patio situated just above where we were parked. There was a group of young college students sitting up there who were about to witness me getting checked. I decided to forgo the attitude I planned to toss his way and come humbly, not wanting to create a scene. I was too grown for all this attitude mess anyway, and I definitely didn't want anyone to witness my impending humiliation. I peeped down into the car, and Naomi was still consumed with her new sound system.

"I noticed you when you were standing at the back of the trunk. You're a beautiful woman, and I just wanted to see if you would be interested in exchanging names and numbers."

Huh? That wasn't what I was expecting. Was he for real? I was not looking my best today. My long, thick hair was a bit frizzy from the July heat. My waves were not popping.

"Well, I don't think so."

"Why not?"

"I'm not looking to get involved with anyone."

"We can just be friends. I really would like to get to know you. I mean, I've been sitting in my car for a moment checking you out. It was something about you that captured my attention when you were at the trunk. And no, it wasn't when you hit my car," he mentioned with a laugh, after noticing my eyes growing wide.

"Sorry about that," I mumbled in embarrassment.

"No worries. Here, just take down my number, think about it, and if you feel cool, give me a call. Just friends, nothing more. I promise."

I looked down at my phone and contemplated. Friends? Uh-uh, I couldn't do it.

"No, I don't think so. But I'm really complimented by the attention," I replied.

"Well, can you just take my business card? My name's Nick, by the way. Can I at least know yours?" he asked, handing me his card, which I promptly slipped into my pocket. I would toss it in the trash can later. I didn't want to be rude.

"I'm Ambiance."

"Hmm, Ambiance, I like that. It fits a beautiful, mocha woman such as yourself. I hope you change your mind," he said in a rich, deep bass voice. Looking into his slanted, dark-colored eyes was like looking into a pool of sin. I could tell with his one gaze what he wanted to do to me. Yes, I knew I needed to end this conversation quickly. He looked like the devil in a suit. I wasn't interested in getting involved, but I wasn't blind, either. I would be foolish if I tried to deny that I found him very attractive.

His sexy voice and fine body, and just the way he looked at me, let me know it wouldn't be nothing like a friendship. No, he definitely wanted more.

"Have a great day, beautiful," he said by way of goodbye. He touched my wrist lightly, and I felt my heart flutter. It made me think of all the things I had been desiring but could not find in my life. Any man who had the power to awaken every sensual nature of my innermost being at just the touch of my wrist was no good for me.

I waved goodbye to him and turned back to the car. Jon and Sharon chose that moment to walk up with their bags in hand. We were headed back to the office park they worked in. Jon and Sharon worked in the Imperial building with Naomi. I worked in a little boutique across the street from the office park. Because it was such a beautiful day for a luncheon, we had decided to eat at a little park near our workplace. They were chit-chatting a hundred miles a minute.

We had all shared lunch time whenever we could for the last three years. Jon and Sharon worked together at the same consulting firm. They had met Naomi when their office building had an after-hours soiree for the

Christmas holiday one year. Naomi and I? We went way back, like high school way back. And she had introduced me to the two of them.

They hopped into the car, and I took over the front seat where Jon had previously been sitting.

"Ambiance, who was that fine chocolate specimen you were talking to?" Jon asked, turning to stare out the car as it peeled out of the parking lot.

"Some guy talking about a business deal. He was giving me information from his business card about an upcoming seminar in real estate. Nothing much, nothing I'm interested in," I lied.

"Hmph, looks like he was definitely interested the way he was eyeing you and kept looking back over his shoulder after he walked off," Sharon stated.

"Whatever. Come on, Naomi. You ready to roll?"

"Yeah, girl," she stated, putting her car in reverse.

"It's cool, girl, you can keep it real with us, you know," Jon stated.

"Yeah, Ambiance. Besides, there's nothing wrong with having male friends. After all, Jon's our friend," Sharon stated.

"That's different, and y'all know it. Jon is gay, and he isn't interested in getting with any of us intimately. Sharon and Jon, you two are the devil. Don't be encouraging her to get mixed up in foolishness. Plus, Ambiance is married, and I'm sure the man isn't interested in being friends with you *and* your husband," Naomi chided, looking at me.

My stomach turned at the mention of my marriage. I had no business being attracted to him, or did I?

2_NAOMI_MR. KNIGHT

Our youth are the most important resource we have. They are the leaders of tomorrow and as such, it is our responsibility to instill love, honor, integrity and responsibility in them. Especially our young black women. Sisters, I'm keeping it real with you, we haven't actually left them a positive legacy to look up to. High fashion, stylish shoes, money out the ying yang, a nice whip to drive and a fly 'do' to sport. Not to mention a brother rolling in cash. That's what we strive for and that's the message we send to our young girls, get it while the getting is good at whatever cost. That's the true message we send when we perpetuate the myth that chasing after ball players, hip hop artists and the like is something to aspire to.

I'm not saying that there's anything wrong with dating these brothers. What I am saying is be yourself, love yourself, and be true to yourself first. It's just like that Ne-Yo song, "She Got Her Own." Go out and get your own education, your own career, your own money and your own life. Because when you work hard for what you want in this life and not depend on your body or someone else to give it to you, then you respect yourself more. And when you respect you, he respects you. And know who you are, because only then will you know what you have to offer someone else.

I guess you're probably like, 'who are you to tell me what I need to do or don't need to do.' Well I'm the CFO at Edwards Broadcasting System. Single and saved. Alpha Xy Zeta sistah and a Master of Arts graduate of Clark Atlanta. A thick, five foot four inch, cocoa sistah who's a force to be reckoned with in the boardroom. At thirty-three I have no time for games in my life. Despite what my friends say, my motto is 'All business and no play makes Naomi a very successful and determined mother.' My girlfriends, Paige and Ambiance often tell me that I have no time for nothing but my career and my teen daughter, Sasha. That may be true, but at least it keeps me from life's little games that men and women often play.

Sometimes it seemed as if they were on a personal crusade to end my almost two decade abstinent streak. But this lady was just determined to stay focused on seeing my daughter through high school and college. I am very much a present part of every day of her life and will remain that way until she is grown and gone, as the old folks used to say.

But that's not even what makes me qualified to tell you, my sisters, how you should or shouldn't live your life. But my story and life makes me qualified to give my opinion. My name is Naomi Blankenship and this is my story.

****

This was just too trifling. I didn't know what to think about today's youth. I sat parked outside Westland Lakes High School waiting on my daughter to come out. What little clothes these youth wore today could hardly be called fashion. I mean what boy in their right mind would respect these females. They had no self-respect and put everything on display. I watched female after female trying desperately to get some boy's attention. The school's parking lot was filled with them. And look at that one over there, she really needs somebody to whoop her behind. *Honey, if I was her mama, I'd embarrass her behind right here in front of everybody, trying to be grown,* I thought.

Walking out of the school with one boy's arm around her, while another one walked past and smacked her on the behind. Then she turned her head at him and laughed it off. The boy whose arm was around her, said something to the first young boy, but neither of them appeared to take her seriously or respect her. Why would they, when she was walking around in that little white skirt that just barely covered her behind? And what was wrong with the school system? Nobody seemed to enforce dress codes anymore. I would be glad when my daughter came out of the school and we could leave.

I was hoping to catch her before she got on the school bus. I had gotten off work early today and popped up at her school after making a last-minute dentist appointment for her. *Look at that fast thang*, I was thinking, just as the fast thang was passing my car heading to the school bus.

I did a double-take. *Uh-uh*, I knew that was not Sasha Kennedy Blankenship! My daughter in that too short, white mini-skirt? Where did she get something like that from? I hadn't brought it for her, and she hadn't been wearing it before she left for the school bus this morning! And why was she letting those boys disrespect her like that? I hadn't raised her like that.

I was so angry, I was literally seeing red. I had to calm down before jumping out the car and snatching my child bald. I sat there gripping the steering wheel tightly until my knuckles began hurting. I was trying to calm down before I jumped out of the car, forgot my 'ligion, and made a fool of her and myself. But then I changed my mind. I had formulated a better plan. I put the car in reverse and backed up just slightly. I pulled out from behind the car in front of me and drove around the parking lot to the exit.

Never alerting my daughter of my presence, I headed straight home. As I drove through the parking lot and down neighboring streets, I realized what the problem was. My daughter and all these other young ladies no longer had the proper role models to show them how to be a lady. I did everything in my power to teach my daughter, but she didn't respect the struggle I had to endure as a single, black mother. Instead, she watched the women on TV shaking their behinds and making millions, or the women in our neighborhood dressing like hoochies and having men almost wrecking brand new SUVs and luxury cars to stop and take a look or get their phone numbers. Never mind the fact they clearly had rings on their fingers and car seats in the back of their vehicles.

Nope, women as a whole had lowered themselves to a new level of disrespect, all in the name of women's rights and equality. Sometimes I honestly believed we'd lost our proper role and calling in the world. Going toe-to-toe with men was why so many women were single, divorced, used, and abused. Not to mention those that put themselves out there to be used. Prime example? My friend, Paige. That girl had a good man waiting to be her husband. But that child couldn't stay off her back and keep her legs closed to save her life. And the fool thought nobody knew. Everybody knew what she was up to...except the man who wanted her heart. And I prayed for him and her both to be kept by the Lord's grace when he did find out.

I pulled my brand new baby into her special place in my garage and went into the house through the garage door. After setting the alarm, I walked to my kitchen and began preparing dinner. I was so furious, I could scream. What the heck was Sasha thinking, dressing like that? I had talked to that girl until I was blue in the face, explaining what could happen to her if she put herself out in the world to be used. Why didn't she learn from my mistakes? Had I listened to my mother and father, I wouldn't have been raising Sasha alone. Had I listened to them, there would be no Sasha. But I thanked God for her and them. My parents had been very supportive.

When I learned I was pregnant at seventeen, I thought my life was over. It took a lot of prayer, screaming, and pushing for me to realize I could still have my dream of going to college.

My parents placed Sasha in daycare and paid the expense while I went to college to pursue my degree in finance. They wouldn't give up on me, and they wouldn't let me give up on myself. But I had worked too darn hard for this child to throw away all the chances I was trying to give her. I'd passed up relationship after relationship. Why? Not because I couldn't get a man. Being a very humble person, I am not being arrogant when I say this: I was and am a beautiful woman.

I quite often received compliments on my cocoa-colored skin, which I nurtured, and my dark-brown, up-turned, hooded eyes. As a child growing up, I had to learn to love and appreciate my thick, full lips that compliment a strong, down-turned nose. As a woman, I learned to enhance my lips with different shades of lip gloss to make them pop, and in my opinion they were now my best feature. My thick, black hair rested just below my collar-bone, and was rich and full of body. I was a thick sister with shapely hips and legs, voluptuous, and because I worked out, I kept my body in check with all its curves and thickness.

Men quite often tried to catch my eye, or get my number. But my beauty was what got me in trouble as a teenager in the first place. So, I didn't have time for relationships right now. I had to get this child through two more years of high school and off to college before I could worry about my love life. Right now, the only love that I had was for my daughter and her future.

So no, I was not in a relationship. I wasn't in a relationship, because Sasha had become my life. After her sperm donor of a father left the picture, I knew I had to make it in this world as a successful woman. And I would teach my daughter to become a strong independent, educated woman if it was the last thing I did.

I heard the key clicking in the lock of the front door. I looked at the clock over the microwave, which read 3:52. Good, at least she had the decency to come straight home without making any pit stops. I could hear the school bus pulling away.

She would have to come down the hallway past the living room to either get a snack from the kitchen, or go up the stairway to her bedroom. As I expected, she was heading straight in my direction. Sasha's snickering reached my ears long before she reached the kitchen. She was obviously on her cell phone. Her call would be cut short as soon as she rounded the corner and saw me perched at the island in the middle of the kitchen. I sat there with my paring knife, peeling an apple.

I couldn't wait to see the shock on her face when she saw me sitting there and she was busted cold in that white mini skirt. What I did not anticipate was the shock that would be on my face, or the pounding in my ears as blood rushed through every part of me. I sat in disbelief without uttering a single word. It felt as if I sat at that island for twenty minutes or more, but it couldn't have even been one full minute before my daughter spotted me.

Sasha stood with her back to me, as she had backed up into the kitchen. Her eyes were closed and some boy's tongue was all down my sixteen year-old's throat. His hands were making their way down her back, but before they could go any further, I cleared my own throat.

"Ahem! Had any good root canals lately, Sasha?"

They jumped apart so quick, you would've sworn they had been burnt. My daughter had inherited her father's light coloring. And she and the young man had a matching red blush creeping up their faces.

"Mom! What are you doing home?" Sasha's eyes were watering up, and I couldn't tell if it was from embarrassment or guilt.

"Question is...what is he doing here?" I said, nodding my head towards the young man. I was still the epitome of cool legs crossed, with my paring knife carving away the apple peel. I was looking at the two of them as I stopped peeling and took a bite of the apple.

Although I was cool on the outside, I was ripped on the inside. I was devastated at my daughter's actions. But even more devastating? The young man was neither of the two I had just seen her at school with.

"Um...um, we were studying. I...I...I was going to tutor him," Sasha lied, looking all around the room at anything but me.

I sat my apple down on a napkin and twirled the knife around in my hand. I couldn't believe the audacity of this heifer. Who did she think I was? Did she think I had fallen from the turnip truck?

"Mm-hmm, and what subject were you studying? Anatomy?"

"Moommm," she cried.

"What's your name?" I asked, pointing the knife at the young man.

"Anthony."

"Anthony, what?"

"Anthony Knight."

"And how old are you, Anthony?"

"Seventeen."

"Mm-hmm…how did you get to my house, Anthony?"

"I caught the bus with Sasha."

"Do you live around here?"

"No."

"No? Anthony, where exactly do you live, and how do you plan to get home?"

"I live over in Jackson, about twenty-five minutes from here. My brother was gon' come pick me up in an hour."

So they had planned for him to be gone before I got home. If he was leaving at five, that would give Sasha an hour to get herself together, before I walked through the door. Surprise, surprise, it wasn't going down that way tonight.

"Well, Anthony, your plans have changed. There won't be any studying going on between you and Sasha, and you will be leaving now."

"But—"

"There are no buts going on here, young man. Now you can either call your brother to pick you up, or I can drive you home and meet your parents."

"I'll call my brother," he said, quickly sliding his phone from his backpack.

"Sasha, come here," I said, pointing at the stool next to me. I saw the fear on her face. She had no clue what I was going to do.

Slowly, she made her way to where I sat and pulled the stool out and as far away from me as possible. Hopping up on the stool, she looked back at Anthony on the phone in the corner mumbling.

When he finished his phone call, he turned to look at us, and I waved him over, as well. He stood behind the stool on the other side of the island. As much as I wanted to go across both their heads at the moment, I couldn't. I was a strong, professional woman who implemented strategic plans to keep my company on top. I needed to allow that side of me to rule at the moment, to prove a point to my daughter. I would reserve mother for Sasha, later between just the two of us.

"Have a seat, young man. Let's cut straight to the point," I said, as I sliced an apple cleanly in half, with one slice straight to the cutting board. I never had to look up to see Anthony jump, but I knew he had. His stool shook, and he grasped the island with his hands to keep from falling. I could see everything from my peripheral, including my daughter attempting to get an attitude.

"Look, I've been where both of you are. You're sixteen, and he's seventeen. When I was your age, Anthony, I was crazy over this young man, who was also seventeen. We spent as much time together as we could. I was an honor roll student, and he was a pretty decent student. We thought we were both intelligent and had things figured out. We both were planning to go to college, but not necessarily together. We weren't kidding ourselves into thinking we would always be together, but we wanted to have fun for the moment. We had our fun on New Year's Eve. I crept—"

"Momm—"

"Shut up! You're going to hear me out," I said, pointing the knife at both of them. "Both of you will listen until his brother arrives. Anyway, I crept out while my parents were at a party and went to his house. The next thing I knew, I was pregnant with Sasha, and he was nowhere to be found. He went on to school on his basketball scholarship and forgot about me and the baby that was on the way. Because, of course, his parents felt as if I was trying to trap him, and they wanted him to live his dream. They weren't going to let this little black girl get in the way of their next Michael Jordan. Well, I didn't have to, he got in his own way. A motorcycle injury ended his career during the first year. But he never turned back and looked our way one time. I worked my ass off with the help of my parents to go to college and get my degree. It wasn't easy even with their help. But I did it, and the last sixteen years have been dedicated to raising Sasha. Now here you come along, and you plan on having 'fun' with my daughter, too. Well, Mr. Knight, that's not a part of my plans for her future. I get that you two are young, but she's not about to become a teen parent. Sasha's going to college, she's going to get an education, and she will be married before she has children, if I have anything to do with it." I twirled the knife in my fingers once again, looked at Anthony with a smile on my face, and said in an eerily calm and low voice, "And I plan to have *everything* to do with it."

I could tell he thought I was coo-coo for Cocoa Puffs. His eyes would widen whenever he would look at me. When he wasn't staring at me, he was staring at the knife. But he could no longer find it in him to look at Sasha.

"Let me ask you a few questions, Anthony...how long have you known Sasha?"

"Umm, I don't know. I've seen her around the school off and on this year. But, I guess I've known her for the last six months."

"Um-hmm...and what's her whole name?"

"Um, um, Sasha Blankenship," he said with pride as though he had accomplished something.

"What's Sasha's favorite color?"

"I don't know."

"What's she planning to do when she goes to college?"

"I don't know."

"What're her favorite foods, drinks, singer, song, hobbies, and place to go?"

"I don't know," he replied with his hands in front of him. It was almost as if he were pleading with me to stop harassing him.

"What about her sisters and brothers...what're their names?"

Now that was an easy one, because she was an only child.

"I don't know. Mannn, why you asking me all these questions?"

"Because I want to show my daughter how niggas don't care. You just want to get in her panties, get her goodies, and keep rolling. You don't know her, you don't want to know her, and you don't care about anything that matters to her. Do you know that today when she was walking to the school bus, there was some boy with his arm draped around her shoulders like she was his girl? Or, did you know another one came up and hit her on the butt?"

"Moommm," my daughter whined again. I could tell she was startled and wanted to know how I knew this information.

"What, Sasha?" I said turning to face her.

"I thought you and Kahim was through? You told me you weren't seeing him no more," Anthony said, as if he was truly upset. He leveled a stare at Sasha.

"We are. It wasn't Kahim, fool! It was Charles, and he was just fooling around."

"But I'm saying, though…who was hitting you on yo' butt and why you letting 'em?" I was amazed at this kid sitting here quizzing my daughter as though he was her man.

"The same reason that she was sneaking you in my home, knowing that's not allowed. She's having fun, the same way that's all you're doing. Anthony, you can run that game on my daughter, but I'm thirty-three, I know you're not serious about her. I know you only want one thing from her and nothing more."

"Ms. Blankenship, I really do care about—"

I held my hand up to cut off his words. "Uh-uh, save it. Your acting career won't work on me. Like I said, you have one thing on your mind and that's all. I'm cock-blocking every chance I get. So, go somewhere else and run your game. But what I will tell you is that I hope you have the sense of mind to make sure you wear protection with the next female. Because you're not ready for a child, son. Trust me on that."

"I was going to wear protection. I don't eva' not wrap it up when I be with these chicks."

I shook my head and laughed. He was so stupid, the epitome of the quintessential male teenager.

"Whachu mean you was gon' wear protection? We wasn't doing nothing, fool! I don't know what you think of me, but I'm not that girl! And what other chicks you been with, Anthony?" My daughter's ire had come alive.

At just that moment, a horn started blaring in my driveway. Anthony jumped off his stool, looking like he wanted to shout, "Hallelujah! Saved by the bell." He grabbed up his backpack from the floor and headed towards our front door.

"Anthony? You're gonna walk out and not answer my question?" My daughter had followed him down the hall with her hands spread at her sides. She was staring at him in disbelief. I stood behind her with my paring knife and apple waiting for him to show his true colors.

"Pshh…Sasha, you know how your rep is, girl. I mean, I know your moms is here, but everybody know how you roll. And don't be worried about me and no other females. It ain't like we serious or nothing, you be doing your thing, and I'm out doing mine. You ain't my girl, this ain't exclusive…it is what it is. You out to get yours, and I'm out to get mine." He shook his head and walked out the door.

Although I hated to see my daughter's feelings hurt, I was glad she got to see boys for who they truly are. Don't get me wrong, I believe there are good men out there, but notice I said men and not boys. At her age, everybody she was hanging with were mere boys.

3_PAIGE_USE OR BE USED

The men, the men, they all love me! Because I'm a beautiful and sexy honeybee! There's a whole lot of F.I.N.E packed into five-feet and two inches of a one hundred and fifteen-pound woman. With my beautiful, golden-bronze skin and slanted, almond-shaped, green eyes, let's just say I turn heads wherever I go.

Say what you want about women who are out to get theirs. I believe every woman has the right to rule her life and her body the way she wants. Hell, if you ask me, I say we better get ours before they get theirs. It's either use or be used. And I'll be the one using…yep, I'm using men up like my favorite credit card. My favorite gift from them? A roll in the sack to relieve a day's stress.

No, women, despite what men say, that doesn't make me a whore. That makes me a smart and clever negotiator, getting what I want and giving them what they want in return. In the end, nobody gets hurt, and nobody gets burnt, right? Ha-ha!!! Not if you wrap it and strap it, you won't. Or at least that's what I thought!

My name is Paige Dougherty and this is my story…

****

I had just closed the file for my last client of the day. I was tired and needed a little downtime to help me relax. Working with juvenile delinquents all day kept me on my toes and sad about the state of the world. I refused to have children. When I saw how people who couldn't afford children popped babies out at random and then abused and mistreated them, it broke my heart. Yet, worse than that were those who could afford to have kids but chose to lavish material wealth rather than love upon them. They oftentimes left the children to raise themselves or to their own devices. These kids were shouting out for love and attention. And they would use any means necessary to grab that attention: theft, burglary, fighting, prostitution, and even murder.

I pushed the phone button for my OnStar system in my Camaro. After giving the call command, I spoke the name, Rodney. I waited several seconds as the phone on the other end rang. Getting the voicemail, I hung up and selected three more names before I finally received an answer.

"Vic, what do you have planned for the night?" I asked, after receiving a response.

"I don't know…what you want me to have planned for the night?" he asked. He knew what was on the menu and what was on my mind.

"How about Facuito's at eight and a night cap at your place?" I asked.

"Sounds good. I'll pick you up at seven, okay?"

"Uh-uh, I'll drive. I'll meet you there at eight."

"Have it your way," he stated.

"I always do," I replied with a smirk on my face and then clicked the phone button on the system off.

After a night at Fasciuto's, Vic and I had made it back to his place, me following him in my car. He wasn't at the top of my list to relieve my tension for the night, but he would do. After all, he was the first to answer my call.

I hoped he didn't plan on having me stay overnight. That was the only downfall about Vic. He wanted to pretend this was some love affair. I wasn't into that. I had no time for love and romance. I was a woman out to live her life, and nothing was going to stop that.

We had barely made it into the door before I began clawing at his shirt, popping his buttons off to reveal a chiseled, ebony chest. Vic was supremely fine, but I didn't much care for hair on a man's chest, and he had his fair share of hair. The only reason I could put up with it, was because it was silky and not nappy like taco meat.

"Slow down, baby. Don't you want to have drinks or sit and talk for a while?" he asked.

"Talk about what, Vic? We talked at the restaurant."

"I know, but…it seems like you had a rough day, and I thought maybe you wanted to relax and chill for a while before getting down to business."

My mouth pressed against his to stop the flow of words. I didn't want to hear this. I just wanted him to push up inside of me and have his way. Damn, why couldn't I find Rodney tonight? That's who I truly wanted to be with. He would just give it to me like I wanted, no questions asked, and be on his way. It didn't matter if it was his place or mine, he was always accommodating to my needs.

Vic's hands squeezed my arms and held them in place as I tried to unbutton his slacks. "Baby, slow up, and let's take it easy," he whispered.

"Look, you said you were concerned about my day. This is what I need from you now, to help me get past the turbulence of my day. Please, baby, just give me what I need, and we can talk about it later. I'm sure I'll be in a better place afterwards, mentally anyway," I compromised.

"Are you sure?" he asked, looking down into my eyes. I knew I had him once he looked into my almond-shaped green eyes. He could seldom resist them.

"I promise," I lied. If it would get me relaxed and released, I would tell him whatever he needed to hear at the moment.

"I just want you to be okay. You know I care about you, baby," he said, staring into my eyes.

"Mm-hmm," I murmured, kissing him along his neck. He finally released my arms from my sides and I began fumbling with his belt buckle again. This time, he assisted me and our efforts at undressing went much faster than before.

I didn't need to make it to the bedroom or any further than where we were. But because I knew that was important to him, I grabbed his hand and pulled him in that direction. I pulled back the covers on his bed and slipped into the cool, black satin sheets underneath. We could do this his way, as long as we did it; that was all that mattered to me.

Vic hopped in beside me, and I opened the nightstand drawer on my side of the bed. I pulled out a condom for him to use and did a quick mental count. There were the same number of condoms in there from my last visit two weeks ago, minus the one we used that night and the one we were about to use now.

Vic rubbed the nape of my neck, where my hair was cut short at. I wore my black hair short in a pixie cut, with it long on the right side and shorn on the left and in the back. It was easy to manage, because I had a nice grade that allowed me to brush my hair down and simply curl the length that hung over my right eye.

He leaned into me and kissed me softly on my lips. If I were interested in a relationship and wanted to settle down with a good man, Vic would probably be the one. He was family-oriented and very attentive to my needs.

His kisses left me wanting what I had already arrived desiring. I grabbed one of his hands and placed it between my legs so he could feel the heat radiating from within to prove my desire. It wasn't long before I felt his desire press against my thigh. I reached back to the nightstand and grabbed the condom I had just set down moments earlier.

Vic stilled my hand as I attempted to open it. "Baby, don't you think it's time to settle down...maybe start a family?" he asked.

Really? Really? We're in the midst of getting busy and this dude wants to go there with me? Damn! Now I see how niggas feel when women be pressing up on them. How come we can't just satisfy our mutual needs? What's wrong with keeping it real, handling our business, and living our lives? Uh-uh, this wasn't working for me. If he didn't stop, I'd dry up like the Sahara desert. I had been dealing with kids and their horror stories all day. The last thing I wanted was to think about kids right now. I wanted to think about Midnight. That's what I called his sugar stick.

Why did I keep him around? Because he was a great listener, he honestly cared about my feelings, he was fun to be around when I wanted to just hang, and he was good in bed.

But I honestly wasn't interested in settling down with nobody. I had seen too many marriages ruined, because men thought they were supposed to run a woman's life. And the next thing you know, the man's creeping out with everything wearing a skirt. No, ma'am, that was not the life meant for me. I had watched it happen to too many women. My mother, my aunts, even some of my close girlfriends. Hell, look at Ambiance, one of my best friends. All of them sucking up to a man, waiting on him hand and foot, and being loyal till the end of time. And what do they get back in return? Extramarital affairs that result in diseases, broken hearts, divorce, and bastard children.

I wanted more out of my life, and it was my intent to get everything I could out of this life before it got the best out of me. If that required using men for their company and getting my freak on in the process because I loved sex, then so be it.

And tonight, Vic was the one on that used or be used list. I knew he cared about me, but I'd always been up front and open with him. He knew I wasn't dedicated to this, and he knew I wasn't ready for marriage and kids. What he didn't know was that I slept with other men. But, hey, what he didn't know wouldn't hurt him. Or would it?

21

4_AMBIANCE_VANILLA ROSE

I was preparing to leave for work, and Eric had not returned home yet. He had never come home the night before. The only thing I received was a phone call telling me he would be home late. He told me not to wait up for him; he and his brothers were hanging out again.

I was so tired of this treatment from my husband, the man who promised to love me for life. His actions lately were reminiscent of our first year of marriage. When he had stayed out with the boys then, I eventually found out it was a particular girl he was staying out with…Kendra.

Eric and I had gone through a lot to heal our marriage. We had fought, cried, prayed, and sought counseling to get through the devastation caused by his affair. It had taken a lot for me to learn to trust him again. And when I did, things were good for a year. Looking back now, we hadn't had a lot of great times. The first year of marriage he cheated. The second year, we were constantly at each other's throats because of the hurt and pain caused by the cheating. The third year we worked on healing and enjoyed each other the fourth year. This last year, the old habits Eric had displayed were popping up again.

Several nights he wouldn't come home, he had little patience with me, and we seldom went out on dates anymore. We were starting to argue over little things again, and he wasn't as affectionate as I needed him to be. It was lonely lying in that big bed most nights all alone. When he was there, he didn't hold me in his arms, or kiss me, or make love to me anymore.

I left him a note telling him that I would be home early this afternoon and could he please wait around for me. We needed to talk. I was running a couple of hours late for work, trying to wait for him to come home. I couldn't wait any longer. I had done all that I could do from home, but now it was time for me to go into the boutique.

I pulled out a pack of chicken from the freezer for tonight's dinner and set the alarm, preparing to leave.

Just as I opened the front door, I saw my errant husband making his way up the sidewalk to our porch. I knew when he pulled up in the driveway and saw my car it surprised him. Funny how he decided to come home *after* I was supposed to be gone to work.

"Hey, baby, you headed off to work?" Eric was reaching out to me for a hug and kiss. He was still wearing the clothes he had left for work in yesterday. I sidestepped him, not wanting to pretend I didn't smell another woman's scent on him or act as if everything was lovely, when I knew it wasn't.

"Oh, so I don't get a goodbye hug or kiss?" he asked, with his arms held out to his sides. He had a look of disbelief on his face, as though I was the one tripping.

"Eric, I don't want to play your games. I have to go to work, and I don't plan on being any later than I already am just because you can't do what you're supposed to."

"What am I supposed to do, Ambiance?" he asked, frowning at me.

"Be home to take care of, provide for, and protect your wife. Not to mention doing your husbandly duties," I informed my ignorant husband, ticking his responsibilities off on my fingers.

"I don't have a problem performing those duties. If you needed some loving, babe, all you had to do was say so," he said, approaching me again with a smile on his face.

I shook my head and walked to the driveway to hop into my mint green 2010 Toyota Camry.

"Ambi...Ambi, you're just going to leave me like that?" he asked. I couldn't believe the audacity of this man. He's the one that stays out all night, comes home the next morning, after he thought I was gone, and pretends all is well.

"Look, Eric, I can't do this right now. I need to get to work. I sat here for two extra hours waiting on you. I have to go. If you have the time, I'll be home by three. We really need to talk."

"Aight, do you, then." He waved a half-hearted goodbye, turned around, and headed into the house. I headed off to work to plaster a fake smile on my face as though all was right in my world again.

It's amazing how as women we can turn our emotions on and off. Not that they aren't still there simmering under the surface, but we can put them in check when it serves our needs. All the way to work, I had been crying over Eric's potential unfaithfulness. But as soon as I pulled into the parking lot of Vanilla Rose, the little boutique I worked at as a personal shopper during the day, I cleaned my face with a baby wipe. I kept them in my purse and glove compartment. Afterwards, I squeezed eye drops into my eyes to remove the red and reapplied my make-up.

I walked into the shop with a smile on my face and began my day at work with Angelique the owner, and Peggy, our shared assistant. Two of the part-time staff were there already when I arrived. I hustled my way through the expected pleasantries and went into my office to lose myself for a moment.

Around lunchtime, I had gone back into the shop to see if my 12:30 appointment had arrived. Angelique summoned me to her office for a moment.

"Ambiance, I've been reviewing those stats you provided and looking at some of the designs in the portfolio. I just want to make sure you're comfortable with your recommendations," Angelique stated, pushing her long black bangs from her face. She turned the folder around to face me, so that I could see what she was discussing.

I once again, reviewed the file, I had given her two weeks ago. I was certain, with all of the research I had done that my recommendations were on point.

"Angelique, I don't have any hesitations about this. The ROI on this will make it worth your initial investment. People love her designs, and they're lasting."

She pulled the business card from her drawer. "You say her name is Sonya Pierce?"

"Yes, she's fabulous with what she does. Her tie-dye poncho and jumpsuit designs are one-of-a-kind originals. If you collaborate with her, I promise you won't have to worry about your customers seeing someone else with one just like it. You can request colors and specific designs for your customers based on the feedback and sales reports," I explained.

I really wanted her to partner with Sonya, because her designs were not only original but phenomenal. I had rocked quite a few of them myself and received many compliments on them or people asking where they could purchase them. I believed it would be a great business venture for them to partner up. It would boost Vanilla Rose's sales, while getting Sonya the attention she needed to grow her own company, The Poncho Girl. She had gone into business for herself a couple of years back, selling her fashions online. But she definitely could use more attention to boost awareness of her company.

"Well, I love the fact that she designs an eclectic selection of clothing items which are novel designs. Do you think she would be open to starting with just her ponchos and then moving into offering the jumpsuits, pants, and dresses? I want to start small and see the response before I take on such a jump from my usual selections."

Angelique was always very careful with whatever she offered her clientele. But I wasn't worried, I knew they would love Sonya's pieces and be back for more. They would probably be in hot demand, so much so, that I hoped Sonya would be able to keep up. She would definitely have to consider hiring an assistant now.

"I'm sure that would be fine, Angelique. So, have you decided to look into it?" I asked, with a barely concealed eagerness in my tone.

"Actually, I've already looked into it. I was browsing her website the other day and wanted to look at it once more," she confessed. She put her glasses on and turned her computer monitor to face both of us. "What was that website again?" she asked, reaching for Sonya's business card.

It was imprinted in my mind. "It's www.theponchogirl.com." I was anxious for her to make a decision. I really loved what Sonya had to offer and wanted to support her any way that I could. I believed in her talent and often tried to convince her to create handmade jewelry, as well. I was convinced she had an eye for this type of thing. I had already sent some of my clients from my fashion consulting business, Bleu Diamante, to her.

"Yes, that's it," she stated, as she pulled the site up on her screen. She perused the monitor for a few seconds before turning to me. "I'm going to call her and set up a meeting."

Just as she picked up the phone, Nelly, one of the part-time sales associates, peeked her red head into the semi-open door. "There's a gentleman out front that says he has an appointment with you, Angelique, to purchase some items for a gift," she announced.

"Oh, I completely forgot. Mr. Jackson was coming to purchase some items for his mother's upcoming birthday. I was supposed to assist him with them, because I was unsure of your schedule of clients today, Ambiance. Do you think you can help him?" she asked, looking at me with a plea of desperation on her face.

Of course, I would if that meant her calling Sonya and connecting with her. "Sure, no problem. Let me know how it goes," I stated, smiling at her.

"Of course, darling," she replied, smiling back at me. Angelique had known me long enough to realize this was close to my heart, and really mattered to me.

I stood and straightened my gold lamè off-the-shoulder, sweater dress over my hips and marched out of her office. Hopefully, this wouldn't take up too much of my time. I was anxious to get back to Angelique and hear the results of the phone call.

Speed-walking in my black stilettos with four-inch gold heels, I almost tripped and fell flat on my face when I came to an abrupt stop. This could not be happening to me. My heart was thudding in my chest. What were the chances of running into this man twice in a couple weeks? He must have worked in the area. It was amazing how I had only met him once before but recognized him from the back as if I had known him forever.

"Here she is now," Nelly stated, pointing over his shoulder in my direction. I tried to get the look of shock off my face before he turned around to face me. At six-four he towered over little Nelly, who was only five-one. He would have towered over my actual height of five-four had it not been for my stilettos. I crossed my arms over my ample breasts that were trying to peek out, since it appeared that was where his eyes were drawn to. That simple gesture made him look back up at me and lick his lips like the cat who swallowed the canary. The look in his eyes sent my mind to twirling again. This was not good. Why was this stranger having this effect on me?

"Ambiance, this is Mr. Jackson. He has a 1:00 P.M. appointment to purchase some gift items. Mr. Jackson, this is Ambiance Caldwell, Vanilla

Rose's personal shopper. She will assist you with ideas, selections, and purchases," Nelly introduced.

Nick, as he had introduced himself upon our initial meeting, walked up to me and stretched out his hand. I couldn't believe he was acting like he didn't know me. I stretched my hand out, prepared to shake his, when he pulled it up to his lips and kissed it. I swear if the butterflies in my stomach were real, they would have come straight out my tummy and up through my mouth.

"Ms. Caldwell, it's a pleasure running into you again," he said, acknowledging our previous meeting after all. Nelly walked away to help another shopper who had just entered the store.

"What are you doing here?" I asked in astonishment, trying to hide the fact that I had become nervous.

"It's my mother's birthday next weekend, and she is a clothes horse. She likes unique items, and I've heard great things about this place. So I came to see what I could find. I had no idea it would be you," he said, bestowing a smile filled with pleasure on me.

I wasn't even sure why I found him so attractive. He wasn't my usual type. The kind of guys I had always been attracted to before marriage looked like my husband. The five-foot, ten-inch to six-foot, one-inch average height male, brown-skinned, low-cut hair, and slender built GQ-type guys. Nick at six-foot, four-inches was taller than my husband, who was six-foot, one-inch. His broad shoulders and chest gave the impression that he may have played football at one time. His skin was the color of cool, brown sugar. His full, thick lips seemed to always sport a half-smile over beautiful white teeth.

I could tell by the way he wore his beard and mustache, that grooming was very important to him. The edges were razor sharp, and the hairs gleamed. Nick's almond-shaped, slanted eyes held an element of mystery to them. He seemed as if he would be extremely fun and considerate, yet there was something dangerous lurking in those chocolate brown eyes. However, the greatest difference between him and other men I had been attracted to was Nick wore his hair in long dreads to the middle of his back. I never liked men with long hair and definitely not locs. But there was something exquisite about the way his fell down his shoulders. He wore them loose that day in the shop, unlike when I met him the first time and they were braided in cornrows.

"Come, follow me, and we can get started on what it is that you need." I gestured to my office towards the rear of the shop.

I felt like his eyes were glued to my every movement as I walked down the hallway. It took everything in me not to twist my hips, which had a mind of their own at the moment and were working themselves like they were on a runway. I mean, honestly, men think we do everything for their benefit or to manipulate, but this isn't always the case. How was a woman with thick, natural curves, wearing four-inch stilettos supposed to walk?

I opened my office door and gestured to a chair in front of my desk. "Have a seat."

As he folded his frame into the chair, I went to a side table and pulled a couple of books and catalogues for us to peruse. I used the time to try to calm my nerves and my stampeding heart.

"Okay, to help me get an idea of your mother's taste, we will look through these catalogues for different styles. And these books here," I stated, patting two large crème-colored albums, "are filled with patterns and swatches of fabric. You can actually touch them to see how they feel against the skin and determine what you think she might like."

I looked up and he was staring at me with that look again and doing those things with his lips. "Mr. Jackson, did you hear me?"

"Sure, you stated that we would look through these books and those catalogues to get an impression of my mother's style. Why? Did you think I wasn't paying attention?" he asked, with a hint of a smile in his eyes.

"Umm…well, no, it didn't seem that way." Why was I so nervous around this man? I felt like some little silly school girl with a crush. This was ridiculous.

"What would make you think that I wasn't paying attention?" he queried.

I fell right into the trap. "Because you keep looking at me the way that you do and doing that thing with your lips."

He threw his head back in laughter. "Does that bother you, Ambiance?"

"It's Ms. Caldwell, Mr. Jackson."

"Oh, so we're no longer on a first name basis?" he teased.

But I was uncomfortable, so despite his efforts to lighten the moment, I was tense. "No, we're not. This is my place of work, and we are here to do business on a professional level. If I were to visit your place of business, I'm sure you would expect the same level of professionalism from me."

"But we'll never know until you come to visit me. Will we, Ambiance?"

I held my head down for a moment and clasped my hands in my lap. "Mr. Jackson, would you prefer to wait on Ms. Angelique to assist you?"

"Do I make you uncomfortable, Ambiance?" It was like he wouldn't quit digging into me. And for some reason, I felt my control slipping. Yes, this was very uncomfortable, but I wasn't about to let him know that.

"Give me just a moment, I'll see if she's available." I lifted the office phone from my desk.

He laid a hand gently on mine, and there went those wonderful butterflies again. "No need," he said, with a more serious look in his eyes than I'd seen since meeting him.

"Okay, shall we proceed?" I asked, touching the books lying on the desk between the two of us.

He nodded his head, giving me permission to proceed. We spent the next hour going over catalogues and fabrics before he was ready to order.

After writing up his slip an idea popped into my head. I pulled out my personal laptop. This wasn't something that I usually did, but I felt a strong urge to share the site with him.

For the second time that day, I visited www.theponchogirl.com and turned the screen his way. "This is something else that you may want to look into for your mother. I noticed she enjoys punches of bold color and unique patterns and designs from your comments and the pictures you shared with me of her. The Poncho Girl is a site that creates unique ponchos, not your typical rain ponchos, but big blousy fashions for women. See, she can wear them as a shirt, blouse, a shirt dress, and she even offers jumpsuits and dresses," I said, scrolling excitedly down the website.

We looked at a variety of designs from pinks, oranges, russets, greens, blues and so much more. All of the patterns had other colors splashed throughout, but some of the designs blended colors to create an entirely new color. He was completely taken with the designs available. We discussed how he could purchase some of those as well.

From the pictures he had shared with me earlier during our meeting, I noted that, she was a beautiful and fashionable woman. He told me that his father had passed away when he was only two, and his mother had raised him alone. When he spoke of her, I could see the love and fondness he had for her reflected in his eyes.

Our meeting was over all too soon as I looked at the clock and noticed it was a few minutes after two. I had promised Eric I would be home by three. I wrapped the meeting up and walked him to the front to pay for his purchases ordered from the catalogue and some directly from the boutique. He stopped me by placing a hand on my wrist. "Ambiance, it appears as if I came right at lunch time. I know you couldn't have had a chance to eat yet. Would you like to have lunch with me?" His chocolate brown eyes sparkled with intensity.

"Actually, that wouldn't be a good idea."

"Are you still making a stance on not wanting to become involved?" He spoke in a low tone to ensure others wouldn't overhear him.

"Yes, and because now that you're a client, it would be a conflict of interest."

"Hmph, the irony. Okay, what if I canceled my order?" he asked.

"No!" I stated a little too loudly. Some of the patrons in the boutique, including Nelly, turned to look our way. "No," I said a little softer.

He laughed and shook his head. "I was only teasing you. I wouldn't do that. But it would be nice if you would consider it afterwards. I mean, it's not like I would frequent this shop. I only came here because it was recommended, and I wanted to get my mom some different clothing items."

"As I stated before, Mr. Jackson, that wouldn't be a good idea."

"Okay, I see. We're back to the formalities again. Well, thank you for your time, Ms. Caldwell, and you have a beautiful day." He walked ahead to the line where another part-time clerk waited to serve him.

"Ramona, can you please ring Mr. Jackson's items up? Most of his purchases were ordered via catalogue and will be delivered within three to five business days. The other purchases are already boxed up on the shelf over there and ready to go," I said, pointing to a shelf behind the counter.

"Sure," she replied, as I placed his purchase order slip on the counter in front of her. I swiftly turned and headed back to my office to get my emotions under control.

For some reason, when he dismissed me and accepted my excuse that I couldn't have lunch with him, it bothered me. I wasn't sure why. I needed a moment to be alone with my feelings to analyze what I was going through. But I didn't have much time, I needed to head home and meet up with Eric. I had forgotten all about Angelique's call to Sonya and wanting to see how that turned out. There were other things on my mind.

5_NAOMI_HAVANA'S COCINA

For the last week, I had been working shorter hours at the office. Most days I spent ten to twelve hours in the office. But ever since I had come home to find my daughter sneaking some boy into the house, I had changed my hours. The company was still getting as much of my attention and time as it had before, but now I did a lot of work from home, too.

Sasha was no longer allowed to ride the bus to or from school, and she didn't have one moment during her day that wasn't supervised. I had met with the principal and shared my concerns with her about the image my daughter was projecting at school. Because her grades weren't suffering, I hadn't received any phone calls as they didn't deem it necessary. The principal hadn't heard rumors about my daughter being promiscuous but shared that she had seen Sasha hanging around with several different boys. Principal Cheryl Jacobs also stated that she seemed to be a bit "friendly" with several of them but she had heard of nothing, so she left it alone.

After disclosing everything I knew in that meeting along with my concerns, Sasha was now being escorted to and from all of her classes by a pre-designated teacher or monitor. I dropped her off at school every morning at 8:05, just as the ten-minute warning bell rang, and I was there to pick her up every afternoon. Then I worked from home the rest of the evening until it was time for her and me to spend quality time. She no longer had access to her tablet, cell phone, or computer. I deleted all of her social media accounts.

Yes, she was furious with me. But I couldn't care less. I had a reputation and coochie to protect. I wasn't on her attitude.

I was sitting in the office park having lunch with Ambiance. Sharon and Jon couldn't get away that day, so it was just the two of us.

"Girl, I'm surprised you didn't snatch her bald with your mean self," Ambiance stated, before taking a bite of her chicken salad sandwich.

"Child, please, I wanted to. But the entire time I sat there, I swear God was speaking to me. All I could do was recall what I took my parents through and how they must have felt. A part of me felt as if to physically hurt her would just be me being a hypocrite. My parents didn't handle me that way. And I got pregnant. At least she hasn't gotten pregnant."

"I can't believe you said she's getting a reputation already. Naomi, I think that little boy was lying. I think maybe he was embarrassed because of how you handled him, and that was a parting shot on his way out the door. Maybe he didn't want Sasha to go back to school and tell them how his big bad butt was punked out by her mom." Ambiance said the last with a giggle.

"I thought of that, too, but I know it was more than that. I told you how I found her at school dressed in something different than what I had purchased. Not to mention she had one boy draped all over her, another smacking her behind, and a third she actually had the nerve to bring home." I picked over my cranberry tuna salad. I had lost my appetite just thinking about what my daughter had done. I was so disappointed; it almost felt as if I had failed as a mother.

"Mmm, maybe. Have you taken her to get birth control? You know you won't always be able to keep those legs on lock. I mean, seriously, I know you're a mom and all but think back to us when we were teenagers. We were both fast. When we could, we would skip out on Bible study and sneak off with them knot-headed boys. Then we'd sneak right back into the church like ain't nothing happened," Ambiance confessed.

"But, girl, we weren't gone the whole time. Sure, we snuck out, but we weren't doing nothing more than kissing and hugging. Not that our fast behinds should've been doing anything," I admitted.

"Yeah, that's all we were doing, but that's not all our girl was doing." I laughed, thinking back on old times.

"Yeah, that Paige is something else. We always knew she would be a hot number."

"I know, I just wish she would be careful. She scares me sometimes. Especially how she plays around with Vic. You can hurt a man something terrible, and when his heart breaks, he's liable to lose his mind. I find myself praying for those two all the time," I shared.

"Mm-hmm. Me, too. But we have to let her make her choices, Naomi. And that's the same thing I'm saying about Sasha. She's a teenager, about to be a senior next year. It's natural that she's going to want to explore these feelings she's experiencing. And if you don't talk to her about them, she can't help but learn out there in the streets," Ambiance lectured.

"Who says I don't have those talks with my daughter?" I quizzed, frowning at her for judging me.

"Girl, chill," she said, patting my hand, "I know you. Your stick-up-the-butt, straight-edged self ain't shared nothing with that girl. You might need to let her spend a weekend with her aunts Ambi and Paige," Ambiance teased.

"No, ma'am! She'll be a whining whore by the time she comes back." It was my turn to tease Ambiance back.

"Excuse me?" She began to choke on her food and grabbed her water and sipped it.

"You heard me. You're always whining about how Eric doesn't have time for you. And we both know Paige is a pot-a-let."

Ambiance fell out laughing. "Naomi, don't you dare let her hear you call her that."

"Well, if it lays on its back like a duck and it spreads its legs like a duck then it must be a…"

"Pot-a-let!" Ambiance roared with laughter, finishing my sentence.

"Alls I'm saying is, it scares me when I look at my daughter and she's turning into Paige. I worked so hard to raise her the right way," I shared.

"I know you did, Naomi. But you have to think about it. She sees her Aunt Paige living a life of fun and luxury. I mean, it was easy to shelter her from Paige's ways when she was a little girl. But these days, we often run into her out in public, and she's with a different man every time. So when you're out with Sasha and this is what she sees, she can't help but want to be like her. She's always been glorified in Sasha's eyes. She dresses nice, has a nice car and home, professional career, she travels, and she's beautiful. But above all, you raised Sasha to respect both me and Paige. So, if you teach her to respect Paige, then that comes with everything Paige represents. You've never taken the time to talk to Sasha and clarify that some of Paige's behaviors are wrong."

I continued to chew on my tuna salad and mulled over what she said. My best friend was right. I had never distinguished between my other best friend, Paige's, behaviors, which were wrong and the ones I attempted to teach my daughter to exemplify. I had assumed she would know better. To me, it was obvious that what Paige was doing was wrong. And I thought, not for the first time, how that was why God intended for children to have two parents. We couldn't always account for every area that needed to be covered. And when one parent missed something, the other parent could catch it. But it wasn't something I chose to do…her father was never there.

I was tired and wanted to lay down for the evening. But Sasha wasn't having it. Despite being on punishment, she was bored and wanted to be entertained.

"Mooommm, pulleezz? It's Friday night," Sasha begged.

"I don't care if it's Sunday morning. You're on punishment, and you're sticking to it."

"But Mom, we still have to eat. Dang! You act like I'm asking to go out with my friends. I'm talking about me and you, Mom. We can't even go out to dinner? You're just being mean!" My recalcitrant sixteen-year-old daughter stomped up the steps.

She was the only one in this world who had the power to get me as furious as she could. I shook my head, sensing so much of my headstrong ways in her. But that was where the similarities ended. She looked just like her deadbeat father, Jaime. They had the same upturned nose and smooth, beautiful, honey-colored skin. She was tall and slim like him, too. She had already reached five feet and eleven inches, which was no surprise to me. Jaime was six feet, six inches tall. However, looking into her round, grey eyes was always like looking at him. And I couldn't help but to think about him every time I got mad at her. As a teen, besides my parents, he had been the only one who could get me so furious.

I couldn't help but wonder if maybe I had been punishing my daughter for the sins of her father. I would push her away when I got angry and wouldn't want to deal with her or even be near her sometimes. Thinking back on my conversation with Ambiance earlier, I also realized it was time to have a serious discussion with my daughter, especially where by best friend, Paige, was concerned.

"Sasha!" I called to the top of the stairs from the kitchen. I heard a muffled reply. "Sasha!" I screamed again.

She came to the top of the steps with her arms folded and her lips pouting. "Go ahead, and get dressed. We're going to Havana's Cocina," I announced.

Her face lit up like a kid on Christmas day. Havana's Cocina was her favorite Cuban restaurant. We didn't go often, because it was about forty minutes from the house. So, it was a treat whenever we did. I knew she wanted to know what was up, but she wouldn't ask me. She would be too worried I would change my mind.

I loved the atmosphere at Havana's Cocina, especially the outdoor patio where most people chose to eat. Brown and gold marble tables sat a few feet apart with a comfortable wicker couch on one side, and flanked on the other side by two wicker chairs. Comfortable weather-proof custard, green, or tan cushions sat in each. Metal lanterns hung from swaying palm trees overhead, with a lantern placed in the middle of each table. A fire pit sat in the middle of the large, outdoor patio. There were two exits that led from the patio to the actual restaurant. Both entrances to the restaurant showcased matching waterfalls. Spanish ivy crawled along the cream stucco outer wall of the building.

The energetic Son music poured outdoors from the live band playing inside. Sasha loved the twangy sound of the Spanish guitar, while I was partial to the percussions pounding out African rhythms.

We made our way to our table as we followed our hostess. Without having to look, we knew we were attracting numerous stares. It wasn't unusual. Although my daughter and I didn't look anything alike, people often stared when they saw the two of us together. She may not have had the dark beauty with strong African American features I had, but she had an exotic beauty of her own, stemming from her Latino father.

After being escorted to our table, she looked around and finally ventured to ask the question she wanted an answer to. "So, Mom, why are we here tonight?" she asked in her rich, husky voice.

"I just thought that maybe we needed some bonding time. I mean, I know that you're on punishment, but you were right, that doesn't mean we can't still spend some time together. I had a moment to think about what you said, and I agreed with you."

"But why Havana's?" she asked. She knew something was up.

"I want this to be a new relationship between the two of us. Today is the start of something new. You're going to be a young adult soon. And I've done everything possible to raise you the right way. But so often, I have fussed at you and told you what not to do, rather than what you should do. You'll be leaving home in a couple of years, and I want these last two to be beautiful. I'm going to miss you, Sashaberry," I shared, calling her by her nickname.

"Aww, Mom, I'll miss you, too." She smiled that dazzling smile my way. She swayed to the beat of the pulsating, soulful rhythms. The atmosphere made me want to get up and dance, as well, but now was not the time.

"I want us to form a relationship where you feel comfortable talking to me about anything and asking any questions. I don't want you to feel like you have to go to your friends or complete strangers to find out what you want to know. And unfortunately, I've been pushing you in that direction the last several years."

"Mom, talk to you about what?" she asked, raising an eyebrow. Her once loose, shaking body suddenly went still as if the music had stopped. She was on full teen alert.

"Anything, honey. Books, school, college, your changing body…boys." I didn't have to fend off defensive comments, because the waiter chose that moment to pop up. He took our orders and politely disappeared.

"So, Mom, what's this new relationship you're trying to create?" she asked, folding her hands beneath her chin.

I thought I had escaped. Not quite. I had some 'splaining' to do to my sixteen-year-old. "Honey, I am honestly worried about what's going on with you." I decided to be truthful.

"What's going on with me?"

"Your reputation. I'm worried about—"

"Mom, are you talking about what Anthony said?" she asked, putting her hands on the table.

"Yes. That's exactly what I'm referring to. Not to mention that I saw two other boys all over you on that same day." I had to struggle to keep my emotions under control. I felt myself getting angry at my daughter all over again. I wasn't trying to be her friend, but I wanted to develop a close relationship where she could talk about anything with me and trust me. We wouldn't get there if I kept blowing up. I realized through the years my daughter had a certain fear of me. That was good, but she also needed to know she could trust me. And I wasn't sure she felt that way.

She sat shaking her head and turning two different shades of red. "Mom, that's so unfair. Anthony lied on me. I told you he did that to get back at me. He was upset about getting busted. I don't have a reputation at school."

"What about Principal Jacobs? She seems to think you're quite often 'friendly' with the boys around school." I shared the principal's disclosure with Sasha, because she needed to know how people viewed her.

"Mom, she's wrong. I have lots of male friends. But that's all they are. I don't get along with females too much, because some of them are jealous of me and downright mean. Other girls don't have the same interests I have. I mean, I have a couple of girlfriends at school that I kick it with from time to time, but not so much. Guys are cool, they don't judge you, and I can talk to them about anything."

"Guys are quite often trying to get to one thing, Sasha. They'll tell you whatever you need to hear or want to hear to get you to drop your panties. I'm not saying there aren't good ones out there, because I truly believe there are. But, at your age, guys aren't thinking about settling down or being serious. They're out to satisfy the desires of their flesh. And truthfully, I'm not mad at them, because they're still young. They have so much to learn and go through before they're sure that's what they want to do. And truthfully, females play a lot of games of manipulation and control. These young boys aren't trying to get tied down with that. I don't want them using my beautiful, intelligent daughter to fulfill their desires."

"Mom, you think I'm stupid? I don't allow anyone to use me. If I were to find myself in a situation, I would know how to handle myself. They can't tell me anything and I just believe it. Yes, I like some of the guys I've met, but it's nothing more serious than going out on dates, kicking it, and that's it. Sometimes it gets a little physical, but I know how to take care of myself Mom."

"What do you mean, get a little physical, and how do you take care of yourself?"

"Mommm, really? Are we really having this conversation?" Sasha asked, looking around to make sure no one could overhear us.

"Well, if I have to learn to trust you again, you have to learn to trust me. You've definitely betrayed my trust, Sasha. This is about you taking on self-responsibility, and you won't make me feel guilty about it. I love you, and it's my job to protect and guide you. And I will do it with every breath in my body."

The band had switched to another, more engaging number. The guitar player and trumpeter had come from the stage and began dancing around the restaurant and out through the patio doors. Many of the patrons had left their seats and followed the musicians. Their bodies swayed to and fro, while others engaged in more frenetic movements, keeping up with the beat of the music. I loved this place but thought maybe it hadn't been the best choice for the conversation I wanted to have. We needed a quieter place with more solitude. There was too much going on around us for either of us to stay focused on the conversation at hand.

The waiter popped up and served our food. Sasha had ordered Enchilado de Camarones. The big shrimp in the Creole sauce was releasing mouthwatering scents. They sat on a bed of white rice with onions and peppers. A steaming serving of plantains was placed next to her plate. Then he sat my Palomilla in front of me. The top sirloin was pounded to perfection, the way I loved it. I inhaled the scent of the lime garlic sauce with sautéed onions and began salivating. I loved Havana's food. I also had a side of plantains with my dish, but I had ordered the house special of Frijoles Negros. There was nothing in the world like Havana's black bean soup.

We dug into our food after saying our grace. Food was a common denominator among most people, which induced a peaceful atmosphere. And my daughter and I were both enjoying one now. But that peace only lasted so long.

As we finished our meal, I heard a distantly familiar voice behind me. I hadn't heard that voice in a while and thought maybe I was mistaken. Something told me not to turn around in my seat, but I ignored that natural instinct and turned.

My heart dropped to the pit of my stomach as I watched a very familiar face making its way in our direction. When he passed our table, I felt a sense of relief wash over me. But it lasted only for a moment. I set my napkin on the table and looked up at my daughter.

"Mom, are you okay? You look like you just saw a ghost."

"I'm fine, Sashaberry. I'm not feeling so well. I don't know if it was something I ate or what. Come on, I'm ready to leave."

"Just like that, Mom? What about dessert? We always have dessert."

"Not tonight, Sasha. Come on, let's leave."

"But Mom, you haven't even paid your bill, yet. Can we at least order it to go?" she pleaded.

"Sure," I replied. "Look, I'm really not feeling well. Baby, let's just pay it at the bar and order your dessert from there."

"Okay, Mom," she stated. "But you sure are acting strange."

We left our table and headed to the bar. I paid for our food after ordering the dessert. It seemed as if that dessert couldn't get there soon enough. It arrived ten minutes later, and I was relieved we could finally leave.

"Come on, baby, let's go. I just need to lie down for a while. I'm sure once we're home and I get some rest, I'll feel better."

"I hope so," Sasha replied. "What came over you anyway?"

"Oh, nothing, baby. I think just the taking you back and forth to school and the altered schedule is taking its toll on my body."

"Do you want me to drive home?" Sasha had had her license for six months. I quite often allowed her to drive for small errands in our community or drive to her friends' homes. But I wasn't about to let her drive that far at night in my baby. It didn't matter if I would be sitting in the passenger seat.

We had discussed getting her a little vehicle, because I wasn't comfortable with allowing her to drive my baby. I had recently purchased that Mustang as a rare gift for myself. But I knew with all the hard work I put in, I deserved something special. So on my thirty-third birthday, I had gone out and paid cash for her. No car notes, no strings attached.

"Uh-uh I'll be just fine, baby. I can make the drive, come on."

I headed towards the door as we passed the restrooms, and my heart stopped once again. "Naomi." My heart plummeted to the floor. That smooth smile carved that honey-colored face into a familiar grin. And those smoke-grey eyes shined brightly at me. I had been looking at that smile and those grey eyes for the last sixteen years. And now they were back in the flesh to haunt me.

"How've you been?" Jaime asked.

6_PAIGE_GETTING MY LIFE

"Mommy, I've told you that I don't like you driving anywhere. How come you can't just wait for me to get over here?" I was furious. I had called my mother and told her that I was on my way over after work. I guess I didn't get there fast enough, because she drove herself to the store. Problem? She didn't make it back to her house before I did. I was waiting in the driveway when she pulled up.

My mom, Helena Yvonne Dougherty, wasn't supposed to be driving anywhere. She was an alcoholic, and the last thing that she needed was a DUI.

"Look, girl, I'm grown. I do what the hell I wanna do. I don't owe you no explanation, and that's what the hell I gotta car for. If I need to go somewhere, I go. What I look like waiting on you when I have a vehicle that's working just fine sitting in my drive?" my mom replied, rolling her eyes at me and then sucking her teeth.

She was a little woman, but she was so feisty. That feistiness had come from her having to deal with my father and his abuse all those years. Instead of moving on, she had become stuck in the past somewhat. Never becoming involved in another relationship, alcohol had become her method of dealing with her hurt and pain. She simply shut the world out.

"You look like my mother, who's playing it safe, that's what you look like. I don't have time to be bailing you out of jail, nor the funds," I declared.

"Well, hell, if I did get locked up, you can bail me out, and I'd just pay your ass back when I get out," she retorted.

"But why even play that game, Mommy? I have no problem taking you where you want to go," I stated.

"I know you don't. But instead of babysitting me, you need to get out and get a life of your own. It's time to start planning a family. You're not getting any younger. You'll be thirty-three this year, and honey them eggs are getting older. I don' told you, I ain't gon' be babysitting no retarded grandchild," she said, screwing her face up at me.

"Mommy! That's mean. Why would you say something like that?" I asked. I was going through her refrigerator, counting her beers. It didn't matter, because I knew she had so many hidden throughout the house that I could never account for.

"Because it's true. You sitting up over here worried about me driving instead of getting a man and some babies. I ain't going nowhere but around the corner. It's not like I'm driving to the other side of town. Hell, ain't shit gon' happen to me around the damn corner. You need to get a life and quit popping up at my house all the damn time anyway," she fussed, taking another sip of beer.

"If I didn't, Mommy, who would check on you?" I asked, firmly shutting the cabinet doors underneath the sink. I had completed my exploration of her kitchen.

"For all you know, I might have a man." She stood up and joined me in her kitchen, pulling a container with leftovers from her refrigerator.

"But you don't, and why would you?" I folded my arms across my chest, waiting to see what smart remark she would have next.

"You don't know what the hell I got! And what you mean, why would I? I need to get my chimney swept just like the next woman. I need some good lovin' between these legs just like you do," she commented.

Eeww! Now that was just disgusting as hell. Why'd she have to go and say something like that?

"I'm not out here getting anything done, Mommy. I'm career-oriented. I don't have time for foolishness from no man," I argued.

"Is that why you sleeping with all those different men, including the married one? Girl, yo' ass betta be careful. You always worried about me; your life in more danger than mine. Something gon' catch up to you if you keep doing wrong. Paige, you mark my words, one day one of these diseases is gonna get you in the ass, somebody's woman's gonna catch up to you, or some crazy ass man gon' take you outta here," she predicted.

She straightened up from where she had been pulling a pot from underneath the counter to warm her food in. I don't know why she just didn't use the microwave I had purchased her. My mother began laughing at the expression on my face. I hated when she called herself warning me about my future because of my lifestyle choices.

"Look, I'm careful with what I do and with whom I do it. My life isn't as wild as you make it out to be. I think that you just do that, because you're bored and it makes for interesting conversation with Aunt Laura. You two need to stay off the phone gossiping and find something productive to do with your lives," I reprimanded.

"Mm-hmm, like laying on our backs and spreading our legs for random men, because we couldn't face our life challenges?" she said, turning her back on me to place her food in the pot.

"Why do you have to be so mean? You make me out to be some whore, and that's not what I am. I just decided I'll use men before they use me. I won't go through the hurt and pain you and Aunt Laura suffered. I'm just saying, there's some things for you older ladies to get into that will keep you out of trouble. Discussing your fallacious tales about my life isn't one of them. Get it together, Mommy."

"No, Paige Antoinette Dougherty, you need to get it together before something happens to your little hot-tailed ass," she warned.

I was beyond pissed and wanted to tell her about herself. But I got tired of arguing with her all the time. "Mommy, we need to get you into some rehabilitation center. You've got to start dealing with your drinking. It's getting out of control the older you get. Do you know your speech is slurred during the middle of the day?" I asked in disgust.

"You've got to start dealing with your freak bone. Do you know a man doesn't respect a whore in the morning?" she asked, as she placed her glass cup on the countertop a little hard after taking a swig of her favorite malt liquor.

I was done. I couldn't talk to this woman. I hadn't come over here to discuss my personal life. If she hadn't been so damn difficult while I was growing up and set such a horrible example of how to deal with relationships, I wouldn't be in the situations I found myself in most of the time anyway.

"Mommy, have a great evening. I'm leaving," I said, stomping out of the kitchen as I did when I was two. I picked up my purse, cell phone, and keys from her living room table and made my way to the door.

As I opened the front door, I heard her call out to me. "Paige!"

"Yes, Mommy?" I called out through clenched teeth as my nails dug into my palms.

"I'll be calling you next time I need a ride around the corner to the store," she yelled, then fell into fits of laughter at me.

I pulled out of the driveway as fast as I could, tires screeching and rubber burning. I was so furious, and there was only one person in the whole entire world who could get me like this…my mother.

What had she done this time? Absolutely nothing. I mean, don't get me wrong, I loved my mother with everything in me, but I couldn't take her drinking. As an only child, it was difficult for me to deal with her sometimes, because I had no one to vent to about it after being around her. I hated the way her words slurred, I hated the way she started drinking early in the morning, and I hated how no matter how much help I tried to get for her, she lied about it. And I hated how she talked to me and down at me.

It was embarrassing. I couldn't and wouldn't take her anywhere. I didn't want anyone judging us. And the worst part was that she made me so mad knowing she was sneaking around driving within her community. I often worried about her getting a DUI, but what could I do about it? If I approached her about it, we fought and argued to no end. We exchanged heated words that we couldn't take back and both of our hearts were ripped apart more and more. The worst part was that I was so afraid she would be taken from me. I couldn't live in this world without my mother. I often prayed that she didn't get locked up for a DUI or kill someone or be killed, herself. Another fear that I had was that she was going to drink herself to an early grave. But these fears I kept locked inside. I could share them with no one.

I understood her drinking stemmed from her relationship with my father and the hurt and pain she endured with him. Not to mention the hurt she experienced watching her own father abuse her mother. She never dealt with her problems, she drowned them in her drinking and made excuses for it.

OnStar began to alert me that I had an incoming call. It was David, and he was pretty cool, so I decided to answer it.

"Hey, babe, what's up with you?" he asked, in that silky smooth voice.

"Nothing much, headed home." I was being blunt and to the point. I was still infuriated with my mom, but I was quickly shedding my frustrations.

"Want company?" he asked.

"Sounds good."

"Paige, what's going on with you, baby girl? You sound a bit tense. Everything cool?" David was one of the people that I could talk to when I was stressed. He didn't pry if I didn't want him to, and he listened when I needed a friend. But above all, he knew my body like no one else. He could make me sing, sending me from soprano to alto to tenor in one stroke. He was just that damned good.

"Just leaving my mom's, that's all."

"Everything all right with her?"

"Yeah, she's fine. We just had a bit of a disagreement," I shared.

"Okay, well, I tell you what. I'll stop by and pick up something to eat, and if you still feel like discussing when I get there, we can. But I promise to release all of that tension in your voice I hear tonight, okay?"

"All right, baby. Can you stay the night?" I asked. He wasn't Rodney, but he was second on my list of desirables.

"We'll see. My wife's flight in from New York got canceled, and she was trying to see if she could catch another one back in to Hartsfield. If she does, I'll have to head home. If not, I'm all yours tonight, baby."

"Okay, David, I'll see you in a bit." I clicked off the OnStar, and then Ambiance called in.

"Hey, girl, what's up?" she said when I answered.

"Nothing much, heading home. What's going on with you?" I asked. I figured she may have had a fight with Eric. Whenever they were on the outs, she wanted to be all up under me and Naomi. If they were in love, which wasn't too often these days, she had time for no one.

"Oh, nothing. I was wondering if you wanted to go out for dinner tonight," Ambiance whined.

"I'm sorry, honey, I've already got plans. Maybe tomorrow night?" I suggested.

See, what'd I tell you…that married heifer only had time for us when she was lonely and wasn't getting any love. *She might as well head over to Naomi's, because my well isn't running dry. Not tonight.*

"Well, I have a few clients lined up tomorrow, and I have to go into the shop. I won't be free tomorrow. I just wanted to spend some time with my girl tonight," Ambiance stated.

"Well, have you tried Naomi?" I asked through gritted teeth. Ambiance got on my nerves when she started lying like that. She knew good and damned well that she didn't want to spend time with me. She must have been bored and ditched by Eric, and I was her back up.

"Yes, she and Sasha are having a mother-daughter night," Ambiance confessed.

Oh, okay, so I was her last resort. Damn her, then. I hoped she felt bad being left alone. I decided to dig into her. "Girl, you need to get some friends or get a man who's got time for you. Every time I turn around, Eric is too busy to spend time with you. What's the point in being married if you are gonna be alone, anyway?"

"Because I love him and he's my husband, Paige. Besides, I wasn't going to keep laying up with him without being married. I don't do that kind of thing," Ambiance stated in a snooty tone.

I had one better for her, because this chick was getting on my nerves. "Oh, well. That's why I don't do marriages. Because when you do, you get done. Men always running around with their boys, knowing they are laying up with some other woman. I can't have that. Nope, I'd rather be the one doing the laying up…know what I mean? I gotta go, Ambi," I stated in my own snippy tone when I heard her gasp.

Now before you get started on me, I know I was wrong. But Ambiance always starts in on me first. I get tired of her holier-than-thou attitude, as though she's better than everyone else on the face of the Earth.

I stepped out of the shower and dried off with a thick, fluffy yellow towel. I reached inside my bath cabinet and pulled out a bottle of almond oil and vanilla and cinnamon lotion from my favorite friend's Secret place, which I rubbed all over my body. Then I applied a hint of the almond oil to my genitals. He loved the smell and taste of that.

I went to my lingerie drawer and pulled out a sexy black number that was sure to leave little to David's imagination. Just as I finished tying the last bit of lace, I heard the doorbell rang. I threw on a black silk robe over my teaser and headed for the door.

"Mmm, baby, you smell so good," David greeted me at the door with a bag of food in one hand and a bottle of champagne in the other. He also had his gym bag hanging over his shoulder.

"What's the special occasion?" I asked, nodding towards the champagne.

"My wife called right after I got off the phone with you. She says I'm all yours tonight." He laughed.

I laughed back with him, sure that she said no such thing. We closed the door behind him and locked it.

I didn't want to bother going to the dining room to eat. We headed straight for the bedroom. The Italian meal he had picked up got set to the side as he began to take the Little Italy tour that I was offering. I moaned as he began to explore the taste of my body. Yep, I knew my man. David was a freak for the scent of almond.

He kissed me briefly before tugging the robe off my shoulders. He backed up just a moment to look at me.

"Damn, Paige, you are so fine. Turn around and model that for me," he said, as he began removing his shoes and undoing his belt buckle.

I strutted from one end of my bedroom to the other, making sure he didn't miss a twist, jiggle, or shake. The deep, sexy, commanding voice of Teddy Pendergrass was pouring into the room from the overhead speakers.

"Are you gonna keep those heels on?" he asked, nodding his head towards my feet. My size sixes were clad in black, five-inch stilettos with gold heels. They were sexy and took the hot little number I wore to another level.

"Only if you want me to, daddy," I stated with a teasing smile as I began to dance and gyrate to the music. I toyed with the lace strings on my teddy.

"Uh-uh, let me do that for you," he said, coming closer to where I stood by the bed.

The top of my teddy crisscrossed in the front, hooking around my neck halter-style. There was only a lace band underneath my breasts and nothing but tassels covering my nipples. A band around my waist tied into a neat little bow in the back sitting on top of my ample, honey-colored behind. The ribbons teased him by swinging between my cheeks. Just underneath both of my round apples was another band of lace which hooked onto my black, lace stockings. A simple swatch of cloth covered my mound, mocking David.

I knew there was only so much he could take. He lifted the tassel from over my left nipple and licked, taking my breast further inside of his hot mouth, all the while working on untying the ribbon swinging down my behind. I spread my legs wide, inviting him to insert one finger inside of me. I didn't want the foreplay tonight. I wanted only to forget my troubles.

He did exactly as I wanted him to, inserting one finger in and out of me quickly. Lowering his head to kiss me, he moaned against my mouth. Feeling his desire pressing against my stomach, I opened his zipper and began to tug down. David stepped back long enough to remove his pants. That was all I needed as I hopped onto my bed.

He came at me with so much aggression, it almost startled me. He flipped my legs open, and since he had already untied the ribbon in the back, the rest of my bottoms slid down easily for him. David's dark brown eyes looked up at me one last time before he lowered his head to feast on my almond-coated fruit.

I grinded my hips in an upward motion, meeting his face, inviting his tongue to come in further. He moaned against it, and then like clockwork, began saying the alphabet. Every time he did that, it drove me crazy. Every stroke of his tongue, as he clearly enunciated each letter of the alphabet, threatened to drive me over the top.

"Oh, David," I moaned, as I grabbed his shoulders and pushed my mound further into his face. No one could make my clitoris feel the way he did when he went oral. He was almost the best around. And trust me, I knew, because I had experienced quite a few.

Later that night after eating, and having sex twice, I heard a vibrating sound. Sitting up in bed where we had fallen asleep, I looked around to determine where it was coming from. Spotting his phone on top of his clothes in a chair, I jumped out of bed to grab it.

I heard him murmur something in his sleep, but continued my naked prance to the chair. I looked at the phone and saw a picture of his wife's face and the time illuminated as 2:03 A.M. No wonder he messed around. If I was that homely-looking, I would beg my husband to mess around, too. A woman has to take care of herself. She can't get all relaxed and let herself go. David's wife had clearly done that; with her hair pulled back in a ponytail and no makeup, she looked like a Plain Jane. Not that she was ugly, just homely. I continued to look at the phone, contemplating whether or not I should answer it. A part of me wanted to be mean and ugly. These women needed to know the truth about their no-good-assed men. I didn't have a chance to make the decision, it was taken out of my hands.

"What are you doing, Paige?" David grumbled, wrapping his big, brown massive arms around my waist. He took one hand and removed his phone from mine. He pushed one button to silence the ringer, but her face continued to show up until the call ended. David kissed me on my shoulder and tossed the phone on the bed. With his free hand, he began to caress me between my legs.

I moaned and threw my head back against his shoulder. "Mmm, nothing, baby," I replied, answering his question about what I had been doing and working my hips side to side.

"This is our night. Didn't I tell you not to worry about nothing else?" he asked in those silken tones. His tongue flicked inside of my ear.

"Yesss," I slithered out.

He turned me around and picked me up in his arms. He walked backwards to the bed and tossed me on it. Walking back to his pants, he pulled a condom out of his back pocket and slid it down his massive length. I continued to stroke my folds as I watched him.

"What happens when you're a bad girl, Paige?" he asked me.

I shuddered. "I get punished," I murmured. David moved my legs apart with his knees, pushed them up towards my shoulders as close as they could go, balanced himself on one hand, and used the other to guide himself inside of me. With hard, forceful thrusts, he began his punishment.

"What...I...tell...you...about...trying...to...answer...my...phone?!" he shouted at me. With each powerful thrust of his penis, he spoke a word. Every time he slammed into my body, I felt like someone was hitting me with powerful gut shots.

I could barely catch my breath, let alone answer his question.

"Answer me, Paige!" he shouted again.

"D...d...don't answer it," I cried. It felt so good, but it hurt so badly.

"What...I...tell...you...would...happen...if...my...wife...found...out...about...us...through...you?" he asked, slamming me again with those powerful thrusts.

"Y...y...you would hurt me," I stuttered.

"I'll hurt you bad, baby. And...what...I...tell...you...would...happen...if...she...left...me...because...of...you?" he asked again. This time, his thrusts were more painful than ever. I knew in the morning my vagina would be swollen. He had my legs bent back over my shoulders, to the point that the entire area from my vagina to my rectum was opened wide. Every thrust had me feeling ripped from the front to the back.

"Y...y...y...you said...you said, you'd kill me," I choked out through the sobs catching in my throat.

"Damn, right!" he shouted. He flipped me over onto my stomach, and I would have to endure another round of that as he questioned me the same way. But this time, the thrusts would be more painful as he entered from the rear.

This went on for what seemed like an hour, but I know it couldn't have been any more than twenty minutes. All the while, David's phone continued to ring and his wife's homely face continued to plague me. He had laid his phone on my pillow, forcing me to look at her as he took me over and over again and as she called him repeatedly. I couldn't turn away from the phone, because his large, beefy hand was wrapped around my neck, squeezing tightly. Tears streamed down my face as I wondered how I let myself get to this point in my life. I briefly thought about Vic and how much he cared about me. I wasn't ready to take on that kind of responsibility, yet. I had some more purging to do.

After David was all finished, he collapsed on his back and pulled me close in his arms. He kissed my shoulder and then my ear. He rolled me towards him and kissed my tears away before kissing me on the mouth. His tongue was a mixture of my almond sweet nectar and the citrusy champagne we had drank earlier. After he finished kissing me, I turned my back to him again and we spooned. He moved my legs apart and slipped a couple of fingers inside of me and played with my sore fruit for a while, before he drifted off to sleep. As he lightly snored in my ear, he kept his fingers inside of me, and I let my tears silently fall, streaming sideways onto my pillow.

When he acted this way, I somehow tricked myself into believing he honestly cared about me. It wouldn't matter in the morning, anyway. It would be a brand new day with new inventions to keep me going and running from the emotional pain which had plagued me since my childhood. Another day, another memory, none as unpleasant as the past.

Why did I accept his punishment? Because deep in my heart, I knew I was wrong. Seeing that woman's face on that phone had me feeling a sense of guilt I had never known as long as I had been sleeping with David. I felt that I deserved punishment not only because I was sleeping with another woman's husband, but also because I had allowed myself to be used and abused. I tricked myself into thinking I was doing the using, and that was the explanation I gave to anyone who asked. Somehow, deep inside, I knew that wasn't true. I knew I was being used by these men. Just as I knew the teasing that Ambiance and Naomi did back and forth calling me a pot-a-let was true. But I wasn't ready to admit that to myself…not yet.

7_AMBIANCE_ANOTHER LONELY NIGHT

"Eric, I'm tired of this. If you're going to keep leaving me, you need to just leave and not come back." I was standing with my arms crossed over my chest, in my long flannel night robe, tears streaming down my face.

"Mannn, don't start this shit tonight, Ambi!" he shouted at me, turning to head for the front door.

"Don't start? You don't start, Eric!" I shouted to his retreating back. He had gotten dressed up once again to go out with his brothers. I had begged and pleaded with him not to go, but he had made up his mind.

"I'm tired of your shit, Ambiance. You're always accusing me of doing something. That's why I don't want to stay at home. Who wants to be with a whining-ass woman all the time? Nothing is ever good enough for you. When I am home, you constantly complain. When I leave, you still complain. What the hell is it that you want from me?" Eric probed.

"I want you, Eric. I want your time. If it's not your brothers, it's your job. And Lord knows you work crazy hours and shouldn't have to," I reminded him.

"I do have to. If I want to make partner, it's what needs to be done," he explained, as if he was talking to a four-year-old. He had been working at Roberson and Klein since he passed the bar. But they had consumed his life.

"You always say that, Eric. What happened to wanting to open your own practice? Huh? You used to have dreams, Eric. We were both going to have our own businesses, and I'm working on mine, but all you do in your leisure time is run with your brothers," I accused.

"Woman! Are you crazy? Do you realize how much time I would have to dedicate to building my own practice? You think you complain now, you couldn't handle it, Ambiance," he said, shaking his head. His voice had taken on a solemn tone.

"But what happened, baby? You used to dream about it all the time. What happened, huh?"

"You!" he shouted and walked out the door. His slamming of the front door on my pleas was his way of terminating our conversation.

I had gotten home that afternoon a little after three, and his brothers were there. I was irate, because I had purposely left work early so we could have our discussion. I was going to tell him maybe we needed to separate for a little while but didn't have the time to have that discussion. His brothers hadn't left until an hour and a half ago. They claimed they were getting dressed and would meet him at the club. I knew if he was going out with them, they weren't going anywhere but to those strip clubs. I didn't understand it. I really held true to being a lady in the streets and a freak in the bed. There wasn't nothing I wouldn't do for my husband, but he wasn't satisfied and I didn't know why. If he would just tell me what it was, I would be willing to work on it. But how could I work on something I didn't understand?

I threw off my old flannel robe over the jeans and t-shirt I wore underneath and tossed it on my bed. I grabbed my slides from underneath my bed, my keys from my dresser, and my purse, and ran down the stairs.

I set the alarm on our home and jumped into my Camry. Easing out of the driveway, I took a left, heading towards the highway, which I believed my husband would have taken. After about five minutes, I quickly caught up with him and had to slow down so he wouldn't spot me. We drove onto the highway and traveled for almost half an hour until we reached downtown. I kept a safe distance, knowing he hadn't spotted me. He was on his cell phone for the entire ride, and it was dark outside.

Eric eased into the parking lot of Candy Stripes. It was the wildest known strip club in the city. Men were already pouring out of their cars into the red brick building. I drove slowly past and turned around down the street in a dark alleyway. I was a little scared, because it wasn't the best neighborhood. I drove past again, and this time saw my brothers-in-law, Stephen and Marc, getting out of Stephen's car. They headed inside the club next. I looked at the marquee over the club and noticed the special headliner of the night was a dancer named Taffy. Really? How trifling this all was. I pulled into a parking space across the street and set up for a stakeout.

I sat with my music turned down low and continued to watch the club. A loud rattling scared the heck out of me and caused me to jump and bump my head on the steering wheel. I wiped my hand down the side of my face and realized I had been asleep, and slob was coming out of my mouth. I was disgusted and grabbed a wipe from the open console between the two front seats and cleaned my face off. Then I looked up, and to my horror, saw that it was a police officer.

Rolling my car window down, I looked up at him with a smile on my face. "Yes, officer?"

"License and registration, please."

"Did I do something wrong?" I asked, fearing I had broken some law I was ignorant of.

He continued to stare at me, and filled with trepidation, I reached into the glove compartment and pulled out my registration and insurance card. Next, I reached into my purse and grabbed my license. Handing it over to him, I stole a peek around him and looked into the parking lot. The lot was still full of cars, and Eric and his brothers hadn't left yet.

Taking a quick look at the clock, I realized I had been dozing for almost an hour. It was a few minutes after midnight.

"I'll be back in just a moment. Do not get out of the car, Ms. Caldwell," he stated, after looking at my license. After straightening up his big, bulky frame, he strode back to his car, and I watched him in the rear view mirror. He was gone for what seemed like fifteen minutes before he returned. Throughout that time, I prayed that Eric wouldn't come out of the club. I could still see his car parked in the lot as well as his brother's.

Finally, the officer strode back to my vehicle and handed my paperwork back to me. "Why are you parked outside of this club, Ms. Caldwell?"

"I was…I was…doing some light surveillance work," I stated. There wasn't any law against that, was there?

"Who are you doing surveillance work on and for?" he asked, with a confused look on his face.

"Well, um, I, well, see…today my husband told me that he was going out with his brothers. And they were at my house, too. They all said they were coming down here. But then I thought maybe my husband wasn't, because he said the same thing a few years ago. But then I learned that he was having an affair. So, when he started acting strange again lately, I began to think maybe he wasn't coming down here. So, I decided to—"

The officer held his hand up, stemming my flow of words. "Ma'am, that's enough. I really don't need to hear anymore." He no longer held a stern expression on his face, but a slight smirk, which also lit up his dark brown eyes. He chuckled just a little before continuing his statement, "Mrs. Caldwell, trust me, you aren't the first one to do this. But as I tell the others, you can't park out here. There's a clear no parking sign there," he said, pointing to a sign just ahead of my car. "You can park on the side street over there," he said, gesturing with his hand. "But this is a really dangerous neighborhood. And just like I tell the dancers, you shouldn't be out in this area without an escort," he explained, lifting his eyebrows at me. "I won't give you a ticket this time, just a warning. Why don't you head on home, Mrs. Caldwell?" the officer suggested. "I'm sure your husband will be home soon enough."

I felt like a chastised child, but I caught the hint and thanked him for the warning. I started up my car and planned to go to the side street he had pointed out. But he followed me as I went around the block and rather than doing a loop, I hopped back onto the highway and headed home.

The next few days passed by with my husband and me barely seeing one another. He made it his business to be up and off to work before I woke up and came home long after I had gone to bed, if he came home at all. He would send a quick text message to me throughout the day to say hi or see if I was fine. Then he would text later to say he would be late or not coming home at all.

I was angry and lonely by the time Monday morning rolled back around. I had spent the weekend alone with no one to talk to or hang with. Naomi must have been busy spending time with Sasha, because she never returned my calls. And after the nasty comment Paige made towards me, I didn't want to talk to her anymore. She didn't have to be so indecent or nasty. I didn't know what was wrong with that girl half the time. But she was one of my besties, and I still loved her. All I could do was pray that God would show her the error of her ways.

I was pulling some boxes from my car to take into the shop that morning when I heard a voice behind me.

"Need some help with that?" came that deep sexy tone. It took everything in me not to allow my shiver to be visible.

I sighed and rolled my eyes turning to face him. "Nick, what are you doing here?" I asked.

"Oh, so we're back on a first name basis again?" he asked, with a slight smirk.

"What do you want?"

"I'm just trying to figure this thing out. You change from one day to the next, and I'm never really sure what it is."

"Okay, Nick. Yes, we're on first name basis again if that's what you want."

He shot a gleaming smile my way before walking closer. "Here, let me help you with those. And I'm here, because my mom was talking about getting something for my aunt. My aunt has been helping my mom out since she had knee surgery. She wanted something special, and I told her I would get it. She gave me a very good description of what she was thinking of, so I knew the perfect place to pick it up."

"Thanks for coming back to patronize Vanilla Rose. I'm sure Angelique would appreciate that," I said, as I passed underneath his arm. He was holding the door open with one arm and held a box between his other arm and hip.

"Well, you all have a fabulous shop here."

He followed me to my office and sat the box he was holding down on top of the one I had placed on the floor in a corner.

"Thanks so much. I guess I'll be seeing you around," I said after walking him to my office door.

"Aren't you going to help me find those pieces I need?" he asked, with a frown crinkling his smooth, brown skin.

"I thought you knew what you needed," I said.

"I do. Well, kinda, but I need a female's input, and your clerk seems to be tied up with other customers," he explained, pointing out the office door as if we could see the shop from where we stood.

What else could I do? After all, I was the personal shopper and this was my job. Angelique wasn't here, and Nelly had been swamped with three customers when I arrived. I couldn't very well throw another person on her.

"Okay. Do you at least know the particular articles of clothing you're here to pick up?" I asked, leading the way out of my office back into the shop.

"Umm, I know she wanted to purchase a jumpsuit, a blouse, and a couple of bracelets. I think I can do fine on my own with the bracelets. I saw a couple the other day I know my aunt would love. But the jumpsuit and blouse, I'm not so sure about." He looked completely confused and like a lost little boy.

He gave me a description of his aunt's size, favorite colors, and favorite fabrics. I pulled a few items and put them together and he shook his head, indicating that it wouldn't do. We went through that three times before we finally hit the jackpot.

After selecting two jumpsuits, a blouse, and a skirt, I coerced him into getting a couple of scarves that would just put the outfits over the top. His aunt apparently liked more neutral tones as compared to his mother's flair for the bold, vibrant colors he selected on his last visit.

We took those purchases to Nelly at the cash register, who was now joined by Claire, our other part-time clerk. "Ladies, could you please wrap these items up for Mr. Jackson? I'm going to head over to the jewelry station to help him select a couple of pieces."

"Sure," Claire replied, moving to grab a couple of gift boxes.

We walked over to the jewelry counter, and I unlocked the cabinet with my keys. "Which pieces did you want to see?" I asked, stooping down to pull out a selection of bracelets.

"That one right there and the one over there," he said, pointing to a twisted gold bangle and a simple white gold tennis bracelet. "Can you try them on, please?" he asked.

I eyed him carefully before complying with his request. Many male customers had come in with similar requests and we complied. At any given time, it could be Claire, Nelly, Peggy, Angelique, or me, if not one of our other part-time staff who tried jewelry on depending on the size of the woman they were shopping for. I put the twisted gold bangle on my right wrist and showcased it for him. He shook his head and thanked me before indicating he wanted me to try on the other.

Nick had to clasp the tennis bracelet around my wrist, because I couldn't quite make the connection between the clasp and the hook.

I turned my arm sideways so that he could get a good look at it. He shook his head once again.

"I'll take the bangle," he stated, pointing at the first bracelet. I placed the other bracelets back into the cabinet and took the bangle and wrapped it up in gift paper, then handed it to him with a flourish.

"You make that look so easy. I can't handle wrapping a gift for the life of me," he chuckled.

"Oh, it's no biggie. You get used to it after you do it for a while. I do this all the time, now. I wasn't too good when I first started out, either."

"Ambiance, can I ask you a question?"

I felt my nerves getting irked again. I really wanted to tell him no, but business was business. I put on my professional face, smiled at him, and handed him the box. "Sure."

"We are hosting a dinner Thursday evening for local business owners in the area. There will be a couple of guest speakers, raffles, and a lot of networking going on. I wanted to invite Angelique to represent Vanilla Rose, but I also wanted to invite you."

"I can't do that, Nick. Thank you for the offer, but as I told you before—"

He held up a hand to stop me from speaking. "You told me on my last visit that you are a fashion consultant with your own business, Bleu Diamante. I think this would be a wonderful opportunity for you to come out and meet some new people. You don't know what doors would be open for you. It's not a date, simply business."

I pondered it in my head, not sure if I should accept his invitation. "I don't know, Nick."

"Look, it's just a business function. I'll have my hands tied up with a few other investors anyway, but I will introduce you around. Just take a chance."

I contemplated a few moments more. "When is it?" I asked.

"This Thursday at seven. Business attire, or cocktail wear and all you need is this ticket," he said, pulling a little envelope from his jacket pocket.

I opened the ecru-colored envelope and pulled the invitation out. Reading over it, I had already decided to accept. What did I have to lose? My husband probably wouldn't be at home, my girls were caught up in their lives, and I had just decided I needed to get a life of my own. This would be perfect to take my business to the next level. Not that my growth had been stagnant, but I really wanted to soar it to new levels.

"What do I need to bring?" I asked, unsure of how these events work.

"Just yourself. And if you would please give this invitation to Angelique when you see her, I would greatly appreciate it," he said, pulling another envelope from inside of his jacket.

That Thursday night I pulled up to the Regency Galleria and handed my keys to the valet. Angelique had said she wasn't going to be able to make it on such short notice but encouraged me to attend. I had decided I wasn't going either but I didn't tell her that. At the last minute, I changed my mind and decided to go after receiving a call from Eric.

"Hey, babe, how was your day?" he asked in a tired-sounding voice.

"It was okay. What about yours?" I asked, listening to background noise to determine if he was in the car on his way home.

"It's been a long one. I'm still at the office. I thought I would've been out of here by now, but this case has me tied up. It's going to be another hour or two before I get out of here. Then I forgot I've got a ticket for that Hawks and Nuggets game tonight. Marc called and reminded me," he said of his younger brother.

I did recall him telling me he was going to the basketball game with his brothers. It looked like it was going to be another lonely night.

"Can't you give your ticket to someone else, Eric? I haven't seen you in almost a week," I whined. I hated that I allowed myself to be reduced to that when I spoke with my husband.

"We just saw each other this morning."

"For less than fifteen minutes. You were headed out when I was waking up. And that's been a constant. You come in after I've gone to bed, if you come in at all, and leave before I wake up. Eric, we haven't had sex in almost two months," I complained.

"It hasn't been that long, Ambi," he denied.

"Yes, it has, Eric. If you're not getting it from me, I know you must be getting it somewhere. There's no way a sex fiend like you can go that long without it," I accused. I knew my husband's habits, and he usually didn't care how tired I was or he was, he wanted sex and expected it when he asked for it.

"Come on, Ambi. Don't start this again. I just told you I've had a long day. I need a night with the fellows to unwind."

"Mm-hmm, of course you won't deny it. You always get a night with the fellows. It seems like you should've married your brothers instead of me," I uttered.

He chuckled, but I didn't see anything funny.

"I'm serious, Eric." I needed my husband to validate me, and I needed and wanted him to make me feel desired, beautiful, and loved. That wasn't on his agenda tonight…as usual.

"Look, when we first hooked up, you understood that my being an attorney would mean long hours, and you said you had no problem with the time I spent with my brothers. Or have you forgotten those conversations? Was it that you would say anything just to have your way and get in my pockets, Ambi?"

I was furious that he had the audacity to say those things to me. I had never depended on his money for a thing! Of course, he paid the bills, but I contributed, as well. It was because of his stingy pockets that I was still driving a 2010 Toyota Camry, while "Mr. Lawyer Man" was driving a brand new 2015 Audi A4 Sedan Quattro. "*Mr. I just have to have the latest because it does things for my career,"* did not care that his wife was still putting around in the car I had purchased five years prior.

I wanted to hang up on him so bad. But I knew if I did it would lead to more trouble down the road. I didn't want that, and our marriage couldn't afford it. So, instead as I always do, I simply took the low road and tried to be the supportive, submissive wife. "I'm sorry, Eric. I just miss you, that's all."

"And I miss you, too, baby. We'll have our turn. The weekend's coming up, and we'll spend the entire weekend together. How about that?" he compromised.

"All right. You have fun with the boys, okay?"

"All right. I love you," my husband said. I hadn't heard those words from him in several days.

"I love you, too," I said, recalling how I used to get chills whenever he spoke those words. Now it seemed as if he was trying to appease me whenever those words fell from his lips.

After hanging up the phone, I sat on the bed for a little while feeling sorry for myself. But then I began to get angry. It just wasn't fair that I had to accept this treatment from him. Something had to give. If he was going to be out all night, so was I. What he didn't know wouldn't hurt him. Besides, it was a business venture, and I was tired of sitting in that big house all alone.

I showered and washed my hair, leaving my naturally curly strands wet. I loved the look when they air-dried. I selected a red sexy, deep V-Neck, slim pencil cocktail dress with cap sleeves. It stopped one inch below my knees but hugged my curves like a well-versed lover. It was paired with black, peep-toe suede shoes and a black, suede cocktail purse.

Getting off the elevator in the Galleria, I noticed signs pointing in the direction of the conference room where the dinner would be held. The room was decorated in tans and golds, and smooth jazz poured softly through the overhead speakers, creating a relaxing atmosphere.

I entered the room and saw a large gathering of people scattered throughout the room, speaking in hushed tones. I was slightly uncomfortable in the sea of unfamiliar faces. Men and women alike glanced my way and nodded a hello or smiled by way of greeting as I weaved my way through the room, looking for Nick. Feeling my nerves become rattled as I failed to locate him, I stopped a waiter passing by and removed a glass of white wine from his tray. I took a sip from the glass and murmured a thank you to him before I sensed a shift in the atmosphere. I turned around and came face to face with a smiling Nick.

I felt my heart fluttering and a deep heat flushed across my body as he took me in slowly from head to toe, not missing an inch. I felt as if I should turn around and model the dress for him, the way he was appreciating my curves. I felt lost in the moment and had to pull myself back together.

His presence caused me to feel slightly off-guard. Wearing black slacks and a white, open-collared button-down shirt with the sleeves rolled up to his elbows, his attire had a casual appearance, but he pulled it off as sexy. I was losing myself again as I visualized threading my hands through his locs, which were caught up in a ponytail at the moment. He must have realized I was unsteady on my feet, because he reached out for my hand with a slight smile. His scent was so masculine and intoxicating, leaving me feeling a bit heady, or maybe it was the wine. I was unsure. But, then again, I had only taken one sip, so I grudgingly acknowledged to myself that it had to be him.

"I'm so glad you could make it, Ambiance," he said, steering me in the direction of a small group of people ahead. "You look beautiful," he whispered in my ear.

I took a deep breath to stop the feelings that were flowing through me. This was all wrong, I was a married woman, but I was feeling very desirable at the moment, and vulnerable.

"Thank you, Nick. Angelique asked me to send her apologies. She couldn't make it on such short notice."

"That's fine. I'm glad you didn't let that stop you. Ed, Roland, Teresa, this was the young lady I was speaking with you about," he introduced me to an elderly white male and a middle aged black male and woman.

After introductions were made all around, they began quizzing me on my business. I finally began to relax, because I could talk about fashion all night long. It was at that point that Nick excused himself.

"Ambiance, I have to greet a few other guests who just arrived. I want you to enjoy yourself, but I'll be back to check on you. Okay?"

"Sure, I'm a big girl. I can handle myself," I replied with a gracious smile. I was a bit relieved to not have to be in his presence any longer, because I didn't know how much longer I could fight back the feelings I was experiencing. Just the mere thought of him was stoking flames inside of me that hadn't been stirred in such a long time.

Nick left my side, and I turned my attention back to the group. They were all looking at me expectantly, and I realized that I missed a question.

"I'm sorry, what was that?" I asked.

"Do you have a business card?" Teresa repeated in a patient manner. There was a certain awareness in her eyes that told me she knew I had been enraptured with our host.

Scrambling in my purse to cover my embarrassment, I pulled out several business cards and passed them around. Apparently, the three of them worked in the non-profit arena, specializing in placing homeless, abused, and welfare recipients back into the workforce. Teresa worked with domestic violence victims, helping them to get on their feet again. And Ed and Roland headed up an organization assisting the homeless and welfare recipients with training and job placement.

They each needed help with their clients and sought someone who could come in and put together a wardrobe for them based on their personality and the jobs they were applying for. I learned there was a government grant which would fund the wardrobe. It was important that their clients regained their self-confidence as they entered the workforce, and part of that was influenced by how they viewed themselves.

After I'd spoken with them for twenty minutes, Nick was back by my side to whisk me off to another group. This went on for an hour before it was time for dinner. At eight o'clock, we were seated for dinner. I was seated at a table with five other people. There were two women; one was the head of an adoption agency, and the other owned a beauty salon. The beauty salon owner, Olivia Ellsworth, was a very spiritual and inspirational woman. She was the guest speaker of the night, and I learned she owned a couple of salons, The House of BeJeweled I and II, located in downtown Atlanta and Buckhead. I had heard of both. There were also three men at the table: a jazz musician, a museum director, and the CEO of a local bank.

Light talk around the table made for a fun and exciting evening. When it was her turn to speak, Mrs. Ellsworth glided up to the podium to give her speech. She was all elegance and class, and I admired her. Mrs. Ellsworth, or Olivia, as she insisted I call her, gave a speech about pursuing our dreams, living to our full potential, and opening the gates behind us to pull others up along the way. What I wasn't ready for was that Nick was the next speaker on the agenda.

I soon realized I had never inquired about what he did for a living. During his speech, I learned that he was a real estate developer, creating projects, having builders build them, and working out real estate deals. He was in charge of marketing them, getting the financing to back the projects, and then selling the completed product. I didn't know much about this type of investment, but it sounded a bit risky.

His speech was geared more towards turning downtown Atlanta around to continue to support its growth and development. When the evening was over, he was bogged down by many guests who wanted to make donations or simply had questions. I knew he would be busy for a while. I wanted to thank him for a great evening, although I had not had much time to speak to him. I had enjoyed my time at the dinner and definitely didn't look forward to an evening at home alone again. It was shortly after 11:30 at night. As I waited for the valet, I called Eric and received no answer. When the valet pulled up, a text beeped on my phone, my husband telling me he was at a bar and that the place was loud. He couldn't talk.

Just as I was getting into my car, Nick called my name. I turned around to see what he wanted, surprised he had been able to get away.

"Hey, there, I saw you leaving and did my best to catch up with you. Why did you run off so fast?" he asked, slightly out of breath.

I laughed. "You were busy. I didn't want to be rude or anything, but I knew you would be tied up for a while. Listen, thanks for inviting me tonight. I had a great time and met some wonderful people. I believe some of these are going to be great contacts. I've set up four consultations already," I gushed with excitement.

"Great. I'm glad to hear that, Ambiance; that's what I was hoping for you to accomplish tonight. Look, my partner is handling everything up there for me. Can we go to the little coffee shop down the street for a quick cup of coffee? I promise not to hold you up too long, but I never really had the time to talk to you tonight."

I looked at my phone. I didn't have to work tomorrow, but it was really late. "I don't know, Nick. I should be getting home; it's getting kind of late."

"Come on…just ten minutes, pullleezz," he begged, with those beautiful eyes, pouting his lips out in an imitation of a spoiled child.

I laughed and shook my head at his antics. I thought about Eric's text again. I had nothing else to do, so why not? "Okay, just ten minutes," I conceded.

"Do you mind if I ride over with you since you've already grabbed your car?" he asked.

"No problem," I lowered myself into my seat and started the engine. I was unsure if I would be able to take sitting this close to him and his stimulating scent.

I couldn't believe it was one in the morning when I glanced at my phone again and I was still at the coffee shop with Nick. It had been so easy to talk to him once I let my guard down. He had told me all about his real estate development company, how he got into the business, and his future projects. I had learned he was an only child but came from a large family of cousins, aunts, and uncles.

"I'm glad you enjoyed yourself tonight. But I have this sense that you keep running from me. What is it about me that throws you off, Ambiance?" he asked, turning his head to the side as he stirred the sugar in his third cup of coffee.

"I have the sense that you're looking for so much more than I could ever offer you, Nick. And I honestly don't want to waste your time."

"How would you know unless you give it a try?" His chocolate eyes had turned serious, and the look he was giving me was doing something to my insides.

I didn't want to share with anyone what I was going through in my marriage. But I couldn't keep lying to this man. And that's exactly what I was doing, lying by omission. He deserved the truth. But the scary part was that I didn't want him to walk away after this. I wanted to be friends with him, but I knew it had to be on my terms. And if I couldn't have it on my terms, then I didn't know what would happen.

Holding my head up and looking in his eyes, I saw something there that made me wonder at our connection. I had only known this man for a short time, but there was something special there. What it was I was uncertain of. "I'm married, Nick." There, it was out. So, if he decided to get up and walk away at this point, I was okay with that.

"I know." I didn't expect that answer. That was all he said. No explanation, no shouting, no questioning. What did he mean, he knew? How did he know?

"How?" I asked; this time it was my turn to look confused.

"The wedding ring you used to wear has left a mark on your left ring finger. You're very evasive, and I can look in your eyes and tell that you hurt. You seem to have a shield of protection around yourself, but not quite as though you're protecting you, but someone else."

"Wow, you're good," I confessed. He was either very perceptive or just that good.

"And…I asked Peggy the last time that I was in the shop over the weekend. You weren't there, and I asked if you would be in. She said not until Monday, and then I point blank asked if you were in a relationship. She told me you were married. But that she thought you weren't too happy."

I looked back into my cup of coffee, fighting back the tears that were threatening to spill. I realized in that moment as I was going around trying to pretend I had the perfect marriage and family life, I was kidding no one but myself. I was the only one who couldn't see the truth for what it was.

He reached out, grabbed my hand, and squeezed it to let me know everything would be all right.

"What's wrong? It's been a beautiful night, and you should be enjoying it," he coerced, as he tilted his head to catch my attention.

It was like a magnetic pull as I lifted my eyes from looking down into my coffee cup back into his beautiful, chocolate eyes.

"It is. It's just that…" I hesitated, trying to find a way to put what I was feeling into words.

"It's just what?" Nick was still holding my hand and lightly squeezed it, urging me to share what was on my mind with him.

"Have you ever worked so hard to put up a front on the outside when what was going on in the inside was nothing like what you were portraying?" I asked.

"Yeah, we all do at some point," he admitted.

"Well, that's how I feel. I work so hard to portray this happy, beautiful marriage, and in reality, I'm empty inside. I mean, don't get me wrong, I love my husband and want to work things out. I just sometimes feel as if he doesn't see the problems that I see," I shared.

"Have you discussed that with him?"

"I have, but he still doesn't get it," I replied, shaking my head. I took a sip of my coffee as I questioned myself about why was I sharing my business with this man.

"Counseling?"

"Well, we've done it before. He's not really into that. So, I don't want to force his hand." I felt that if I were to force Eric to go to counseling again, it would create more problems for us and he would be resentful.

"You have to determine what's most important to you. And then that's what you do. Your happiness, your marriage, and life balance…whatever that thing is, that's what you dedicate yourself to, and don't give up until you arrive at that place," Nick advised.

"Sometimes I feel like just hollering, 'Jesus, take the wheel,' because I know He didn't mean for us to go through this. I don't know, sometimes I wonder if we've grown apart," I mumbled.

"It's gonna be okay. Whether you work through this or not, you'll grow stronger at the end of it," he said, smiling that disarming smile of his at me. "I get the sense that you really need a good friend in your life right now. And I'd like to be that friend, if that's okay with you," he offered.

I wanted it to be okay, but I knew deep inside it wasn't. The only good male friend that I needed was my husband. Many women feel that it is okay to be friends with men despite the fact they're in a committed relationship or even married. To me, this was true in some instances, but not ones where you knew that other person was attracted to you and you found yourself attracted to that person, as well.

And I was definitely attracted to Nick, but I couldn't turn him away. The funny thing is, he was a good-looking man, but that wasn't what my attraction was solely based on. He stimulated my mind, I was very aware of his presence when he was around, and I felt beautiful and desired by him. I knew that was wrong, but I had been missing that in my life for such a long time. Every woman needs to feel beautiful, intelligent, and desired. And if she wasn't getting that from her husband, she was bound to get it from somewhere. And as long as no lines were crossed, everything would be okay.

Wouldn't it?

8_NAOMI_MEETING JAIME

The nerves bundled in my belly were being released as I stood there. I wanted to scream, to have a hissy fit, to punch him, to do something to release the years of pent-up anger. I had always dreamt about this moment. What would I do? Well, here I was in the moment, and I wouldn't do anything that I would regret. I wouldn't lose my head and become a ghetto fool. Not the one that he used to know. I would be the classy and elegant professional lady I had grown to be.

"I've been wonderful, Jaime, and you?" I asked with a smile pasted on my face, holding back the tears and anger.

"I'm doing well. I'm teaching social studies and coaching basketball at a private school close to my home. It's rewarding spending time with the youth and giving back, you know what I mean?"

"Mm-hmm, I sure do," I said, narrowing my eyes at him.

"What are you doing these days?" he asked, making small talk.

"I've been busy building my career in finance, and now I am the CFO at Edwards Broadcasting System."

"Wow, sounds like you have been handling your business. They're a large mega broadcasting company here in the southeast. And you said you're the CFO?" he asked. His round eyes had grown larger at the mention of what I did for a living. I could tell he was calculating my dollars. Too bad he would never be a part of that.

"Yeah, I'm doing fine."

"Momm, are you ready?" Sasha interrupted from behind me.

"And who do we have here?" Jaime asked, with a smile on his face.

Sasha had been standing behind me, bored and impatient, looking at the pictures on the wall of the restaurant. She had always been fascinated with Cuban culture, and Havana's Cocina did a wonderful job of depicting the country and its culture.

I prepared myself to do the inevitable, because I wouldn't lie to her. She didn't deserve it.

"Come here, sweetie. I would like to introduce you to someone. Sasha, this is your father, Jaime Fernandez-Garcia. Jaime, this is your daughter, Sasha Kennedy Blankenship," I introduced. There was no amount of pleasure in me as I heard my daughter's sharp intake of breath. I never wanted to cause her a moment of pain. But I had no right to withhold this vital information from her. I would have loved to prepare her for this moment, but life doesn't always give us those choices.

Although I wasn't thrilled with the emotions she must have been experiencing at that moment, I did take immense pleasure from the look on Jaime's face.

"Whaa—" He couldn't finish his sentence. I pulled Sasha from behind me and put her front and center. Jaime's face went pale at the sight of his daughter. I knew he must have felt as if he were looking in a mirror, seeing the light, honey-colored skin, the exotic look, and those stormy, grey eyes.

"Naomi...are you kidding me?" Jaime looked as if he didn't know what to do at that moment.

"My father? Where have you been? I thought you were dead!" Sasha was turning red and outraged.

"Naomi? Why would you tell her something like that?" Jaime actually had the nerve to look hurt as he looked between me and Sasha.

"She didn't tell me *anything*. Mom always told me that you just left. But I couldn't believe that. I mean, all these years in my mind, I figured you had to be dead not to come and see about me. Never to be curious of what I looked like or if I was doing okay! You had to be dead, right? Who would do that to their own child?" Sasha was taking deep breaths in and out. I had to get my daughter out of there.

"Come on, Sasha, honey," I said, tugging at her arm. She was becoming more upset by the minute.

But she wasn't having it; she remained planted in the spot she stood in. She wanted to hear what he had to say.

"It wasn't my fault. I mean, I didn't know about you!" he exclaimed.

It was my turn to be outraged. And he had to know he had provoked my ire by the slack-jawed appearance I took on and how my almond-shaped eyes narrowed to slits. "You have the audacity after all these years to stand here and lie?" I asked in a forced whisper, pointing my finger at him. "I mean, even now you can't stand up and be a man and take on your responsibility? Your parents wanted me nowhere near you, afraid I would mess up your professional NBA career. Jaime, don't you dare pretend like you didn't know about this baby! You went along with their precious plan to secure your career," I accused, in an outraged whisper.

I was struggling to hold on to the last bit of dignity I had. I was ready to get real ghetto on him. How dare he come shooting lies at my baby? Punk!

At that moment, a woman appeared behind him, coming from the restroom with two small children. They appeared to be about three and four. The little boy reached up to Jaime. "Daddy! Dey got foam soap in dey bafwoom," he announced.

"Hey, honey, what's going on out here? What is she talking about?" the woman asked. She was extremely short beside him; they were almost comical-looking. The woman, whom I assumed to be his wife, was about five-two, light-skinned, thick, and really pretty.

"Uh, nothing, honey. Natalie, this is just an old friend of mine from high school. Go ahead and check on our table for me," Jaime ordered.

Was that all he recalled me as? Well, I guess when his wife is standing there, a man wouldn't hardly be interested in introducing another woman as his ex from seventeen years ago, who he had fathered a child with.

"Oh, o...o...okay," she said, not questioning her husband. I was all for respecting men, but I'd be damned if I would come out the bathroom and see my husband arguing with two females and not get to the bottom of it.

"Really? If you won't tell her the truth, I will!" That was Sasha pushing past both of us. Like mother, like daughter...she was headstrong, but she was also fearless like her father had been before he turned into a coward.

"Wait!" Jaime hollered out after her and turned to follow her. I grabbed him by the arm.

"Jaime, I used to honestly respect you. I couldn't believe how you turned out. I couldn't believe you never stood up to your parents. But even then, I got it. Okay, you were a young teenager with a bright future ahead of you. A baby on the way? That would be enough to scare any male, especially one whose future was being jeopardized. But what about when you were grown? How come you never came back, then? My parents have been living in the same house forever. You never once lifted a finger to see about your seed. What kind of man are you?" I was breathing deeply, filled with anger and loathing for this man.

He couldn't answer me. He turned to run after Sasha to see what damage she was causing. I ran after him to go rescue my daughter.

"What do you mean, his daughter?" Natalie was asking. Fear had consumed her features, and she was holding her two children close to her. Sasha was standing with a strong expression on her face, but her eyes were red with tears, and she appeared as if she was holding everything inside, trying not to explode. My daughter was devastated and suffering from the pain of a broken heart.

"Come on, baby. We don't need to make a scene. He's got his own ghosts to deal with," I said, pulling Sasha by the arm.

"No, Mom. I want to know why he left me. I want to know how he could never come and look for me. I want to know why he went on and lived his life, having another family as if I never mattered!" Patrons around us were looking our way now, because my daughter's thick, husky voice was carrying to those tables close by.

"I have no clue what's going on here, Jaime. What is she talking about? She says she's your daughter. You never said you had other children. Jaime, she looks just like you...honey, she's got your eyes and coloring. Jaime, answer me, damnit!" Natalie shrieked.

I knew our work there was done. Whatever he needed to do to make his family right was not my concern. I had to go home once again and pick up the broken pieces of my daughter's heart.

Jaime couldn't tear his eyes away from his daughter to answer his wife. He kept staring at Sasha, and finally, he spoke.

"I'm sorry. I'm so sorry. My parents forced me to turn away," he apologized.

"But you never once came back to check on me. You are a grown-assed man! Your parents aren't still stopping you now. It's your cowardice and ignorance that's stopping you. Well, you know something, you have missed out on a beautiful life! I am an honor roll student and have been every year I've been in school. I'm on the basketball team at school, I'm a member of the National Beta Club, the Teen Deliberators Club, and the Junior Volunteer Leaders of America. I don't need or want anything from you. If you were afraid we would need child support, we don't. My mom makes more money in one month than you probably make all year. She has more courage in her pinky finger than you have ever had in your life! My mom has dedicated her life to loving and raising me to be strong and independent. And where were you? I pity your children...because you're a poor excuse for a father. And even now you can't stand strong and tell the truth! You're pathetic!" Sasha ran towards the door, heading for our car.

I looked at Jaime and Natalie one last time. I had no sympathy for him whatsoever. But my heart went out to his wife and their children. The kids appeared afraid, and his wife looked as if her whole world had just been turned upside down. But so had my daughter's, and that was who I had to take care of.

I was thankful it was the weekend. That prevented Sasha from having to go to school or me from going to work. She was going to need some time to deal with her emotions, and I had to be there to help her through. She hadn't wanted to discuss it on the car ride home, preferring instead to sulk and go to her room to cry herself to sleep.

I had ignored the phone calls from Ambiance the entire weekend. I had no time for her pity parties or her whining about her marriage. I also didn't answer Paige's calls, because I wasn't interested in hearing about her latest dalliance. I had received confirmation more than ever that I had to protect my daughter. And I would do it at all costs.

Saturday afternoon, I finally gathered the courage to call my mom and tell her what happened.

"Oh, no, my poor precious angel. Do you want me to come over, sweetie?" she asked.

"No, we'll be fine. I just hate seeing her hurting the way that she is. I never realized she had really convinced herself that he was dead," I admitted.

"Naomi, that's because you didn't want to realize. Honey, remember that day I told you she was over here playing in the front yard with the neighbors' grandkids? She told them that day her daddy was dead when they asked her her parents' names."

"I know, Mom, but she was a little girl back then. I mentioned something to her and explained that he wasn't. But I honestly had no clue she still felt that way after all these years," I shared.

"Well, did he have the decency to explain what happened to him, why he left her?" my mom asked. She gave the benefit of the doubt to everyone. But I could hear the doubt in her voice as she posed the question.

"No, ma'am. He simply lied. At first, he claimed that he didn't know," I stated.

"Hogwash! He knew about her, because he sat his pitiful self right here in my living room with his head held down when his parents came to say that he couldn't do this now. He sat right there as they suggested you have an abortion. Did he say anything about that?"

"No, Mom. I think he just wanted it all to go away. His wife and kids were standing there, and he looked fearful more than anything. I honestly felt sorry for his wife."

"For what?"

"Because Mom, she hasn't done anything. It was like she was caught in the crossfire, and she had such a hurt look on her face. She knew nothing about Sasha. Imagine being married to someone all that time and one day realizing you don't know them."

"Well, she married a coward, so that's what comes with the territory," my mom stated.

"I know, but that still doesn't make it right."

"No, sweetheart, it doesn't. But I thank the Lord that He knows what He's doing. He took you out of that boy's life for a reason. There's no telling what you'd be going through if you two had stayed together. Your father would've killed that boy."

"I know, Mom."

"What are you going to do about Sashaberry?"

"I'll keep talking to her, and we'll take this one day at a time. That's all we can do now, Mom. And pray."

"That's it baby. I'll be praying for you, too. Take care of my grandchild, now. I have to get off this phone and get your dad's meal started."

"All right, Mom. Love you."

"Love you to pieces, sweetie." She blew a kiss at me, and I ended the call.

I sat back on the couch and thought for a long time. I thought about the choices I had made throughout my life. The choice to ignore my parents and get involved with Jaime, the choice to have a baby as a teenager, the choice to fight for her future and mine, the choice to remain single throughout my life, and the choice to not search for him.

I was proficient on the Internet and with technology. I had a friend who owned his own private investigating firm. I had at my disposal the tools to find Jaime for my daughter for the last several years now, but I never once lifted a finger to find him. Why not? I owned some of the blame for this, maybe not as much as he did, but I was partially responsible, too.

After doing some true soul searching, I realized I feared being rejected a second time. What happened at the restaurant was my greatest fear. Now that I was on the other side of it, I was better and stronger. I had worried all those years that if I saw him again, he would deny my child once again. The humiliation of being rejected or having a man claim a child isn't his is unbearable. Especially when you know the child is his and no one else could have fathered it. But the implications that came with his denial put in the air the insinuation that maybe you were a loose woman with low morals. It projected the image that you slept around. That was always the fear I held inside.

I was a young woman who did care what the world thought about me. I was a good girl growing up. I was a young lady who made a mistake by having sex before marriage. I made the mistake of falling for and trusting the wrong guy. As a young lady, I made the mistake of having unprotected sex with that guy. My daughter was the result of those choices, but she was the best blessing God had ever given to me. I would no longer punish her or myself. I would teach her to love herself in spite of her parents' failings. She would be a part of the healing process, and together we would come out refined like gold.

I let her sulk for two days, but Sunday it was over. I went up to her bedroom early that morning and sat down on her bed. Looking around the fuchsia and teal room, I knew I was proud of my daughter's accomplishments. She had made some not-so-great choices lately, but she had to know that she was better than the choices she made.

"Honey, how are you feeling?" I asked, as she lay in that bed.

"Mmm," she groaned. Sasha hid her head under the pillows after I walked to the windows to open the blinds and curtains.

"Look, baby, I know you're upset about what happened on Friday night, but I'm not going to let you hide away from the world. It's like you said, Jaime lost out on a beautiful life. Now, for you to come in here and succumb to this misery and spirit of depression would be admitting that he won. That would be stating the coward had the last word. You are too bright and too beautiful to allow this to take your spirit. What has changed? Huh, Sasha?"

She removed the pillow from her head and turned red swollen eyes my way. "I thought he was dead, Mom," she hiccupped out.

My daughter was breaking my heart, and I was angry at that good-for-nothing sperm donor of hers.

"Baby, I never told you he was dead. I was always truthful with you about that. So, now that you know for a fact he isn't, what has changed?" I asked.

"He doesn't love me!" she spat out.

"You...don't...need...his love to define you, Sasha," I ground out through gritted teeth. "Look at me! Whether he is dead or alive, you are still Sasha Kennedy Blankenship. You are still a point guard on Whitaker High's basketball team. You are still an A, honor roll student who holds a position in all those clubs you told him about. You're beautiful and intelligent and have so much to offer this world. That's who you were before you believed he was alive, and that's who you still are. His existence does not change that. Him being alive and breathing does not stop you from holding your own special place here on this earth, dedicated to living the purpose God created you for. The best way you can live your life is to live it for you. To live it like you own it and nothing is going to stop that. Not your father, not me, not anyone."

She sat up in bed and sniffed, wiping her long, curly hair out of her face and back over her shoulders. "It just hurts so bad, Mom."

"Why, Sasha?"

"Because I thought he loved me. And now I realize he doesn't," she cried out. Her body shook with sobs and I pulled her close.

"Oh, Sashaberry. I'm so sorry, baby. I should've addressed that a long time ago. Does that change how you feel about yourself?"

"Nooo," she wailed.

"Does it change how me, or Papa, or Nana feel about you?"

"Mm-mm," she continued to whine.

"Then you need to get strong and move past this. You don't need his love. I know you want it, but you were doing just fine and we were getting along very well without him in our lives."

She stayed in my arms and continued to cry a while longer. I let her purge herself until she was all done.

"Now, I want you to get up out this bed, get showered, and get dressed. Papa and Nana are expecting us at church this morning. Do you understand?"

"Yes, ma'am." She sniffed.

I could only hope and pray that some of my words had penetrated the fog in her mind. I prayed that she could now possibly understand some of the sacrifices I had made for her. Most important of all, I hoped she would take this experience and grow from it, that it would make her stronger and not break her. I didn't want her to allow his mistakes to define her future the way I had allowed them to define mine. He had robbed one of us of our life, he couldn't have both. Because in my soul-searching, I realized I had chosen to stay away from relationships to protect my heart, as well. I never wanted to feel the hurt and pain I had experienced in the years since Jaime walked away from our daughter…and from me.

9_PAIGE_A RUN AWAY

I sat at my desk staring at the file in front of me. As a senior social worker, it was my job to connect children and families with the resources needed for them to live a productive life. I was also called in to handle clients who had severe behavioral issues and those who had experienced severe traumatic incidents in their lives.

I was very familiar with the current child, whose case file sat before me. She had been in nine foster homes in less than two years. Her mother had been murdered by her father, and her mother's family didn't want to take her in. According to them, she had a multitude of issues they didn't want to take on. Her father appeared to have no family. So, the child had been put into foster care. The first family couldn't deal with her, because she was constantly wetting the bed at the age of thirteen, and her recurring nightmares caused her to scream out loud in the middle of the night.

The second foster home had begun neglecting her after they had a child of their own. This wasn't anything uncommon. Sometimes families who couldn't have children wanted to adopt and started out as foster families first. But when they had children of their own, they'd decide they no longer wanted the foster child. They would want to return them as if they were products from a store that didn't work or unused or damaged goods.

The third foster family had been a nightmare. Allegations of sexual abuse arose from one of the other foster children in the home. An investigation into the allegations revealed not only was that child being abused, but so was the child in my case file. She had been raped repeatedly during her stay there by the teen foster brother, and it came out that the foster father had been molesting her, as well.

The fourth, fifth, and sixth foster families were overwhelmed by the complications she brought. If she wasn't fighting the other children, she was physically destroying the home. Her behavior grew worse from there as she bounced to her seventh, eighth, and ninth foster homes. She was now dealing with complications stemming from seeing her father murder her mother and from being raped and molested. Her promiscuous behavior in the last three homes created complex matters for the foster parents. On a few occasions, she attempted to approach the fathers in an inappropriate manner. Eventually, she was kicked out of the last three. She was currently residing in a temporary group home until we could determine her next step.

She was waiting in the lobby with her caseworker to meet with me. We were going to determine whether we needed to place her in a group home or if we needed to implement other alternatives for her. I needed to address her promiscuity. She had been diagnosed with a couple of STDs on a few different occasions. And if we didn't get matters under control now, I was afraid of what her future might look like.

I closed the file and took a sip of my coffee. I was ready to start my day. Walking into the lobby, I spotted Gail Edmonds, the case worker, and beckoned her and her client into my office. Trying to discuss her options and the consequences of her behavior with her was to no avail. She was obstinate and didn't want to talk to either of us. She sat sulking, staring out the window behind me the entire time.

After our meeting was finished, Gail and I sat in my office while her client sat in an adjoining office under supervision.

"I recommend she goes to the Angela Simms Home for Girls or the Mattie Simpson-Billings Home," Gail advised.

"Why the Billings Home? It's an orphanage for young children, not a group home."

"I know, but there is a couple that started off as volunteers, and now they're on the board of directors. Courtney and Pierce Brennen have started a new mentoring program for orphaned children who have experienced traumatic events in their lives. It's designed to help them with the healing process, reconnecting with society, and discovering the gifts they have to offer. I believe it would be instrumental in helping Madison recover from her past," Gail advised.

I thought it over for a moment. "Well, my concern is that she would be exposed to males, as well. With her promiscuous behavior, I think it's advisable to place her in an all-girls program at this time. At least until we have had the opportunity to address these issues and put a plan in place to help her overcome."

"I agree, but with 'round the clock supervision, we can definitely prevent her from having any more episodes," Gail countered.

I detested her terminology. What did she mean, episode? She wasn't a schizophrenic or a person with an illness like epilepsy. She didn't have episodes, she had promiscuous behavior. The child had suffered abuse, and as a result, she acted out her feelings of pain, hurt, anger, and love by the use of her body as a weapon. There were no episodes! I struggled to rid my intonation of disgust. A voice in my head reasoned that I possibly could have been taking this a little more personal than I should have.

"Gail, she cannot possibly have 'round the clock supervision. And that type of thinking is a fallacy. The system is understaffed and underpaid. No matter what they tell you in those homes, make no mistakes about it, they do not have those kind of resources or that kind of time to dedicate to any one particular child. Don't get me wrong," I said, holding my hand up to ward off her comment, "I'm sure they mean well, and I have heard nothing but great things about the orphanage, but what you're suggesting to me is close to impossible. We cannot continue to let these children slip through the cracks. That orphanage isn't the place for her at this time. If we fail her now, we will just be another kink in the system. She needs to know that she can trust someone. If she can't trust her social worker, who can she trust?"

"I understand, Paige. I really do, I just thought—"

"Don't think about it, Gail. It's your job to know. You have to know what's best for your client and place her in the environment that will foster growth, structure, and healing for her."

"So, what do you recommend, Paige?"

"I recommend the Angela Simms Home for Girls. I have researched it, as well, and that was my first and original thought. She will have daily counseling there, be placed on work detail in a male-free environment, and attend classes every day. They have mentors and therapists to pair her up with to help her on the road to recovery. We have to do everything possible to keep her out of the juvenile system. And right now, the decisions she's making are putting her on track there. When is her next doctor's appointment?" I asked.

"In two weeks, on the seventeenth," Gail replied.

I consulted my calendar and thought about it for a moment. "You are escorting her there, correct?"

"Yes, ma'am."

"Okay, I will meet you all there. What time is it?" I realized I had that day open so far. There were no appointments currently scheduled.

"Umm, 10:45 that morning," she replied. Gail looked shocked. She knew I was, in effect, prepared to take this case off her hands. She was already on probation for not handling a previous case properly. I was looking over her cases with a firm hand, and I had no plans of relenting any time soon. These girls couldn't fall by the wayside. They needed someone to fight for them. I knew what it felt like to not have someone fight for you. Eventually, you were no longer the victim, but you victimized those closest to you. The cycle had to end.

The rest of my day went that way, and I couldn't wait to get home. It was one abused or unloved child after another. Some with hope, and others with what some would say was no hope. But I believed in them and wouldn't give up. The job of a social worker is never over, and sometimes you get calls in the middle of the night. It took its toll on you emotionally and physically. Because I had dedicated myself to this line of work, I had no time for relationships or family. I focused solely on the job and enjoying myself after hours. The job left me empty inside, too empty to give myself to others. My job could be rewarding when we saw positive outcomes, and at other times, it could be draining. Or at least I wanted to believe it was the job doing that to me.

I was soaking in the tub when my cell phone rang. I grabbed a towel close at hand and wrapped it around myself. Walking to my bedroom, I glanced at the caller ID. A smile slowly spread across my face. I needed him tonight. I hadn't heard from him in about a week. But that was not abnormal, Rodney popped in and out of my life as it suited him. And I allowed it. He was just what I needed. He didn't ask questions, never held me accountable, and he didn't feel the need to explain himself to me. He wanted one thing and one thing only. He was my thug in the dark, and I loved him for it.

"Hello?" I greeted in a sultry tone.

"Hey, wassup with you tonight? Can I come through?" he asked in his no-nonsense tone.

"Sure," I replied, with a smile lighting up my features.

"Good, I'll be there in ten minutes." He clicked the phone off, no explanation, no terms of endearment, and no questions. Straight from the hip. That was Rodney.

As promised, my doorbell rang within ten minutes. I simply had time to finish my bath, dry off and lotion down. There would be no lingerie for him. He didn't care for that stuff, and he didn't stay around long enough to appreciate it.

Rodney was the same light caramel color I was. He was slender built with muscles, light-colored eyes, and wavy hair. Although he was no pretty boy by any means, at first glance, people might assume he was. Rodney was a rough neck through and through.

"Come on," he said, locking the door behind him. We never made it to the bedroom, and he didn't bother removing his clothes. He reached inside his back pocket and removed a condom, unzipped his pants, dropped them around his ankles, and made me bend over at the waist. I held onto the countertop dividing the living room from the kitchen.

He sheathed himself and there were no words exchanged between us. Rodney shoved himself inside of me with one swift motion. Holding my waist to keep me as still as possible, he began swiftly pumping in and out. I continued holding on to the countertop to balance myself and opened as wide as possible to accommodate him.

"Mmmm, baby, that's it, big daddy. Aiggh give it to me just like that!" I shouted. I didn't care if the neighbors heard or if the cops came knocking, as Maxwell said. It felt good to let him relieve himself inside of me, and it felt good for me to discard the frustrations of my day. At one point, he pulled me away from the countertop and bent me over to touch my toes. As he pumped, he also smacked my behind. And every time it would jiggle against him, he would hit it again.

We went at it like that for a few hours off and on. He would let me take breaks here and there, and then he would start all over again. Kissing me from the crown of my head all the way down to my feet, he was a lover that truly made my toes curl. And when he tasted me, he sucked me dry. I would scream and holler his name out loud. If I was on top riding the horses he brought, I would hold on for dear life as he shoved his length completely inside. There was no stopping him from getting where he wanted to go. I was like 7-Eleven, open twenty-four-seven, giving him complete access.

When Rodney was finished with me, I was drained of all emotions, doubts, and fears. I lay in the bed beside him as he gently snored. My phone began ranging. It was David. I ignored it. I dared not hit the decline button, because that would signal to him that I had purposely cut his call off. He hung up and called right back. His wife must not have been around.

Rodney stirred in his sleep. "You gon' answer that?" he asked.

"Uh-uh, you ready to go again?" I asked.

"Nah, I gotta go. What time is it?"

"Ten-thirty-five," I responded. I walked to the windows and closed the curtains to shut out the night.

"All right. I'll see you around."

And just like that, he grabbed his keys and he was out.

I felt relaxed from my head to my toes. That only lasted a moment as my phone started ringing again. It was David. I decided to answer the phone. I didn't want to argue with him later, and there would be a later.

I heard a niggling little voice in the back of my mind that sounded very much like my mother. It was warning me that I needed to be cautious about sleeping around, but at the moment, I didn't want to focus on that. I was a grown woman, and I knew exactly what I was doing. Besides, I had protection…and not just the kind that came in little square foil packs or little round dispensers with multiple colors and labeled by the days of the week. No sir, I carried my little .25. Just like American Express, I didn't leave home without it.

"Hello?"

"Where you been?" he barked.

"Here at home."

"You been with another nigga? Cuz if so, you need to tell him to bounce. I'm on my way."

"Ain't nobody been here, David. Not sure why that should matter to you anyway. By the way, where's your wife?" I was getting fed up with his possessive act. Hell, Vic was all into me and he wasn't involved with anyone else, and he didn't act like that.

"Don't worry about her. I'm on the way."

I pulled my sheets off and took them into my laundry room. I didn't know how long he would be, and he didn't give a heads-up. I hurriedly put a fresh set on, took a quick shower, and lit the candles in my bedroom.

It had been a mistake to ever allow David to come to my home. Rodney was the only one I had ever allowed to come over, and that was because he respected my space. David acted as if he owned it.

David had been there for only thirty minutes before my work cell phone rang. It was not unusual to get a call in the middle of the night, but David had never experienced it.

"Shut that phone off," he grumbled. He was pushing hard into me at that moment. But my first responsibility was to my job. That was the prime reason I had not entangled myself into a relationship. I had been thinking it was time to cut my strings to David. There were any number of men out there willing to service my needs. He was not the only one. I didn't know what it was about him, but it was almost like he was becoming emotionally attached. I had no time for emotional attachments, especially not to a man who was married and had nothing to offer me anyway.

"David, get up, I have to answer that," I stated.

"Uh-uh," he replied.

"What do you mean, uh-uh? I said get up, David!" I demanded. I began bucking to push him off me, but his grip around me grew tighter. It seemed the more I fought him, the more excited he became. I began thrashing around in his grip and using my fingers to claw at his arms. And then he released me.

I was furious! How dare he think he could control me like that! I was not going to see him anymore after tonight. But I wasn't dumb. I didn't trust David, and I wouldn't tell him that I couldn't see him anymore. Not in person, anyway. I preferred to ignore his calls, or tell him over the phone.

Some may think I was a coward, but I knew David was a bit on the crazy side.

"What's wrong with you?" he asked, gathering his senses.

"Me? There's nothing wrong with me! But if I tell you to get up, you get up!" I declared. I was moving to my phone on the dresser.

"Man, you tripping. I didn't come over here to be tripped on," he grumbled, heading to my bathroom to wash up. I didn't bother arguing with him.

Looking at the caller ID, I knew it was Jenny, the director of intake at my organization. She was covering the night shift. Every night, there was a different employee manning the emergency line, a dedicated line available for both emergency and non-emergency personnel to contact us. All calls were routed to the director on duty's work cell phone or home phone. Social workers, case managers, directors of the various group homes, foster parents, and all emergency workers had this line. I listened to Jenny's voicemail and then dialed her back.

"Hi, Jenny, this is Paige."

"Hi, hon, I'm sorry to wake you," she stated, "but it's an emergency. Madison is missing."

"Have the police been called?" I asked. I didn't acknowledge her statement about waking me. The less people knew about me, the better for me. I was living a double life, and that was okay by me. The Paige at work who promoted and preached good ethics and morals was not the same Paige who slept with various men behind closed doors to gain some sense of release and self-fulfillment.

"Not yet. But Mara Dixon, the director of Rock-Stone Manor, says she has been gone less than an hour. She had just left Madison's room around two this morning, because Madison was having nightmares again. Ms. Dixon says when she went back to check on her, she was gone. It had been less than forty minutes at that time. They have organized a group to go out looking for her in their community, and she will keep me posted."

"Are any other children missing, Jen?"

"No."

"All right, I'm on my way to the Manor," I said, and then hung up the phone. Rock-Stone Manor was a transition house where juveniles stayed while they were waiting to be transitioned to their foster family or group home. Mara Dixon, the home's director, was one of the best in our world. She really cared about the youth, and she was a rock.

Madison had run away. She had never been a run away before, and it scared me. It sent the message that her problems were getting worse. If we didn't find her soon, we would have to involve law enforcement. The last thing that I wanted was for her to become involved in the juvenile justice system. I knew I had a job to do, but I cared about the welfare of these kids. And Madison struck a chord of familiarity with my soul. I would make the decision on how to handle it when I arrived.

For now, I needed to get David on his way and get out. I walked in on him running a bath.

"David, you'll have to make it a quick wash up. One of my clients needs me," I announced, grabbing my washcloth and going to one of the "his and her" sinks.

"Oh, so you just gon' throw me out like that? You got yours, and now you have no time for me."

This Negro did not just say that to me. Yeah, it was time for him to get his roll on. I could have any other man I wanted. I did not want a married man with separation issues. Hell, if I wanted that, I could've had children.

"Look, first of all, I didn't get mine. Second, I've told you time and again that when my work cell rings, I have to go. No questions asked, and no answers given. This is the first time that it's ever happened with you here, but that line comes first and foremost. Don't be in here treating me like I have to answer to you. I'm not your woman. You're a married man, and we have no commitment to one another. You know what this is…I told you what it was when we first got involved a year and a half ago. Now, I don't mind you coming over and handling your business, but at the same time, we're not going to do this. I can't do this commitment-type thing. If you want that, you need to take it back home to your wife!"

The entire time I was speaking, I had my back turned to him and was washing up. I could see him in the mirror walking towards me. He was getting angry, and I didn't care. He slammed his fist into the mirror.

"Damn you, Paige! You ain't nothing but a two-cent ho'! I ain't gotta take this shit from you!"

David didn't even wince when he broke my mirror and cut his fist. I bent over into a ball when he did it, praying the glass didn't cut me. That was it. He was no longer welcome in my home. I stood up, taking a moment to regain my composure. I would not say another word to him. And I damn sure wouldn't display another sign of fear. I listened as he threw his clothes back on and stormed out of my condo, slamming the door behind him.

I shuddered for a moment and ran to the front door and locked it. Within fifteen minutes, I had washed up, dressed, and jumped in my car, heading for Rock-Stone Manor.

10 AMBIANCE LUNCH DATE

It was two weeks after I had coffee with Nick before I decided to use his number. I had not seen him since that night. He hadn't even dropped by the boutique. Not that he had a reason to, but I was hoping he would anyway.

Eric and I had had another one of our infamous blow-ups. He walked out the house and by the next morning, he had not come back. I called and texted him. He simply texted back and let me know he was at his brother, Steven's, house. Hmphh, well, we'd see who would be sitting around moping today. It surely wouldn't be me.

It seemed at times the clock stopped altogether that day at work as time dragged on. My eyes glanced up at the clock a few minutes after eleven, and I couldn't take it anymore. Business was really slow, and I had no appointments scheduled. I pulled out my cell phone and closed the door to my office.

Changing my mind, I walked to my desk and picked up the office phone. I didn't want my cell phone number to pop up on his caller ID. I had thrown his business card away after saving his number in my phone under a false name. I dialed the number I had saved under Weight Loss two weeks ago. I shook my head at my ridiculousness. Eric had a habit of checking my phone even though I had never given him reason to.

"Hello?" came that sexy voice.

"Hi, it's Ambiance."

"Hey, I'm glad you decided to hit me up. Did you enjoy yourself that night?" he asked.

My insides were quivering; his voice was so sexy. It caressed me up and down like silk on soft skin after a fresh bath. Mmphh. *Breathe, Ambiance...breathe, girl,* I coached myself. It felt good to have someone looking forward to hearing from me and I could tell in his voice he wanted to hear from me.

"Umm, yeah," I managed to squeak out. Now that I had done the deed, I was trembling. What was I going to say? I had not put too much thought into this.

"So, what's going on with you today?" he asked.

"Well, just a little work and not too much of anything else. I was thinking, I really appreciate you inviting me to the dinner. I had lunch with one of the ladies that I met that night, and I have three meetings scheduled with the three gentlemen you introduced me to. I think these contacts will take my business to the next level. So, I wanted to take you to lunch to thank you for the opportunity."

Yeah, that sounded good. I hadn't known why I wanted to call him other than to hear his voice. But this excuse sounded as good as any.

"Well, I'm glad it worked out for you. That's what it was all about. And I would love to have lunch with you," he confessed, with a slight chuckle.

I knew he was thinking about how hard he had tried to get me to go to lunch previously, but I wouldn't give him the time of day.

"Okay, well, do you have any particular day in mind?"

"How about today? It's good for me if it's good for you," he declared.

"Sounds good. I usually go at 12:30."

"Can you get away early today, perhaps for an extended lunch?"

I thought about my calendar. I had no meetings scheduled that day. This would be perfect, because I could skip out for lunch and get back in time to head home for the day. We had two other personal shoppers on duty that day. I wouldn't be missed, I reasoned.

"Sure, that won't be a problem," I confirmed. "Where do you want me to meet you at?" I asked, grabbing a pencil to jot down any notes or directions.

"I'll be there to pick you up in about ten minutes, is that cool?"

I panicked, "Um no." People at the boutique knew that I was married. How would I explain Nick's constant popping up at the boutique? There were only so many clothes a man could come to buy for his mother and aunt before people started getting suspicious. Not to mention I didn't want to explain getting into a car with some tall, dark, and sexy man driving a nice whip.

"Are you sure? I don't mind picking you up."

"No, thanks. I'll be fine driving myself. Where do you want to meet?"

"Let's go to the Shepherd's Place," he said, referring to an upscale restaurant three blocks from my job. I didn't know if he planned to pay or if we were paying for our own meals. Well, after all, we were only friends, right?

There wasn't anything going on that shouldn't be. So, of course I would pay for my own meal. Just because he had paid for both of our coffees that night meant nothing. There went my shopping money for this paycheck. I was a clothes horse and had to buy at least two outfits every paycheck along with a handbag and a pair of shoes. The Shepherd's Place didn't cost quite that much, but it was definitely not cheap.

"Okay. I'll meet you there in say ten?"

"All right, pretty lady. I'll see you there," he said in that voice that made my insides quiver.

I hung up my office phone, grabbed my purse, phone, and keys, and headed for the door.

"Peggy, I'm taking an early lunch. I should be back in about a couple of hours."

"Sure, Ambiance. Do you want me to reschedule your lunch date with Marc and Sharon?" Peggy knew that Marc and Sharon quite often popped up to get me on their way to lunch. She was the keeper of both mine and Angelique's calendars, as well.

I had forgotten all about our lunch date. Oh, well, I would hook up with them another time. "That would be great, Peggy. Just see if they can reschedule for tomorrow. Tell them I had an important meeting."

"Sure," she said with a smile. She was a very reserved and professional older lady. Before Nick told me he had attained very personal information about me from her, I would have said she didn't gossip. Peggy was efficient at the work she did keeping me organized, preparing my materials for every meeting, and producing timely reports.

I fast-stepped down the hallway to the back of the boutique and made my way into the ladies restroom. Slipping in, I locked the door behind me. I checked my image in the mirror to make sure everything was on point. I wore my naturally-wavy, jet black-hair in a ponytail. I pressed my full, red lips together. My Relentlessly Red M.A.C lipstick was holding up smooth as usual. My eyes were flawless, and my makeup only enhanced them. I turned around in the mirror to check out my style. I wore a black, short-sleeved dress today that stopped just a few inches above my knees. And those oh-so-beautiful, sexy red heels that adorned my size six feet made my calves pop, along with other unmentionables. Yes, your girl was looking fierce.

Subconsciously, I had dressed with the thought that I just might see Nick today. I tucked my little red and black purse under my arm and trotted out the bathroom.

Hopping in my Camry, I started feeling the first flaring of my nerves. To quell the feeling and the second-guessing of myself, I popped in my Dru Hill CD. It wasn't long before Jazz began belting out the words to *Never Make a Promise*. Mm-hmm, that was what Eric used to sing, but he didn't keep any of his promises.

I quickly ejected the Dru Hill CD and inserted another one of their CDs, *Enter The Dru,* and selected *Beauty. Yeah, that's more like it.* I opened my purse and searched for a piece of gum or some mints. I came across some watermelon gum and popped a piece in my mouth. Mmm, so juicy and flavorful. Whew! That wasn't the thought I wanted to have. For some reason lately, my mind had a habit of wandering into places it had no business. I put the car in drive and pulled out of my parking space as I bobbed my head. This was more like it.

My heart picked up its pace the closer I got to the restaurant. It wasn't long before I pulled up and parked right next to his charcoal beauty. I didn't know the model of whip he drove, but it sure was pretty.

I hopped out and secured the locks. Just as I was preparing to head in the direction of the restaurant, I heard my name. "Ambiance." I would know that voice anywhere. There went my heart and everything else. How could someone I didn't know and had just met have such an effect on me? It had to be the issues I was going through at home with Eric.

I turned around, and a smile involuntarily took over my face. Nick was standing there in black slacks, a white, open-collared shirt, and a black jacket thrown carelessly over his shoulder. That was one fine man, if I could say so myself, and I was definitely saying so.

"Hi, how are you?" I greeted in a shy manner, so unlike me.

"I'm doing well now that you're here," he professed. He lightly placed his hand on my lower back for a moment, ushering me towards the doors of the restaurant. I briefly looked around to make sure I didn't see anyone I knew. When he removed his hand to open the door, I instantly missed his touch.

"Why, does this mean you can finally eat?" I teased.

"Yeah, okay, something like that." He looked confused.

"What is that supposed to mean?" I asked.

"I was just happy to see you. I'm glad you're here and looking forward to spending some time with you."

I let out a huge sigh. It was bad enough I was battling my own reactions to him. I didn't need him adding his feelings and thoughts to that.

"I told you that I wasn't looking to get involved, and you're saying things like that. Nick, honestly, I just need a friend," I pleaded.

I was doing an award-winning act of trying to convince him and myself. Because deep inside I needed more than what my husband was willing to offer at the moment. I wanted more, but it couldn't be my fault. I just didn't want it to be my fault. I was a good girl, but my husband was a bad boy. A real bad boy. I had grown tired of his cold ways, and the way he virtually ignored me as though I didn't exist. He tolerated me, that's what it was. He had cheated earlier in our marriage a couple of times, and I thought I had forgiven him, but after a while, I realized I hadn't.

As time moved on, Eric started pushing me away after he grew tired of my emotional state about his infidelity. We had erected a barrier between us, and in the last couple of years, I had tried to pull it down. He wasn't willing to.

Nick belted out a deep laugh. "Look, I can't help myself. You are a beautiful woman, so as a natural man, I react to that. I enjoy your company and talking with you. I heard you when you said you weren't trying to get involved, but let me ask you this, then…why are you here standing in this spot with me?"

"I told you. I wanted to take you to lunch to thank you for the opportunity you gave me. And I think we could be good friends. Sometimes, I just need someone to talk to, someone to kick it with, that's all. A man and woman can't be friends?"

"Sure, they can, if they can ignore the mutual attraction they have. But I can be cool. I have no problem with that. If you're sure that's what you want," he remarked, raising an eyebrow at me.

"It's what I want," I stated firmly.

"Shall we have lunch, *friend*?" he asked, placing emphasis on the word friend.

I followed him inside the restaurant.

As time passed we fell into an easy and convenient flow of having lunch together daily. It happened without either of noticing it. After our first lunch together, Nick invited me to lunch the next day on the premise that he wanted to run an idea by me. Then I invited him back to lunch the day after that to prepare for a meeting I had with one of his business contacts. He was so easy to talk to and share a couple of laughs with. I looked forward to spending time in his presence, and his opinions mattered to me.

"So, why aren't you dating anyone?" I scooped a forkful of crab salad into my mouth.

"I don't know. This business keeps you going, and you have very little time to date. Most of my business partners in this industry are married. Their women understand the long hours and dedication to the business. You pretty much make this your life if you want to be successful at it. And I am relatively successful."

I finished chewing my salad. "But you make time to have lunch with me every day. You could be spending those lunch hours with some special woman, wining and dining her."

"Yeah, but most women want to go out in the evening or spend time together on the weekend. I just don't have that time right now. I'm usually in the office until late in the evening or night, and on the weekends, I am at one project site or another. Don't get me wrong, I get time in here and there, but more often than not, I'm tied up in work. But then again, I choose to give myself to my work, because it's really the only life I have. I mean, you should understand. Didn't you tell me your husband was an attorney who worked long hours?"

I sipped on my glass of tea to wash down the salad and compose my thoughts. Yes, I had told him that, but it wasn't the complete truth.

"Nick, my husband is an attorney who spends long hours and days at the office and in court. But the truth?" I took another sip of my tea as I contemplated what I would say.

Nick nodded, urging me to go on.

"My husband often has late nights at his brothers' and boys' houses as well."

"Maybe you're just assuming that, Ambiance," he said, attempting to get me to see a positive side.

"No, it's not an assumption. It's what he's told me."

"Well, he could be out running the streets. Have you told him how it makes you feel?"

"He knows. And that's just the problem, I'm not so sure he isn't running the streets. As a matter of fact, he was doing exactly that the first year of our marriage. He gave me the same excuses he gives me now, and I learned he was having an affair with a woman named Kendra. I couldn't understand why he would marry me if he wasn't ready to settle down," I confessed.

I was feeling the rush of pain all over again as if it had only been yesterday. To a certain extent, I felt it could have been. I had no clue what my husband was out there doing these days. He could tell me whatever, and I had to trust him. But a gut feeling inside told me not to.

"Most nights he doesn't come home. I mean, he probably comes home two or three nights out of the week. The rest of the time, I just get a text telling me he's with his brothers or at one of the fellows' houses. Most of his friends and both his brothers live in the downtown area near his job. So, it's a convenient excuse."

"A text, huh?" There was something brewing in his eyes and I couldn't detect what it was.

"Yeah. It hurts, because he chooses not to come home, and I'm left there feeling like…I'm not worthy of a phone call?"

"Ambiance, do you have children?"

"No. I refuse to. I don't think we should have children until we get our marriage right. In the beginning we agreed we would enjoy the first two or three years of marriage before we started a family. But we haven't been able to enjoy that much. Why would I want to bring children into it?"

The waiter came by to check on us and refresh our drinks. We thanked him.

"How long have you been married?"

"Five years."

"So, what are you doing on those nights he's gone away from home? Do you go out with your female friends?" Nick was sitting back in his chair running his fingers down his beard.

"No, they're usually busy with their own lives. I've no one to hang with or talk to. I watch TV or go to sleep early when I'm not working on my business. My consulting hours are usually between four and seven. Afterwards, I just work on different ideas and marketing my business online. But there are many nights when it's just me and my pillow," I confided. I had no clue why I was telling him all of this. I knew I shouldn't, but a part of me couldn't help it.

His smoldering eyes were narrowed and heavy. I could only imagine the thoughts going through his head. A part of me was ashamed, because although I wasn't looking to have an affair on my husband, I was looking to be desired by a man. I wanted someone to look at me the way Nick was looking at me now. It made me feel beautiful, sexy, desired, and womanly.

"Why don't you pick up the phone and call me?"

"I thought you said you kept long hours, too?"

"I do. But I promise I'll make time for you whenever you need it." He reached out and grabbed my hand across the table.

I held my head down and looked at our hands clasped together on the table. This was something more than friends, yet not quite lovers. I felt the heat emanating from the two of us. I tried to ignore the look he was now pinning me down with, and I couldn't. After a few awkward beats, I removed my hand from his.

"I'm sorry, Ambiance. I didn't mean to make you feel uncomfortable," he apologized.

"No, it's okay. I guess I just needed to get that off my chest. And for some strange reason, I feel so comfortable talking to you. I almost feel as if I can tell you anything."

He gave me a crooked half-smile.

"Look, baby girl, you can. You can trust me with anything, and I won't let you down. Whatever you need, simply ask, and I've got your back. I think I've told you that before."

"Yes, you have, and you're so sweet for being so attentive to my needs. Whew! How did we get on me, anyway? I thought we were talking about you and your need to date."

"We were. I wanted to talk about you. And hey," he said, reaching out to grab my chin and lift my head up. He drew closer to me across the table, "I meant what I said. Call me on those nights. That's what *friends* are for." His mouth was saying friends, but his eyes were saying something else entirely.

I had lost my breath and my words. His eyes had me quaking on the inside. I knew that everything I was feeling in that moment was wrong. I had grown up with loving parents in a household filled with love and support for me and my two brothers and sister. They had instilled in us good morals and values. So, if what I was feeling right now was so wrong, why did it feel oh so good?

I had always been a strong black woman, standing for what I believed in. I had never backed down from a challenge, and fear wasn't my middle name. I refused to allow situations to take control of me. Instead, I preferred to be in control of every situation. Some would say throughout the years of my marriage, I had been weak. I wouldn't call it weak, I would call it a woman who was willing to do whatever was necessary to make sure her marriage worked. But what I was feeling at this moment would have me admitting that for the first time in a long time, I was weak. I was weak, because I had allowed my husband to break me down emotionally. But because I was so weak, I knew it was time for me to stand stronger than ever before. I would not make that phone call tonight. If I did, it would be my undoing.

11_NAOMI_BONES & STIX

Sasha and I had resumed our regularly-scheduled lives after the brief interruption. Attending church with my parents that Sunday had been a cleansing process for us both. We enjoyed dinner with them that evening and returned to school and work as if all were well. I continued to take her back and forth to school until I could re-secure my trust in her. Just because we had run into Jaime, did not mean I had forgotten the things Sasha had done prior to that.

It was a couple of weeks after our run-in with Jaime at the restaurant that I once again experienced an upheaval in our lives. I was analyzing the forecasts that were submitted by each department for the month when my internal line buzzed.

"Yes, Nadia?" I answered after pushing the button to respond to my assistant's call.

"There's a gentleman in the lobby downstairs insisting he needs to speak with you. Security did not allow him up; however, he has persisted, stating it was an urgent family matter," she explained.

I could not think of any male that would be attempting to reach me about family matters. I was an only child, and my father, uncles and grandfather all had my cell phone number as well as my direct extension at work. Everyone here was very familiar with my father. I knew it couldn't be him, otherwise they would have allowed him to come directly up.

"Did he leave a name?" I inquired. I removed my reading glasses and rubbed my tired eyes. I knew they were probably red after hours of staring at my computer screen.

"No, ma'am. Security says he appears to be a Hispanic gentleman?" A probing tone rang out in Nadia's voice, as though she were questioning rather than informing me.

Hispanic. That could only be one person…a Cuban man by the name of Jaime Fernandez-Garcia. What the hell did he want, and why was he here at my job? Truthfully, I could answer the second half of that question easier than the first half. He dared not go to my parents' home. He probably knew I had shared what happened with them, and my father would be waiting to break his puny behind in half. He knew that I worked for EBS, so he had shown up here instead.

What I did not know was the why, and curiosity was getting the better of me. I wanted to know the why, but I wanted to do it on my own terms. I knew I needed time to get my emotions under control. And when I really thought about it, I realized I wasn't as surprised as I first thought I was. Honestly, I had been expecting this visit. I even suspected that his wife might be behind it, but, where he was concerned, my emotions were a wreck. He was the last man I had truly cared for or trusted, and he had taken that care and trust and tossed it out like yesterday's garbage.

"Okay, I know who it is, Nadia. Please have them buzz him up, but leave him in the waiting room. Tell him I will be with him when I finish my conference call," I ordered.

"Yes, ma'am." Nadia hung up the phone, and although this entire situation had to be an oddity for her, she did not dare question me. She knew I would never leave anyone waiting who stated it was a matter of urgency, just as she knew I did not have a conference call. The only thing I had on my schedule today was meeting Ambiance for lunch. I had not seen her in some time, and we were supposed to get together for an extended lunch today. That would be canceled.

I went back to my forecasts and resumed reviewing them, but my mind had difficulty focusing. I picked up the phone and called Paige. Although she had her issues, I could trust her to shoot straight from the hip.

"Hey, girl, I need a word of advice. You got a moment?" I asked.

"Sure, what's going on?" Paige asked.

"Well, I've only spoken to you and Ambi briefly here lately. I haven't had a chance to tell you what's really been going on, because I've been trying to wrap my mind around it," I began.

"What's up, girl? Everything all right? My baby okay?" she asked, referring to Sasha. She and Ambiance were crazy about Sasha and had always been a large part of her life. With me being an only child, Paige and Ambiance were the only aunts Sasha had ever known. And there wasn't a thing they wouldn't do for her.

"In a way she is, and in a way she isn't. We went to dinner a couple of weekends ago, spending some time together. I started listening to what Ambi had to say about me talking to Sasha more. After catching her at school and then her bringing that boy home, I decided she was right."

"Good, I'm glad you're listening, now," Paige interrupted.

"Well, that day we went to Havana's Cocina. You'll never guess who we ran into," I confided.

"Jaime?" Paige asked in a nonchalant tone.

"How…how—" I couldn't even finish my sentence; I was in so much shock. He was the last person I expected to see, but somehow, the primary person Paige suspected.

"Look, Naomi, I'ma keep it real with you. A long time ago we knew that was his favorite restaurant. His parents always took him there when we were younger. That's how you became introduced to the place. All these years you've been taking her, I figured you were hoping to run into him again sooner or later. It was no secret to me what you were doing."

"No, that's her favorite restaurant," I denied.

"Yeah, I know it is. But it became her favorite, because you explained to her at an early age that she was Cuban and African American. She understood that this was a part of her heritage, and so it was a matter of great importance to her. But you never took her to any other Cuban restaurant. You two enjoy fine dining at all these different places. You eat at three or four different Italian, Middle Eastern, or Mexican or whatever kind of restaurants you choose. But you only visit the same Cuban restaurant over and over again. And you drive halfway across the city to do that when there's one right there in your community. It's clear to me and Ambi what you've been doing. Wake up, sister, you're the only one who doesn't see it. And do me a favor…close your mouth," she stated.

I did just that. My best friend knew me well. I was sitting there like a fool with my mouth wide open. Paige had just read me like the writing in a book, and I couldn't deny it. She only stated to me what I had always known deep inside but refused to admit to myself.

"Okay. Well, that didn't go so smooth, because she really got upset. Not to mention he was there with his wife and kids," I shared.

Paige sighed, and I knew she was empathizing with me. "Oh, honey. Are you okay?"

"Yeah, I'm good," I replied.

"No, I mean deep down on the inside…are you okay with seeing him like that?"

This was Paige; if I didn't keep things real with her, she would call me on it.

"Okay, I was somewhat rattled, but not surprised. Yeah, it would've been great to see that he had been suffering in misery all those years without me and his child in his life. But the truth is he's been doing well. The only retribution I received was all those years ago when his NBA career came to ruins. But other than that, he appears to be okay."

"Well, that's a good thing, Naomi. I know you don't see it that way now, but eventually you will. It's time to start the healing process," Paige shared. She sounded like the social worker that she was.

"His wife was completely caught off guard. She had no clue, and Sasha read them both the riot act," I imparted.

Paige giggled uncontrollably, and I shared in on the laugh with her. It felt good to release that.

"So, what's your problem now?" Paige asked after getting herself under control again.

"He popped up at my office today," I shared.

"He's at EBS? But how did he get past security? Y'all like Fort Knox up in there and shit. Hell, I've been there dozens of times, and I know them heifers know me, but they won't let me up there."

"Well, they didn't. They called and spoke with Nadia, and she informed me."

"Oh hell, mouth almighty knows, now everyone will know," Paige teased. She didn't much care for my assistant. She was great at what she did, but Nadia took nosey to a new level.

"Well, she doesn't know anything, yet. He's out there in the waiting room expecting me to pop up, and I'm gonna make him wait."

"For how long? You don't want to wait too long, or Ms. Nosey Nadia will sure get him to spill the beans, and then she'll be telling everybody on y'all's next newscast. She surely did go into the right industry, because that girl is definitely good at communications and broadcasting," Paige continued to joke. But she was only telling the truth.

"Well, I wanted him to sit and squirm a while. I wanted things to be on my level," I shared.

"Look, you're going to have to get over your high and mighty controlling ways, Ms. CFO. Get your behind off this phone, and go handle your business. And truthfully, Naomi, can I offer a word of advice?" Paige added in a serious tone.

"Sure, go ahead, girl."

"Take him out of there. Whatever he has to say, give him your full, undivided attention. I mean don't put up with no lies or mess from him, but listen to everything he needs to say to you. Use your discerning spirit that the Holy Spirit gave you, and filter the truth from fiction. And then decide where to go with it from there. But above all, whatever you do, do it away from EBS. Take the brother to lunch, and sit down for a one-on-one chat without all the ears y'all got around that place."

I knew she was telling the truth, and her words were sound wisdom. So, I grudgingly agreed. I finished my call with Paige as she wished me well and looked at the clock on my wall. It was 12:45. He had already been waiting for almost half an hour. I guessed that was good enough. I made another call.

"Hello, may I speak to Ms. Jacobs, please? Yes, it's Ms. Blankenship." I held the line for less than a minute before the principal answered.

"This is Cheryl Jacobs; hello, Ms. Blankenship," she greeted in a friendly tone.

"Hi, Ms. Jacobs, I wanted to thank you so much for keeping me posted with everything that's going on with Sasha. And thank you for keeping a closer eye on her now after the information that I shared with you."

"No problem, Ms. Blankenship. She's a tough young lady, and she still is holding her own. She actually seems a bit more focused since meeting her father. I worried that maybe she might start to act out at first, but it seems she has gone further down the path she was already on. Her grades are still on track, and she's giving her all to her clubs. Is there anything else that we should be looking out for or anything else that I can do to assist you?"

"No, ma'am. You've been great, and I appreciate all you've done already. Can you please notify Sasha that I need her to ride the bus home this evening? I won't be able to pick her up today," I informed the principal.

"Sure, that won't be any problem."

"Thanks, Ms. Jacobs. And you have a great day."

I was unsure how long I would be with Jaime, and even more, I was unsure how long it would take me to compose myself before having to face my daughter again.

"You, as well," Ms. Jacobs said and disconnected the call.

I headed into my private bathroom. I freshened my makeup and brushed out my hair. I was the picture of professionalism in my beige skirt suit. I wore a navy, sleeveless blouse with a navy and beige polka-dotted scarf around my neck. My suede beige, sling-back three-inch heels clacked across my bathroom floor as I walked back into my office. I grabbed my navy-blue Chanel handbag, my keys, purse, and two-button, V-neck slim blazer and headed for the door. Yes, your girl was looking good as always, but I was especially glad about that today.

When I left my office, I gestured for Jaime to follow me. No words were exchanged in front of Nadia. We didn't speak until we were outside in the parking lot. I informed him that I had been preparing to head to lunch and he could join me. He followed behind me in his car. On the way there, I prayed for God to give me the grace to hear him out and to be somewhat cordial.

We settled on Bones & Stix for lunch. It was an upscale jazz restaurant a few miles away from the office. I didn't want to encounter anyone from my job while I was on this mission.

I ordered the Salmon served with pasta and green beans in a lemon garlic sauce. Jaime ordered shrimp scampi with a glass of wine. I planned to return to the office, so my beverage of choice was a sweet tea.

"So, to what do I owe the surprise of this visit?" I asked, as we waited for our meals to be delivered. I wanted to get straight to the point and not mince words. There would be no small talk. There had been several lost years, and he had so many explanations to give. I didn't have enough time in the day for all the explaining he needed to do. So, I only wanted to know what was most important to me. Why? Why did he walk out and never look back?

"You've raised Sasha to be a beautiful girl. I can tell just by her spirit that she's strong, and I know she must've gotten that from you. She looks just like me, but she's got your spirit."

I smiled at what I perceived to be a compliment. "She does, but she also has some of your ways."

He smiled and nodded his head. "I've been doing a lot of thinking. Naomi, I can't get back all the years I've lost. I made a choice and listened to my parents. When I look back now, I know that had to be a scary time for you, because it sure as hell was for me. But I'm not lying when I tell you I really believed you had gone to have an abortion after that. I didn't think you would go through with it."

"You thought that little of me?" I had leaned forward across the table with my arms crossed in front of me.

"Not that little of you, Naomi. We were just kids, and I knew how bad you wanted to go to college. I just didn't think you would go through with the pregnancy."

"Jaime, don't do this. You didn't care. You hoped that I wouldn't. Not once did you ever come back to check to see whether I did or not."

"You're right, it was a convenient thought to believe you hadn't gone through with the pregnancy. It was easier to look at myself in the mirror each day as long as I believed I didn't have a child out there somewhere. Then I got caught up in focusing on my NBA career. And then after the motorcycle accident, I spiraled into depression for a while. When I finally bounced back, so many years had passed I thought you wouldn't accept me back into your life. Then time continued, and life just went on. I thought about you quite often," he explained, as he fiddled with his fork and napkin.

"Did you ever think about her?"

"No. I didn't allow myself to dwell on it too long. In the moments when I thought maybe you didn't have an abortion, I began to wonder if it was a boy or girl. But then I changed my thoughts, because truthfully, I couldn't handle what I had done," he admitted. He turned red in the face. "What I need you to understand is that I've been torn throughout the years about this. I would start thinking, 'what if?' But then, as soon as I would begin to think maybe you had kept our baby, I started wondering where your life was headed now. And then as time passed, it got easier and easier not to handle it. I had no way of knowing if you had gone on with your life. I mean, it could've been anywhere from point A to point B. I began imagining you in a relationship with some other dude. And when I did, I didn't know if maybe he had stepped up and been the father I hadn't been. I got to thinking about how it would interrupt your life if I just popped up on your doorstep one day, not knowing whether or not you had told your significant other or our child about me. I didn't know if you kept the baby or what. I knew I had made the wrong choices, and I didn't want to make another wrong choice that could hurt the life you were now living."

"And you didn't care to know, Jaime." The waiter approached at that moment and served up our dishes. "Thank you," I said. "Thank you," Jaime replied to the waiter.

"May I?" he asked, reaching across the table for my hand. It was so weird touching him again. But I recalled he had been big on prayer as a teenager, as was I. It was good to see some things hadn't changed. After he said the grace over our meal, we both proceeded with caution and began to eat our food and ponder our own thoughts.

"Well, I'm glad you had such high thoughts of me as to preserve whatever life you thought I had," I said, my voice dripping with sarcasm.

"Ease up on me, will you, Naomi?" he asked, setting his fork down.

I set my own fork down rather hard, and I knew fury shone in my eyes. "Ease up on you? Ease up on you? Let me explain something, Jaime! I've had no one to ease up on me in sixteen years! I've had to work my ass off and give up any life I may have thought of having during this time. I have dedicated my life solely to raising our daughter alone. Now, don't get me wrong, it was my choice to keep her, and it was my choice not to become involved in a relationship. I'm not putting that on you but please don't think it cruel of me if I don't have any sympathy for your plight. Just like I made choices, Jaime, you made choices. I chose to stay and put the work in. You chose to walk out on us!"

There, I had had my say, and I was very clear on how I saw things. As I regained my composure, I looked at Jaime. I saw something in his eyes. It was like a veil was being lifted, and he was being awakened.

"I hurt you."

"Damn right you hurt me, Jaime. You weren't there for our child all these years, and I had to do it alone."

"No, Naomi. I know that hurt, but I mean I hurt you, too. All these years, I never thought about that. You're still hurting over me leaving our relationship."

My eyebrows furrowed up. "What are you talking about? I'm not hurting over whatever relationship we had. We were kids, I've gotten over that," I stated in no uncertain terms.

"I don't think you have. I think that's why you chose to stay away from relationships, too. You didn't trust anyone with your heart again. I'm sorry, Naomi. I'm really sorry for all the pain I've caused you and our daughter." He reached out for my hand again, but this time I snatched it back.

I shook my head back and forth for a few seconds. "You walked out on me after almost two years of dating. We discussed going to the same college, we talked about your NBA dreams. I helped you prepare for the SATs. Everything you needed, I was there for you on. But when I needed you most, you disappeared without as much as a goodbye. You walked out of my parents' living room that day, and I never heard from you again. How could you be so callous? Do you want to know something even more pitiful? All these years, I've been taking our daughter to Havana's Cocina, her favorite restaurant. I taught her about her culture from both backgrounds. And Paige said something to me that I've had to acknowledge. I took her to the restaurant all those years with the expectation of possibly running into you again," I confessed. I grabbed a napkin and dabbed at the tears threatening to flow from my eyes.

"I'm sorry. I had no clue. Naomi...do you know I've been going into that restaurant all these years, too? I never once saw you. But then again, I wasn't expecting to. I mean, my parents always took me there as a kid. But even after I left home, I continued going there. I always remembered our time there, and I haven't stopped going even now. I guess a part of me always hoped you would pop up there, as well, but I wasn't so certain it would happen. After all, you never went to that restaurant unless you were with me and my family," he stated.

I laughed a bitter laugh. "Isn't it funny how you always imagine what you're going to do in a given situation? And then when faced with that situation, it's never what you expected? I wanted to run when I saw you. I spotted you long before you saw me. I heard your voice and didn't dare turn around. You passed me and Sasha's table, and I pretended to be sick to get her to leave. She knew something was wrong, but I pressed the issue hoping to get out of there before you saw me. We were almost home free before you came around."

"I'm glad I didn't miss you. I'm glad we ran into each other." He took a sip of his wine and sat back for a moment. We were both lost in our own thoughts, not quite sure how to proceed.

"Naomi, that was the proudest moment of my life."

"What was?" I was confused and had no idea what he could have been referring to.

"Seeing my daughter. All these years, I've questioned her existence. All these years, I wanted to right my wrong and step up. I wasn't sure if she existed, but I wanted to find out and do right by her if she did. I didn't know how to do it, especially as the years ticked off, because it became harder. So, I immersed myself into becoming a school teacher and coaching the boys' basketball team at school. I threw myself into becoming the best father I could be to my other two. I just could never make up for where I failed when I was younger. I didn't do the right thing then, but I want so bad to do it now. I want to right wrongs, Naomi. I want to be a part of Sasha's life and get to know the young woman she's become. I mean...look at her, she's beautiful, intelligent, strong, and has so much fire inside of her."

I don't know what I expected him to say, but that wasn't it. Somewhere inside, I was numb. I felt nothing, and then it slowly began to come to me, the shocking pain and fear. What did I have to fear? In reality, nothing. But my mind created this image of me losing my daughter. It had always just been me and her, and I had wrapped my life around her. I mean, sure, I realized someday she would go off to college and leave me behind. I was mentally prepared for that. I also knew that my life would begin at that point. But she had two school years to complete before I was ready for that realization. I wasn't sure if I was ready to share her with a previously absentee father. How did he think he had the right to just pop back into our lives now? Yet, how could I believe he didn't have the right to do just that?

I'm sure I looked like someone had just knocked the wind out of me.

"Naomi? Naomi? Are you all right?"

"Yeah...yeah. I'm okay," I replied slowly.

Realization dawned in his eyes. "Naomi, I'm sorry. I'm not trying to be presumptuous. Let me reassure you, I understand it's up to you to decide if I can be a part of her life. I'm not trying to come in and take over, or take your place, or anything like that. I just want to get to know her."

He watched me as I continued to sit there in silence. "Please, Naomi. I just want a chance to step up. I'm sorry, and I can't ever make up for my failings, but I just don't want to be a failure. Not where she's concerned. I've failed her enough already."

I let out a huge sigh. I had decisions to make, but I wouldn't refuse him his rights. However, the decision was not mine alone to make.

"Jaime, I've heard you out, but give it some time, please. You have no idea what she's been through. She took finally meeting you pretty hard, and it was an entire weekend before I could even get her out of bed."

"I didn't know. I'm so sorry," he said, wiping his hand down his face. I saw sincere regret in his eyes. I didn't know the man who sat before me, I only knew the boy he had been. I wanted to believe he had grown and matured. But then again, I had seen a glimpse of something I didn't like at the restaurant that day, the fact that he still stood there and didn't take responsibility for his actions. The fact that he tried to lie and deny knowing we had a child.

"Jaime, she had convinced herself all those years that you were dead. That was preferable to believing she had a daddy who didn't love her. Your love was so important to her, and she needed that. She needed to believe in it and when I think back, I'm starting to realize that love she imagined you had for her helped her to shape her belief of who she was. I can't and won't let you hurt her again, Jaime," I declared.

"I promise you I won't. Just please give me a chance. I'm not that boy from sixteen years ago. The only reason I didn't come clean that day was because I was in shock. I had no idea how to handle the situation, or how to handle my wife and children being faced with that situation."

"Speaking of, Jaime, how come you didn't tell your wife you possibly had a child out there?" That was another question I needed to ask, something that had been bothering me.

"How could I? I had no details or nothing to provide her with. All I had was a maybe, and I couldn't throw that at her. I couldn't have that hanging over her head all these years. It's almost like a competition of some sort. I mean, what was I supposed to say? 'Natalie, a woman that I was in love with sixteen years ago possibly has a baby out there by me somewhere. I don't know if she went through with it or not, but baby, one day a child could pop up on my doorstep.' Who does that?" he asked, his eyes widened with confusion.

"It would've been a start. At least you would have acknowledged the possibility, and it would have shown you cared. Not to mention I'm sure your wife would've appreciated knowing, rather than being caught off guard and learning about it in a restaurant full of people the way she did."

I knew as a woman, if I had learned about something regarding my husband that way, there would've been hell to pay. Not only was it embarrassing, but it had to be hurtful to know your husband didn't trust you enough to share all of his past, mistakes included.

"I see how you, as a woman, would feel that way. But coming from a man's perspective, I did what I thought was best for my family. As you stated earlier, you made your choices, and I made mine. And trust me when I say, I'm paying the price for mine now," he confided.

"Is your wife okay?" I really didn't want to see her hurt. I didn't know the woman, but it was never my intention to see any of my sisters hurting. Although there was no way to avoid it, enough people had been hurt by this situation already.

"She's fine. I mean, we'll get through this. Yeah, it took something out of her, and we've got some things to work through now. But it was more important to her that I establish a relationship with my daughter."

"So, she's the reason you're here?" I asked.

"No. Sasha's the reason I'm here. But it's nice to know that my wife supports me in this, and that she isn't trying to hold me back or be self-conscious about it. She understands her place in my life, and she's not threatened by what I'm trying to do. She's furious it hadn't been done before now."

I shook my head and took a sip of my tea. I contemplated for a moment. Maybe I had things all wrong. Maybe I could have been pursuing a relationship and could have found a good man who would have loved me and my daughter, too. Nah. I shook my head, clearing it of that train of thought. I mean, don't get me wrong, I had had my share of lonely nights. But I wouldn't trade them in for nothing in the world. I had made my choice, and I was proud of her.

We continued eating our food and making small talk. I got to know Jaime all over again, and he got to know me. If he was going to be around Sasha, it was important to me that I knew him, and he needed to know how I had raised her. I promised to speak with Sasha about seeing him, but I needed to do it in my own time and on my own terms. Jaime told me that he understood that. We exchanged phone numbers and headed out of the restaurant. It had been an extended lunch, and I quickly realized it was going over into the dinner hour. I looked at my watch; it was almost 4:30 P.M.

I wasn't sure what it was about leaving restaurants lately, but I was beginning to feel as if I needed to avoid them altogether. For the second time in less than a month, I was startled by what my eyes had seen.

Just beyond the bar, seated at a table for two was Ambiance, and the gentleman whose car she had bumped my car door against. I knew it was him, because I had gotten a clear view of him the day she had hit his car. I saw him clearly in the rearview mirror, although she had thought I wasn't paying any attention. He was a very attractive, tall, brown-skinned brother with dreads.

There wasn't anything wrong with her meeting with a man to have lunch or dinner. After all, she was a fashion consultant with her own business. She had been known to have lunch or dinner with clients, although they were more often female than male. But this wasn't a client meeting. No, this man was caressing the side of her face with one hand and holding her hand with his other. And she was so into him with that faraway look in her eyes that she never saw me. Lord, have mercy. What had my girl gotten herself into? I strode quickly from the restaurant with Jaime, never missing a beat.

12_PAIGE_BOOTY CALL

Madison had been found safe just a few blocks from the Manor. She was hiding in the restroom of an all-night convenience store. The shift clerk, who was familiar with the Manor and the work that went on there, had alerted one of the volunteers who worked at the manor. He watched as she snuck into the store while he was busy with customers and then looked around surreptitiously before creeping into the bathroom. Initially, he thought she was coming in to steal something. But after cautiously watching the bathroom door for her exit, he thought something else might be going on.

When she didn't leave after twenty minutes, he dialed the number to the Manor to see if they were missing a child. He reported that she had gone in there about twenty minutes prior and had not come out. He thought it was odd for a child of that age to be out that time of night.

Because this was her first offense with running away, she got off lightly with a stern warning and a revocation of her household privileges. She was placed under all-night supervision until we could send her to the Angela Simms home. I explained to her the consequences of all future attempts to run away, as well as the fact that any privileges she would have had going into the home would now be suspended. Everyone else looked at her and saw an angry and sullen child. I saw a child who was afraid of change and tired of being sent from one place to another.

I had come back home around four-thirty in the morning. Most people were just getting up to start their day, and mine had already begun. I tried to lay down for at least a couple of hours to get some sleep. I knew I would be running on empty for most of the day, but I would get off early and come home to catch up on my sleep.

No sooner than I laid down, my phone started ringing. I tried to ignore it, but whomever it was hung up and called back two more times. I stared at the phone on my nightstand as if it were some evil entity. Finally, I rolled over to that side of the bed and looked at the caller ID, David. Really? What did he want this time of morning? I was not up for his foolishness, now. I hit ignore; he started calling again.

The next time I turned the phone on vibrate, and rolled over to go back to sleep. A light buzzing like the sound of a bee was going off in my ear. I began swatting at it, but it wouldn't stop. I was finally pulled out of my sleep by the incessant noise and realized it was the doorbell.

Who in the world would be ringing my doorbell at…5:45 in the morning! What the hell? I threw the covers off of me, and stomped to the front door. Whoever it was at the door was about to feel the wrath of a sleepless woman!

I peeped through the peephole and was furious. This man had the audacity to come to my home. Didn't he get it when I didn't answer his phone calls? I thought he had lost his mind and was starting to act like an obsessed man.

"What do you want, David?"

"Open the door, Paige!" he roared.

"I'm not opening the door. I just got back from checking on that child, and I need my sleep. Now, please leave, and I will call you later."

Why did I think it would be that simple? He started banging on the door again. "Open the damn door!"

"I said I'm not opening it and I'm telling you to leave now!" I commanded in a forceful voice that I didn't quite feel.

"I ain't going no damn where until you open this door!" he hollered.

"If you don't leave, David, I'm calling the police," I threatened. If he didn't leave, I wouldn't have to call the police. My neighbors would be calling the police on him for disturbing the peace. I didn't want him to get in any trouble, I just wanted him to leave.

"So, that's how it is now, Paige? That's the game we playing?" he asked.

"Yes, that's the game we're playing. When you left here, you called me a whore, remember? So why would such a respectable man as yourself want to be laid up with me, rather than at home with his wife?"

"Come on, Paige. I'm sorry; let me in…pullleeezzz?" he begged.

I started walking away from the door, determined to ignore him. I had only gotten a few feet away before he started kicking on my door.

"Let me in before I break this muthafucka down!" he screamed, and began a new round of banging and kicking on my door.

He wasn't going to leave, and I knew I had a decision to make. I ran to the kitchen and grabbed the cordless phone off its station and dialed a number I had memorized by heart, after blocking my number. After it rang a few times, I walked back to the door and listened to the sleepy voice answering on the other end. I placed it on speaker phone, muted the part on the other end, and laid it down on the table next to the front door. I turned on the intercom so that David's voice would come through the house on the speakers installed throughout.

He was still banging on my door, screaming my name. "Open up, Paige, I'm not playing!"

"Why, David? Why do you want me to open the door? If you're acting like this now, how do I know you're going to act right if I let you in?"

"Paige, baby, please let me in. I promise I won't hurt you. I miss you, baby...I was just upset, because you had to leave me tonight. Please, let me in. I just want to be with you again...feel your body up against mine. I need to make love to you, Paige. Please, open the door!"

"David, where does your wife think you are right now, honey?"

"I told her I had to leave for an earlier shift at work. Come on, baby. Let me in; we can take a day off and make love all day. Please let me in, Paige."

"No, David. I can't take a day off. I have so much going on at work, and I need to get some rest. Please leave before I call the police."

"You bitch! I'll kick this door in!" he shouted.

"David, I'm begging you to go home to your wife. If you kick my door in, I promise you I'll have something waiting on the other side for you. And I'm not afraid to kick start a little fire. Trust me!"

I picked up the phone and placed it to my ear. I could hear frantic hellos on the other side.

"Hello, Victoria. This is Paige."

"Paige, who? What is my husband doing at your house?" she cried into the phone. I didn't wish her no harm. I really didn't. Most women might think that I did, but not only was I tired of David's foolish ways, I was tired of him making a fool of his wife. She needed to know about his misdeeds.

"He's going to be locked up if you don't call him and tell him to come home. I don't want him to come visit me anymore. I've been sleeping with your husband for a year and a half now. He's angry because I'm breaking it off."

"What kind of woman are you to sleep with a married man?" she sobbed into the phone.

"A woman who is hurting and running from the truth. A woman who just doesn't give a damn." I hung up the phone and slid down onto the floor in front of my refrigerator and sobbed.

I could hear his phone ringing outside. I assumed his wife was calling him, and a couple of the men that lived in my building had come out to address him about the noise. Somehow, they convinced him to leave.

I headed off to bed. I would definitely be taking the day to work from home. I had to catch up on my sleep. My job required that I make life-changing decisions for children. I refused to make a decision that I would later regret or that could damage someone's life. I had damaged enough lives, and I was tired. From this moment on, I would never sleep with a married man again…not knowingly. I was not out to tear my sisters down. Just because I had my own issues didn't mean it was okay to take it out on them. Every other sister deserved the love and support of her black sisters. My actions had done everything but that. Yes, I was done with married men.

I received a call from Naomi around three that afternoon asking me out to dinner after work. I suggested she come to my place instead. I was still dragging and too tired to put up with people in public. She informed me that Ambiance would be coming along, as well.

I ordered Chinese to be delivered so that no one had to cook. It would be quick and simple. Naomi and Ambiance rode over to my condo together, arriving just before seven.

"Hey girl, did you see your car?" Naomi asked, gesturing over her shoulder to the parking lot behind her.

"What do you mean?" I asked, panicking and feeling as if I couldn't catch my breath. I ran out the door with my two friends hot on my heels.

When I arrived in the parking lot, tears fell from my eyes. Not because my baby had been attacked, but because of what it represented, hate, evil, anger, and rage.

All four tires had been slashed, and the front driver side window had been bashed in. On the front windshield, $0.02 had been scrawled, and on the back windshield, the word "ho" had been spray-painted.

"Who in the hell did you piss off?" Naomi asked.

"I don't think it was something she did. It looks like the work of a horny teenager. Paige, which one of those babies on your job you been teasing again?" Ambiance laughed.

I turned tear-filled eyes her way and shot her a venomous look. I was in no mood for jokes. I knew who had done this, but I had no way to prove it.

"Come on, honey. Let's go back in the house, and you can call the police to file a report. If for nothing else, at least for insurance purposes," Naomi coddled. "And you need to take out a restraining order if you know who did this."

I sniffled and shook my head *okay*. I was consumed with rage and couldn't think straight.

After we called the police and filed a report, my next call was to the insurance company. They would send someone out first thing in the morning and also have a rental car delivered to me.

"So, what's going on, girl?" Ambiance asked, tucking her feet underneath her on the floor where she sat.

We finally had a moment to sit down and dig into our food. I didn't have much of an appetite and toyed around with it. I would probably have it for my lunch on tomorrow at work.

"David, the guy I met at the conference on workplace safety a year and a half ago…" I began, and then spooned a small bite of food in my mouth.

The ladies nodded their heads, assuring me they remembered him and wanted me to go on.

"Well, I broke things off with him, and he obviously didn't take it too well."

"I thought you weren't in a relationship?" Naomi queried.

"I'm not. It was just one of those things, you know?" I shrugged it off, hoping to leave the subject alone.

"Was he getting attached to you like Vic?" Ambiance questioned.

"Mm-hmm…but he doesn't even have the right to be jealous. Being a marr—" I cut myself off, realizing what I was about to say. I hadn't meant to allow that to leak.

"Come on, Paige…don't tell me he's married?" Naomi probed, quickly picking up the vein of conversation I had purposely dropped.

I looked all around the room, avoiding the gaze of my two friends. I felt so ashamed, I didn't know what to do.

"Paige…Paige, look at me. Is he married?" Ambiance demanded.

As I shook my head *yes*, she let out a deep breath. I knew she was furious, especially knowing she had issues with her husband and his infidelity. I didn't mean to hurt my best friend. Ambiance stood up and walked to the bathroom off the hallway.

"Paige, what were you thinking?" Naomi asked me.

"I wasn't thinking, Naomi. Truthfully, I didn't care. It's only been lately that it started to bother me. To be honest, it was one day when we were together that she called him and he forced me to look at her face on his phone while he continued to do it to me. That was the first time I felt any shame," I revealed.

I sighed deeply, not knowing what my girl was going through. I pointed towards the bathroom. "I never meant to hurt her, either," I shared.

"She'll be okay. She's got her own issues to deal with," Naomi stated. I shook my head, figuring she was referring to Eric's affairs.

"Well, I'm glad you learned your lesson. I am assuming you don't plan to do that again?" she asked.

"No. I'm tired, Naomi. And truth be told, I don't think it's over. Now, he has his wife to deal with."

"What do you mean?" Naomi asked. At that moment, Ambiance walked back into the room. Her eyes were red, and we knew she had been crying. When Naomi moved to comfort her, she put her hand up, stopping her.

"I'm okay. I really am. And it's not you alone, Paige. Everyone has choices to make, and that man made some poor choices, too. But go ahead with your story."

"Are you sure?" I asked.

"Yeah, I am. Finish telling us what led to this," Ambiance encouraged.

"Well, he was upset with me, because I got a call about one of my babies who had run away. I had to leave and sent him home." For some reason, I didn't share with them what he had done to the mirror in my master bathroom. Maybe because that was too personal. Everyone knew I had been sleeping with the man, but somehow sharing that information was putting it out on a different level.

"Oh, no, is she okay?" Naomi asked. Naomi and Ambiance both knew how much the children I worked with meant to me. Even if they were only around for a short time, they were the most important thing in the world. They were what kept me whole and gave my life any substance, the possibility that I could make a difference and give someone a shot in this thing called life.

"Yes, we found her. All is well with that. But I didn't get back home until four-thirty this morning. He was calling me no sooner than I got in and then at my door when I refused to answer. He started banging on it and kicking it when I refused to let him in. I threatened him with the police, told him I was packing, and nothing I said would deter him. He acted a fool in the hallway, until some of the men in the building got him out of here."

"But why did you say you didn't think it was over, and he has his wife to deal with?" Naomi asked.

I looked at Ambiance. I didn't want to upset her any more than I already had, and I was sure this next confession might do just that. She sensed my hesitation and pulled her eyes from her lap, where they had been focused, to look at me.

"I'm okay, Paige. Go ahead and tell us what happened," Ambiance stated.

"Well, in the midst of him acting a fool, I called his wife."

"How did you get her number?" Naomi asked.

"The day he forced me to look at her picture on his phone while he had sex with me, I saw it, and that number stayed in my head. So anyway, I called her and put her on speaker and turned on the house intercom. She could hear everything he said. I said some things to him to calm him down, and he started talking intimately. Then I got on the phone with her and I told her. Call me selfish, but a part of me felt she needed to know," I said, attempting to justify my actions.

"Damn!" Ambiance said. She stood up and was rubbing her arms up and down. I knew she was trying to get control of her emotions and thinking of her own troubles with her husband.

"What did she say?" Naomi asked. She was not only worried about Ambiance, but I could tell she was worried about my state of mind, as well.

"You know, she was furious and I could tell that she was hurt. But I swear, I didn't do it to hurt her. I did it to help her. She needed to know. If she chooses to stay with him, that's her business. But at least she knows what's going on in her marriage."

"Did you use protection?" Ambiance's voice came out a little shaky.

"Always," I replied. I didn't feel as if I owed anybody that explanation, but I knew where her question was coming from. If I could offer anything to ease her pain for what she was going through, I would give that to her.

"I wish someone had told me." Ambiance muttered that under her breath, and I barely heard her.

Naomi simply nodded her head.

"Look, I know you two look at me one way. We see life in different perspectives, and I don't judge you about the routes you choose to go. So, I just ask for the same respect," I shared.

"That's not fair," Ambiance began. "You're always judging me. You talk about how you wouldn't put up with the stuff that I go through with Eric. You talk about how you're going to use them up before they use you and you wouldn't be sitting home at night alone, crying while you know he's with another woman."

"And that's true, I wouldn't. Hell, but that's how I feel. I don't get you, Ambiance. You've known that man was sleeping around on you before, but not only did you stay with him, you still put up with his mess. You don't have a life, because everything is centered on him. If he wants you to stay at home alone…then guess what you do? I won't be sleeping with a married man again, but I won't be letting them make a fool out of me, either. And that's exactly what you do every time you let Eric get away with that. I just wish my sisters would wake up," I stated matter-of-factly with a simple shrug.

"Really, Paige? You're the one who needs to wake up. First, you said that you don't judge me for the routes I choose, but you just bashed me for staying with Eric along with everything our life represents. Then you say you wish your sisters would wake up, when it's you that needs a reality check. You're out here sleeping with every Tony, Derek, and Hakim. You don't care if they're married or single or gay or straight. As long as he's swinging it your way, then you're soaring on eagles' wings and spreading for him. You dangle poor guys like Vic on a string, and he follows behind you like a puppy dog. You go to work and preach to those young kids about morals and making the right choices in life, but you live yours like a pot-a-let ho'! And yes, I said that, because that's how you portray yourself. Not me, not Naomi, not Rodney, not David, or anybody else. You sit there and claim that you called that man's wife because she needed to know the truth. Well, truth is, you did it to be spiteful and vindictive because that's just who you are. And the sooner you face the truth about yourself, the better off you will be and everyone else around you! Just because you don't love yourself and haven't dealt with your past, doesn't mean you have to punish everybody else. We all have our struggles, Paige! We've all had our failings and disappointments in life, but we don't turn around and shit on others. I love you, Paige, but I will not continue to stand here and be disrespected by you. I don't get why you act like you hate me or my husband. Neither of us have done anything to you, and you can't find it in your body to have a kind word to say to me or him. I've known you since we were teenagers, and I've watched you throw yourself at men, lose self-respect for yourself, and get sloppy drunk at times. I've been here to help you pick up the loose ends in your life. Well, you know what, Paige? I'm not here anymore. When you get your shit together, call me!"

I was sitting on my couch with my arms folded across my chest. I refused to let one single teardrop fall. I didn't need her. I knew everything she said to me was true, but who the hell was she to tell me how I needed to live my life? I only said I wouldn't live my life the way she chose to live hers, but I didn't tell her how she needed to do that.

Naomi had been sitting back looking between the two of us. Throughout all the years we had known one another, Ambiance and I had seldom had words. Usually, she was making peace between me and Naomi, because we were the two strong-headed ones. Now, Naomi was looking aloof. No sooner than Ambiance hit the door, Naomi stood to follow her.

"I'll take you home," I said to her. I knew she had ridden with Ambiance to my house.

"Girl, I'm good. I need to talk to her and calm her down, and I think you need some serious think time. I love you, girl." She came and hugged me tight, ending it with a little squeeze.

I followed her to the door, locked it behind her, and went to my bedroom and threw myself across the bed. I picked up the phone and called Sherrod, another one of my fly-by-night lover boys. I needed a night of good loving to relieve my pressure and stress.

"Hello?" I had answered my phone without looking at the caller ID as I was hopping into my car to drive to Sherrod's house.

"Hey, Paige, you busy?" That was my mama.

"Kinda," I replied.

"What you got going on?" she inquired. That woman sure was nosy. I had to get her off the phone before I arrived at Sherrod's house, or I wouldn't be able to get rid of her at all. And I didn't want her ruining my mood.

"I'm heading out on a date," I lied.

"You going on a date after ten at night? He ain't got but one thing on his mind. Girl, you know that ain't nothing but a booty call!" my mother declared.

I ran my hand down my face and sighed. Why me? I thought I had found a way to escape.

"Mommy, it's not a booty call. We're going out tonight," I lied again.

"Going where? Huh? Where you going, Paige? Yeah, just like I thought, nowhere but to his house. A booty call," she ranted, after I took too long responding to her question.

"Mommy, what did you call for? I have to leave now," I said, as I pulled up to his house. Sherrod lived right around the corner from me, but he didn't know that I lived that close.

"Oh, so it is a booty call?" she probed.

Damn! What was it with that woman? I had to get her off the phone and I didn't want to be rude, but…she was messing up my flow. My natural juices had dried up after being on the phone with her. By the time Sherrod saw me in my little white mini-dress, my unrestrained nipples wouldn't be pert and poking through the material anymore. And the heat that was between my legs wouldn't be so hot. But he probably wouldn't give a damn. As long as I showed up at his house with no underwear on underneath my dress the way he liked it, he would be happy.

"Yes, Mommy. I'm going to his house for a booty call, and when I finish with him, I'll send him over to your house to take care of you," I snapped, and hung up the phone on her. Damn, she was worrisome!

I eased out of my car just as Sherrod opened the door to his home. He stood there stroking his penis through his sweat pants. Yeah, he was hot and ready, and just seeing him standing there like that with no shirt on to cover that dark, ripped chest and those sexy abs made me hot and bothered all over again.

No sooner than I stepped onto his porch, he grabbed my ass with one hand, squeezing and kneading it over and over again as he gently pulled at my bottom lip with his mouth. Reaching underneath my dress, he released a deep moan, satisfied that I had no panties on. Mentally preparing myself for what I knew was next, I could never become physically used to the hard twist he always gave my nipples to make sure there was no bra underneath.

"Ow!" I shouted at the painful sensation after pulling away from our kiss. He had left my nipple sore and tender with that move.

"Come on here, girl," he said, letting go of my behind and kicking the door closed with one foot after we entered through the doorway.

Sherrod's house was decorated in brown leather and dark, rich woods. He kept the lights in the living room off and pulled me back towards his bedroom.

Two of his bedroom walls were covered in mirrors, and there was one on the ceiling. Sherrod was not only a freak, but he was also arrogant. He was actually the type to watch himself in the mirror having sex to make sure his positions, faces, and body were on point. The first time I learned this little fact about him, it was enough to send me running.

One thing kept me coming back for more. The boy could eat the hell out of some coochie! Whew! Nobody ate my kitty the way he did. And for that reason alone, I was willing to put up with some of his little idiosyncrasies, like watching himself make love, or singing in an off-key voice while he did. Now don't get me wrong, the brother could lay pipe, too. But there was nothing like his mouth humming on my honeypot.

I noticed several changes as I looked around his bedroom. The walls, formerly a brownish-gold hue, had now been painted a beautiful silver. White pleated panels hung at the window, but I would say the biggest difference was his bed. The prominent California king with a mirrored headboard which dominated the master bedroom had been downsized to a queen-size. Silver fabric and little fake diamond buttons covered the headboard, giving it a look of elegance and class. Not his usual style at all, but it was very nice. Beautiful white bedding with silver threading throughout the covers and pillow cases looked like something straight out of a Homes and Garden magazine.

"Redecorating in here, I see," I said, smirking at him before turning back to him to begin stroking his swollen manhood.

"Yeah, something like that," he said, picking me up and spreading my cheeks as far apart as they could go. As he continued to squeeze them, he began grinding against me and captured my tongue in a lover's dance. My legs gripped tightly around his waist to make sure that I wouldn't fall. With the muscles that rippled along his broad chest and arms, that wasn't really a concern I needed to have.

I was throbbing and ready for him to taste me by the time he finished kissing me. I quickly pulled my little white dress up and over my head, tossing it to the foot of the bed.

"Damn, girl, your body is so fine!" he said, kneeling in front of me. I was standing on the side of the bed in my five-inch stilettos, watching as he ducked his head between my legs to get his first taste of my fruit for the night.

I don't know what turned me on more, the way his tongue went to work inside of me intermittently with his fingers, or the way he moaned and groaned, expressing his need for more of me. Head back, knees bent, and squatting over his face, I let him work me for several minutes. My legs began to shake as I continued to hold on to the back of his head. And just when I thought I couldn't take anymore, I began pulling away from him. But he wasn't ready to let go, yet. His hands squeezed tighter around my waist, not allowing me to get away from his greedy, hungry, searching mouth.

"Aww, Sherrod! Oh, baby, you know you can do the damn thang! Oh, yes, daddy, come on, that's what I need," I pleaded.

He pulled back and looked up at me, "Ride daddy's face, Paige. Ride it, baby," he begged, holding my waist tightly in place.

"O...oo...okkkay," I stuttered out, as I bucked to and fro, rocking my hips in a gyrating, fast-paced motion. And when it all became too much, I gave him exactly what he was looking for as I squirted in his mouth.

And that's the way she found us.

"Sherrod! What the hell! Who the fuck is this? What the hell you think you're doing?" I heard a woman's voice screech.

I opened my eyes on the downside of my ecstasy and saw a tall, heavyset, light-skinned female standing in the doorway, eyes wide and in shock at the sight before her.

"Who the hell is this bitch?" she screamed, as Sherrod pulled his face out of my dripping jewel.

"Baby, she's...she's...she's just a friend," he said, standing up, holding his hands out in front of him as she came flying at him with a shoe in her hand, prepared to do damage.

Whelp, time for me to hit the road! I had gotten what I came for and then some. I snatched my purse from the side of the bed and looked around for my dress, and that's when I saw it in her hands. She was trying to strangle Sherrod with it as he was trying to fight her off.

"Excuse me, I hate to interrupt this lover's spat, but I'm gonna need that back," I said from behind Sherrod, pointing to my dress in her hands.

"Bitch, please!" she screamed, turning her wrath on me.

"Look, I'm not gonna be too many more of your bitches." I was speaking in a very calm manner.

"You'll be—"

"Shirley, calm down, baby. It's not her fault," he explained.

"Not her fault? Not her fault? Oh, so what? You taking up for her now?" she asked, turning between him and me. "I knew I shouldn't have moved in with your trifling ass, Sherrod!" she screamed.

All I wanted was my dress.

"It's not like that," Sherrod stated.

"It's not like what, Sherrod? Please, baby. I'm begging you to tell me what it's not like. Because to me, it looked like she was riding the hell out your face! You told me you don't do that, because it's nasty, but I come in our home and catch you with this trifling bitch and you're doing to her what you won't do for me? I'm your fiancé, Sherrod!" she screeched again.

If it wasn't so pitiful, it would've been funny.

"Sherrod, your fiancé? Really, Sherrod? You didn't tell me you were in a relationship, let alone engaged," I remarked, standing with my hands on my hips in all my naked glory.

"You didn't tell her about me? So, maybe it wasn't that serious to you?" She burst into tears.

"You *are* that serious to me. It's just that…well, she's a good friend and she was kinda stressed tonight and asked if I could help her out," he explained. I couldn't believe his lame-ass excuse. If she went for that…even though it was true, well, she deserved whatever he dished out.

I was mad, too, because other than David, I didn't typically do men who were in relationships. I shook my head and started laughing. This shit was really pitiful and comical.

"What the hell you laughing at, bitch?" she screamed, suddenly lunging at me.

I was ready to fight, if that was what I needed to do. I wasn't that type of person, but after all, I was the one caught up. I didn't know anything about his woman. All I wanted was to get my dress and go the hell home. Sherrod grabbed her around the waist, picking her up and holding her in the air. She was swinging and kicking at him, trying to get out of his embrace.

"You!" I said, tossing her a look of pity and one of disgust at Sherrod. "Give me my dress back, and I'll be out your hair tonight," I replied.

"You ain't getting shit back, skank!" she cried.

Sherrod attempted to pull the dress from her hand, while still holding on to her tightly. I grabbed at it with the other hand to no avail. With all the pulling and jerking, the dress ripped. I was pissed.

I had placed my purse down on the bed before fighting for my dress. I reached and picked it back up. "Sherrod, good bye. Get yo' life, and I'll send you the bill for that $350-dress your bitch just cost me!"

I stalked out of his house as naked as a jaybird, with nothing but my stilettos, purse, and keys. I was thankful that it was dark outside, knowing no one could see me. Luckily, I had a gym bag with workout clothes in it in the back seat of my vandalized car. I expected the rental to be delivered in the morning.

Pulling the bag to the front with me, I hurriedly threw on some clothes before him and his crazy chick could bring anymore drama outside to me. After tossing on the t-shirt and shorts, I put my car in drive and sped out of the driveway. My condo was less than a five-minute drive away.

13_AMBIANCE_MY HUSBAND & MY FRIEND

I was so furious, yet so refreshed at the same time. I loved Paige with all of my heart, but she only got what was coming to her. My hands were shaking so bad, Naomi had offered to drive my car, but I politely declined. I wanted to pretend that I would be just fine.

"Girl, are you okay?" she asked, glancing at me using her peripheral vision.

I huffed a little before saying a word. Looking out the window to try to find the right words to say, I felt her eyes boring into me as we sat at the red light.

"I will be. I'm just so tired of Paige's nasty ways. Why does she have to be so mean and say such hurtful things?" I asked. I knew the answer, but I needed it confirmed from someone else.

"You know why she says those things. She's hurting inside, and that's how she deals with her pain. She places this wall of armor around herself and tries to act hard."

"Well, she needs to deal with her issues. I know it wasn't easy for her having an alcoholic mother and all, especially with her father walking out, but that's something she has to deal with. She needs to talk to her mom about her feelings and get her into some detox or AA program. That's the only way she'll start feeling good again," I reasoned.

"It's easier said than done. I know she wants to get her mother some help, but Ms. Helena has to want it first. And there's no telling that woman how she feels. If Paige starts to talk about her drinking, sometimes she'll listen and agree with Paige. But before long, her mother will be cursing her out and putting her out of her house. It hurts Paige to see her mother that way," Naomi explained.

"And it hurts me to see her doing what she's doing to her life. Never mind how she treats me and the things she has to say about my marriage. I'm standing strong for the woman that I am regardless of what people think about my marriage," I stated. I was beginning to calm down and get back in control of myself once again.

"Is that why you were in Bones & Stix the other day with a certain gentleman that you met the day we were at Shakers?"

Thank God I had come to a stop, because I sure would have crashed into the Volvo just ahead of us. It was bad enough she had caught me off guard, but then I couldn't think of a word to say. A lie or otherwise. My heart sank to the pit of my stomach, and you know the butterflies that float around when you're nervous? Well, they had nothing on the dragonflies that were taking over my insides.

"Ambi?" she inquired, with a light note of curiosity in her voice.

"Ye..ye…yes?" I stuttered out.

"Did you hear me?" she asked, knowing that I had.

"Uh-uh," I lied.

"Girl, please, you know you heard me," Naomi teased.

"No, I didn't. I was lost in my own thoughts; what did you say?" I tried so hard to be smooth with my lie, but I was failing miserably.

"I asked, is that why you were in Bones & Stix the other day with the gentleman you met the day we were at Shakers?" she repeated.

I cleared my throat, knowing full well I had heard her loud and clear the first time. Her repeating it the second time didn't make it any better.

"I'm not sure what you're talking about." Why was I lying? This wasn't even my personality. I always kept it real, especially with Naomi.

"The gentleman who was holding your hand, Ambi, and caressing your face," she stated.

Dang! She had seen all that? And since I decided to play the role, she was going to really bring it to me.

"It wasn't what it looked like, Naomi," I pleaded my case.

"What did it look like, Ambiance?" she asked. "Because I clearly didn't call it." I could hear it in her voice; she was enjoying this so much. "It looked as if you were enjoying the company of a very attractive gentleman," she said, in now what sounded like a soothing tone.

"He's just a friend, that's all." I turned my eyes back to the road and continued with my drive, wishing I could disappear.

"It appeared to be more than friends to me. But hey, I'm not the one you have to explain it to. I'm just thankful that Eric didn't walk up in there."

I exhaled deeply, wondering why I had never thought of that. Suddenly, it occurred to me, I was never concerned about whether Eric would catch me spending time with Nick or not. And a part of me also realized I didn't really care. Yet, I knew if he did see the two of us together there would be trouble.

The day Naomi saw me, I had called Nick up at the last minute. I wanted a break from the shop, because it had been a stressful day. I needed someone to vent to, and he agreed to be that one.

What Naomi had seen was him reassuring me that everything would be okay. He had simply told me it was always darkest before the dawn. Coming away from that extended lunch, I felt better about my life than I had in a long time. He had shared with me that three more of his business contacts wanted to do business with me. My home life may have been looking down, and the job may have been tiring, but my business was definitely looking up.

"He wouldn't have anything to get mad about. Especially with the choices he makes, and besides, it was an innocent lunch."

"Okay, okay, I hear you. All I'm saying is just be careful. I heard you checking our girl, and everything that you said was true. Ambiance, I know you're in a challenging marriage and whatever your choices are, I support you one hundred. But, be careful with whatever you decide to do. No one would fault you if you wanted to go a different route in life. And if that's true, all I'm saying is make sure you tie up all of your loose ends before you move forward with someone else. If they're truly interested and care about you, they'll wait," Naomi lectured.

I let out a nervous laugh. "Well, then I guess I have nothing to worry about because I'm not making any changes."

Then a thought occurred to me. "Hey, why were you at Bones & Stix anyway? I thought you said you needed to cancel lunch."

"I did. Jaime had popped up unexpectedly at my office, and we had some things to discuss and some closure to bring to the past."

My friend's face no longer looked happy, light, and teasing. She looked as if she had retreated into the past and appeared to be sad.

"Oh, I'm sorry, honey. Was everything okay?" I asked, reaching across the console to pat her hand.

She simply nodded. The rest of the ride to her house, she proceeded to tell me what the two of them had discussed.

A couple of days later, I found myself at Macy's early in the morning, shopping to purge myself of my negative energy. Church had always been my refuge in the past when I was feeling low, but I no longer sought God as my refuge after marrying Eric. I still had what some would call a decent relationship with the Lord at that point, but I wasn't as close to Him as I used to be. Now, whenever I needed solace, I found myself pulling out my plastic cards. A little retail therapy was just what the doctor ordered.

I had been standing in line waiting to check out, responding to emails for several minutes before my turn finally arrived.

"Good afternoon, how are you today?" the sales clerk asked.

Smiling at her, I simply stated, "I'm blessed, and you?"

"Oh, I'm wonderful. Just wonderful. Did you find everything okay?" she asked, as she began ringing up my items.

"Yes, thank you," I mumbled, fishing in my purse to pull out my wallet. I stood waiting on her to finish scanning and bagging my items.

"That will be $323.01," she stated, placing the last of my items in the shopping bag.

I handed her my Visa and waited while she swiped the card. My thoughts were on my dilemma about my friendship with Nick.

"Ma'am, I'm sorry but your card has been declined. Do you have another one you would like to try?" she asked kindly.

"Sure, but can you swipe it again?" I asked, pulling out my MasterCard and American Express.

"Ma'am, I swiped it twice already," she said, still wearing a patient smile.

"Okay, here," I said, trying to determine what could be wrong with my Visa. That was my most frequently used card, but I knew that it wasn't maxed out. Eric had recently paid the bill. I would call the bank once I left the store.

Placing the Visa back in my wallet, I looked back up at the sales clerk who wore a frown, shaking her head again as she handed me back my MasterCard. What in the world was going on? I wondered as I handed her my American Express card next.

Of course, the third time is always the charm, but my luck ran out on me that day as I watched card after card be declined, including my debit cards. The line behind me was growing, and people were getting frustrated. I didn't care, I was determined I would get these items.

"Ma'am, would you like to try cash?" she asked politely.

I was furious and confused. What was going on with my cards? I didn't carry that much cash on me at any given time.

"No, ma'am. Can you please hold these items while I contact my bank and my husband? I'll be right back," I pleaded.

"I will hold them for you for the next half an hour, but after that, they have to go back on the floor," she explained.

I made a mad dash from the store to my car. Sitting in the parking lot, I found myself in tears. I had called bank after bank only to learn my cards had been canceled.

"Eric, call me as soon as you get this message!" I punched the end button on the cell phone. What had happened?

I sat in the car for a moment to get my emotions together. After not receiving a phone call back, I decided to drive home and wait for my husband's arrival.

Eric finally came home late that morning just before noon to find me tossing dishes in cabinets and slamming drawers like I had lost my mind. I was in a mood, and I was fit to be tied. There were so many reasons I was angry with my husband. I ticked them off in my mind: Eric had canceled my credit cards, I didn't want to let my friendship with Nick go, I was concerned about what would happen if Eric ran into the two of us one day, and my husband was a married man living the single life.

It was unfair that I had to feel this way. Eric went around acting like an unmarried man and never gave an explanation for anything he did. Most days, I couldn't reach him by cell, only by way of text when he felt like it.

I was fuming and was ready to pounce on him as soon as he walked through the door, but he threw me another curveball before I got a chance to deal with him.

"Hey, babe, I've invited Steven and Danielle and a couple of my frat brothers and their wives over," he announced, walking into the kitchen with a smile on his face. "Oh, yeah, I also invited Randy and Tiffany, and John and Miesha," he said, referring to our neighbors on both sides of us.

I wasn't in the mood to play hostess, and I was ready to pop his bubble. To say that I was surprised that he wanted to do anything with me was putting it mildly. We hadn't entertained in our home for quite some time.

"Uh-uh, Eric, it's not happening today," I announced, tossing the last dish back into the suds and grabbing an envelope I had placed on the table after drying my hands.

"What the hell you mean, 'it's not happening today'?"

"Exactly what I said. You know you've been dancing around our issues for such a long time now, Eric, but you will face the music today if you want to stay married!" I said, narrowing my eyes at him. I felt a jolt of confidence that I hadn't had in a long time.

"Look, girl, I don't know what's gotten into you, but you better back down a bit. And why are you walking up on me like you're about to do something to me? What the hell is wrong with you?" he asked, as I came to a sudden stop only inches from him.

"You, Eric! You're what's wrong with me!" I shouted, opening the envelope and allowing all the pieces of my cut-up credit cards to fall to the ground.

His response was not one that I had anticipated. He looked at me and started laughing. He actually began to laugh at me.

"What the hell is so funny?" I asked.

"You. You're a joke, Ambiance. You don't need those damn credit cards anyway. Every time I turn around, you're running them up again. I can't afford to keep paying for your damn expensive-ass shopping habit. You have two closets in this house in bedrooms outside of your huge, walk-in closet in our bedroom filled with clothes, shoes, hats, and purses! And lots of them still have price tags on them and aren't being used. Every time I turn around, you're out spending my money again," he accused.

"Your money? Your money, Eric?" I was all up in his face at this point.

"Damn right, I said my money, Ambiance! I pay those bills, not you! Every month I'm paying your credit card bills again, and you don't care how much money you spend or how much I'm spending trying to keep the bills down. Matter of fact, you don't even look at the bills when they come, Ambiance. I open those damn bills. You probably don't know that I've been paying them down to the point that they were finally paid off. Today was the start of a new cycle, and that's why your cards were canceled. I didn't want you to start another damn cycle running up those bills. Now, if you want to get some credit cards, go ahead, but not on my dime!" He turned his back and walked away from me, heading towards the stairs at the front of our home.

"You're an asshole, you know that, Eric? I've offered you money to pay those cards, and you refused it," I said, walking behind him as he went upstairs to the bedroom.

"That was at the beginning of the marriage. That was before you started running up a crazy-ass bill. I've done everything I can think of to persuade you to get your shopping habit under control, and nothing has worked until now," he stated firmly.

I could see a vein throbbing at his temple. He was clearly upset, but I didn't care. His wrath would not outdo mine. Not today.

"Everything except love me, Eric. I beg for your attention, and I'm tired of begging. So, I do what makes me happy. I'm sorry if it's at your expense, but your decision to live your life the way you have has been at mine," I revealed. "I'm tired of being alone in this big, empty house."

"This big, empty house is what you wanted, even more than I did," he said, shaking his head sadly. "You forgot about my dreams, too, Ambiance. I begged you years ago to give me kids. You didn't want any, because you felt the time wasn't right. You keep telling me how the time hasn't been right. I'm tired of some shit, too, Ambi." He sat down on the bed and began removing his shoes and then his socks.

"It wasn't right, Eric. We were having too many problems in our marriage, and I didn't think it was fair to bring children into that. We need to make a home before we can fill the home," I declared.

"Look, I'm the head of this household, and I determine when we do what. Not you!" he stated, pointing a finger at me.

"I determine what happens to my body, Eric, not you!" I shouted, pointing my finger back at him.

"Yeah, whateva. Look, I've invited people over today. You can stay up here moping about credit cards, or get with it. I'm putting meat on the grill whether you like it or not."

"Oh, so I'm just supposed to get in line like nothing's even happened and play the role of the perfect hostess?" I asked, placing my hands on my hips and following him into the bathroom. Out of habit, I found myself picking up his clothes as he discarded them behind him.

"If you can't do it, I'll find someone else who will."

I stood in disbelief as I watched him turn on the shower, adjust the nozzles, and hop in. *He did not just say what I think he said.*

"Excuse me, what do you mean you'll find someone else who will?" I asked, stepping up to the glass shower doors.

"I didn't stutter, Ambiance. There are plenty of women who wouldn't mind stepping into your role and giving me the support I need. If you can't do your job, I'll find one who will." He closed the glass shower doors on me.

I was fuming inside. This was not over.

His guests had arrived around two in the afternoon, and now it was after eleven at night and they had just left. Eric came trying to be sweet, as if nothing had happened earlier. What was up with him? He had canceled my credit cards, not paid me any attention in months, and told me he could be with other women if I didn't get in line, and all of a sudden, now he wanted to be on my good side? I was not sharing the bed with him tonight. Uh-uh. I didn't mean that literally, because we did share a bed every night when he chose to come home. But we hadn't been intimate in a couple of months now.

I had begun to lose my interest and desire for my husband because of his treatment of me. So, my attitude tonight was another way to keep him from trying to get too close. I was hoping, if anything, it would push him away. I felt like if my husband didn't care about our marriage, neither did I. I was tired of putting all the hard work in while he ran the streets.

"Ambiance, what's wrong with you, girl? You're acting like it's the end of the world. You're going to break those dishes if you keep tossing them around like that."

That was my husband, Eric. At six-foot-one with a warm, brown sugar complexion, piercing dark eyes, and full kissable lips, he was definitely a charmer and a looker. Women had a hard time ignoring his looks, and that was what kept him in trouble. The fact that he was a very nice dresser and always smelled so delicious didn't hurt either. His physical build was more like that of a baseball player. He was definitely muscular and toned, but not overtly so…like a certain man named Nick. But none of that was swaying me tonight.

Eric was standing in front of me now with one hand on the counter and the other wiping down his face.

"Come here, quit acting so mean and hateful," he stated.

What did he mean? What did he expect after years of his ignoring me and his treatment of me earlier? I really didn't want to discuss it with him. He had gone too far, and I didn't know if I wanted him to turn back now. I didn't want to work things out anymore, and it seemed as if that was exactly what he was trying to do.

"Look, Ambiance, I know things between us have been off for some time now, and I know it's my fault. I messed up the first year of our marriage, when we should've been getting to know one another as husband and wife. I know it took some time for you to forgive me, but...it was hard being pushed away during those times. And I'm sorry about my attitude earlier."

He had placed both of his arms on either side of me, not allowing me to move away from him. I was trapped as he pressed his manhood against my behind. I tamped down the feelings for him I felt swelling up inside of me.

"Well, good, now you know how I felt when you weren't around. When you were out whoring around and running the streets. Even now, you don't always come home at night. I don't know where you've been, or who you've been doing," I huffed, slamming a dish into the soapy water, causing bubbles to fly back up in my face.

"You mean, *what* I've been doing?" he asked, as he began pressing little kisses down my neck. I took a deep breath and held it in.

"No, I said it right the first time. I don't know *who* you've been doing."

"Girl, I'm not doing anybody. You know sometimes when I'm hanging out with the fellas or my brothers, I get caught up. It's hard coming home at night to another argument or you ignoring me. Most of the times I've been out drinking, and you know I don't believe in drinking and driving. So, I usually stay at one of their houses until I sober up in the morning." He turned me around to face him and looked me in the eyes. "Why are you acting brand new, Ambi? We had an agreement that I would never do that anyway," Eric stated. His eyebrows were furrowed as if he was expressing his confusion to me.

I knew we had that arrangement. But how convenient for him.

"Look, what is it that you want from me?" I asked him, pushing him back from me.

"You, baby. I want you back. I want us to get back to the way we used to be," he pleaded, placing his hands on my behind. He looked down into my eyes and rubbed his hands up and down my back.

I refused to speak to him.

"Come on, babe. Look at how we were today while we had company. We have a beautiful synergy. We can work through this. I miss you," he stated, kissing the tip of my nose.

"I can't just turn off what you did to me, Eric. It's not all about those credit cards. I can get my own cards. But it's because you played it the way you did. You didn't have enough respect for me to discuss it with me. Do you know how embarrassing that was standing in that line and having card after card declined? Not to mention you even canceled my debit cards! Did you forget that my checks go into that account, as well?"

"Come on, Ambi. You act like you have no access to funds. Your money from your business goes into a separate account. You could've used that money," he replied. His body had stiffened up, and I knew he was getting upset again. It was only a matter of time before he would say something out of line.

"You know that money is for my business, Eric. I use that money to continue to grow the business," I defended.

"And I applaud you for that, but don't act like you don't have access to funds. Look, I'll get your debit card reinstated, and we'll work out something about your shopping. Just work with me, girl. That's all I ask," he pleaded.

"All right, Eric," I gave in.

"Good. Now come on and give me some," he urged.

I knew it. It was too good to be true. He only wanted to get some that's why he was behaving himself.

"Uh-uh," I declined.

"What?"

"I said no. You're all horny because you couldn't keep your eyes off Tiffany's ass. I saw how you were watching her all day in those short shorts. If it hadn't been for Randy insisting they leave early, I think you would've ejaculated in your pants," I accused.

Yes, he had been all over me that day, but I never missed how he couldn't tear his eyes away from Tiffany's behind whenever she hopped up to do something or bent over to make sure he caught a glimpse. I had long suspected there was a mutual attraction between my husband and my neighbor, and truthfully, I wouldn't be surprised if something had happened between them. I didn't want to think like that, but my husband was a man-whore.

"Really? I was only looking at her because of how she was putting herself on display. You know I don't respect a woman like that. And I can't believe you think that less of me. She's not as fine as you, as beautiful as you, as classy as you, or as sexy as you. And the bottom line is…she ain't you!" He said this last as he began grinding against me and ran his tongue along the side of my jaw.

Damn! I had to put up some type of front. He was really getting to me, and I didn't expect this. I knew my husband had the power to awaken these dormant feelings. I had worked hard to make sure that he didn't. And after he refused to for so long, I had begun to lock a part of myself away.

I was only desirable to my husband when he wanted something from me. And that wasn't too often these days. But Nick, on the other hand…Nick made me feel beautiful, intelligent, thought about, and loved.

I had taken into consideration the things Naomi had to say a few weeks earlier when she disclosed the fact that she saw me with Nick. I was cautious in all of my dealings with him. I never wanted anyone to misinterpret what was going on with us again. He accepted the fact that I was married and there would never be anything between us. But he was always there when I needed someone to talk to.

I now looked forward to Nick's phone calls in the morning on his way to work and me calling him on my way home. I looked forward to talking to him in the evenings when my husband didn't make it home at night. But I had not taken it a step further than that and had no plans to. I just enjoyed the presence of his company. We still had lunch together every day, but now I went out of my way to meet him. It was important to me to meet him in places I knew Eric wouldn't be. Not because I was doing anything wrong, but because I didn't want the drama that would surely come.

Nick had left town a few days earlier on a business meeting, and I had missed our lunches, but he made sure he called me now more than ever.

During my lunch hour, I sat in my car and talked on the phone with him for almost an hour. He was scheduled to come back the next day, and I couldn't wait.

Now here my husband was trying to unlock the part of me that I was protecting from his hurtful ways. I was a woman broken, tired of being mistreated and unloved by my husband. But now, all out of the blue, my husband wanted to be with me, and all I could do was think about how much I missed another man.

"Come on and give daddy some of that good loving," he said, as he lifted my chin. He began plying me with his soft, smooth kisses. I couldn't do this. Not now.

"No, Eric. We can't just go back to what was. You destroyed that," I said, trying to pull out of his embrace.

"Okay, we can create something new. We can be like the phoenix. It doesn't have to be the way it used to be. We've both been through some things, and we've changed. We've grown and matured in so many ways, and I know that we still have something beautiful," Eric replied in an attempt to convince me, of what I wasn't sure.

"I'm glad one of us feels that way," I admitted.

"One of us? You don't feel the same way?"

I looked at the floor and refused to meet my husband's eyes.

"How you acting, Ambiance? Why you tripping on me?"

Tears began to fall from my eyes. I couldn't do this. I had to make a stand one way or the other. I was a one-man woman. When my man didn't want me anymore, I just went into a shell. I had begged my husband to pry that shell apart, but he wasn't interested. Now that I was working my way through it and finding me again, he wanted back in.

I didn't know what had changed for Eric in his life. I didn't know why he was all of a sudden interested in me or how long it would last. Maybe his lover had turned her back on him, but I was fed up and couldn't take it anymore. I needed and wanted more than what he was willing to offer but I had taken vows for better or worse. Wasn't I supposed to be ready to forgive him and let him lead the way? But how could I when all he did was rip my heart straight from my chest, throw it on the floor, and do the samba across it? I was tired of hurting, and I knew in my heart of hearts he would cast me aside within a few days and return to his old ways.

"I'm not tripping on you, Eric. I'm learning to love me, now." I said this last bit and flicked the dish towel I had been holding down onto the counter, pushed past him and stormed off upstairs to our bedroom.

If I had thought that was the end of things, I had another thought coming.

Eric came into the bedroom that night after I had fallen asleep and began to pull at my nightgown. No matter how hard I tussled, he fought me for it until it ripped.

He smiled down at me as if he had accomplished some great feat.

"So, you're just gonna take it now?" I asked.

"Come on, baby, don't be like this. I want us to make things better. And we start here. We've gotta connect through the body. What's that scripture about couples being apart for only a little while to fast?"

I couldn't believe he had the audacity to attempt to quote any scriptures.

First Corinthians seven and verse five flashed clearly through my mind, as though the Bible were open before me.

"No, Eric. It says that we shouldn't deprive each other except for mutual consent, which we have not, for prayer devotion. Then we would be expected to come together again so that Satan won't tempt us because of lack of self-control. The only thing I have to say about that is, I never agreed to being deprived, and at some point, he obviously got to you."

I was still lying underneath my husband who now had my arms pinned at my sides. A look passed through his eyes. It came and went quickly, but it looked like contempt.

He moved his hands away from my arms and began tugging at my panties. I finally lifted my hips up and let him remove them. It would not be said that I deprived my husband for any reason. If things went awry, it would be his fault not mine.

He entered me and pumped a few times. It didn't seem to matter to him if I enjoyed it or not. I wrapped my arms around my husband and stroked his back a few times. He continued to push inside of me and I allowed him. Eric never saw the tears rolling from my eyes. When he was finished with me, he simply rolled off and turned his back to me. Within five minutes, he was snoring and sound asleep.

For the first time ever, I was glad that I was on birth control. I crept out the bed and went to the bathroom and showered. I couldn't wait until tomorrow.

As usual, when I woke up that morning Eric was gone. I didn't have to go to work that day. I was working from home on my business. I focused on a few loose ends for a fashion show that I was putting together for one of the clients I had met through Nick. I was so excited about this project that nothing could stop my shine, not even what happened between Eric and me the night before.

The fashion show would feature a group of women who had recently become employed through the non-profit agency, Real Gems. I had taken each woman on a personal shopping trip and helped her pull together a new wardrobe, which would allow her to be professional and successful in the workplace. I had also taken the women to The House of BeJeweled in the downtown Atlanta location, and the owner Olivia Ellsworth, had allowed each of them to be professionally styled at no cost.

Now these women would have the opportunity to walk the runway in a community fashion show. The show was free for the community and other people who wanted to participate in the program to get on their feet again. Donors were donating money to the cause, and it seemed as if it was going to be a great success.

Nick and Marla Devonshire, CEO of Real Gems, had been responsible for most of the donors. However, I had recruited the assistance and donations from Naomi, Marc, Sharon, and Angelique. In turn, Angelique and Naomi had gotten donations from other professionals they networked with. Naomi had even contacted Paige, who also pledged a donation.

Paige and I still were not on speaking terms, but she knew I was serious. I wanted her to get her act together before she called me again. I was done with letting people use me. My husband may have been using my body, but no longer would he have my heart to use and abuse. If he wanted to make love to me, fine, but there was a wall up to protect me now.

I looked at the clock on the wall and realized how fast time had flown. It was almost one o'clock, and I was supposed to meet Nick in Stone Mountain in half an hour. I knew there was no way I would make it. I called him to let him know I was running late. I finished up some last-minute touches for the fashion show, sent out a couple of emails to clients, and ran to shower and change.

Strutting into the restaurant, I knew my simple summer outfit was looking good. I don't know why it mattered to me that I was fierce, but it did. I hadn't seen Nick in almost a week now, and I wanted to be spot-on. Why? Because the truth was I was attracted to that man. I had no business being attracted to him, and I knew it wouldn't lead to anything, but it didn't stop me from wanting to be desired.

I wore a black, halter tank top with ruching on the bra area. My tan, wrap skirt sported a split up to the middle of my thigh. I paired it with gold and black bangles, gold tri-hoop earrings, and a pair of black espadrilles. Every step I took showcased my toned right thigh and gave a little glimpse of the left one. I was a woman who knew how to be sexy without being sleazy, and I could do it in the simplest clothing. Sexy was a state of mind, an attitude more than the clothing you wore. Many women didn't get that and thought that the less they wore, the sexier they were. I knew the reverse to be true.

I was meeting him at Flaming Rio, a Brazilian restaurant in Stone Mountain. When I approached the table he had reserved, he stood to greet me. I saw his eyes light up the moment he spotted me, and then I saw his gaze slowly roll down every inch of me and stop at my thighs.

Nick pulled his bottom lip in between his teeth and stretched out his arms to welcome me. He gave me a nice hug and squeeze before releasing me. But in that brief moment, I felt something I had never felt before. It was some spark or connection between the two of us. I wondered if I had imagined it, because I had missed him so much.

He was dressed in a pair of black jeans, a white t-shirt, and a tan linen blazer over his shirt. His casual appearance caught me off guard, as I was used to seeing him dressed in business attire.

"Well, hello there, look at you. Looks like someone took the day off," I remarked, addressing his casual attire.

He laughed a deep, sexy laugh and shook his head full of loose locs. "I had to visit a couple of the construction sites today. I tend to dress down on those occasions. So, did you miss me?" he teased.

"Of course, I did. I have had no one to have lunch with or toss all of my issues on," I pouted, teasing him.

"Awww, I'm sorry. I wish I could've taken you with me," he said, as he grabbed my hand across the table. I felt it again! It was almost like an electric shock. I looked into his eyes and saw a longing desire. He held my gaze for several moments before I finally turned away.

I cleared my throat and made an attempt to resume the conversation. "Mm-hmm, I bet you do," I replied, slipping my hand from his grasp. I decided it was the perfect moment to take a sip of my iced tea, which I grabbed with both hands to keep them occupied and out of his hands. He had ordered drinks and our meal just before I arrived, after I called him when I was five minutes away.

He smiled at me again. "I really wish I could have taken you with me. It would have made the trip more interesting. How's the show coming along?"

"Everything is falling into place. I tell you, I am so thankful to you for the connections you have provided. This is taking my business to a new level faster than I imagined. But above all of that, it's so rewarding working with these women. I am experiencing an entirely new level of fulfillment in my life that I never could have anticipated."

"Well, I'm glad to hear that. How are things on the home front?" Nick asked, looking into my eyes, imploring me to be honest with him.

Nick was the only person that I truly opened up to about my marriage these days. The girls knew that Eric stayed busy at the law office and when he wasn't billing hours, he ran the streets. But I didn't share my feelings about my marriage with them. I had known eventually I would need someone to air my grievances to, and Nick had proven to be that sound shoulder. He never uttered a word against my husband; instead, he always encouraged me to stand strong.

Some days, I didn't feel as if I could, like today. "It's still the same. I'm so tired of it all, Nick. I just wish he had cared when I cared. These days, I'm not even concerned if he comes home or speaks to me at all. He could call me up tomorrow and say he's never coming back and it wouldn't phase me. The only thing that means anything anymore is building my business and being able to work with those wonderful women, and these lunches I share with you. I look forward to it every day. I actually rush my weekends by, just so I can see you again on Monday." I stirred my sweet tea with my stirrer, and looked back up at him before going on. "That's sad, isn't it?"

It appeared as if he was looking into my soul, he was staring so intently at me.

"No, it's not sad. Your heart just longs to be loved, and you're missing a part of you right now. I've come along and provided friendship, something you crave, along with attention, and it's making you feel alive again. I can understand that. Believe it or not, I look forward to these lunches, too. It does a man's ego good to have a beautiful woman to share a meal with. But girl, you gotta stop coming around me in skirts like the one you're wearing today. There's only so much temptation a man can take."

He smiled that beautiful smile at me that warmed my heart. I thought about what he said, and I wasn't upset that I had achieved my goal.

"It's about time you took notice. And I'm glad you like it." I was bold in my choice of words. I left them open for interpretation.

Nick leaned back and placed his arm along the back of his booth and then grabbed his glass of wine and took a sip. He looked at me over the rim, those smooth, chocolate-brown eyes darkening with something mysterious behind them. I was glad I wasn't drinking. I began blushing when I thought about how forward and provocative I had been.

"Yeah, I like it very much," he answered. He shook his head, and I could tell he was thinking. He confirmed that after a few moments when he posed his next question.

"Let me ask you something. You just said you didn't care if he called you up and said he's never coming back. Then if you feel that way, why don't you initiate a divorce?" His facial expression was blank, as though he were holding back his emotions. I had come to know him well enough by now to know that he didn't want to influence my answer one way or the other.

I pondered his question carefully. I didn't want to just throw any answer out there to him. Searching deep within, I was surprised at what I discovered.

"Because I'm afraid of living this life on my own. I left my parents' home to go to college. After college, I had a couple of roommates before I met Eric. I moved away from them to move straight into the home we live in now a few months before we married. I've never done this thing on my own. I worry what would happen if for some reason I lost my job, or my business failed. Nick, I'm not a risk-taker. And I couldn't handle living alone day after day with no one to share my life with. I honestly fear the loneliness."

"But you don't have anyone to share your life with now. You leave an empty house behind you every day, and then you come back home to an empty house in the evening. And most nights, you go to bed alone. Aren't you now living the life you fear?"

As callous as it sounded, I didn't want to point out the obvious. He had forgotten that I mentioned worrying that I could lose my job or my business failing. So, I went to the other points instead.

"Not really. I always have the option that he might come home. I mean, just yesterday he was talking about working things out," I shared.

"Oh, yeah?" He glanced up from his meal that the waitress had recently delivered to our table.

I saw the hint of curiosity in his eyes and something else that was akin to fear. Was he worried what would happen to our friendship if I worked things out with my husband? I had to know.

"Yes. He let me know that I hurt him when I continued to push him away. He said he missed the way things were." I continued to pour out information to see what reaction he would have to this news.

There was none; he had thrown the wall up to block out whatever I had previously seen. Nick continued to eat his food, almost as if we were discussing the weather.

"You don't have anything to say about that?" I asked.

"What's there to say, Ambiance? I mean, in one breath you tell me you don't care what he does and make it sound like you want out. Then in the next breath you proceed to tell me how he wants to work it out. What am I supposed to do? It's ultimately your choice, not mine. You've been clear from the beginning that you don't want to get involved and that you are a very married, one-man woman. So, what exactly are you asking me?" he asked, placing his fork down.

"Don't you care?" I asked, holding my breath.

"Look, I don't want to play any games with you. You've been a cool friend that I enjoy spending time with, and I've tried to be a good friend to you. But I keep my feelings tucked away in this thing, because I don't want to confuse you or create problems for myself."

I wanted and needed to know what those feelings were. I wasn't sure why they mattered to me, I just knew that I wanted to know and to understand what he was feeling.

"Nick, I share everything with you. I want you to share with me, as well."

We sat in silence for a few moments while he contemplated something in his head. I could only guess he was trying to determine how much and what he should share with me.

"Ambiance, it's no secret I've been physically attracted to you since the day we met. That's why I stepped to you the way that I did. I wanted to get to know you better, and I was intrigued by you. But after I learned you were married and you made your feelings clear about that marriage, I was careful of how I handled you. I've gotten to know you, and I want to know more about you. I want to be very much involved with you emotionally and physically. It's a struggle for me, too. I respect you, but I won't lie. Ambiance, I wouldn't be angry if your husband left tomorrow. I just want to step in and pick up the pieces to let you know it will be okay. I want to love you, I want to make love to you, and I want to share your lows and celebrate your highs. I want to touch and taste every inch of your body. I want to take away the loneliness you experience on those nights when there's no one to hold you close. I want to take away your fears and let you know your financial worries will cease to exist. But more importantly I want you to want me, too. But I can't have that, so I accept what you offer me…your friendship."

Wow! I had not seen all of that coming. This man had left me longing and craving for what I could not have.

"Now that I've shared that with you, what do you plan to do about it?" he asked, sitting back in his seat.

My eyes grew wide. I didn't know what to say; the ball was back in my court. A part of me wished my husband would up and leave so that I could run away with Nick. But that was only because I didn't want any of it to be my fault. I was a coward!

"Yeah…that's what I thought," he concluded.

"What's that supposed to mean? I can't just up and leave with you, Nick, and say let's spend the rest of our lives together. That's why I was up front with you about where things stood from the beginning. I never thought it was a good idea to have this friendship. I knew that it would leave both of us longing for more," I confessed.

"Is that what you want, Ambiance? Do you really want more? And if so, more of what? Me, him, both?"

I held my head down and stared sightlessly at the table. He was right. I wanted my cake, and I wanted to eat it, too. I knew I couldn't have him and my husband, but I wanted both. I wanted the security that came from being with Eric all those years, but I also wanted the love and compassion I knew I could have with Nick.

I laughed.

"What's so funny?" Nick asked, narrowing his eyes at me.

"The fact that you have me pegged. I want the safety I feel in knowing what to expect with my husband. There's no surprises there; it's just one big disappointment after another. But you…you're the game changer. It scares me to know that not only do I want you, but I can even see myself risking it all to be with you. I know it might sound crazy, but I'm starting to feel like I'm addicted to you. I can't wait for your calls, I can't wait to see you, and I always find myself wondering what's next when it comes to you," I confided.

Nick licked his lips and shook his head. "Yeah, I figured as much. But baby, you gotta know…it won't always be like this."

"Be like what?" I felt my heart racing. Was he threatening to take back his friendship?

"One day, Ambiance, it's gotta be all or nothing. One day you will have to decide what you want to do."

"Why?"

"Because eventually you'll get tired of this thing we're doing. Hell, I don't even know what we're doing. But there will come a time when if it's not us, you'll have to put everything into making your marriage work. And with that comes honesty, being truthful with Eric about our friendship…where you're spending your lunch breaks, who's on the phone with you all morning and night. You can't keep hiding me if you want to make your marriage work. And once the truth comes out, I don't think he'll be too happy with it."

"No, I don't think that will be a problem. Eric's pretty secure in who he is."

"That's where you're wrong, Ambiance. Most men like to project the image that they are secure, but in reality, they're anything but. The way you say he has to run around on the marriage and never comes home, he's either a fool, insecure, or an insecure fool. And you're a fool if you think your husband will be okay with us being friends."

I laughed so hard, tears ran down my cheeks like they were in a marathon.

"What the hell is so funny?" Nick's head was cocked to the side, and his eyes crinkled when I opened mine long enough to look at him. For some reason, this made me laugh harder than before. Eventually, I regained my composure.

"Just what you said. My friend told me the same thing one day when the topic of you came up. It's nothing, really," I said, reminiscing on the same statement Naomi had made about Nick.

"Now, here's the reality check. So, we both know your husband won't be excited about this friendship, but I'm almost sure my girl won't be too happy about it, either," Nick stated, looking me in the eyes.

What the hell? What girl? Since when did he become involved in a relationship? He had never mentioned a woman before. I knew he hadn't. Come to think of it, we often talked about him needing a special woman in his life. Who was this chick and how long had she been around? Was she cute? What did she have to offer him?

I averted my eyes and quickly took a moment to sip my iced tea to try to cover the fact that he had just caught me off guard. Not to mention I was extremely jealous and had no right to be. I only hoped he didn't notice. I risked a glimpse at him, and he was spearing a piece of asparagus onto his fork and not looking at me. Was he teasing me? I couldn't tell, but I needed to know. I had to know.

"So, what's your plan?" I asked.

"It all depends on you."

"No, I mean about your girl. What's your plan? Are you going to tell her about me, Nick, or what?"

"Like I said, it all depends on you." Nick was buttering his roll and talking calmly, as if nothing had just happened.

"I'm sorry, but when did you get a girl? You never mentioned that you were in a relationship." There, it was out. I couldn't take the suspense anymore, it was killing me.

It was his turn to laugh, and his was a bit sardonic. "There's no girl, Ambiance. But I am saying that one day there will be. One day, I'll be moving forward in my life. Not that it doesn't mean we can't be friends still…after all, that's what you wanted. But my point is that things will eventually change, whether it's because of your husband or a relationship that I become involved in. Things won't continue to remain the way that they are now. And I just want you to begin to think about that."

"Why, Nick?"

"Because I don't want you to take it too hard when it happens. I want you to be able to withstand the disappointment and still be strong in spite of it.

I'm here in your life for a reason and a season, and who knows what it is or for how long. Only the Almighty has the answer to that one. But the one thing that I do know is I'm here to make you better and stronger, not worse. So, when I exit the stage, I want to know you're going to be all right."

It was my turn to be silent. I needed a moment to ponder what he had said. I just assumed he would always be there. I didn't even want to contemplate what life would be like without him there. And I had never truly considered the alternative of him not being there, or the possibility that Eric would give me an ultimatum.

We finished the rest of our meal making small talk, staying away from the hot button issues of my relationship with my husband and my friendship with him.

He walked me to my car afterwards and stood in front of me holding both of my hands in one of his.

"Hey, look at me. Come on, girl, hold your head up and look at me," Nick stated, grabbing my chin and tilting my head upwards toward him.

"What?" I replied.

"You're a beautiful woman, inside and out. You need to know that, because the sooner you do, the sooner you can heal and know what it is you have to offer this world and what you expect to take from it. Until then, you're no good to anyone, not me, not your husband, and especially not yourself. Right now, you're vulnerable, and another man would try to take advantage of that. I'm not here to do that. I want you to be strong and beautiful and know your worth. I want you to know your value in this world. You feel me, beautiful?"

Nick bent down, and holding my face between his hands, he pressed a sweet simple kiss to my lips. He turned and walked his sexy self away from me to his charcoal, sleek Nissan 370Z Coupe Nismo. Yes, I had finally asked the man what type of car he drove and memorized the name. But at the moment, I wasn't in awe of his car, I was in shock. I couldn't believe he had just done what he had done. Worse? I couldn't believe that my husband was parked directly across from Nick's car and had seen the entire thing.

14_NAOMI_MENDING FENCES

Convincing Sasha to give her father half a chance was not easy. She wanted no parts of it and let me know she felt betrayed by the fact that I was even speaking to Jaime, let alone wanting her to spend time with him.

"Maybe you fell for his story, Mom, but I didn't!"

"Sasha Kennedy Blankenship, get back down these stairs, now!" I was standing at the island chopping vegetables for the grilled steak burritos I was making for our dinner. My tempestuous daughter had stomped up the stairs at our latest disagreement about her at least calling her father. This had been going on for almost two weeks now. I was getting worn down and ready to give up. Jaime had called again this morning asking if I had made any progress. It took everything in me not to get angry with him.

Here I was picking up the pieces once again where he had failed his daughter. It seemed as if I had been doing that ever since the day he walked out. I was tired, but I had to know that I had given it my all before I gave up.

She marched back down the steps with her arms crossed over her chest and her lips poked out.

"You know, you look like you did when you were four and I told you that you couldn't wear your tutu and ballerina slippers to school."

Sasha didn't so much as crack a smile. I blew out a breath and set my knife down. I walked to the sink and washed my hands, dried them on a paper towel, and walked over to where my daughter stood. I pulled her into my arms.

"What are you scared of, baby? All these years you wished you had gotten to know him. All these years you visualized him in your head, and now that he's here, you won't give him half a chance. Are you worried that he's going to take you from me?"

Sasha shook her head *no*, not saying a word. I felt her shoulders shake and knew that she was crying. "Then, baby, what are you afraid of?"

She still refused to say a word, and then it began to dawn on me. I don't know how I didn't see it before. Sasha was so much like her father in so many ways. I had told her that throughout the years, and in her head, she had made him up to be fabulous and convinced herself he had died. Now it had to be a blow to her knowing he was alive and not as fabulous as she first thought. I realized my daughter was projecting Jaime's failings onto herself, and it was impacting how she felt about herself. She was worried that getting to know him would reveal all of his flaws. And if they were revealed, she would be disappointed. That was scary to her, because to her, she was him.

"Come here," I said, pulling her into the family room. I sat her down on the couch and went to the bookshelf to grab a photo album. I showed her picture after picture of herself at the various stages of her life. She saw pictures of herself as an infant with me, Ambiance, Paige, and my parents. She saw her at dance recitals, soccer games, swim lessons, award programs, birthdays, and so much more. I had shown her these pictures throughout the years at various times when she just wanted to sit down and look at them. But this time was different.

"What do you notice about all these pictures, Sasha?"

"I don't know. He wasn't in them?"

"No. That you were beautiful, and you were strong, and you were loved, and you were cared for. You even see yourself having a tantrum in some of them. But what you notice above all is that I was there. Your family was there. And no matter what, love was never withheld from you. But more than that, you have to notice that Sasha was Sasha. You were who you were then, and now. No matter who comes or goes in this life, you will remain you. He cannot break you or make you baby. Only you have the power to give someone else that type of control over your life. And it's up to you how you decide to be happy, how you decide to live this life, and how you decide to move forward. No one has that power but you. In all these pictures and stages of your life, you dictated your outcomes. We could want the best for you, but we couldn't reach those goals, create beautiful art through dance on stage, or win those awards you won in life. Only Sasha could do that. Only Sasha held the power all those years ago, and only Sasha holds that power now. So, if your father isn't who you wanted him to be, if you find that you're disappointed in the image you created in your head, it's your choice. You can continue to carry around an illusion created by you all those years ago, or drop the image you've held all these years and get to know the man he is. Learn the other part of your culture and what makes up Sasha. It gives you more power, more freedom, and more control over your life."

Sasha took a deep breath within my arms and sat up. "I don't know, Mom. I have to think about it."

"That's fine. It's better than the resolute no and the shouting you've done the last couple of weeks. Just remember this, regardless of what your answer is, I love you and I support you. But keep it real with yourself."

"Okay. I love you, too, Mom," she stated, wrapping her arms around me.

Later that evening after dinner was complete and the kitchen was done, Sasha was in her room with a girlfriend from our church listening to music. My cell phone rang, and when I glimpsed at the caller ID and saw Jaime's name, I released a pent-up breath.

"Hello?"

"Hey, wassup?"

"Nothing, sitting here watching TV."

"Did you talk to her again?"

I waited for a moment as I gathered my thoughts. I didn't want to make him any promises. I owed him nothing, but a part of me felt sad for him. I felt sad that he had missed out on so many wonderful years of knowing and loving that beautiful young lady.

"Yes, Jaime, I spoke with her again. I don't know what to tell you. She said she would think about it. I don't know how long it's going to take, and I won't keep pressing her on it."

"Thank you, Naomi. That's all I ask just, that you don't give up and give me half a chance."

"It's not me that you need a chance from, Jaime. It's that young lady in there whose heart is broken in half."

"Well, I did need a chance from you, because I couldn't even begin to form a relationship with her without your support, Naomi."

"Mm-hmm, well, just remember this: don't break her heart. I promise you, if you disappoint her, I will personally hire someone to kick your ass! It's been hell since you walked back into her life and these last couple of weeks, the flames have been burning hotter. Jaime, she's worried that you'll disappoint her. She really has connected her image of herself with you. She feels like you're such a part of her that any of your failings will reflect on the person she is. I have worked hard to craft her into the beautiful young lady she is. She may look like you on the outside and have many of your ways, but there is so much of me and my hard work intertwined within that."

"Naomi, I know, I know. I'm just…sometimes, I don't know what to say. I wish I could erase the mistakes and turn back the hands of time. All I can do now is make it right. I promise you, I won't hurt either of you again."

I shook my head and wiped away the tears that were falling down my face. I didn't want him to hear them in my voice, so I muted the phone for a minute. All I heard was him breathing. I unmuted the phone.

And then there was a knock at the door. "Hold on, Sasha." I called out, attempting to clear my throat and getting up from my bed at the same time, in search of a tissue.

"Can I come in for a sec?"

I guess she didn't hear me say hold on as I was grabbing a tissue from the dresser to wipe my eyes, because she came barreling through my door.

"Mom, me and Sabrina were wondering if…Mom, what's wrong?" she asked, rushing towards me.

I had wiped the tears away, but I couldn't cover the red in my eyes. I was still holding the phone to my ear.

"Hello? Hello?" That was Jaime on the phone, calling out to me.

"Yes, Jaime, hold on for a second."

"Okay," he muttered. I think he heard Sasha's voice in the background.

"Mom…is that him on the phone? Is that why you're crying? What did he do?" Sasha's voice was turning shrill to my ears.

"Sasha! Stop right now! Your fa-Jaime hasn't done anything."

"Then why are you crying, Mom?"

"Because, there are some things that you just will never understand until you're grown. If you don't mind, would you please speak to your father?" I asked, holding the phone out towards her.

I had said that I wouldn't push her again, but I couldn't pass up on this opportunity. It seemed as if the timing was perfect. She stood in front of me with her arms crossed over her breasts, attempting to be stubborn.

I lifted an eyebrow at her and pushed the phone towards her once again. Sucking her teeth and doing that sickening eye-rolling thing that she did, she reluctantly grabbed the phone.

"Hello?" she muttered, full of attitude.

She listened for a moment, mumbled a couple of yeses, and then walked out of the room with the phone. I followed behind her and then turned towards her bedroom when she went to the guest room. She closed the door behind her.

"Sabrina?" I called, peeking my head into my daughter's bedroom to check on her friend.

"Yes, ma'am?" the teen called back, as she shuffled through songs on Music Choice.

"Sasha will be back with you in just a moment. She had a phone call to take."

"Okay, Ms. B," she chirped, and turned back to what she was doing.

I walked back into my room, making the decision not to check up on Sasha. I would give her the privacy she needed. But I was antsy with anticipation as I waited for her return. I could only pray that he wouldn't say anything that would cause her to blow up. A part of me hoped that she would give him half a chance, but another part was hesitant. Sasha had been mine all those years, and now, I just might've had to start sharing her, and the thought of that made me a bit jealous. I began to wonder what type of relationship she might form with her dad and his wife. The thought of another woman being over my child caused a sour feeling to develop within my stomach.

I knew I had to speak to my parents; they were the only ones who would understand my pain and could help me sort through the feelings I was experiencing.

"Mom?" Sasha peeked her head back through the door, handing me the phone. I took it and looked at my daughter, who had an apprehensive look on her face.

"He wants to speak with you."

"Hello?" I didn't know why my daughter couldn't tell me whatever needed to be said.

"Hey, Naomi. I spoke with her, and for once, she didn't scream at me. I don't know what you've been saying on your end, but thank you. I mean, she listened to what I had to say. She didn't have much to say, but I did ask if I could spend a day with her. She said she would be open to it, but I needed to talk with you first. You raised her well; she won't do anything without your approval," Jaime stated.

Hmph, if only he knew. She had done quite a few things lately without my approval, starting with a white mini skirt and a boy in my home. But I wouldn't go there for now. I would focus on helping her build a relationship with her father, and maybe we could address any future issues that arose together. This may have been just what was needed to get my daughter back on track.

"Yeah, well, I did my best. So, what do you want to do?" I asked.

"Well, I was hoping next weekend I could get her on Saturday and hang out with her. I don't know, maybe go jet-skiing, shoot some hoops, and grab a bite to eat. I know you told me she plays ball, but I don't know how she'll feel about jet-skiing."

"You can ask, but I think she'll be open to that." It was my turn to get up and walk out the room. I didn't want my daughter to hear the jealousy that might rise in my voice when I asked my next question.

"Cool, maybe we can grab a bite to eat at Havana's Cocina and talk about our culture."

"That sounds like a good idea, too. Is it going to be just you and her, Jaime?" I asked, walking down the hall and looking back to make sure my daughter wasn't following me.

"Yeah. I thought maybe it would give her a chance to get to know me and me a chance to get to know her without any other distractions. Would you like to come?" he invited.

"No. I think it should just be the two of you," I responded. I didn't want to give his wife any reasons for concern or jealousy. After all, she was just learning her husband had another child they would have to share him with. She didn't need another woman to share his time with, as well.

"All right, if you're sure," he agreed.

"I'm sure."

"If you change your mind, Naomi, I would love to have you. I kind of thought fishing would be good, because of that one-on-one time, but she might get bored by that," he shared.

"She definitely would. I'm sure whatever you settle on will be just fine for the two of you. With the exception of fishing, though. Neither of us have ever been fishing kinds of girls," I joked.

Jaime laughed softly and then spoke. "Yeah, I do recall that you weren't the outdoorsy type. And you always hated worms, especially after the rain," he reminisced.

"They were always so slimy and gave me the creeps. Just nasty, even when I think about them now, ewww!" I exclaimed.

We both laughed and then went silent on the phone for a moment.

"Thank you, Naomi. Thank you so much for giving me this opportunity. And I'm sorry, I'm so sorry for hurting you and—"

"Don't do this. You don't have to keep apologizing and going down that road. It's not about me anymore, it's about our daughter. If we're going to move forward in this, it's time to leave the past behind. At least with me anyway," I corrected him. I couldn't do the reminiscing thing; it would only serve to hurt me further and I had worked hard to move on from the past.

"Okay, Naomi. You got it. I was thinking...I mean I know you're doing okay financially, but I need to give you child support. I can work on paying some for the last several years, but I'll need time to get that together. But I can start now."

"Jaime, I appreciate what you're trying to do. I really do, but let's not do this. If you want to do anything at all, just put some money in an account for when she goes to college. She has a debit card now, but I would like to make sure she has a steady monthly allowance when she goes. With both of us contributing, she won't have to worry about getting a job for clothing, social activities, or anything else she might want."

"Cool. Sounds good," he stated.

"All right, well, what time do you want to pick her up on Saturday, or would you like me to meet you somewhere to drop her off?" I asked. The more I thought on it, the more I realized I didn't want him to know where I lived.

"What's best for you?"

"Umm, where do you live?" I asked.

"In Lithonia."

"Okay, let's meet at Oasis," I said, referring to a popular mall in an upscale area of town. It was a halfway point for both of us, about twenty-five miles from my home and his area.

"Cool, will 11:00 A.M. work for you?"

"Yeah, Jaime. I'll talk to you then."

"Sure. Let me know if anything changes," he stated. I knew this was almost too good to be true to him.

"Hopefully, nothing will. But I will be in touch if it does," I agreed. Clicking off the phone, I went back to converse with my daughter.

"Hey, baby, how are you feeling?" I asked, sitting next to my lanky child, who was sprawled across my bed on her stomach.

"I'm good," she said, chin propped on her folded arms.

"Are you sure? I don't want you doing anything you don't want to do."

"It's okay, Mom. I've been thinking a lot, and I have a lot of questions scrambling around in my brain. So, I'll kick it with the old man for a moment and see wassup with him."

"Old man?" I asked, lifting an eyebrow. I tickled her, and she scrunched up into a fit of laughter. If she was calling him an old man, what was she calling me? He and I were almost the same age.

"You grow finer with time, Mom. His age shows on him." She wiggled her eyebrows up and down at me.

"He wants to go jet-skiing and shooting hoops with you." She shrugged her shoulders at my comment. "Seriously, are you okay with this, Sasha?" I asked.

"Yeah, I'm good. Let me get back to Sabrina before she thinks I've ditched her…and Mom, you're the best. I'll never love anyone as much as I love you," my daughter said, grabbing me and hugging me.

I guess she had seen through my insecurities after all. My daughter knew me as well as I knew her.

15_PAIGE_JUST ONE NIGHT

Life had turned upside down for me, and I wasn't too thrilled at the way it was going. I was headed on a fast track downward, but I wasn't ready to give that up. I had certain expectations of life, and one of them was to drown my hurt by using men before they used me.

I had not heard from Rodney since the last time we had sex and David popped up later that night. I had been calling him and leaving voice mail after voice mail. He hadn't returned my calls, yet. Unfortunately, David had not stopped calling me. He was leaving vulgar voicemails on my cell phone, telling me what he wanted to do to me. When I refused to call him back, he began leaving voicemails calling me out of my name and telling me how he meant what he said about me screwing over his marriage. I continued to ignore him. Once I got in touch with Rodney, I figured I would simply change my phone number and not have anything else to do with David.

I wanted and needed Rodney to come over and spend more time with me. I knew if David ever popped up and Rodney was there, David would not be a problem again. Rodney wasn't someone to be fooled with. Everything about him was hardcore, thuggish, and real. David was a bunch of talk with a penchant for bullying females. He wasn't about to bust a grape, and I knew if he ever threatened me around Rodney, he wouldn't do it to another woman again.

I had left work once again and was heading to The Olive Garden for a nice quiet dinner alone. I wasn't quite ready to go home yet, so I figured I would hang out and eat. I had called my mom to see if she wanted to have dinner, but she was already drunk at five in the evening. My mom had been drinking for as long as I could recall, and it seemed as if it got worse with time. I hated calling her in the middle of the day and her speech was slurred. I hated even more that she actually thought she could get behind the wheel of a car and drive. She drowned all of her life's disappointments and sorrows in the bottle. I drowned mine in men.

As I was leaving the restaurant, I caught a glimpse of Rodney from behind. I began walking up to him just as some other female caught up to him and he leaned down and kissed her in the mouth.

Okay, that was cool, I mean, we weren't exclusive or anything. I saw other men, he dated other women, and we both knew it. No biggie. But I did want him to see me, maybe that might jog his memory to give me a call.

I walked around a group of people heading to their table to give him a chance to see me. Rodney looked up and caught my eye, then he looked away as if he hadn't seen me. Okay, so maybe he didn't want the other woman to get jealous. I could definitely respect that. But somehow, I needed to speak to him. The waitress was already cleaning my table, so there was no way I could return and wait him out.

My opening came when the female he was with stopped a waitress passing them by and asked her a question. The waitress pointed in the direction of the restroom, and the woman left Rodney's side. I quickly swooped in.

"Rodney…hey, baby, I've been calling you," I said. I wanted to get straight to the point. I knew I didn't have long before his date returned.

"I know. I've been busy, Paige." He tried to walk past me with a dismissive air.

I placed my hand on his arm to stop him in his tracks. He looked down at my hand and then back up at me with a scowl on his face. "Wassup, Paige? Whachu want?"

"You. I just wanted you to stop by sometime. I need you. I miss you and Baller," I said, with my eyes lowering to look at his manhood.

He laughed at me. "Need me? Girl, you don't need nobody. You got all your bases covered. I ain't mad at ya'."

"What are you talking about?"

"You know how you roll." He shrugged his shoulders before continuing on, "Look, it's never been a secret that you sleep around. It's what you do, and we've talked about it several times in the past. That last time I was at your house, I did my business that night. You got a phone call before I left. And I don't know if you know, but when I left your house, there was some dude in the hallway at the other end of the stairwell. He walked up on me asking if I had just been with you. I don't know who dude was, but I let him know don't be rolling up on me like that. He let me know he had just called you, so I knew he was telling the truth. I wasn't all into it like that. However you live your life is your business, but when I got somebody rolling up on me because of how you handle it? Then it's time for me to bounce. So, that night I handled my business, then somebody else came and did what they had to do. You should be all good, girl; ain't no shortage of men in yo' life, l'shorty."

I felt a chill flow over my body. That freaking psycho David! He was watching me? There was no telling how long he had been doing that and what all he knew about my personal life. I had the creeps. I would deal with that later. Right now, I had to deal with what was standing in front of me.

"Rod, are you really talking to me like that? I thought we were better than that. I thought we understood one another. I roll the same way you roll," I shared.

"Nah, baby girl. I do what I gotta do and I'm out. I ain't sleeping with all these different females. I mean it's a couple of y'all I would chill with every now and then, but you ain't even chilling with nobody. You just fucking and rolling on, like that's the thang to do. And if that's how you wanna get down, that's cool. But I'm doing something different now."

"What do you mean, something different?" I asked.

"That woman you saw me with? That's my baby. It's time for me to set shit straight with her, that's all I'm saying. I promised her I would give up the other women, and it's just me and her now. I always kept it real with her, and I ain't 'bout to mess that up now."

"But, Rodney, I always told you that I would leave everybody alone for you. You know that. Out of all the men I date, you're the only one that I care about, Rod." I couldn't believe he didn't understand that. I had never pressed him about being in a relationship, but I had always explained that I would be there if and when he needed me to be.

"I hear you. But that's part of your problem. The only one you cared about was me, so you just letting these niggas roll up in you, and you don't even care about them. How much are you caring about yourself, then? Come on, Paige. Think about what you're saying. Hell, you're not the type I'm trying to settle down with. I can't see myself being with a woman who I know open her legs for everybody that's hanging low. For all I know, my boys been up in that. I can't get down like that. But you cool. I mean, you do you, I'm just doing something different now," he said, pushing me aside like I didn't matter.

"You dirty ass—"

"Whoa! Watch your mouth. There ain't no reason for you to make a scene, Paige. You made your choices in this life, and I made mine. I'm laying it all down for my one and only. I ain't hating on you, but I don't wanna do you no more. 'S all I'm saying. You feel me?" He was looking me up and down like he was about to check the hell out of me. With one eyebrow raised and his hands out at his sides, I knew Rodney would go hood on me if he needed to. I didn't want that.

I felt like I had just been scraped across the floor. I ran from the restaurant with tears blinding me and hopped into my Camaro and hit OnStar. I called Dedric, Leon, Maurice, and Xander with no results. I called Vic, praying he wouldn't answer the phone and was relieved, but confused, when he didn't. He never missed any of my calls. What could he possibly be doing that he couldn't answer my phone call? Oh, well, I would try someone else. My next call to a dude named Jacob was answered. I had met him downtown a week earlier when leaving the juvenile courthouse after one of my clients' hearings. I hadn't had a chance to see what he was packing.

He had invited me out on a date a few nights ago, but I wasn't able to make it. I had to drop by and see about my mom, who had been sick after going on one of her alcohol binges. Tonight was the night I would hook up with him.

"Hello?" he greeted.

"Hi, Jacob, it's Paige."

"Hey, little lady, how are you?"

"I'm doing well. What about you?"

"Cool. Just got in from work, thinking about going out. You want to join me for drinks?" Jacob invited.

"Nah, I was actually headed home. I just finished grabbing dinner at the Olive Garden. How about I come by your place for drinks?" I didn't want to invite any new males to my home. I was over that after David. It was a practice Naomi and Ambiance had warned me against, anyway. Ambiance.

Whew, I missed my girl, just a bit. I wasn't really on her shit either, though. I pushed her out of my head and tuned back into the conversation I was missing.

"...long?" Jacob was saying. I had missed everything except long, and for some reason in my mind, I instantly thought about the size of his penis.

"Huh?" I replied, choking.

"I was asking how long before you could be here?" he asked.

I coughed a bit more to get myself together.

"Are you all right?" he inquired.

"Um, yeah. I was drinking a soda and it went down wrong," I lied. "Where do you live? I can pop it into my GPS and head over there now."

He gave me the address, and I punched it in and told him that I should be there within half an hour.

When I arrived, I was impressed with his home. The brother was living in a nice area of McDonough in a gated community. His two-story, brick home had a well-landscaped, four-acre lot with a three-car garage. He was the first man that I had met in a while that appeared to be doing well for himself. The others were thugs or just working a routine nine-to-five.

He met me at the front door in tan slacks, a sky-blue, silk pullover shirt, and some tan loafers on his feet. Jacob smelled nice. He was wearing a light, sporty fragrance that wasn't too overpowering but nicely enveloped you.

"If I didn't know any better, I would swear you were peeping through my window when you dressed this morning," he teased.

I smiled as I realized, I, too was wearing tan and sky-blue. My tan skirt stopped at my knees but hugged my curves so lovingly. Of course, my strappy sandals matched my skirt and my tan and sky-blue bag. But nothing was as hot as my sky-blue halter top that showcased cleavage galore and allowed my smooth, golden back and shoulders to be exposed to his lips if he so desired. I had left my matching tan suit jacket in the car.

I looked up at him with green eyes that I knew melted any man's heart and sashayed my way through his door. "Hmph, I'm sure it was the other way around," I teased him back about our matching colors.

Jacob led me into his den where Bobby Womack was singing from surround sound. I was counting on Bobby's words...that I would not be lonely tonight.

I took a seat on his couch. Jacob walked to his fireplace and rested one arm on the mantle.

"So, why would a man like you need a house this huge? There wouldn't happen to be a Mrs., would there?" I asked after he took me on a tour of his home. I had not seen any pictures of women or children. The décor of his home was nice, but definitely lacking a woman's touch.

He laughed a gentle, teasing laugh. "Not quite. If there was, trust me you wouldn't be here. I'm not that type of man. When I find the one...she will be the only one."

"So, am I to assume there are several now?" I asked, as I took a sip from the glass of wine he handed me.

"You're free to assume what you like. But you can also ask, and I'll tell you point blank."

"I like that. A man with no reservations and no games. Straight to the point and keeping it real," I confessed.

"Good, that's how I like my women." He smiled at me.

The smile that split that pretty, earth-brown skin in half showed a beautiful string of pearls behind those luscious lips.

We made small talk for a little while, until we had finished our second glass of wine. His eyes looked like pools of dark chocolate, upside-down, half-moons. "Tell me about you, Ms. Dougherty," he said, as he poured me another glass of wine.

"There's not much to tell. I love to shop, eat at nice restaurants, save money, save the children in my life, and have sex."

He slowly shook his head as he took me in from head to toe.

"And what about you, Mr. Hawthorne? What do you like?"

"I love to ski, sky dive, go rock-climbing, ride my bike, eat good food, drink good wine, and to have passionate sex."

"Okay, so we have two things in common. I've had dinner and I believe you have as well, so let's cut straight to the other thing that we have in common and see how compatible we are." I don't know if it was my normal "I don't give a damn" attitude taken to another level by the glasses of wine I had consumed, or our spirits connecting, but I was ready to throw it all out there.

It seemed as if Jacob glided across the room. He was standing right in front of me now with his hand extended pulling me up from my seat towards him.

He lowered his head, and with his right hand caressing the nape of my neck, he kissed me, taking the lead and not bothering to ask for permission. But, hell, why did he have to when I'd already given him an all-access pass to my body lock, stock, and barrel?

His tongue was thick and luscious with a strong, fruity taste and a slight hint of alcohol. As he ran his hands down my sides to hold tightly to my waist, I felt my nipples hardening, and the tingling in between my legs had begun.

I slipped my hands underneath his silk shirt and felt the hardening of his muscles around his abdominal area on up to his chest. Oooh, good, no hair! I loved it!

His lips slipped down to my neck, and his hands lowered to my behind as he squeezed it and moaned into my mouth.

It wasn't long before I pulled away and turned my back to him, allowing him to unsnap my halter top and unzip my skirt. I shrugged out of my body-fitting skirt until it pooled at my feet and then pushed the top down my hips and to the floor with my skirt.

I now stood before Jacob in a hot pink lace thong. I wore no bra. He could see how pert my breasts were and how my nipples stood at attention, waiting for him to taste them. Jacob didn't disappoint; he grabbed my left breast with one hand and sucked it so gently and lovingly. I arched my back, making sure he didn't miss out on one single drop.

Before I could make another move, Jacob swooped me up in his arms, left the den, and carried me upstairs into his master suite.

Jacob begin by kissing the arches of my feet, and then he took my toe into his mouth and sucked on it. Now, I might be a freak, and you can call me what you want, but that was some freakish shit right there! But even more surprising was it got me all tingly down there. He slowly kissed his way up from my feet and pressed little kisses to my inner ankle, working his way up my calves to my thighs. In little teasing bites, he took the flesh of my thighs into his mouth until he reached my Mother Pearl.

I tensed as I felt the sweet heat of his mouth near my glistening jewel and anticipated the feel of his tongue licking and sucking at me. I arched my back, ready to let him explore my inner sugar walls. He blew on it for several seconds before moving up to my belly and skipping my mound altogether.

To say I was thoroughly disappointed was putting it mildly. Why had he teased me, if he wouldn't eat my fruit? Oh, well, he was missing out on a good thing. But I couldn't be mad, because I barely knew him, and I damn sure wouldn't be taking him into my mouth.

As his mouth made its way to my breasts, I began to arch up, pressing my throbbing jewel against his protruding muscle. But once again, he pulled back.

"Give me just a sec," he stated, pulling away from me long enough to grab a condom from his nightstand.

After he ripped it open, I took the condom from him and rolled it down his manhood, squeezing it as I went along, watching the head contract. I couldn't wait to feel him inside of me. And I didn't have to wait long, because as soon as I lay back on the bed, he placed his fingers inside of me as if checking my moisture level. In and out he allowed his fingers to glide, and I worked myself up and down on them, waiting for the real thing.

Soon after, he replaced his fingers with his shaft. The wicked gleam that came into his eyes and the pounding he was giving to my lotus flower took me to a new high. Oh, this man was the best I'd ever had up until this point. I was glad that Rodney had walked out, because he had definitely been replaced…him and David both!

When I say that man loved me all night long, I mean he loved on me allll niiiight longggg! When I thought we were finished, he would contort my body in a new position and show me moves I had never seen before. And I was a woman who was very experienced sexually in the karma sutra, something I felt I'd mastered. But Jacob took my experiences to new heights.

It was 6:45 when I woke up the next morning. I looked to my right, and Jacob's smooth, hard body was nowhere to be found. I squinted at the sun peeking in at me through the blinds. It was time for me to get moving, too. I needed to get home, but not before washing up.

Pulling the cover back from my lean body, it was then that I heard the shower going. I stretched a bit and looked around and smiled. His floor-to-ceiling windows were beautiful in the large, open space of his bedroom, looking out over a beautiful, wooded lot. His furniture was dark and masculine, but it didn't overpower the space. Sensual and erotic paintings and sculptures of men and women decorated the space, giving it the feel of a lover's nest.

After taking in much of what I had not seen last night when I was engaged in relations with this man, I walked my naked body into the bathroom to join him in the shower. But he was toweling his body dry and turning off the shower when I opened the door.

"Hi, sexy, I was just about to join you," I greeted with a warm smile on my face.

Maybe he wasn't a morning person, because he didn't return my smile.

"Sorry, but it's time to go. I'm running late for work this morning, and I've got an 8:30. So, we have to get moving," he replied, tossing his black towel into a clothes hamper and grabbing a bottle of lotion from the counter.

I couldn't help but follow the trail he made as he applied the lotion to his body. I appreciated every nook and cranny of his beautiful, muscled physique. He looked like a work of art, carved by the hands of God, Himself!

"Yeah, I need to get moving, too," I agreed.

I looked around to see if he had extra washcloths and towels handy, as he squeezed past me out of the bathroom door. There was a shelving unit with doors directly across from the shower, which I assumed held the towels and washcloths. Upon opening it, I found that wasn't the case. He had lots of bath salts, lotions, gels, and other things stored in there.

Walking back into the bedroom, I watched him laying his suit on his bed. He had already dressed in his underclothes. Matching boxer briefs and t-shirt, I liked his style.

"Jacob, can I get a wash cloth and towel?" I asked, walking back towards him.

"For what?" he asked, as he pulled his light-green, button-down shirt on.

"So that I can wash up."

"Sorry, Paige, it's time to go. I told you…I'm already running late, and I have got to hit the highway. You know 75 and the Connector is no joke this time of morning. You have to get dressed and make those preparations at home. Besides, you'll have to change when you get there, anyway. Your clothes are folded on that chair over there with your purse," he said, pointing to a chair by the doorway. "I brought them up for you this morning from the den."

I watched him in disbelief. I felt as if he was giving me the cold shoulder and kicking me out of his house. Okay, I understood he was running late, but he could've awakened me earlier so that I could have gotten ready with him.

"Thanks," I mumbled. I grabbed my clothes and quickly dressed as I began to feel uncomfortable. When I finished putting my clothes on, he was dressed, with his briefcase and keys in hand.

"Oh, yeah, by the way…there's a little something for you on the dresser," he said, pointing and heading out of his bedroom.

I walked to the dresser to see what he had left. I couldn't believe my eyes as my mouth dropped open. That bastard! He had left a one-hundred-dollar bill with a note that read, "Thanks for a great time. Here's a little gas money for your troubles."

What the hell did he think I was, a whore?

I ran down the stairs after him and found him preparing to set the alarm.

"What's this all about?" I asked, waving the money and the note in his face.

He crinkled his eyebrows and momentarily looked away from the alarm keypad at me in confusion. "What do you mean? Was it not enough?"

"You left me money like I'm some whore?"

Jacob grabbed me by the hand, pulled me out of the house, and closed and the locked the front door behind us.

"Hey, little lady, I didn't mean any harm. But usually women who play it like you do expect payment for services rendered...whether they're a dancer or a lady of leisure. Was I mistaken in my assumptions?"

I slapped his face so hard my hand was stinging. Then I ran as fast as I could to my car, while clicking the unlock button on my keychain. I wasn't that crazy. I knew you didn't just hit a black man and expect he wouldn't do anything back. By the time I made it to my car, he was standing in front of his garage, shaking his head with a smirk on his face.

All I wanted was to get home and have a hot shower. I thought it might be a good idea to work from home today.

****

I pulled up to my condo and parked, breathing a sigh of relief. I had to come up with a new game plan. I had been attracted to Jacob and liked what I thought he had to offer. I was even thinking of maybe just kicking it with him for a while, thought maybe he was the one that could hang around. But after the way he played me, I knew we had nothing more to say to one another. Why the hell was it that men were allowed to sleep around and no one said anything, but us women were called whores when we did it? I was tired of the double standard and couldn't care less what anyone had to say about me.

My thoughts turned to Vic, and I knew if I ever decided to settle down, he was the one I would have to consider. He really cared about me and respected me in a way none of the others ever had. After the things Rodney had said and the way Jacob had treated me, I knew it was time for some sort of change in my life. But I was still scared. What was I scared of?

I was scared a man would dog me the way my uncle dogged my aunt by sleeping around with every woman that passed him, including her friends. I was scared that he would beat me and cheat on me with my best friend and leave me for another woman to start a new family, the way my father did my mother. My mother had turned to alcohol to drown her sorrows and shut me out, when we should have been turning to one another for comfort a long time ago.

I had made up my mind in high school when I first became interested in boys that they wouldn't rule me, I would rule them. And I knew I had power over them the way they all chased after me. I had always been a beautiful girl. My hair, now worn short, had once curled down to the middle of my back. I had always been a slim girl, but God had blessed me abundantly with breasts and a nice, firm behind. And I was a tease, or at least I had been until I turned nineteen. Escaping to college allowed me to be carefree and give it away.

My first time having sex, I didn't lose my virginity to some guy I fantasized about spending the rest of my life with. Nope, I had sex with one of my classmates who was really cool. He knew I was a virgin, and after a night of drinking at a party, we ended up at his place. He made it easy for me, and over the course of six months, he taught me so many tricks. After that six months was up, he unleashed me on the world! Rihanna had nothing on me. I wasn't a good girl gone bad…hell, I'd never been a good girl!

I laughed as I thought about my old friend, Ronnie, who was now married with five kids. Getting out of my car, I looked forward to my hot shower as I clicked the lock mechanism on my key chain.

I walked up the steps, made it to my door, and unlocked it. After closing the door behind me and locking it back, I headed to my bedroom, stripping along the way. When I arrived in the doorway and saw what awaited me there, I couldn't believe my eyes. I had to do a double take. David sat there on my bed stank bucky naked!

16_AMBIANCE_MRS. CALDWELL

I knew regardless of how I handled the situation, my life would be different from that moment on. I had followed my husband from the restaurant as he took curves and roadways at break-neck speeds. Once we were home, he began ranting and raving and throwing things around.

"You have the nerve to come at me like I'm the one having an affair, and you're out here screwing around on me?" he screamed, as he threw a vase against the wall in the living room. I huddled in the corner with my hands over my ears in an attempt to drown out the ear-piercing sound of the porcelain shattering. I had never seen this side of Eric before...hurt and furious.

He was experiencing a similar hurt and pain to that he had taken me through the last few years, with one difference. I hadn't had an affair.

It was about an hour and a half before he calmed down. There was much destruction done to our home during that time. Eric had broken a few vases, a mirror, some dishes, and even a precious painting we had selected during our first year of marriage. His tirade had taken him from downstairs to upstairs and back downstairs again. When he calmed down, he sat in front of his TV in the den staring at a black screen.

I sat on the couch next to him, where he refused to look at me sobbing uncontrollably.

"You are never here for me, Eric. I need someone who understands me, who listens to me, and makes me feel desirable. Every woman out there is more interesting to you than I am. You love going to the strip clubs and hanging out at the clubs with other women. What about me, Eric? What about taking me out and spending time with the woman you vowed to spend the rest of your life with? If it was going to be like this, why did you ever get married? Why didn't you leave me where you found me? I need you. I need your time and attention. I am a married woman alone in my own home and heart. I don't feel like a married woman. Not because I don't try, but because you don't give a damn! Didn't you think eventually some other man would notice and pay attention to me? You can't just sit me on the shelf like some of the awards you win at work and let me collect dust. I am a human being with emotions and feelings. I am a woman! I am your wife!"

He continued to sit in front of the TV with his shoulders hunched and ignored me.

"Damn it, Eric, say something!" I screamed at him and tossed a pillow, hitting him in the head. He grabbed the pillow off the floor where it fell at his feet and held it in his arms. Eric turned to look at me with tears pooling in his eyes. It broke my heart, because in all the years I had known my husband, I hadn't seen him shed a single tear.

"How long has this been going on?" he asked in a hoarse voice.

"Whether you believe it or not, there's nothing going on between me and Nick. We're just friends and nothing more," I mumbled.

"Since when did friends go around kissing each other in the mouth?" Eric's voice broke at the word "mouth."

"He gave me a sweet and simple kiss on the lips. It's not like we were tonguing each other or making out in the parking lot. He was consoling me, because I was feeling down."

"I'm your damn husband, Ambi! I'm the only one that should be consoling you!" Eric shouted, throwing the pillow back to the floor.

"Really? Well, how can you do that when you're never home? I bet you don't even know what my problem is," I accused. I stood up and went into the bathroom off the den and grabbed some tissues.

I came back and he was shaking his head back and forth. "I can't do this, Ambi. I cannot have my wife cheating on me," he mumbled.

"What the hell is that supposed to mean, Eric? I told you I wasn't cheating on you. Have I ever given you a reason not to trust me? I can't believe after all these years of me putting up with—"

"Putting up with what? I haven't done shit, Ambiance!"

"You think I don't know every time you go to your brother's house that you're not with some other woman? You think I don't know his wife, Danielle, doesn't like me, Eric? She's been trying to hook you up with someone since you met me. You use the excuse that you never take me over there, because I don't get along with her and her friends, but tell me this...why would you want to go somewhere your wife isn't welcomed? Why is that the one place you always want to hang out at?"

"Come on, that's my brother. Of course I'm going to go to his house and spend time with him! But don't you dare turn this shit back around on me. This isn't about my brother, Stephen, Danielle, or me! It's about you, Ambiance, and the fact that you're out there whoring around! Look at you, dressed like a slut!" he said, pointing at my outfit that earlier had made me feel sexy. I wasn't even revealing much.

I couldn't believe he allowed those words to come out of his mouth at me. I slapped him in the face and turned to leave the room, but he grabbed me roughly by my right arm before I could escape. I looked down at his hand on my arm and could see that it was trembling. Slowly turning around, I was aware of the deep inhalations he was taking to calm himself.

Looking up into those coal black eyes, I saw the fury within. He wanted to hit me back so bad, but he didn't dare.

"Don't you ever," he said through clenched teeth, "don't ever put your hands on me again! Especially not over some other nigga...you hear me?"

I pulled out of his grasp and ran up the stairs and into our bedroom. Throwing myself on the bed, I cried until my throat was raw and my eyes stung. I didn't realize I cried myself to sleep until I woke up to see the alarm clock showing 3:20 in the morning.

Dragging myself from the bed, I felt like I had gone one round in a boxing match. My entire body ached from being curled in an uncomfortable position. I had not covered myself with a blanket, and the air from the air conditioner had been blowing directly on me. My throat felt like I had been coughing all night long, and my eyes were puffy, and I knew they would be red and swollen. My clothes clung to my body and made me feel grimy.

I went downstairs to the den looking for my husband and couldn't find him. I went all over our four-thousand square-foot home and could not find him. I then checked the garage and noticed his car was gone. Going back into his office, I saw that his briefcase and laptop were also gone. I figured he wasn't coming back for the night.

I retrieved my purse from where I had left it in the living room earlier and climbed the stairs and took a shower to properly prepare for bed. When I climbed into bed, I pulled my cell phone from my bag to see if he had called. I had missed several calls, one from Naomi, one from my dad, and three from Nick, with his last call coming shortly after one in the morning. None of them were from my husband.

I called Nick back; it wasn't uncommon for us to speak in the wee hours of the morning.

"Hello?" came his sleepy voice on the other end of the line.

"Hey," I whispered into the phone.

"What's wrong, Ambiance?" His voice quickly cleared up and expressed more concern than tiredness.

"Nothing," I lied.

"Come on, girl, don't lie to me. I can hear it in your voice. Besides, we usually don't call each other this late. If we're on the phone this late, it's because we were already on the phone from an earlier conversation. Sweetheart, tell me what's on your heart tonight."

His words and his tone had the ability to soothe me and make everything all right. He cleared his throat, and I could hear him shuffling around as if he were pushing his covers back.

"I think he left me," I shared.

"Oh...why do you say that?"

"We had a horrible fight tonight, and it got physical," I whimpered.

"What the...he hit you, Ambiance? Where the hell you at?" he shouted into the phone.

"No! No, Nick! It's nothing like that. I was the one being physical because I didn't like the words he spoke to me. He never laid a hand on me. He was angry and tore up some things in our home and caused some destruction, but he didn't hurt me. Not physically, anyway."

"How did he hurt you, baby?" Something about his tone and the way he called me baby shook me to my core. I felt like he was right there caressing me.

"He knows about our friendship, Nick."

"What do you mean, he knows...what does he know?" There was a slight hesitation in his voice.

"He was at the restaurant today and saw you kiss me before you left."

He blew a rugged breath into the phone. "Damn! I'm so sorry, Ambiance. I am so sorry, baby."

"Don't be! It wasn't your fault, and I explained to him that he took it the wrong way but he didn't want to hear it. He got angry and started ranting about how I'm always accusing him of an affair and I'm out having one."

"I wish," he muttered into the phone.

"Huh?" I asked. I wasn't sure I heard him properly.

"I said, I wish. I wish you were involved with me. That idiot doesn't know how good he has it. You're a good woman, and he should appreciate you a whole lot more than he does. Don't get me wrong, I always try not to shoot him down and I'm not about to start now. I'm just furious that he didn't hear you out," Nick explained.

"I know, Nick. I tried explaining to him that you and I were just friends. He wasn't hearing it."

"Honestly, I wouldn't either if I were your man. But then again, if you were my woman, you wouldn't be in this situation to begin with. What do you need from me tonight, babe? Do you need to meet up and talk?"

"No, Nick. I'll be okay. I do wish I could just know my life was going to be okay. But just having you on the phone with me and hearing your voice is good enough."

"I'll always be here for you, Ambiance. I know what I said earlier at the restaurant, but I promise you I'm not going nowhere. I just wish I could hold you in my arms right now and wipe away those tears I hear in your voice. I wish I could kiss you one more time. I swear just thinking about your lips drove me crazy all afternoon. I haven't been able to get you out of my mind. I called it an early day, because I kept thinking of you and couldn't focus." His voice, so deep and so sincere, was soothing to me.

For the first time in several hours I smiled. "Really?"

"Yeah, really," he agreed.

"You're so sweet and just so nice." I wished I had met him first.

"Nah...I just care for you that much, girl."

There went those butterflies in my belly again. This man had the ability to make me feel like a little girl all over again instead of the grown woman that I was.

"I care about you a lot, too, Nick. I care about you so much that it scares me," I confided.

"Why does it scare you?" he asked.

"Because I am a married woman, and I am too grown to pretend like the feelings that I have for you are simply platonic. It's so much more than that, and I find myself thinking about you almost every hour of the day. Right now, I want to be held by you so badly."

"Well, we can make that a reality. All you have to do is say the word. I can come pick you up, or you can come over, or we can meet someplace. Just say it, baby."

There was a warring in my mind and in my heart at that moment. My mind, with its logical self, explained that the rationale I was using to be with this man was wrong. It was reassuring me that this was not God's will for my life and reminding me that He doesn't bless a mess and my life was a catastrophe at the moment. But my heart yearned to spend time with this special man that I believed God allowed me to meet for a reason. I just didn't know what that reason was.

"I can't, baby," I said, trying that word out on my lips. It felt strange calling some man other than my husband baby. But it felt so right. I could get used to calling Nick baby. I heard his light chuckle in the background.

"What's so funny?" I asked, feeling a bit unsure of myself.

"You are. You said 'baby' like you were asking permission to use the word or to call me that. If it's my permission you're seeking, I'm letting you know you have it. Sounds good to hear you call me that...sounds like home. You know what I mean?" he asked.

"Mm-hmm. Yeah." I thought it felt right as well, but knew that it wasn't.

"So, what's your next step? Are you staying there to see what he does next, getting counseling, or what do you have planned?" His querying nature was very careful, and I assumed he didn't want to overturn the apple cart just yet.

"I don't know. I have a lot to think through. I've made my share of mistakes and I'm far from perfect. I just want the chance to get it right this time. I need to know what I'm doing before I take another step. Maybe we need to talk in person," I suggested.

"Okay. Will I see you tomorrow for lunch?"

"Sure. Just let me go ahead and get some rest, because I still have to go to work tomorrow," I shared.

"All right...and baby?"

"Yeah," I whispered, in what I considered a low and sexy voice.

"Call me if you need anything. I'm here for you, girl."

"Okay. Goodnight, Nick."

"Goodnight, my love," he whispered, blew a kiss, and then clicked his phone off.

My heart was running a Boston marathon and all of me was tingling inside. What was this school girl feeling inside? I knew that this newest development was not something I could share with Naomi or Paige. I was in too deep, and I knew I couldn't just let this man go. Uh-uh, he was down deep in my soul and in my blood. What was I going to do?

A part of me hoped Eric would leave me for another woman of his own accord. Then it wouldn't be my fault, it would be all his and so easy to get with Nick.

Lord, have mercy on my soul! What was I thinking, and when had I allowed the devil to get in so deep? I was going to hell in a hand basket and in a hurry. I slid out of my bed and began to pray over my situation.

"Lord, you know that my heart has been lonely for some time now. I've prayed and asked You for guidance and to give me the love that I long for. Well, God, I know that You don't make mistakes, so I'm not going to even ask if this is from You. I know the enemy comes to steal, to kill, and to destroy. And he comes to seek whom he may devour. Lord, I have been running with the enemy for so long, I don't know my ups from my downs anymore! Help me to turn from my wicked ways and to pray for my husband and my marriage. I know that what You have put together no man should put asunder. You have brought my husband and me together as man and wife, and I am to honor and submit unto him. But, Lord, tell me how do I overcome what we are going through now? Jesus, I feel like a piece of me has come to life since I met Nick. Why is this happening to me? Why am I enduring this type of hurt and pain, Lord? This type of thing can come to no good, it's only meant for a wicked end. I need You right now, Father, to step in on my behalf and strengthen me. Fortify me against the tools of the enemy. Help me to find strength in You, oh God, because I know that Your strength is made perfect in my weakness. Well, I'm weak right now, Lord. Oh, Father in Heaven above, I am so very weak. Please step forth and take me into Your arms. Carry me safely to the other side of this thing that I not bring defilement to my marriage. Forgive me, Father, for my transgressions and cleanse me from all my iniquities. Help Nick find a woman who is free to love and give of herself to him. Protect my husband through the night, Lord, and give him vision that he can see we were meant to be together. And Lord, give him a heart that forgives and protects above all. It is Your sweet and holy name that I bless. And in the name of the Lord Jesus I pray. Amen."

****

When I awoke the next morning, the first thing I did was to call Eric.

"Look, I don't have nothing to say to you, Ambiance. I just wanted to answer the phone to make sure you're okay," he answered, by way of a greeting.

"Eric, look, I know this isn't anything but the devil trying to attack our marriage. Can't you at least consider the pain I felt when you cheated on me and how I tolerated everything from you to make this marriage work? No matter how much it hurt and how others pressured me to leave, I stayed for the sake of our marriage. I have fought, cried, and went to therapy to get past what you've done. Now when you think that I'm having an affair, you can't even talk to me?"

I was quiet as I listened to him breathing. After a few seconds, he finally spoke up.

"Are you through?"

"Yes, Eric," I replied, preparing my heart for what he would have to say.

Click. I couldn't believe he hung up the phone on me.

I continued to get dressed and prepare for my work day. Halfway through the morning, Angelique called me into her office.

"Hi, honey, come in and have a seat." She gestured with a smile on her face.

I pulled the chair out and wondered why she was grinning like the Cheshire cat.

"Well, first I want to thank you for connecting me with your friend, Sonya Pierce. The numbers are unbelievable," she said, pushing some reports across her desk to me. "Her designs have been such a hit here. There have been requests for different articles of clothing for her to design, too. So, we have come up with another concept. She and I have had several meetings, and I have decided for a time that part of the shop will be dedicated solely to her designs."

"That's fabulous, Angelique!" I shouted, clapping my hands.

"Yes, it is! And because you were the reason behind the success, I want you to manage it. I would like for you to pair up with her and create a sample of designs to be showcased in our fall catalogue. Is that something you would be interested in?" Angelique held a mischievous grin on her face. She knew that I would love to work on that project with Sonya.

"I would be honored, Angelique. I would truly be honored," I shared.

"Okay, so here's what I have in mind…" She began to state numerous little ideas that I recorded on my notepad. I became enraptured by her enthusiasm, prattling off more details to take the concept to a higher level.

There was a knock at the door, and Angelique mumbled for them to come in. It was Ms. Peggy, and she wore a grim look on her face.

"Yes, Ms. Peggy?" Angelique asked.

"There was a call for Ambiance," she noted.

"I thought I asked you to hold all of our calls?" Angelique probed.

"I was, but then...there's been an accident," she stated, with a serious look of worry on her face as she wrung her hands.

I grabbed the arms of my chair, sitting forward in it. "What is it, Peggy? Is it my husband?" I immediately sensed in my spirit that something was wrong and it had to be him.

Peggy nodded her head *yes* and was having a hard time getting her voice together.

"Damn it, Peggy, what is it?" Angelique demanded.

"He was in a bad car accident. They air-lifted him to Atlanta Allied Health Center, and he's there now. His brother called and said he was going into surgery and they needed you to get there as soon as possible."

I jumped up out of my chair, heading for my office to grab my keys and purse.

"Wait, Ambiance!" Angelique called after me. "I'm driving you over," she said.

Everything from that moment on was a blur. It seemed as if it were taking forever to get to where I needed to be. All thoughts of everything else had left me, and I could only focus on Eric. I knew this was God's way of punishing me for the wrong I had done. No, I had not slept with Nick, and I had not even kissed him, not a real kiss. But I was spending time with a man who wasn't my husband, and I was having feelings for him that were not right. I could only pray over and over in my head on the way to the hospital. *God, please let him be okay. I will change my ways and won't even be with Nick again not even for lunch,* I prayed.

"Where is he? Is he okay, Stephen?" I asked, running into the emergency room towards my brother-in-law.

He turned a tear-streaked face to me, with deep-set, chocolate brown eyes so much like his brother's.

He grabbed me and held me tight. "We gotta pray, Ambiance...we gotta pray he makes it, honey, okay?"

My normally laid-back and in-control brother-in-law was a nervous wreck. "Where are Mom and Dad?" I asked, referring to my parents-in-law.

"They're on the way," he stated.

At just that moment, my mother-in-law and father-in-law, Hope and Stephen Sr., walked in followed by their youngest son, Marc. The men came rushing into the waiting area with deep concern etched across their faces, and my mother-in-law had been crying.

Stephen released me to grab his mother into a tight hug, and my father-in-law began commanding someone to give him some details. The retired military general was always in control when he stepped on the scene.

He flagged down a nurse who let us know that my husband was still in surgery and it could be a while before he came out. We would just have to sit and wait for further news.

I was on the edge of my seat with worry when I remembered I hadn't called my own parents. We had been at the hospital for half an hour at this point. I stepped away into the parking lot, followed by Angelique.

"Honey, what can I do for you?" she asked.

I sniffled and wiped away my tears with a tissue I had pulled from my purse. "Nothing, Angelique. You've been great, sweetie. You can go back to the shop. I'll be just fine."

"Honey, I will stay here with you. You need a support system," Angelique worried.

"I'll be fine. I'm going to call my parents now, and Eric's family is here. Please, Angelique, I'll be just fine. Just go back to the shop, and I'll keep you posted."

"Are you sure?" she asked, with an uncertain expression on her face.

"Yes, I'm sure," I assured her, as I wiped my nose once again.

"What about a ride, sweetie? We left your car at the shop," Angelique brought to my attention.

"I'll get a ride. I'll be fine, just go ahead and get there. And please let Ms. Peggy know I'm going to be just fine. I can tell she was worried today," I stated.

"No problem. And honey, if you need anything, I mean anything at all, please call me," Angelique pushed.

"I will." I watched her walk away, and I pulled my phone from my purse. I tried my father's cell phone and couldn't reach him, so I tried my stepmom, Alexis, next.

"Hi, Mom," I stated. I had been calling her that since I was about nine years old. She was the only mother that I knew.

"Hey, Ambi…what's going on, baby?" I knew she detected the emotion in my voice.

"It's Eric. He's been in a car accident, Mom."

"Oh, no! Honey, where are you now?"

"I'm at Atlanta Allied Health Center."

"All right, honey let me go wake up your dad, he's taking his old man nap. We'll be right there," she assured me.

"Okay, thanks, Mom. Be safe, please," I pleaded.

"I love you, Ambi," she stated.

"I know, and I love you, too," I replied.

I hung up the phone and made a call to Naomi. I reached her voicemail and figured she may be in a meeting. I left her a brief message and asked for her prayers.

I had missed two calls from Nick. I would not be calling him back. If it were not for my relationship with him, my husband wouldn't be in this situation. If God brought Eric through this, I would return to church give my all, and be faithful to my husband in every way.

When I walked back into the emergency room, the family was surrounding a doctor who was finishing his explanation.

"…is out of surgery, and she's doing just fine. Her left leg is broken along with a couple of ribs. She also has a broken jaw, which we have wired shut. I know that sounds like she's not doing fine, but considering the fact that their car wrapped around that telephone pole the way it did, she's doing very well. We have her in an induced coma because of the extensive pain she's in and that also gives us a chance to monitor her."

The family had not seen me walking up behind them.

"Dr. Eckenbaum who is this lady you're talking about?" my father-in-law probed.

"The woman who was in the car with him at the time of the accident. Mrs. Caldwell…" the doctor proclaimed, with a confused expression on his face.

"Sir, I'm not sure who was in that car with my son, but I assure you that it was not his wife. Mrs. Caldwell is out there in the parking lot. We just spoke with her briefly when we arrived," my father-in-law announced.

"It was Kendra, Dad," Stephen announced, turning to his father.

"That slut?" my mother-in-law questioned.

"Don't tell me my son was still mixed up with that woman!" This last bit came from my father-in-law, who was outraged.

Stephen slowly shook his head. "Dad, they have a six-month-old son together, Eric Jr. He never left her alone."

I tried to cover the gasp from my mouth with my hand but was unable to stifle my cry. And then I all I saw was black.

17_NAOMI_FAMILY EMERGENCY

My daughter and I had made it through her first visit with her father unscathed. I had spent the day with my parents, sharing my thoughts and feelings with them on this newfound relationship. They had worked hard to let me know that I was doing the right thing, or at least my mother did. However, my mom and dad felt that the feelings of insecurity and envy I was experiencing were normal. But they also assured me of what I already knew. I had nothing to worry about. I had raised my daughter to be a wise, independent, and intelligent young lady. She knew where her strength lay, and our relationship was solid and stable. Nothing could shake that.

"Look, baby, I think you're doing the right thing letting her get to know her father," my mother stated, as she spooned a serving of cabbage onto my plate next to her famous Sunny Golden Fried Chicken.

"Hmph, father my a—" my father began.

"Gene! Don't you dare say that. Now you just hush up and eat your dinner," my mother warned him. She often sat quietly by and upheld his word. But she didn't play that about cursing in her home. She said she wouldn't allow the Lord's presence to be disrespected in her home, and He surely was in my parents' home.

"I'm just saying, I don't know why he wants to pop up after all this time. He wasn't nothing but a sperm donor. He ain't never contributed to that child's growth. Now, when she 'bout grown and ready to head off to college, he all of a sudden want to pop up and get the daddy of the year award! Well, I'm tellin' you, it ain't happenin', not on my watch, Cathy!" he argued back.

"He didn't just pop up. They ran into each other. I'm sure if he had known about her, he would've tried to contact Naomi after he'd grown up and matured," my mother defended.

I turned my nose up at what she was saying, because I knew it was a bunch of hogwash and so did she. Her purpose for saying all of that was because she didn't want my father to turn my mind against allowing Sasha and Jaime to build a relationship. But she didn't have to worry about that, I was determined to give it an honest shot.

I looked at my phone for probably the tenth time in the last hour. She still hadn't called.

"You ain't got nothing to worry 'bout, Naomi. We all raised that girl right. She ain't gon' just let him step in her life and take your place. She probably ain't had a chance to call you, yet," my father stated, reading my mind. "I'm sure he's probably right over her shoulder at every moment," he complained.

"Richard Eugene Blankenship, give that man half a chance!" My mother set her serving bowl on the table with a clatter to convey the severity of her stance to my father.

But Pops wasn't having it. "Catherine Aileen Blankenship, he's had more than sixteen years to get a chance. He didn't take it. All I know is he better not do nothing to hurt neither one of my babies again. Or he's gon' have me to deal with. And that's all I gots to say on the matter." My father punctuated his statement by taking a sip of iced tea from his glass and glaring at my mother over it.

She shook her head and looked down into her lap. And with that one simple movement, I saw my father's hard core softening. He reached out to his right where she sat and grabbed her hand in his and softly rubbed it.

"Okay, I'll give him a chance. But one wrong move, and just like white on rice, I'm gon' be in his a—"

"Eugene!"

"Just saying…that's all." He picked up a forkful of cabbage and shoved it into his mouth, going silent for the remainder of the meal.

I admired the two of them. I was sure they had their share of challenges along the way, but they truly loved one another and had each other's back.

Sasha had shared with me that she did enjoy the day she had spent with Jaime. It would take some time to build something solid, because she still struggled with why he left her in the first place. She was rocking between wanting to get to know him more and being angry at him over his choices. I didn't touch it with a ten-foot pole. I knew she had to work through it on her own.

I had just come from a meeting about capital projects for the next year when I noticed I had missed a call from Ambiance. We had not had lunch in a while, and I knew she probably wanted to hook up today. I wouldn't be able to because I had a couple of performance review meetings to conduct before the day was out. I was determined that I was not staying late that day. My evening had already been promised to Sasha; we were going out to the movies after having dinner.

I called Ambiance back and got no answer. *Oh, well*, I thought, *she'll call back later.* It was then that I realized I had a voicemail. I checked the voicemail from her, somewhat surprised because she didn't like leaving messages. Usually she texted if she couldn't get through to me.

"Hi, Naomi. It's me, Ambi...I'm at Atlanta Allied. Eric's been in a bad car accident, and he's in surgery now. Can you please pray for us?" I could hear the tears and the fear in her voice as I listened to her message. Her voice broke off in a sob before she hung up. My hand flew to my mouth in shock.

I could only imagine what she might've been going through at that moment. Despite the problems they were having in their marriage, I knew Eric was her world. I prayed that she was not suffering from guilt over her friendship with the guy she had met at the restaurant.

I sat down at my desk and quickly checked my calendar. Satisfied with what I saw, I shut my computer down for the day, grabbed my keys and purse, and left my office.

I stopped at my assistant's desk before heading for the elevators.

"Nadia, I have a family emergency. Can you please re-schedule the performance reviews for Doug and Jackie for Thursday?" I inquired of my assistant.

"No problem, Naomi. Do you want them at the same time they were scheduled for today?" she asked, as she pulled up my calendar in Outlook.

"Yes. And I won't be back in today. Just forward all of my calls to voicemail. If you need anything, I can be reached on my cell," I replied.

"Thanks, Naomi. Is everything all right?" she asked, with a true look of concern on her face. I could tell it wasn't her nosiness this time, but that she really did care.

"It will be. Do me a favor, please call Jon and Sharon and let them know that Ambiance's husband has been in an accident and that I'm on the way to the hospital now."

"Will do, Naomi. Do you want me to send some flowers?" she inquired, as she picked up the phone to dial my friends.

"No, that won't be necessary. And Nadia...thanks for all you do, girl."

"No problem. Be safe, Naomi."

"I will." And with that, I was off, running my thick self towards the elevators.

****

When I arrived at the hospital, I found a nurse and asked her if she knew where the Caldwell family was. She pointed me in the direction, and I found the group huddled in a lobby area.

"You need a breath of air?" I asked Ambiance, as she opened her arms to hug me close.

"Mm-mm," she murmured, shaking her head *no* as we held each other tight. We stayed that way for a moment, before she finally pulled back, swiping at her tears with a well-used tissue.

Afterwards, I was embraced by Ambiance's parents, Jerry and Alexis, whom I was close to. "Hi, Moms and Pops," I said, affectionately calling them by the nicknames I had been calling them since I was a teen.

"Hey, baby," Alexis replied.

"How's my gran?" Jerry asked. He considered Sasha among his grandchildren and loved her just the same.

"She's wonderful...she met her dad recently," I informed them.

"That's great!" Alexis enthused.

"Yeah, Gene told me," he stated, referring to my father, "and it's about time!" Jerry's deep voice roared. He was one of my dad's closest friends and was very angry when Jaime had walked out. He had wanted to go over there and meet with Jaime and his father and give them a piece of his mind, in a physical way.

"So, what's the news?" I asked, grabbing a chair and pulling it close to theirs. Ambiance had walked away after I arrived and was huddled close to Stephen in a whisper session. His wife, Danielle, didn't look too happy. But that was no surprise, because she had never liked Ambiance, anyway. No one knew why, and if they did, they weren't telling.

"Well, he's out of surgery now and in recovery. Apparently, he has a dislocated shoulder, a broken femur, and some type of brain injury that has him in a coma," Jerry explained.

"It's called diffuse axonal injury, honey," Alexis interjected.

"Don't nobody need to know all that stuff, woman. All she wanna know is that the boy is hurt in the head, baby," Jerry snapped.

Alexis ignored her husband and went on with her explanation, "According to the doctor, it's affected a large area of his brain. They don't believe the coma will be long-term, however."

"Oh, my. Well, that's good. How is she holding up?" I asked, nodding my head in Ambiance's direction.

Jerry and Alexis both shared a look with one another and went silent.

"What?" I asked. They couldn't just leave me out of the loop like that. Ambiance was practically my sister.

"Well, she should be the one to tell you this, but when we arrived, they had a doctor administering care to her. She had fainted," Jerry shared.

"What?" I knew my voice was a little louder than it should have been, but their simultaneous efforts to shush me didn't go unnoticed, either.

"Yeah, there's something else going on outside of this accident, Naomi," Alexis whispered, her pretty, light-brown unlined face frowning up.

"What is it?" I queried. At that moment, Ambiance walked up to our little group.

"Mom, Dad...I need to get away for a moment. If you don't mind, I'm gonna have Naomi ride me around for a bit," Ambiance stated. She looked as if she had aged ten years since the last time I saw her. I felt bad that I had not been around for my friend lately. She looked as if she could really use a friend right now.

"Okay, honey. But do us a favor. After this, don't come back. You need to go home and get some rest. Naomi, take care of Puddin' for us, okay?" Jerry asked.

"Sure, Pops. No problem. Come on, girl," I said, grabbing her by the arm and pulling her from the lobby. I looked at the faces around us and saw what appeared to be pity with the exception of the look of joy on Stephen's wife, Danielle's, face. At the time, I figured the pity was in response to what lay ahead for Ambiance's and Eric's future as he began the healing and recovery process. I had no idea she was about to blow my mind with what she had to say.

****

"Thanks for coming, girl. I needed to get out that place," Ambiance said, sipping on her third strawberry daiquiri since our arrival. We had opted to go to the Midnight Bar and Grill to have a light dinner of grilled Tuscan chicken salad for me and a tuna sub for Ambiance that she had only picked over. But she was sucking those daiquiris down like she had just returned from the Sahara. We had engaged in small talk since we had arrived, up until now. I hadn't pushed her for details, but I could tell she was ready to talk.

Ambiance shook her head back and forth a few times and then ran her fingers through her long, curly hair and finally pulling it. "Argggh!" she exclaimed loudly, before bursting into tears.

I moved from my side of the booth to hers and grabbed a few napkins and wiped her face. I just held her in my arms and rocked her back and forth for a little while.

"It's okay, honey. Everything's going to be alright. He'll make it through this and you two will be just fine," I murmured.

"Mm-mm," she moaned, shaking her head.

"Yes, it will. You must have faith; you know God will bring you through this, too. He's brought you through so much."

"I don't want to go through this, though, Naomi. You don't understaanndd," she wailed.

"What don't I understand, honey?" I asked, pulling her hair from her face.

She sniffled and grabbed two more napkins and wiped her face. She turned her tear-streaked face towards me. "He never left her alooone!" she sobbed and laid her head on our table.

I carefully moved the plates out of the way so they didn't crash to the floor. I didn't like the way this conversation was going.

"Who never left who alone?" I asked.

It took her a moment to regain her composure enough for her to speak again. "Eric. He never left that slut, Kendra, alone that he was messing with!"

"How do you know that, Ambi?" I asked. I wanted to believe with everything in me that she was wrong.

"She was in the car with him, Naomi. She was in the accident, too. I walked up and heard the doctor telling the family what was going on with her. He thought she was Eric's wife. Then his dad clarified who she was, and that's when Stephen told his dad that they never quit messing around. And what's worse…is she has a six-month-old son with him!" Ambiance burst into a fresh batch of tears.

My heart sunk to my feet. I was done. I had honestly thought he had gotten his act together and that Ambiance was just being paranoid. Patrons close to our table looked our way, but I gave them the stink-eye as I attempted to console my friend. After all, it was a bar, and I was sure this wasn't the first time someone had gotten drunk and bawled their eyes out in here. It didn't matter if she wasn't really drunk, she deserved to have her cry, too.

"Baby girl, you have got to get your act together," I consoled in a low voice.

"Mm-mm," she whined and blew her nose loudly into her napkins before going on. "Stephen told me everything. He told me that my husband was getting ready to leave me. The times that Eric was telling me he was at Stephen's house, he was with Kendra all those times…overnight, on the weekends, early mornings, whenever he could. Stephen said he rarely saw Eric these days. That's why I wasn't allowed to go over there, because he wasn't there. He said a few times Eric even brought her and their child around, but he told him he wouldn't be a part of him disrespecting me. But then Stephen's wife, Danielle, said he couldn't push his nephew away. All this time, I knew in my heart he was still messing around. We just got into it yesterday, and I was feeling so guilty," she cried.

"About what, honey?"

Ambiance looked at me out the corner of her eyes. I could tell she was determining if she wanted to share this next piece or not. I knew right then that she had done something she had no business doing. Call it a woman's intuition or a girl just knowing her girl.

"I had lunch with Nick at Flaming Rio yesterday, right? So, I had shared a lot of things with Nick that Eric and I have been going through. Getting a man's take on it…you know?" She was twisting her napkin in her hands, giving me a pitiful look. Yeah, my girl had done something wrong.

"Well, honey, of course he's going to be on your side, because he wants to get with you," I interjected.

"No, no, no…it was nothing like that. He doesn't say anything bad about my husband. He gives me different views to look at things in and forces me to be real with myself. That particular day I was feeling really blue and he had been encouraging me. When we left out, he gave me the sweetest kiss on the lips."

"What? I told you he wanted you!" I shouted. When I noticed patrons looking our way again, I lowered my voice. "That's like the day I saw him caressing your face. That man is so in to you, Ambi!" I honed in on my point as I pointed an accusing finger in her direction.

She scrunched her face up again, looking like she was about to burst out into another fresh batch of tears. "Would you just hush and listen, Naomi? I know he's into me and I won't lie, I'm into him, too. But we wouldn't let it go any further than that. He just pressed a kiss against my lips and pulled away. When he got into his car and left, that's when I saw Eric parked directly across from him. I knew he had seen it all, and he pulled out of that parking lot like a bat out of hell. I followed him home, and when I got there we went through it. He accused me of having an affair and everything," she said, taking another sip of her drink.

"Well, what do you expect? The man kissed you on the lips and you're married, honey." I attempted to reason with her, because for some reason, she wasn't using logic.

"I know...I know," she murmured and took another sip of her drink before continuing. "But I tried to explain it to Eric, and he didn't want to hear it. I brought up his affairs, and he denied it and then he left. I tried calling him this morning, and he didn't want to talk. I went on to work, and then I get the phone call about the accident. Naomi, I had asked God to forgive me of my sins. I had not only repented for having feelings for another man, but I committed to never seeing or speaking to Nick again. I swear! I did all of that before the accident. Then, after the accident, I thought this was God's way of punishing me for my wrongs."

"Honey, our God is a just and forgiving God. He loves you in spite of all your wrongs, and He only wants what is best for you. It isn't your fault that this happened," I encouraged Ambiance.

"I know that now, Naomi. But I just don't know what to do. My husband is laid up in ICU, and I don't know what his future holds. He has a child outside of our marriage and I learn that he was going to leave me anyway? A part of me is relieved and says that I can go on with my life. But the other half says that there are so many loose strings and I don't know where to go from here. I want him to be all right, I really do."

I looked at my longtime friend and wished all the hurt and pain would go away. "Honey, you pray. When you can't do nothing else and it seems as if you've done all you can, you just be still and let God be God. He don't need your help in this. You pray to Him for guidance and follow how He leads you. If He wants you to stand by your man, then that's what you do. If it's over, then you be strong and pick your head up and move on. You don't get involved with someone else until you're sure where your marriage stands. I know it hurts that Eric did what he did, but two wrongs don't make a right. I think for right now, by his side is where you belong."

"I know. It's just that—" Her cell phone rang cutting her off mid-sentence. "Hold on, let me see who this is."

I took a sip of my margarita that I had barely touched all evening and then got up to scoot back into my seat.

"That's him now," she confessed, with a look of guilt on her face.

I didn't have to ask the question, but I did. "That's who?"

"Nick. This is the sixth time he's called me today and I haven't answered."

"Why, honey? Are you scared to tell him you can't talk to him anymore...or are you holding out, hoping you don't have to tell him that? And why is he calling you so much, Ambi?"

She let out a deep sigh and finally looked me in the eye. "When I talk to him, it needs to be one-on-one and not here with you. And no, I'm not holding out on anything. We usually talk every morning on our way to work, we eat lunch together almost every day, and then we talk again on the way home in the evening and before going to bed."

"Damn!" I said. I put my hand over my mouth politely when I realized how loud I had spoken that word.

"Well, we just keep each other company, and we enjoy spending time together and talking together. He's a great friend. The only reason I haven't answered his calls was because this morning I was still reflecting on my prayer from last night. I didn't want to talk to him just yet, because I wasn't ready. I was going to tell him at lunch, but then the accident happened. He called me while I was on the way to the hospital, and I couldn't answer it then. Then he called me three more times, probably trying to figure out where I was at. And now, this is the time we usually call each other when he's heading home for the evening," she explained.

I looked at my cell phone and noted the time of 7:30 P.M. I had already called Sasha and told her what was going on. She loved Ambiance so much, and her heart was breaking knowing that Ambiance was hurting. She had forgiven me for skipping our dinner and movie date.

"You didn't even have the decency to tell the man that you weren't going to be at lunch? You stood him up?" I asked.

"Well, I didn't mean to," she whined. I hated when she got into her crybaby mode. She only used it when she wanted me to feel sorry for her and not chastise her about her wrongdoing.

"Look, you have a lot to clean up. And it starts with calling that man and at least offering him an apology for standing him up. Then you need to pray about how to deal with this mess and decide what you're going to do about your husband one way or another. That's after you pray about it, that is. Because I know God won't steer you wrong on this. You just have to be patient and wait on Him to answer you. But before all of that, let's get our check and get out of here."

"I'm not ready to go home," Ambiance said, shaking her head.

"And that's fine, you don't have to. But you and I are going to go on a little shopping excursion to pick you up some items, and then we're heading to my home. We'll have a girls' night all night long…just you, me, and Sasha. You aren't going to work tomorrow, I'll work from home, and I might just let Sasha skip school depending on how long we're up tonight. How does that sound?" I asked.

"Sounds like a winner to me. Can we get some more booze?" Ambiance asked, wiggling her eyebrows. It was the best mood I had seen her in all day.

"You little lush, you. Girl, come on and get your fast tail out of here!" I scolded, with a light smile on my face.

18 PAIGE POT-A-LET

My eyes had to be deceiving me, right? Because I just knew David was not sitting up in my bed naked as a jaybird wearing nothing but a smile on his face, and my remote control in his hand.

By this time, I had stripped of everything except a pair of panties. "What the hell do you think you're doing, and how the hell did you get in my house?" I questioned with my hands on my hips. Then I held one hand up. "As a matter of fact…no, you don't need to answer that question. Don't bother explaining it to me," I said, going to my cordless phone on the other side of the bed. I pressed nine and one to call the cops, but he had reached around me just as quickly and hung the phone up.

David wrenched the phone from my hand and flung it to the other side of the room where it crashed against the wall.

I thought this fool had lost his mind. What I said was, "David? You just broke my phone! What are you doing?"

"I'm coming to claim what's mine. What it look like I'm doing?" he asked, with that same silly grin on his face.

"It looks like you done lost your damn mind!" I screamed. He pulled me close to his body and placed his hand over my mouth before whispering into my ear. The heat from his breath had me recoiling from him.

"Baby, I told you if my wife found out about us through you that I'd hurt you, right?" he asked in a low tone in my ear.

"Mm-hmm." I was just beginning to get scared now. I thought I had been scared at first, but now he was revealing that psychotic personality that I knew had been hidden underneath all of this time.

"And what I say would happen if she left me because of you?" he asked in that same eerie tone.

"You'd kill me?" I asked.

"Ding, ding, ding! You're the next winner on the Ho' is Right!" he announced in a crazy, sing-song voice.

Awww, shit…what the hell was I going to do now?

"But, baby, guess what? You're in luck. Cuz I thought about it real hard. And even though she kicked me out the house, I don't completely lose. That just means I can have you all to myself now. Yeah, baby, it's gon' be just you and me. So, I ain't gon' kill you. I'm just gon' hurt you real bad."

He squeezed me so tight that I thought my rib cage was going to explode. If I could just get myself twisted around and kick him in his family jewels, I could possibly escape. But he had my body flush up against his. His left arm was wrapped around my abdomen, and he had his right arm looped between both of my arms, which were twisted behind my back.

I focused on trying to stay calm, because that was all I had left. If I panicked now, there was no way I could think myself out of this situation.

"See, the way I figure it, I had a nice little setup going. My wife's got a damn good job, and she's a good woman. But between her and her kids, she stays too busy for me all the time. Them little shits bad as hell. If they was mine, I'd kick they asses, but since they ain't, I don't give a damn what they do. So then, I had you on the side to take care of all my personal needs, and you do it so damn good. Hell, a man could get addicted to a woman like you, Paige. And that's exactly what I had done. I got so addicted to you like a drug I couldn't leave you alone even when I wanted to. I tried to stay away from you, but that sweet stuff be calling out to me in my sleep. I wake up some nights, and I gotta have you. I get up and leave the house while she sleep, and I don't care what she think. And then I come over here to you, and you take care of Big Daddy just like I need you to. But then one day you want to start tripping on me. You don't want to answer my calls no more. And see, as long as you was giving me your loving, the rest didn't matter. It didn't matter to me when she was sitting there crying and wondering where I been. I could tell her anything, and she believed it. She asked me if I had someone else, and I lied and told her no. I swear I would try to be a good man to her…and then I'd pull your panties out the secret compartment under the driver's seat in my car and sniff them, and I'd need one more hit of you."

What the hell? Did this bastard just tell me he had stolen my panties and was carrying them around with him? Nasty ass fool! *Lord, help me out of this mess I'm in*, I thought.

I tried wriggling my hands from his grasp again. And he only squeezed me tighter. "Uh-uh, baby. You ain't going nowhere 'til I say you go. You hear me?" he breathed in my ear.

I shook my head *yes*, affirming that I not only heard but that I understood, as well. If we could just make it to the bed, I could get my gun that was underneath the mattress on the right side. As if he read my thoughts, he ushered me back into the living room, never letting me go. We walked like two bugs stuck together until we entered the living room and he threw me onto the couch. He stood over me and then kneeled down at the bottom of the couch like he was worshiping me or something. He was waving his hand up and down the length of my body. Then he began sniffing my private area. What was he doing? I wished I could contemplate his next move, but when a person is crazy all of their thoughts and moods are sporadic and cannot be predicted.

In a flash, David reached underneath the couch and pulled out a knife he had obviously hidden there earlier. He lay on top of me and then pressed the blade underneath my right breast and smiled a sick smile at me. And to think I had shared my body with this bastard! I guess Naomi was right. She always warned me about laying down with men I barely knew. Something about soul ties or something like that. I'd have to ask her about it if I got out of this situation…not if, but when. If I had to take this Negro out and come up on murder charges, then so be it. His crazy ass wasn't taking my life!

David leaned in and kissed me on the lips softly. He kissed me a second time, and then I bit his lip. I was hoping he would jump up and I could move from underneath his body. Not likely.

"Damn it!" he shouted, and then slapped me hard across the face. I bit my own lip and felt the blood beneath my tongue as I flicked it out to soothe it.

"Girl, I swear you're gonna make me hurt you!" he declared, and he pressed the knife under the tip of my breast. I felt a stinging and knew that the bastard had cut me. This was confirmed when he lifted up slightly and put one finger underneath my breast and then put it against my lips, trying to force me to taste my blood. I turned my head from side to side, trying to resist his sick and twisted ritual.

He quickly slashed the knife across my cheekbone. The stinging cut that separated the skin of my cheek left me in astonishment and pain. I hollered out loud, praying someone would hear and call the cops.

"Bitch! Shut up! I mean it; if you scream like that one more time, I swear I'ma kill you. I've always kept my word to you, and this is no different." And with that, he reached down and slashed the knife across my thigh, leaving another stinging cut. This time, he placed his left hand over my mouth, stifling my cry.

I often thought of myself as a strong woman, but every bit of strength I had was leaving me. Not because of the pain, but because I was in the hands of a psycho. I felt the need to scream, fight, or do something, but I didn't. Tears leaked from my eyes, and my body was wracked with pain, but David took no notice. Instead, he pushed the knife against my throat and whispered in my ear.

"Paige, open your legs for me. And I don't want no static from you. You ain't never had a problem opening them for me before, and obviously, none of these other niggas you let up in here, so let's not play any games a'ight?"

I slowly nodded my head. I didn't want to do it, especially knowing he wasn't protected. People could say what they wanted about me, but I always used protection. I hadn't allowed any man to go bareback, not even my beloved Rodney, or Vic, who I trusted with my life.

When I didn't instantly open my legs, he pushed the knife further into my throat and I knew he would cut me if he felt it necessary. He had already proven that to me.

I parted my legs, and David pushed himself inside of me. I could never understand how a man could enter a woman when she was bone dry like the Mojave Desert. I always thought it had to hurt him. Well, if it did, I couldn't tell with David, because he began pushing inside of me and I felt as if I would rip. The excruciating pain was more than I could bear, so I lay under him stiff as a board. Screaming inside of my own head, hating myself for what I had become and what I had allowed men to see me as. I lost myself in the misery and the nightmare of it all. I refused to believe that I was being raped. My mind traveled of its own accord back to a day when I was at Ambiance's house with Naomi.

They were having a Super Bowl party, and there were several men over. A conversation started about women and men dating and the double standards. I asked a question that later I wished I hadn't asked.

"Why is it there are double standards for men and women?" I asked.

The men all threw out their various answers, none of which made sense to me. But then one of Eric's friend's, Marvin Ramsey, spoke up. "Women were originally designed to be the nurturers and caretakers of the family. As time went on, society made them believe they were less if they weren't doing the same things men did and had the same rights. But God didn't make it that way. He made the woman to be the nurturer when He made Eve from Adam's rib. She was supposed to be by his side and be that caretaker. He was supposed to be the protector and provider. But our people have gone through so much hurt and pain and a legacy of self-hate imposed on them by the slave masters, we got caught up in that Willie Lynch mentality. Now the black family has been successfully infiltrated by that mentality all these years later. Women believe they have to be equal to or better than men. So, they go toe to toe with us in front of the children, teaching our daughters a legacy of disrespect towards the man. Men have begun to lose that respect for women because of the way they portray themselves and the hurt and pain that we endure. As Black men, we are often seen as and treated as the lowest creatures on the totem pole. And when our black women lose respect for us, what do we have left? I'm not excusing men for sleeping around, because I don't condone that behavior. To me, there has to be respect for the person that I'm laying with. Women come a dime a dozen, and they always seem to be willing as long as we can keep it under wraps. Now for me, if there's no mental connection, then there's no physical connection. I respect myself too much for that as a man. But for our women...I expect them to love themselves more than that, too. Otherwise, if they're just laying up with every man they run into, then they're nothing more than a pot-a-let ho'," he explained.

"What does that term mean, anyway?" I asked him, before turning to send a glare towards Ambiance and Naomi. They had called me that on several occasions, and I got the gist of it, but I wanted a deeper understanding. I wondered if they really knew what they were saying to me.

"Well, it's kinda like those port-a-potties. Everyone goes in and uses them. Just like all those men at the construction site go to relieve themselves in the port-a-potty...ain't no flushing or nothing, just plop, plop, and they

head on out. Ain't no cleaning it out or none of that. If you lucky, they might have a little sanitation sheet to sit down on, but for the most part, they don't. Everybody is in and out of it, and it's nothing more than a trash receptacle to receive someone's refuse. Same thing with a woman who sleeps around. She is nothing more than a receptacle to allow a man to dump into her whatever he's disposing from his body. There's no spiritual or mental connection there, and he has no regard for her well-being. He is simply using her to relieve himself. And every man she lays down with, she gives a piece of her soul away to, and she takes a piece of him. The good and the bad."

I was silent for the rest of the party. Angry that my girlfriends had been calling me that, and angry that I had allowed myself to become that. But it didn't stop me. No, I went harder into what I knew was wrong. And that was what had led me to the place I was at now. Underneath this monster who was humping and pumping and dumping his refuse in me and not giving a damn. Because that was exactly what happened when he came. He relieved himself inside of me and got up after a moment.

"See, what you been missing out on all this time? Always making me strap up. I ain't laying up with nobody else 'cept you. Hell, my wife barely got time for me, so she ain't getting the shit that I save for you. And yo' ass creeping around with every damn man that come within a five mile radius of you. You wanna be a ho', Paige...then that's what I'ma treat you like. You should be *grateful* that I feel you the way I do. Most men don't even think twice 'bout no ho'. Me? I keep coming back for more like a dumb ass. And all I asked of you was not to involve my wife. You coulda told me to leave yo' triflin' ass alone, and I would've done it. You was wrong to call my damn wife and get her involved in our shit!" David roared.

By this time, he was sitting on a chair next to the couch staring at me. I was lying on the couch, still staring up at the ceiling with silent tears seeping from the corners of my eyes. He kept rambling on about how I had messed everything up. I began to tune him out after a while and think about all the things I would change in my life if given half the chance. I had vowed I would let no man hurt me after my mother and aunt were mistreated by my father and uncle. But I had been treated worse than they ever had. I had done the mistreating. After all, if I didn't respect and treat myself right, why should anyone else? At least they still had some dignity and self-respect. What did I have? A psycho who was hell-bent and determined to make my life miserable, if he didn't end it first.

19_AMBIANCE_MY FRIEND & HIS MISTRESS

For three days, I went back and forth between the hospital and work. I barely went home. The first night of the accident, I had gone to Naomi's and she and Sasha had worked so hard keeping my mind preoccupied. It didn't take long before my thoughts would wander back to either Eric or Nick and my predicament. I had been praying and asking God for guidance, and He had been silent. My family had been by my side constantly, calling or dropping by the hospital to make sure I was okay. And what was worse was that I was missing Nick and wanted to call him badly. But I refused.

Angelique was upset when I returned to work two days after the accident, but I explained to her I couldn't sit at home twiddling my thumbs and being at the hospital was driving me crazy. She didn't know my situation, and I wasn't eager to share it. So, I threw myself into the Poncho Girl project, working side by side with Sonya to create a selection for our fall catalogue.

In my spare time at the hospital when I wasn't sitting at my husband's bedside, I was downstairs in the lobby using my laptop to work on my business. The fashion show was coming up soon, and I didn't want to ruin my business before I had a chance to grow it.

The Friday after the accident, I was at the shop sitting alone in my office, contemplating designs Sonya had sent to me to be included in the catalogue. A knock at the door distracted me from my thoughts.

"Come in," I mumbled somewhat absentmindedly.

"I thought you had disappeared off the face of the earth," Nick murmured.

I looked up, caught off guard by his sudden appearance.

"Heyyy…who let you back here?" I asked.

"Miss Peggy. She said she thought you needed a break." He grabbed a chair and sat across from my desk, not waiting to be invited.

I blew out a breath and pushed my hair behind my ears and turned around in my chair to face him. "I'm sorry. I didn't mean to stand you up like that. It's just that…my husband was in a bad car accident that day, Nick."

"I'm sorry, is he okay?" His eyebrows furrowed with concern.

"He's currently in a coma. He suffered a dislocated shoulder, a broken femur, and a diffuse axonal injury, which is a form of a brain injury," I explained.

"So, what does that mean?" Nick inquired.

"The doctors were worried about swelling on the brain, because it can decrease blood flow to the brain and cause further injury. They are constantly monitoring him, but all the signs right now look good for a positive recovery. He's on steroids, and once he's awake, they plan to begin the rehabilitation process. You know, speech and occupational therapy, physical therapy, and counseling. "

"Wow. I hate to hear that. I'm sorry to barge in on you like this. I didn't know. I was just worried about you and thought maybe...I honestly don't know what I thought, Ambiance. I just know I missed you. I missed you so damn much," he confessed, and stood up in his chair.

I held my hand up and stopped him as I anticipated he was moving around my desk to hold me. "Stop, Nick. I can't do this anymore," I said, rapidly shaking my head.

"You can't do what, Ambi?" he asked. I could see the hurt taking over his eyes.

"I can't do me and you anymore. I have to be there for my husband at this point, Nick. I just don't know how long his recovery will take. All I know is that I can't ask you to place your life on hold any further."

I was fighting back the tears, because telling him this was so difficult. He had been nothing but a great friend to me. I didn't want to do anything to hurt him.

"Ambi...please, please don't do this. I'm not pushing you into anything, but I know you need a friend right now. Someone to be strong for you. Even if you don't see me, you can still at least call me...just every now and then call me for support, or if you need someone to talk to. I don't care how hard you push, I'll always be here," he replied. He had finally made it around my desk and pulled me close to him.

I broke down in tears standing there in his arms. They felt so strong and sure around me. My body shook for a while as I contemplated how much I would miss him. But I knew I needed to do this. I hadn't told him of my husband's plans to leave me. If I had, he wouldn't let me go, of this I was sure. Right now, I needed to focus on Eric's recovery process. Who knew? Maybe this was God's way of giving us a second chance at our marriage. Wasn't this what I had wanted, after all? Then why was I hurting so bad inside?

I pulled out of Nick's arms as I could no longer stand there and pretend I wasn't feeling something for the man. His powerful, crisp citrus scent danced in my nostrils and messed with my senses. The heat of his body was threatening to consume me, and the feel of his hands on my back was burning me up inside. A woman is built on emotions, we cannot help who we are. But we can help the choices we make. And I had chosen to leave my emotions wide open like a front door for this man to just walk in.

I made the mistake of looking up into Nick's eyes, and I was lost. I wanted what I knew would happen next. I wanted to feel his lips against mine, but a bit more intense than that day at the restaurant. I wanted to share the passion of what he had made me feel these last few months with him. It was at that moment that I realized I had been having an emotional affair with that man. I was all in, my heart and head too far gone…I was just as guilty as Eric was in his choice to have an affair.

"Goodbye, Ambiance. Call me when you're ready." He walked away just like that, and I never got the kiss I longed for.

****

I had been getting little sleep, as my dreams had been riddled with visions of me and Nick, and then again, of Eric racing from the restaurant, racing away from me always. He would look back and laugh at me as I tried to catch up with him. And it always ended the same, his car would hit a light pole and burst into flames.

I was sitting in my husband's hospital room reading a book early that Sunday morning when the door opened. I sat on the left side of his bed, surrounded by flowers and hidden by the bed, which was lifted high. I couldn't see the person who entered the room, which was unusual. Whenever anyone walked in, I could often see their head and chest above the bed. But as I listened, I heard a distinct noise. Suddenly it dawned on me when the squeaking stopped that it was the sound of a wheelchair.

I rose slowly from my seat by his side and walked around the bed. I was still unseen as I stood there with a look of disgust on my face. I took in the light-skinned woman, whose skin was the color of creamy coffee. She wore her long, brown hair in a wavy braid down her back. She was bent over in a wheelchair with her head lying on his bed. Her shoulders shook as she cried. I chose not to say a word, not because I wanted to give her a private moment with my husband, but because I needed to gather my thoughts.

I remained that way for almost two minutes, and then I couldn't take it anymore. "Kendra?" I had never met her or even seen pictures of her before, but I knew who she was.

She turned her head around with her eyes widened in surprise.

"I'm Ambiance, Eric's wife." I stood with my arms folded across my breasts, my face lined with wrath.

She sniffed, wiping her eyes on the sleeves of her robe. "I know who you are." Her voice was bitter, almost as if *I* had done something to *her*. "Can I just have a moment with him, please?" Her voice was somewhat deep, what most would probably call sensual. I couldn't believe she had the gall to ask me if she, his mistress, could have a moment alone with my husband.

"Don't you think you've had more of them than you were entitled to, Kendra? I always thought about all the things that I would say to you if I ever met you. I wondered what you looked like, what you offered him that I couldn't, and so many other things. And now that I see you, I'm not impressed at all. Actually I feel sorry for you. A woman who can't get her own man and has to sink to the level of sharing another woman's man is no woman at all in my book. You have no self-respect, no love for your fellow sisters, and no self-worth. I pity you, because until you've learned how to love yourself you can't truly love anyone else. And don't tell me you love yourself, because if you did, you would have placed yourself in a much better situation than this. You have to settle for his leftover love," I spat out at her in anger.

She shook her head at me as if she pitied me. "Eric loves me, and he loves his son. Despite what you may think, I am the most important person in the world to this man next to my son. I don't have to settle for anything. Every night that he's not home with you, where do you think he is? He's at home with me and his son. When you wake up alone in the morning, I'm waking up in his arms. He's holding me, cuddling me, and making love to me...not you. He probably comes home to your ass only two or three times a week. Home is where his heart is, and his heart is with me, Ambiance. You didn't know who I was and never saw me, because he protects me with everything within him. But I've always known what you look like, where you live, and where you work. He doesn't give a damn about you."

"You keep believing that, and you keep sitting there waiting for him to come to you, Kendra. I promise you he won't be leaving me, sweetheart, to come be with you. I'm his wife, you're just the mother of his child," I retorted.

"You may be his wife, but not for long. I'm the one he chose to start a family with, and I'm the one he'll grow old with. You just wait until he gets out of this hospital bed," Kendra hissed.

"And then what? He has several months of therapy awaiting him, including speech therapy. I have the power of attorney over my husband. You will sit and rot in hell before he returns to you. And you don't mess with a child of God. You better be very careful what you wish on me...your wrong will come back on you. God surely doesn't like ugly, Kendra. I guess that's why you're the one sitting in that wheelchair now and not me."

"Yeah, he told me you were a Holy Roller," Kendra taunted me, with a vile laugh.

"I may be a Holy Roller, sweetheart, but at least I know Whose protection I'm under. I'd rather be under His protection, than his," I replied, pointing to my husband. "You have no clue of the punishment you're setting yourself up for. I know He's going to take care of me," I stated, as I pointed my finger towards the ceiling, indicating Heaven.

I stormed out of the room leaving her there alone with my husband. I had to go and get my emotions together before I lost it in front of her.

"Mommm," I cried into my phone as I sat in my car in the hospital's parking lot.

"Honey, what's wrong?" Alexis asked. Listening to the panic in her voice, I realized I had scared her and that was not my intent.

I sniffled, trying to gather my composure. "I'm at the hospital, and Kendra just came into the room. We had some words and...Mom, I just can't do thisss," I wailed into the phone. I yearned to feel her arms around me.

"Baby, where exactly are you now?"

"I'm in the parking deck in my car," I replied, pulling another Kleenex from my glove compartment, wiping my tears.

"Are you dressed?"

"Yes, ma'am. I've got on some slacks and a blouse, why?" I asked.

"Meet me at the church, baby. Your dad and I are heading there now, and that's where you need to be. Only He can help you with what you're going through. I mean it, Ambi. Bring yourself to church where you belong. We've missed seeing you lately."

"I know, Mom. I'm on the way." I listened to my step-mother's sound advice and knew that I needed to follow her words of wisdom.

****

The choir's soothing voices rang through the church singing praises to the Lord. I loved their rendition of Juanita Bynum's, *You Are Great*. I was standing in worship to the Lord with my hands outstretched, tears streaming down my face. Alexis stood on my left, rubbing my back up and down.

When the song came to an end, Pastor Boyd entered the pulpit smiling. "Praise the Lord, everybody!"

The church called out, "Hallelujah!"

"I said, praise the Lord, everybody!" Everyone shouted a little louder. "Come on, stand to your feet and praise Him like you have a reason to praise Him. If you're here this morning, that's a reason to praise Him, because He blessed you with the most precious gift in the world...He woke you up to see another day. Now, stand to your feet if you're able and give our Magnificent God a worthy, right-now praise!" he shouted.

Everyone stood and began to shout Hallelujah and gave hand claps of praise. A woman in the front row hollered out, "Thank ya, Jezuz!" and went into a praise dance.

"'Let everything that hath breath praise the Lord,' the Psalmist said. So, if you're alive and breathing, praise Him!" Pastor Boyd encouraged harder, as more people began to break out in praise dances, and some danced into the aisles. The music ministers played the keyboard, guitar, drums, and horns harder than they had before, looking at the congregation and back at one another, grinning from ear to ear.

Pastor Boyd began dancing in the pulpit in circles, himself, until he broke out in a sweat, and then he slowed up and wiped his brow with his handkerchief. He began walking back and forth with his hands lifted in worship and uttering praises to the Lord. I felt myself getting caught up in the moment, too, as I thought about all the good things He had done. I could've been the one laid up in a hospital bed or rolling around in a wheelchair. But God! I broke out in a praise dance.

Pastor Boyd began preaching after another ten minutes of a praise session. I listened to him for quite some time. But it was the ending message that pricked my heart and really gained my attention. Before then, I had been listening half-heartedly while thinking about my life, and the run-in with Kendra at the hospital.

"There are so many scriptures in the book of Psalms you can go to for encouragement in your hour of need. His word is there for guidance, power, and enlightenment. God simply wants you to come to Him as you are. Many people say 'Pastor, I don't know the scriptures that well,' or, 'I can't pray the way you pray.' It's not about knowing the right scriptures or praying in a certain way. You talk to your Heavenly Father the same way that you talk to me or your best friend. It doesn't need to be some pumped-up prayer. Psalms thirty and two says, 'O Lord my God, I called to You for help and You healed me.' God desires to be Jehovah Rapha to you, which is the Lord that heals. Whether your infirmity is in your mind, body, heart, or spirit, He is the God who heals all manner of sickness and disease. Simply call out to Him, and He will hear your cry and be faithful to heal you. If you can do no more than say, 'God, I need You!' you can stand in faith knowing that He *will* come to your rescue. Because He loves you just that much. He doesn't want to see His children suffering. He desires for you to live an abundant and prosperous life. No, God doesn't want you to suffer, He longs to make you whole."

"Amen!" a few people shouted out. "Preach it, Pastor!"

"Open your heart to God and allow Him to come and truly enter in. He is to be revered in all areas of your life. As you trust Him with your finances, and as you trust Him with your relationship, learn to trust Him with your heart. He will take care of you. He will heal your broken heart and lift your infirmities from you. His word says, 'Come onto Me all who labor and are heavy burdened and I will give you rest.' God wants to take your burden from you and allow you to enter His perfect rest. Because He lovingly offers it to us, we should accept it. We can only enter that rest through His precious word. Spending time in His word and Presence is necessary to enter that rest. When we have faith in Him and trust Him to take care of our heart and our healing, then and only then have we entered that rest. In that rest, there is strength. There is power in that rest. There is peace in that rest. And there is healing in that rest. God wants to give it to you today, my brothers and sisters."

Pastor Boyd stepped down from the pulpit, flanked by six other ministers with his arms outstretched. "If you need rest today, come. Come to the altar, and give it all to God. If you have never accepted Him as your Lord and Savior, now is the time. Tomorrow's not promised. Or, if you say, 'Pastor, I gave my life to Him a while ago, but somewhere along the way, I fell by the wayside.' It's okay, my child, we all struggle, we all sin and fall short of His glory. You can rededicate yourselves today. Or, if you simply find yourself in the need of prayer, come to the altar now. Come, won't you come and enter His rest?" he petitioned.

I felt a tugging in my heart. I knew I needed to walk down there and accept the offer. The only reason it was so hard was because I had been entrenched in fear that I had allowed to take root in my heart. That was what the enemy wanted. It was time for me to truly give it up to God. I had no answers. I didn't know whether Eric would wake up tomorrow or in a few months. And when he did wake up, I had no clue if he would stay with me or leave to be with his mistress and child. I knew I had been playing a dangerous game of fire with Nick. I had not truly repented from the mistakes I had made. My heart was sorry for the things I had done, and I longed to be forgiven. I pushed past the person standing on my right and made my way down that aisle.

When I reached the end of the aisle, my father, Deacon Richardson, was waiting with open arms. I saw nothing except for my father, who stood to Pastor Boyd's right, waiting for me. I almost flew into my father's arms and bawled my eyes out. I had come home, and it felt so right.

After praying with my father and a couple of the church mothers, I had rededicated my life to God. I understood that I wasn't being punished by my choice to fall into an emotional affair with Nick. However, I realized that sometimes the Lord allows us to go through things to bring our focus back to Him. And the things that had occurred in my life were not the devil attacking me. Instead, it was situations I had created, Nick, and those I had allowed, ignoring Eric's cheating, which God was allowing me to go through so I could focus on Him again.

When church was over, my father handled his normal responsibilities, as my step-mother and I chit-chatted with the other church ladies. We ate lunch at a small restaurant close to the hospital before they escorted me back.

By the time I arrived, Kendra was long gone and Eric had been taken for further testing. My mother-in-law sat in a chair across from his bed.

"Hi, Hope," I greeted in a quiet voice, as if we were in the library. She set her crossword puzzle down on the table next to her and rose to embrace me.

"Hi, honey. How are you coming along?" she asked, sitting back in her chair.

I walked past her and sat in the chair I had abandoned earlier when Kendra came. "If you had asked me that question a few hours earlier, I would have said I was broken. But I know that I'm being healed now and that despite what comes from all of this, I will be better in the end."

His mother nodded, and I could tell she had something on her mind.

"Hope, was she still here when you arrived?" I asked.

I didn't need to mention the name, she knew exactly who I was referring to. Hope rubbed her hands together and stared out the window for a moment. Then she turned back to me with tears in her eyes.

Shaking her head *yes*, she acknowledged that Kendra had not left by the time she arrived. "I had so many hopes for you and my son. You've always been such a welcome addition to the family," she shared.

I laughed a bitter laugh. "You couldn't tell me that by the way Danielle treats me," I said, referring to my sister-in-law.

Hope smiled a gentle smile my way and waved her hand at me. "Aww, honey, Danielle's bark is worse than her bite. Did I ever tell you that she had a crush on Eric in the beginning?"

I was amazed at this newfound news she shared. After being in the family for four years, I never had an inkling of this. "Are you sure, Hope?" I asked.

Hope shook her head again. "Honey, you know me. I don't frivolously toss out information without knowing what I'm talking about. She met Eric when she did her internship at his law office. He constantly ignored the passes she made, and that still didn't stop her. They had a Christmas party one year and she had been drinking too much and she shamelessly tossed herself at him in front of everyone. Stephen had been invited to the party, and he felt sorry for her. You know how arrogant Eric can be at times, and Stephen always felt his brother led her on and then played with her. Somehow, his rescuing her from embarrassment burdened Stephen with becoming her protector. He hasn't left her side since. That's the real reason she hates you, you know."

Hope picked up her crossword puzzle and went back to work on it as if that finished her conversation.

"Did you know he was going to leave me?" I asked.

"Yes...Stephen told me and his dad the day of the accident about that. But I don't think you have to worry about that. My husband won't allow it to happen. Eric listens to his father's advice more than you would think. Besides, Stephen Sr. ran her off when we found her in here. Oh, yeah, you know how your father-in-law can be. He read those nurses the riot act and the doctor, too. Kendra's not allowed back in this room or anywhere near him as long as he's in this hospital."

I released a deep sigh. "Hope, I thank you and Stephen Sr. for all that you do and for your love and support. But no matter how much you try to protect me, you can't change his heart. If my husband's heart isn't with me, he's going to do what he wants. You can't just turn love off and on like that," I expressed.

Hope rose from her seat and walked over to where I sat.

"Sweetheart, sometimes it isn't about love, it's about the vows you took and the commitment you made," she said, patting me on my hand.

She turned to head for the door and turned back around for a moment.

"I'll be back. I'm going down to the cafeteria to get a bite to eat. You want something?" she asked.

I shook my head *no*. It may not have been about love for the older generation, but love was everything to me.

20_NAOMI_BENEFIT OF THE DOUBT

My guess was that everything on Ambiance's front was going well, or as well as could be expected. I had talked to her off and on, and nothing about Eric's status had changed. She did share with me that Kendra had come into his room on Sunday while she was in there. But if you ask me, it was a blessing in disguise. Why? Because it drove Ambiance's emotional self back into the arms of her first love…Jesus. He truly does work all things together for the good of those of us who love Him and are called according to His purpose.

Now, Miss Little Hot Thang, on the other hand, I hadn't heard from in a while. I didn't know if she was mad at me or what. But I had been calling her, and she hadn't returned any of my calls. I had left her a couple of voicemails, and she still hadn't called. If she didn't slow her fast butt down, I was going to pop up at her apartment unannounced. And she knew she didn't want that to happen. God forbid that I run into her and one of her gentlemen friends. *Lord, please have mercy on my friend. Send a rhema word to Paige, Lord God.*

"Moommmm!" Sasha cried from upstairs, interrupting my thoughts.

"What is it, hon?" I called back.

"I can't find my green jeans. Have you seen them?" she shouted back. The poor child sounded as if the world was coming to an end.

"No, honey! Did you check the dryer?" I shouted back. I was attempting to complete a report for work. Although it was a Friday night, I had nothing else planned so this was a working weekend for me. I knew Sasha was nervous about her weekend plans. She was going with her father and his family to the mountains for the weekend. He had planned for them to go water-skiing, hiking, and kayaking. She was excited about the plans until she realized his wife and children would be coming along.

Up until now, she had spent time with her father alone and had not seen his family since the day she first met him in the restaurant. I knew this trip would be a bit overwhelming for her, because not only was she meeting them formally and spending time with them, but she was spending an entire weekend with them, not just one day.

She had been eager to spend a weekend hiking and kayaking with her father. But the disappointment had been evident rather quickly when she learned his wife and children would be coming along for the weekend getaway.

Sasha came back down and plopped on the couch next to me in my office. I had moved away from my desk and sat on the couch to be more relaxed.

I pushed my laptop away from me on the table and turned to face my daughter, whose smile was turned upside down.

"Honey, what's really wrong? This isn't about the green jeans is it, Sasha?" I asked, rubbing her back as she lay across my lap.

"Mommm," my daughter whined, "I just…I don't know. I haven't been around them since that day. And I feel kinda awful about how I hollered at his wife and for telling them that I feel sorry for their children. I acted like a hysterical freak that day."

"Daughter of mine, you're a child and you're only human. As such, you're going to make mistakes in this life, this isn't the first, and it definitely won't be the last. Each mistake will bend and shape you and allow you to grow stronger and better, if you let it. You stand up with your head held high, and you explain your feelings and emotions to Natalie, one on one. I believe she will understand you, respect you because you were mature enough to take on your responsibility, and most of all, I believe she will forgive you. In terms of the children, they're still young. Children move forward and forgive and forget a lot easier than adults. You don't worry about any of it, just go and have the time of your life."

"I guess," she murmured, with her face buried in my lap.

"Sasha. Sasha, sit up and look at me," I commanded, patting her on the back.

She sat up and looked at me with eyes just like Jaime's.

"It's okay for you to build relationships with them, honey. This just means that you're more loved than ever before. You have one great, big extended family on all sides, and God has packed you with so much love inside that He decided it was time for you to share it with others."

"But what about you, Mom?" She pouted her lips out the way she had when she was four instead of sixteen.

"What about me, Sashaberry?"

"I don't want you over here by yourself when I'm out having fun with them. It's always been you and me, and now it feels like I'm betraying you or something," she confided.

I laughed, and I could understand how my daughter would feel that way. Sure, we had Paige, Ambiance and my parents, but the majority of the time it had always been just me and my baby. Now she had another family to share her time and love with. I made a decision right then and there to open up to my daughter.

"Sasha, I have placed my life on hold for such a long time since you were a little girl. You're growing up now, and you're not that same little girl anymore. Soon, you'll be leaving me and your dad and going off to college. He'll still have his wife and children, you'll have your college buddies, and me, I'll have...well, I'll have—"

"Aunt Ambi and Aunt Paige," Sasha cut in with a warm smile.

"Well, yeah. I'll have them, but they have lives. Ambiance has her husband, Eric, and Paige, well...you know she loves to date."

"Yeah, she does. Aunt Paige has lots of male friends, Mom," Sasha stated, raising her eyebrow.

"How do you know that?" I asked, a bit shocked that she had noticed more about Paige's habits than I had given her credit for.

"Mom, I'm sixteen, not six. It's like the two of you are at opposite extremes. I want you to date *someone*, and you won't. Aunt Paige? I wish she'd select one or two. But, she says she's not ready to be tied down."

I was a bit caught off guard, because Sasha had never shared with me her desire to see me involved with someone. I took for granted that she was happy with the way things were.

"I know she says she doesn't want to be tied down, but like you, I wish she'd be a little more selective, too. Not to mention safe. Anyway, this isn't about Paige, it's about you and me. When you leave for college, I won't have anyone. And that's the truth of the matter. So, it's about time for me to get out and start meeting people and building a life for myself. I don't want you to worry about me, Sasha."

"You're going to start dating, Mom?" Her eyes widened in disbelief.

"Well…" I was unsure how to proceed.

"That's great! It's about time you get a life. You know you're not getting any younger, and you need someone to come along and make you smile. You spend too much time doing work and dipping in my life, anyway. And that's not good for someone your age. Besides, you don't want to be an old spinster, do you?"

"Excuse me, I'll have you know that I'm only thirty-three. I don't know what all this stuff about 'someone my age' and being a spinster means. You act like I'm sixty-something years old, girl." I grabbed a pillow from behind my back and hit her with it.

She laughed and grabbed one of her own, and we launched into a full scale pillow fight right there in my office, until my phone buzzed. I was nearly out of breath as I made my way to my phone sitting on my desk and saw Jaime's name pop up on the caller ID.

"Hello?"

"Hi, Naomi. I just wanted to let you know that we're on the way over. And I wanted to thank you once again for allowing me to have her the entire weekend."

"It's no problem, Jaime. She's looking forward to it," I replied, turning to face my daughter and pointing upstairs with my left hand as I cradled the cell phone between my right ear and shoulder. Sasha pulled a face at me giving me the stink eye. I lifted an eyebrow at her and once again pointed upstairs with more emotion this time, urging her to finish packing.

"Well, that's good to hear. But I just want to thank you, because if it weren't for you I know we wouldn't have had a chance to develop the relationship we have. I just hate that I missed out on the last sixteen years of her life."

"Look, Jaime, I've told you that you can't keep apologizing, and you can't make up for those missed years. You can't get those back, you can only enjoy the ones that still lie ahead. So, treasure them and create precious memories with her now. Oh, yeah, before I forget she's a bit nervous about being with the entire family for the weekend and especially being with Natalie after her scene at the restaurant."

"Man, Nat's cool on that. It was just as important to her that I build this relationship with Sasha as it was to me. The kids are excited about her coming with us, too," Jaime attempted to reassure me.

"I understand that, but you still have to tread lightly where your daughter's feelings are concerned. You all may be cool with it, but just help her work through it at her own pace. Sometimes she's harder on herself than she has to be," I shared.

"All right, thanks for the heads up. Well, I'm on the way, and we'll be there in about forty-five minutes," he declared.

We said our goodbyes and I pressed "end" on my cell phone. I continued working on my report for another forty minutes before I took a break. It had been a while since I had heard Sasha moving around upstairs, and I knew her father would be pulling up any minute. I shut my laptop down and climbed the stairs to go and check on her and make sure she was packed up.

"...broke? Whachu mean it broke? And why you just now telling me this? Oh, my gosh!" There was the sound of panic in my daughter's voice. She was on the phone, and I began walking back to my room to wait for her to finish her conversation until I heard the next words out of her mouth.

"...might be pregnant...Mom's going to kill..."

Yes, I was going to kill her! *I know that I didn't just hear my daughter say she was pregnant.* How in the heck did that happen? I had a tight leash on her, and she didn't have time to meet up with anybody. It better not have been that Anthony boy! What I hated worse than a female allowing herself to get trapped in such a situation as I had when I was a teen, was a female who got caught up with a boy she knew didn't give a damn about her. Hadn't she learned from my past? I talked openly with her about it.

I marched back to her room and pounded on her door before opening it.

"Sasha Kennedy Blankenship! Get off that phone, now!" I screamed.

Fury was causing the lines around my mouth to tighten, and my heart was doing some sort of fast, staccato beat. Why was history repeating itself? Hadn't I done everything to protect her from making my mistakes? I had begun having discussions about sex with her at a very early age. I had left nothing out from protection to diseases; we had covered it all, including the option to remain celibate until she married. So, why in the name of Jesus was this happening to me? Yes, I felt like it was happening to me. Was this what my mother had experienced when I first had to tell her that I was pregnant? My mother had always been very mild and soft-spoken, so while it was a difficult conversation to have with her, I didn't get beat down the way I was about to beat my daughter down.

"Hey, let me call you back. My mom needs me…I said I would call back. Look, would you just calm down?" she argued to the person on the other line.

"Look, young lady, when I say get off that phone, you get off that phone right now! You don't owe nobody no damn explanation except me!" I shouted. My cursing caught both me and her off guard, because it was something that I seldom engaged in. But I needed to express just how serious this situation was, and I was in no mood for teenaged games.

She clicked her cell phone off and set it on the dresser next to her purse. Sasha turned worried eyes my way. "Mom, you didn't have to curse me, I was getting off the phone. I was just—"

"No, you don't tell me what I don't have to do, young lady. You're getting too grown around here and you've lost your mind if you think—"

"Can you tell me why you're all of a sudden tripping on me, Dr. Jekyll and Ms. Hyde?" She walked to her bed and plopped down and looked back at me almost as if I had grown another head.

I knew that to her, I had to be coming out of the air with my new attitude, but I had been completely caught off guard by what I had heard. Surely, this wasn't happening.

"You better watch your mouth, Sasha, before I snatch you bald." I had walked up on her, pointing a finger in her face. She slightly turned her head and blew a breath out.

I blew a couple of breaths of my own to calm myself down, once I spotted my finger shaking in anger.

"Sasha, how many times have we had discussions about sex?"

"What?"

"Answer me! How many times have we had discussions about sex?" I repeated.

"Mom, I can't count all the times. Why?" She was looking up at me in confusion.

"Because I have tried to do my best with you. I've talked until I'm blue in the face, I have shown you every DVD I could find, and read with you every book we could purchase. I have enrolled you in sex education classes and been transparent about my own choices and past. Didn't any of that sink in? Where did I fail you?"

"Huh?"

"I know...it must've been with that nasty little boy named Anthony. Or was it Kahim, or maybe Charles? I don't know, but something or someone has made you lose your raggedy mind!"

"Mom, back up and slow down. What are you tripping on?" Sasha rose to stand in front of me.

Her five-foot, ten-inch frame allowed her to look down on my five-foot, six-inch frame, and I didn't like that one bit. I used my right hand and pushed her back down onto her bed. I walked up to my daughter, and with my right index finger, pointed in her face as I began to check her.

"Listen here, little girl, you must think that I'm stupid or something or that I fell off that turnip truck the old folks are always talking about. Well I'm not stupid, and I damn sure didn't fall off a truck. You think I didn't hear your conversation? You think I didn't hear what was going on or know about the choices you've made that have caused you to repeat my situation? Or maybe that's just it, you don't know yet, so since you're not sure, you think the whole world's dumb."

Sasha's eyes widened and were brimming with tears as she shook her head at me. I wasn't about to fall for that pity role. I was so mad; how couldn't I have seen it? Right after I found Anthony in my home that day, I had put a tight leash on my daughter. But here lately, with everything that had been going on, I had fallen slack. I had become consumed, once again, and slacked up on her. Not with work, but with running back and forth trying to support Ambiance while Eric was in the hospital and allowing her a little trust, because she had been working on a relationship with her dad.

"Mom...I don't know what you're talking about. Honestly, I don't, but I wish you would tell me." The tears she was shedding ripped at me a little bit. Just a little. I needed to let my daughter know that I knew about the pregnancy or the maybe pregnancy. After all, hadn't she confirmed that the condom had broken but she wasn't sure if she was pregnant or not?

"Sasha, I was just walking upstairs and overheard your conversation. I heard you say something broke, but I wasn't sure what. I walked off, not wanting to eavesdrop, until I heard you say you were pregnant," I shared. My words broke on the word "pregnant." I couldn't bring myself to quite use that term in the same sentence with my daughter's name. I had such high hopes for her.

"Pregnant? You didn't hear me say that, Mom," she bawled. Her face was all scrunched up now and turning red. She was shaking her head back and forth at me.

"I'm guessing whatever little nappy headed boy that was on the other end of the line told you his condom broke!" I accused. "I know what I heard, Sasha. And I heard it with my own ears," I continued.

"Well, you better clean your ears out, Mom! Because that's not what I said! It's not me that's pregnant, it's Sabrina!" She broke down sobbing after her confession.

I stood there for a moment feeling quite stupid. *Did she just say it wasn't her, but Sabrina?* Not Sabrina from the church, she was a sweetheart. But then, I suddenly became excited because it wasn't my baby. Not that I wished that on Sabrina or her parents, either, but it wasn't my dilemma to deal with. Phew!

"Oh, baby! I'm sorry...I'm so...I don't know...wow. Thank God it isn't you." I said, and I attempted to gather my daughter in my arms. But she planted both hands firmly against my chest and pushed me back from her so hard that I fell on the floor.

Wait a minute, now, I might've been wrong, but that attitude wouldn't be accepted. I pulled myself off the floor and stood in front of her.

"Look, Sasha, you might be upset, but don't you dare ever push me like that again, do you understand me?"

"Mom, you just accused me of being pregnant. You never gave me the benefit of the doubt, you never asked me or questioned me about it in the slightest. You simply accused me, afraid that I had made the same mistake you made. Well, you know what? I'm sorry I was such a mistake! I'm sorry I screwed up your life so bad. I'm sorry you had to sacrifice for seventeen years so that I could have a life. It's like all my life that's all you've ever done was throw down my throat how you had to sacrifice because of me. You only wanted me to know that you didn't have a life because you got pregnant at a young age. That's been my baggage to carry all these years! I'm not you, Mom. I'm my own person with my own thoughts and feelings. I just wish for once you would trust me! Just once, give me the freaking benefit of the doubt!" she screamed at me.

I never knew she felt that way. But at the moment, I didn't care. I was about to put her in her place. She had forgotten she had made several bad choices.

"I did give you the benefit of the doubt, Sasha! Until I caught you at school wearing clothes that I did not buy for you, letting some nasty boy hang all over you and another one grab you on the ass! Not to mention that same day you came home and were letting another one come into the house, and he had his tongue all down your throat. So, to hell with the benefit of the doubt! You tossed it out the door like yesterday's garbage! I don't owe you that. I may have been wrong in my accusations and the way I handled things, but you will still respect me as long as you're living in my home! Is that understood?" I stood firmly planted in front of her with one hand on my hip and another pointing at the floor to indicate the house she lived in belonged to me.

Now, don't get me wrong, I knew I was dead wrong for cursing at her. She wasn't used to hearing me use that type of language. But at the moment, I was disappointed in myself and her and couldn't calm down enough to find a better way to deal with it. I was disappointed in myself for how I had jumped to conclusions and wrongly accused my daughter. I was disappointed in her, because she had the audacity to put her hands on me when I was attempting to apologize and comfort her. I wasn't making this situation easier for either of us, but at the moment, I was all in my emotions. I didn't do that often, but every now and then, I indulged. I didn't realize what it was about to cost me.

"Well, maybe I just won't live here anymore. You don't have to worry about my lack of respect, and I don't have to worry about you not giving me the benefit of the doubt!"

"Where are you going, Sasha? You can't take care of yourself!" I exclaimed.

"With him!" she shouted, slanting those cat-like eyes and pointing a finger over my shoulder. I slowly turned around and saw Jaime standing behind me with his mouth opened in shock.

21_PAIGE_SEX AS A WEAPON

It had been three days since David had invaded my space and taken over my life. Initially, I thought I would wait for him to fall asleep and escape the first chance I got. But those hopes were quickly dashed the first day. He had produced a pair of handcuffs and marched me back to my bedroom at gun point, my own gun I might add, and chained me to my bedpost. I wasn't allowed to get up and do anything. He took my sense of pride from me and humiliated me by forcing me to use a bedpan when I had to use the restroom, and he gave me a sponge bath daily.

My job? I was forced to call in and take several days of emergency leave off, because I was having a family emergency and would be out of town. I was taken off the emergency call list, and no one would be calling my work phone for any reason. I began to think about how it would have been so wonderful had I created some type of code word to use with my employees in the event of an emergency. We always worked with situations that could become harmful to us, but no one had initiated a procedure for this type of emergency in our safety plan. If I survived this ordeal, it would be one of the first things I did with my employees and friends.

Then I had to rethink what I was saying, there was no "if." I would survive, come hell or high water. I was a natural-born fighter, and I would fight until my last breath. I just had to formulate a plan. I began to think about the cases I had and the children who needed me to fight for them. I hadn't prayed in a long time, but I knew God had a plan for my life. The hurt and pain I had gone through was supposed to be used to strengthen other youth and teens going through similar situations. God wanted me to encourage them and stand strong by their side, but I couldn't do it if I was dead. And I couldn't do it living the life I had been living.

My friends? They were the last hope that I had. I had not received a call or visit from Ambiance at all. I knew she was probably still mad about our last encounter. She could be stubborn like that, but then again, so could I. Believe it or not, I actually missed her. I would've given anything at this moment to hear her whining and nagging voice. I would've even liked to hear her preach to me. However, Naomi had called on several occasions, and I was forced to ignore her calls. I had told David that I needed to answer the call, because she would start worrying. He didn't seem to care one way or another. He wasn't in his right frame of mind. Which is why I wasn't surprised when the next step occurred. On the third day, she decided to pop up at my home.

David had been rambling on like the crazy man that was on a karate movie he was watching on TV. Emotionally and physically exhausted, I spent most of my time in a catatonic state, when I wasn't planning my escape. The sound of the doorbell startled me. It had been so quiet around my place for so long, only the sounds of me and David. My eyes widened as I turned to look at him sitting in the bed next to me. He grabbed the remote and muted the TV and turned to me.

"Who the fuck's that at yo' door?" David asked, in a gruff tone.

His eyes were wildly moving about his head, and his pupils were dilated. If I had not been around him every moment of the day, I would swear he was on something. But then again, I had no clue as to what he was doing when he went into the bathroom and locked himself in there. He sure wasn't taking a bath or shower, despite the fact that he would let the water run most of the time he was in there. While he had dedicated his time to keeping me clean, he had failed to do the same for himself. David smelled like sweat, urine, and ass! That was the only way I could describe the funk that emanated from his body.

"I...I...don't know," I replied, rubbing my left hand against my stinging cheek when he slapped me, demanding a response to his question. I honestly did not know, but I could only guess it was Naomi. And as quickly as that thought popped in my head, I knew I had to do something about it. She had a key to my home, and she would use it at the drop of a dime, especially since my car was parked outside and I hadn't been answering my phone.

"You...you know what? I think that's probably Naomi," I replied.

He looked at me with frustration and contempt. I could tell he didn't trust me.

"Who's Naomi?" he demanded, picking up my gun from my night stand where he kept it. Straddling me before I had a chance to blink, he placed one hand around my throat and pointed the gun at my head with his other hand.

I poured every bit of sorrow into my eyes, hoping that he would not kill me at this moment. He released the grip, but didn't remove the gun.

Choking and gasping for air, I rubbed my throat where his hands had previously been. "M...m...my best friend," I stuttered.

"The fuck she want?" he snarled at me, with the look of a vicious dog.

"I don't know. I have to answer the door, David—" I began before he cut me off.

"Why?" he screamed.

"Because she has a key! She'll use it if I don't answer the door. She's been calling the last few days, and you won't let me answer her call. She sees my car outside; she's going to know something's wrong and come in if I don't answer."

"Let her ass come in here if she wants to. She'll regret that shit. Stupid bitch!" He began to mumble incoherently under his breath and started knocking things off my dresser.

I had to think quickly, because I didn't want her coming in. If something happened to Naomi, I knew I would never forgive myself. Sasha needed her mother in her life. And Naomi's concern for me was no reason for her life to end so swiftly. And I had no doubt that David would keep his word.

"Before she comes in, she'll call the police, David. I know she's going to think something's wrong, and she'll call them and then come in. You don't want the police here, David. It won't come out right for you." If I could just get him to let me go to the door, I could stall Naomi from coming in and buy some time. I just had to think of a code to give her when I got to the door. Something David wouldn't pick up on.

He licked his black, scaly, chapped lips as he considered what I had told him. He was standing on my side of the bed with the gun shaking in his hand, watching me and contemplating. It only took a moment for his processors to realize what I suggested was in his best interest. He quickly grabbed the key from the dresser and moved back to my side, holding the gun to my head with one hand and placing the key in my left hand to unlock my right wrist, which was the only one cuffed to the bed post.

I moved as quickly as possible and stood up from the bed. I didn't think about how much energy I had lost lying in bed for three days. My brain felt as if it were rolling around inside of my head like a loose bowling ball, ricocheting from one side to the next. The throbbing in my head was intense, but that wasn't the only issue I had. I instantly wavered on wobbly knees, and had it not been for David steadying me with one hand, I'm sure I would have fallen back down. I felt as if everything he had fed me over the last few days was going to come back up. I put one hand to my mouth and the other over my belly, trying to stabilize everything.

"Here, put your arm around my shoulder," he suggested.

I placed one arm around his shoulder while he balanced me with his right arm around my waist. He continued to point the gun at my stomach with his other hand. I would have to get myself together before I got to the door, because Naomi would notice if I couldn't stand alone or if I appeared ill. David had the same thought I did.

"Look, get your shit together before you get to that door. Cuz if she thinks something's wrong, I swear I won't think twice 'bout busting a cap in her ass. I wish yo' ass would so much as wink yo' eye at her or utter a strange word. You betta' make her think everything's fine," he threatened in a growl.

"Okay, okay! I'll just tell her I have company, and I know that'll make her leave."

"Yeah, whateva'. Say something! Tell her you coming!" he whispered loudly in my ear, while poking me with my gun at the sound of the doorbell ringing again.

"Hold on! I'm coming!" I shouted, with my normal, impatient tone.

We finally made it to the door, and he shoved the gun in my side and gave me another reminder. "Remember what I said. She get suspicious, her ass is dead and you, too."

I was only wearing a bra and panties. So, I would position myself in such a way that she would see my shoulder and bra strap when I opened the door and realize I was indecent. That would allow David to continue to hold me up, and I could lean on the door for the remainder of my strength.

Peeping out the peephole, I confirmed that it was Naomi at the door wearing a worried expression. Her eyebrows were furrowed, mouth crinkled at the corners caused by the tight frown she was wearing, and her hand was on her hip.

I opened the door slightly, leaving the chain intact. "Damn, girl, what's up? You blowing up my phone, and now you popping up at my house. It had better be an emergency," I snapped.

"What's going on, Paige? I haven't heard from you, and you haven't answered my calls. Surely you can't still be mad about that incident with you and Ambi." Naomi squinted her eyes at me, waiting for my answer with a mother-like attitude. I think she believed that she was our mother sometimes.

I waved my hand, dismissing her idea as ridiculous. "Pssh! Girl, n'all! I'm not stuck on that. I've been busy between work and my extracurricular activities," I explained. David poked me in the side with my gun again, indicating he wanted me to hurry up. "Speaking of which, I'm caught up in one, now. You're messing with a sista's groove."

"Well, look, we need to talk. I need you to give me a call soon. So much has happened with me and Ambi since you haven't been around, Paige. Her husband's in the hospital in a coma, she's found out he has a child, Sasha's lost her mind…I just don't know what to do."

"What?" I was astounded by the news that Eric was in the hospital, but even more so that he had a child. There were so many questions firing off in my head, but I knew now was not the time to ask. I had to get her away from my door in any manner possible as soon as possible. "Okay, look, I'll call you later and we'll catch up. But right now, I gotta get back to handling my business. I have a big, stiff horse in my bed waiting to be ridden. Ride 'em, cowgirl!" I laughed, playing things off as if I were cool. I knew it would piss her off, and that was the point. I had to keep her safe. But I needed to send an SOS at the same time, too.

"You know, you can be so damned callous and cold when you want to be." Naomi was shaking her head at me with a frown and a look of disappointment. "I tell you that your best friend's husband is in the hospital and her life's been turned upside down, and all you can think about is sex! I hope you wrapped it up, because one day your sex addiction is going to be the end of you. Quit playing games with your life, Paige," my best friend warned. I couldn't help but think about how ironic her words were. She had unknowingly predicted the situation that I was already in.

"Look, I gotta go. I didn't ask you to come over here judging me. So, to hell with what you and Helena Rose think. You two are always judging my sex life. I gots to get mine." I slammed the door in my friend's face. I turned back to David with a weary smile on my face.

He walked me back to my room and laid me on the bed, once again handcuffing me. David removed my bra and fondled my breasts with rough, calloused hands. My skin was sore and bristled at the touch of his palm against me. I had been lying in bed for so long, my body was sore and feeling bruised all over. When David took a nipple into his mouth, my toes curled, and not from passion, but disgust. I cringed and dug my nails into the palms of my hands. He continued to moan as he sucked on my nipple, which had betrayed me by becoming hard and stiff. Encouraged by this act of abandonment on behalf of my body, he pulled at my panties and began placing two fingers inside of me.

I had to figure out a way to regain his trust. Something had to give. I couldn't continue to lie in this bed day after day, not moving and losing energy and strength. I had succumbed to self-pity, and that wasn't like me. I couldn't formulate a plan in the state of mind that I was in. I was scared I would fall into a state of depression if I didn't change my situation soon. So, I decided to use what I had been good at to get him back on my side.

As David stroked my inner folds with his fingers, I began to gyrate my hips, lifting up slightly to encourage him. Inside my head, I continued to envision myself free and seeing this bastard dead for the cruelty and torture he had inflicted on me. From somewhere deep within, I summoned moans and whispers to make him believe I wanted what he had to offer. I knew that it wouldn't happen overnight, but I knew that if I could get him to trust me again, he would release me from the handcuffs.

David removed his fingers from within me and pulled my panties down around my hips. I lifted my body from the bed to assist him. Once he had me in the raw, he lowered his head between my legs to take a taste of me. This was normally my favorite part of any sexual encounter with a man. But not today. I wasn't working to have any form of release, except the physical release from the handcuffs and punishment that my warden had decided I needed.

"David, mmm, that feels so good, baby. Deeper," I encouraged. Inside, I was coaching myself not to throw up and give myself away. The last several days my jewel always remained dry when he tried to have sex with me, creating soreness and pain for him and me both. I would beg and plead with him to leave me alone and try to fight him off. But those efforts only left me with more cuts and threats until I would finally surrender, lying stiff under him. I knew I had to be careful in my approach today, because I didn't want him suspicious as to why I was suddenly giving him what he wanted, something I had been denying him the last few days.

"Like that, huh?" he murmured, looking into my eyes before lowering his head again.

"Yeah," I whispered in a hoarse voice. With my left hand, I pushed his head further between my legs as he sucked and licked. I clamped my legs around his head, tightening with each stroke that he rendered. Viciously, I began bucking my hips against his mouth and pretending I was in the throes of passion.

He pulled back to prevent me from releasing and prepared to have sex with me as he removed his own underwear. I clamped my legs closed with my hand between my legs as I rolled from side to side, shaking my head back and forth. I released moans of passion, pretending that I had experienced my release despite the fact he had stopped.

"Damn, girl! Why you leave me?" he asked, frustrated as he held his penis in his hand.

"I'm sorry, David. I didn't mean to, but it's just…I've been so mad at you. We can try again later."

"Nah, we gon' do it now!" he exclaimed, as he climbed onto the bed with me and grabbed me around the neck. Tears instantly sprung to my eyes as I attempted not to fight back. I willed everything within me to go still and humble. The moment I was able to do that, it triggered something in David. I could see it in his eyes. He released his hold around my neck, bent down, and pressed a kiss to my lips. His cracked lips felt like a paper cut to my soft, moist ones. I quickly flicked my tongue out to soothe the spot he had pierced with his lips.

Once again, he forced himself inside of me, and this time, I allowed it without any argument or hesitation. It was all a part of my plan. I knew that I had to work the plan and work it well. After all, this man had brought my body to ultimate pleasure so many times. And I knew that he could do it again if I allowed him to. It wasn't about being disgusted at the moment. It wasn't about denying him something that didn't belong to him. It was about survival. It was about the game of manipulation, of power and control. It was about victory and winning in this game of lunacy he had launched. It was about freedom and revenge. And boy oh boy, would my revenge be ever so sweet.

So, while some women would have been miserable over being raped, I took control of my destiny. I knew that I could use this to my advantage, and therefore, I refused to look at it as rape anymore. I would allow him to have me and use me as often as he needed to. Just like I had in the past. But this time, I was doing it with purpose.

David became more excited the more that I allowed him to take advantage of me. The more I opened myself up to him and the more I participated and made him believe I was interested, the more turned on he became. He forgot for a moment that he was supposed to be angry at me and abusing me. He was caught up in the moment, and I used my feminine wiles and passion to control the outcome of this situation.

In the midst of David calling my name, his phone began to ring. Unfortunately, the ring tone indicated that it was his wife calling. It was the first time she had called since he had been with me. My body stiffened, not sure what this would mean for me or my plan that I had launched.

David stopped in stride and turned to look at his phone on my dresser with a frown on his face. For just a moment, it appeared that he had become lucid, realizing what he had done. A look of regret and guilt crossed his face. I had to take control of the moment while it was still on my side.

I knew that if I let go of the control I had, it could turn the tides against me. I didn't want to fathom what the outcome could be. In that moment, I squeezed my PC muscles, pumping against him a little harder. I used my one free hand and pulled him to me.

"Mmm, baby, don't stop. You feel so good, big daddy," I moaned, and then licked my tongue across my lips. The clenching of my muscles was all I needed to regain the little control I had.

David turned his head back to me, stared into my eyes, and went back to work, pumping harder than ever before and moaning, "Paaaige...oh, baby. Yeah, you know how I like it. Work it, girl, work it!"

22_AMBIANCE_A CUP OF COFFEE

Tired. That was the only way to describe what I was feeling. I was physically, mentally, and emotionally exhausted. Eric was not making any progress at all. His last round of test results showed some swelling on the brain. The doctors were working to eliminate the swelling, but the prognosis didn't look too good. In the very beginning, we were told that ninety percent of patients don't recover consciousness, and of the ten percent that do, they often have severe impairment. I didn't want any of this for Eric, and I knew that I served a God who was a great Healer.

Yet, I couldn't help but wonder what would happen to our marriage once he did recover and completely regain the full use of his faculties. Everyone around me tried to prepare me for the worst, including Eric's parents, but I wasn't hearing it. I sat by his bed every day reading to him from the *New York* and *Oxford Journals*. I read scriptures to him from the Bible and prayed with him daily. I talked to him about our future and our past, letting him know that I had forgiven him for the choices he had made, and praying that he would forgive me for the ones I had made.

It was during one of these conversations that Danielle walked into the room. I could only hope that she hadn't overheard what was to be a private moment between husband and wife. I set the crossword puzzle I had been working on down on the table next to me and stood. I wasn't sure why she was there without her husband, but it was her right as family. I would allow her to have her own moment of privacy with her brother-in-law, because I definitely didn't want to be the recipient of her kind of evil. I just wasn't in the mood for it. And to be honest, I had never had the backbone to stand up to her.

"I'll give you some time alone with him," I said by way of greeting as I walked past my husband's bed, prepared to exit the room.

"Ambiance," Danielle said in a soft-spoken voice, one that caught me off guard. I was used to her speaking mean words to me in a hateful tone, but this was a voice that was only reserved for those she cared about…and I was not counted among that fortunate few.

"Yes?" I acknowledged, halting my progress toward the door.

"I actually came to see you. Do you think we can have a moment?" she asked.

"Sure." I couldn't begin to understand why she would want to converse with me. I was hopeful and nervous at the same time.

"Can we go to the cafeteria and grab a cup of coffee?" she suggested.

"I don't see why not," I said, leading the way out of my husband's room. Danielle followed me to the elevator, and we made small talk about his progress along the way. I updated her on the latest round of tests, and she listened intently.

After we grabbed coffee and doctored it to our individual tastes, she glanced at me with an apologetic look on her face.

"Look, I know you're probably wondering what I want with you since I could hardly be bothered to speak to you before."

"Yes, the thought had crossed my mind," I conceded.

"Stephen Jr. and Hope have always been on me about how I treat you. And I've never acknowledged it before, but lately I have had time to think about my actions. Watching Eric in that hospital bed and the effect it's having on everyone has given me time to think. I know we're not promised tomorrow, but it hit home after Eric's accident. I started thinking about how many bridges I've burned through the years, and I don't want anything to happen to me knowing that I haven't given my best here on Earth, or that I hadn't been forgiven by others or forgiven others. You know what I mean?"

I merely shook my head and sipped at my coffee. Sounded like somebody had experienced a "come to Jesus moment."

"You're not going to make this easy for me, are you?" she laughed, and a knowing smile graced her pretty face.

"It's just that I don't understand. I hear what you're saying, but none of it ever made sense to me in the first place. I haven't done anything to you for you to treat me the way you have. You've always acted as if you hated me and treated me like some outcast. You've talked down to me and humiliated me in front of others every chance you've gotten." It felt good to have this discussion and let out my feelings.

"I was jealous of you," she confessed, shocking me to my core.

"Jealous of me?" I asked.

She nodded her head at me.

"For what? I don't have anything for you to be jealous of, Danielle."

"I was jealous, because you got what I wanted. Hope told me that she shared my history with you about Eric and Stephen. But there are parts of the story no one knows. I don't even know why I'm telling you, except maybe to explain why I treated you the way that I did. It might sound crazy, but for a while, I *was* crazy. I was crazy about Eric. That man walked on water in my eyes. I mean, he was so handsome, so sexy and intelligent. Every time I was in his company, I felt like a young high school girl with a crush. I imagined every little thing that he said to me meant something else. Every late night that I had to work with him fueled my hopes of a relationship with him. I found excuses to be in his presence, to have lunch or dinner with him, or just to brush up against him. I would hold whatever blouse I had been wearing that day in my arms at night, sniffing his scent while fantasizing about him. And when that Christmas party came, I had finally drummed up the nerve to approach him…with a little bit of help from some alcohol. Truthfully, I wasn't drunk that night, but I've always allowed everyone to believe it to save myself some pride. I banked on him having enough drinks in him to at least get him in bed that night. I had been constantly by his side all night refilling his drinks in the hopes of getting him drunk. He could handle it better than I expected. I thought surely he would get drunk enough that I would have to drive him home, and I planned to take advantage of him. What I hadn't planned on was his clear rejection of me in front of everyone. I was mortified. Truthfully, when I became involved with Stephen, it was only with the hopes of making Eric jealous. I honestly thought that would get to him and eventually he would realize I was the one for him."

I was stunned at her revelations and the fact that she was being so candid with me. "What about Stephen? Weren't you worried it would hurt him if you left him for his brother? Especially after his brother rejected you?"

"Not at all. When it came to Eric, I couldn't think straight. Nothing else mattered except being around him. I was the one that came up with those boys' nights they always have. It was an excuse to be in the same vicinity as Eric. Stephen and I had moved in together after dating four months. I hoped Eric would see what a good woman I was and make a move on me. But it never happened. After a while, I finally gave up hope of being with him as he brought one woman after another around. I began to lose focus on him and decided to give my relationship with Stephen an honest try. When I did, I was surprised to learn that I had real feelings for him, and we had a beautiful relationship. We still do, actually. I began to forget about my feelings for Eric and feel sorry for him. He was the one missing out on a beautiful relationship with some special person. Every time he brought a date around, it was a different woman, and I knew that it was all about the sex. Until you came on the scene. Everything changed. Although I had accepted the fact that Eric and I wouldn't have this relationship I once dreamt about, and I had gotten over him, or so I thought. I couldn't reconcile him settling down with anyone. I always chalked up his refusal to enter a relationship with me up to the fact that he would always be a playboy. It made it easier for me to accept his rejection. You know, kind of like, it's not you, it's me? And when he settled down and then married you, it lit a fire under me. I was furious and determined to make your life miserable. Then, as callous as it sounds, when I learned he was messing around on you, I gained satisfaction in that. Every time he came to our house with Kendra, I received a moment of pleasure from that. I wanted so many times to call and invite you over out of the blue. But I knew that would create problems between Stephen and I, which wasn't worth it. So, I just basked in the pleasure I got from knowing that he was unfaithful to you. It was a small measure of pleasure, because the truth was, regardless of what he was doing, he was still married to you and didn't plan to leave," she explained.

This chick was on some other kind of crazy. I laughed a bitter laugh. "Well, that's where you're wrong, Danielle. Apparently, that wonderful man that you and I both desired to have as our own, did plan to leave me. He wouldn't be yours, but he was never going to be mine either. I was sharing him with another woman for all these years and didn't realize to what extent I was sharing him."

"Girlfriend, I honestly don't think Eric would have left you. I believe it was just a phase he was going through."

"I would love to believe what you say, Danielle, it would do my ego well. Unfortunately, it's true," I confided.

She took a sip of her coffee, watching me as I watched her with a guarded expression. I didn't know how much I could trust her.

"You know, I feel so bad about all the thoughts I ever had against you. You deserved better than what you were getting. You're a good girl and a helluva wife. I wouldn't have put up with it. I would have taken his sorry ass for everything he was worth a long time ago. He didn't deserve you. There's something else that I want to share with you. Something no one else will want you to know, and I think you should."

"What's that?" I didn't know if I could take any more surprises. I had already had too many since Eric had this accident.

"Just before the accident, he had called Stephen ranting and raving about you having an affair on him. Now, I don't know how true it is, but just listen, Ambiance," she warned, as she held up her hand to stave off my forthcoming comments.

"He told Stephen he had seen you at a restaurant kissing some man, and he wanted to kill you and the guy. He went on and on about how he couldn't believe you would hassle him so bad, when you were messing around, too. Stephen told him it was what he deserved after taking you through the hell he'd taken you through. Said that he was a hypocrite for judging you the way he had and that you deserved happiness. Hope and Stephen Sr. know this as well, but they were advocating for him to leave Kendra alone and work things out with you. I just want to say, whatever decision you make, make the one that's best for your heart, Ambiance. You've put your time in, and I'm not telling you to leave him now, but don't stop your life for a maybe. Eric's always been arrogant and condescending, and he's always taken you for granted. Don't put your hopes in a dream that may not come to pass."

I wondered if she was being honest with me, or if she was still hoping that he and I would break up for her own selfish reasons. It didn't matter. It was time to put all this evil to rest, which was God's will.

I reached my hand across the table to pat Danielle's. "Sweetie, I'm so thankful that you've come to put to an end this warfare that has been going on between us. And I thank you for letting me know the entire family knew about something that I didn't even know about. I have a friend who means a lot to me, but I wasn't having an affair. At least not in the sense that my husband led you all to believe. I received friendship and concern from a man who cared about me when my husband abandoned me. The kiss my husband saw in the parking lot that day was the most intimacy I had ever shared with that man. And while I owe no one an explanation, I do owe it to my husband and to my friend to be free and clear before pursuing anything with him. I'm grateful for your honesty, your kind words, and advice, but the journey that I'm on now has nothing to do with Eric or my friend. It's about my relationship with the Lord. I can't move forward with or without Eric until God releases me to do so."

"I never thought that I would say this, Ambiance, but I admire you."

"For what?" I asked. Danielle seemed so sincere. I couldn't imagine what she would gain from the confessions she was making this day, except to free her conscience as she stated at the beginning.

"You're a strong woman. You've been taken through a lot of hurt by this man, but you've never lost your sense of self. You continue to hold strong to your values and your faith. I would love to enjoy a close relationship with God the way you appear to and be comfortable in my journey with Him, as well."

I smiled at Danielle from the heart. "You can, Danielle. Just get alone with Him, speak what's on your heart, and keep your heart open. But above all, keep it real with Him. He will speak to you and lead you if you let Him. I promise. I know I couldn't make it without Him. The strength that you think you see is all Him."

"Well, I might've already said this before, but I want what you've got. I want Him, too," she joked.

We laughed together, and I knew that she meant it as much this time as she had the previous times. But only this time, we were referring to a different Man. One that we could both share and enjoy, One that would never let us down.

****

Later that evening, I was in Eric's room when the beeping of his heart monitor changed. I looked up from the designs I was completing for the fashion show and tossed my drawings to the side. I didn't know how to read the cardiac monitor, but I knew that everything appeared to be out of sync. The only thing that I did know was there were more squiggly lines on the monitor than I had ever seen. I pushed the nurse's button to call for help, but the doors burst open before I could move away from his bedside.

Nurses and doctors came crashing through the doors, pushing me out of the way.

"What's going on?" I shouted, wanting someone to tell me something. I didn't care who it was, I needed to know something about what was happening to my husband. They had begun to attach wires to his chest after ripping open his gown. New needles were added in his arms that had not been there previously. There was a lot of chattering and bustling going on in that little, tight room. Everyone was calling out codes and colors that I could not understand, and pushing me further back to the door. Finally, a young nurse hustled over to me.

"Come on, honey. I know all of this appears frightening at the moment, but we need as much room as we can get. Come and take a seat in the waiting room, and I promise we'll be with you shortly."

"But what's going on?" I pleaded. I needed to know something. Tears were running down my face like a runaway train. My heart was pounding in my chest, and emotions were swirling through me like a violent storm.

"Sweetie, just have a seat here," she said, ushering me to a chair just down the hall from Eric's room. "I promise, a doctor will be back to talk to you soon." She hurried back down the hall, leaving all of my questions unanswered, with a strong sense of fear attempting to creep into me.

All I could do was call his parents, my parents, and Naomi. She was the first to arrive on the scene, because she had been in the area picking up dinner for me. Naomi's plans had included stopping by the hospital three times a week to make sure I ate, and tonight was one of the nights for her to do that.

She sat calmly by my side, holding my hand and praying. Her prayers were interrupted as Danielle and Stephen Jr. came rushing through the door.

"Hey, Dad just called and told us to get down here. What's going on?" Stephen Jr. queried.

Tears were still pouring down my face. I had no new news to offer Eric's family. "I don't know. I was sitting in there one moment doing some work, and the next thing I knew, his monitor started going off," I wailed.

Danielle grabbed a handful of tissues, handed them to me, and sat on the other side of me. Giving her a thankful look, I wiped my eyes and nose and turned my attention back to Stephen Jr. He had sat down on the other side of me when Naomi had graciously given up her seat to sit across from us.

"I called the nurse in, but they were already on their way in. They started putting all these patches and plugs on his chest and arms and pushed me out the room. She wouldn't tell me anything. She said I had to wait, and nobody's come outttt," I howled into my brother-in-law's arms.

I had been crying, but relatively strong, until the moment he came. There was something about a man's presence in this situation that let me know I didn't have to be strong anymore.

And so it was, when my in-laws, brother-in-law, Marc, and parents arrived, Stephen was holding and rocking me in his arms in an effort to comfort me. Danielle and Naomi were sitting in chairs behind us, holding hands and praying.

"Where's my boy?" Stephen Sr. came storming through the doorways, demanding.

"Dad, we don't know anything right now. They pushed Ambi out of the room while they worked on him," Stephen Jr. replied.

"Well, what kind of work are they doing? Why did they have to work on him?" he demanded to know.

"Dad, we don't know anything different than we knew before. What she told you on the phone is still what we know," Stephen Jr. explained.

"Why the hell not? Who the hell's in charge around here?" Stephen Sr. shouted, as he stomped away from our small group like a general leading his troops into battle. He went towards the nurses' station, raising pure cane as they attempted to calm him down. I silently wished them luck but was glad I wasn't the one having to deal with him.

"Honey, come on, let's get some coffee or something to calm your nerves," Alexis, my step-mom, suggested. She and my dad had arrived at the same time as Eric's parents.

"Uh-uh, I need to be here in case they come out with news. I have to be here!" I was a bundle of nerves and becoming difficult to deal with.

"Okay, honey, it's okay. You don't have to go anywhere. I'll go get you some and bring it back," Alexis suggested. She bent down and kissed me on the forehead, and then she turned to mumble something to my father, who nodded and sat down next to me.

We had been sitting there for almost two hours before my father-in-law couldn't take anymore. He got up once again to get results, because his first efforts were futile. I could hear his voice echoing off the walls as he gave the nurses at the station a hard time. I tried, for the most part, to stay in a place of peace, and ignore what he was saying. I was relatively successful until something got under his skin.

"...and I mean it!" Stephen Sr. thundered.

I wasn't sure what he meant or what he had been going on about, but whatever it was got results, because the nurses jumped to attend to his orders. They came back and stated a doctor would be out soon to give us an update.

Soon turned into another twenty minutes before the nurse came to see us with a doctor.

He spoke with her in private a few moments and then walked up to our group.

"Mrs. Caldwell?" he asked.

"Yes?" That was both Hope and me replying at the same time.

"Umm, which of you is Mrs. Eric Caldwell?" he asked.

Everyone pointed to me. "That would be her," Danielle offered. I wasn't sure that I wanted to be who he wanted me to be at that moment.

"Hi, I'm Dr. Kamdar," he stated, extending his hand to shake mine. "Can I speak with you for just a second?"

For some reason, I couldn't look him in the eyes. I was focused on the gold name plate affixed to his lab coat. I wondered how his first name was pronounced. It was Maneesh. I begin to wonder if it was pronounced like "man-nish," or "man-eesh," as it was spelled. Then I began to wonder if he was a mannish little boy when he was younger. I know...I know, this all sounds crazy, but I couldn't help my reaction. It was the only thing that was keeping me from breaking into tears.

"Mrs. Caldwell, please follow me," He walked away assuming I was right behind him. I wasn't. Everyone noticed my hesitation except him.

"Dr. Kamdar, we're Eric's parents," my father-in-law announced, as he pointed at himself and Hope and my parents, "and these are his siblings," he stated, pointing around at the rest of the group. "We're going, as well," my father-in-law announced. It was a statement that left no room for discussion.

Dr. Kamdar turned his head and nodded. "Please do." The nurse followed us.

A few hundred feet around a corner was a private conference room we were ushered into and the nurse closed the door behind her.

Dr. Kamdar was a Middle Eastern gentlemen somewhere in his late thirties, although by his youthful appearance, he could've easily been in his mid-twenties. He had a gentle and humble appearance. He stood a few inches over six feet tall, with his hands pocketed inside of his lab coat. He wore blue, wire framed glasses that perched on a slightly elongated nose.

"Mrs. Caldwell, Mr. and Mrs. Caldwell, Eric has suffered from complications of swelling on the brain and the pneumonia he was diagnosed with a couple of days ago. There are no cerebral or brain stem functions present…" he stated.

"What the hell does all of that mean?" my father-in-law asked.

"It means he's been declared brain dead," Dr. Kamdar continued to explain. "At this point, we are suggesting that his ventilator, feedings, and fluids be ceased because they are futile. We can continue to offer him sedatives to ensure his comfort, but there's little else that can be done at this point."

"But, what if there's a chance that he will survive? We won't know unless we continue to try, right?" This was Danielle speaking up. I wasn't sure whose behalf she was speaking on…hers, mine, or Eric's.

"No, ma'am. I'm sorry but there's nothing the life support system can continue to do except prolong his transitioning." Dr. Kamdar's voice was sympathetic, and his face filled with compassion.

My heart was breaking at the news he was delivering, but I felt bad for him. I knew he wanted to be anywhere but here at this moment, because I knew I did. I couldn't get past his pronouncement that my husband had basically passed away.

"Can't we dispute your suggestion, Doctor?" Stephen Jr. asked.

"You could, but it wouldn't do you any good. If the board declares it's not in his best interest, you would have to take it further. I can't make the decision for you, it's a strong recommendation his team of doctors have come to. We didn't arrive at our conclusion lightly, but we know there's nothing more that the life support system can do for him. With the fluid on his brain and the complications of pneumonia, wellll...it was too much for Eric to stand. Ultimately, the decision rests with Mrs. Eric Caldwell." Dr. Kamdar made the proclamation and turned towards me. I felt as if a judge had just pronounced me guilty. Ten pairs of eyes turned my way.

Eric's youngest brother, Marc, cleared his throat. "Ambi?" The one word he spoke let me know he, along with everyone else, was interested in hearing what I would have to say. This was too much for me, and my dad knew it, because he chose that moment to speak up.

"Can't she have some time to decide what to do? I mean, you all kind of just threw this in her lap, and that's a huge responsibility. She's still struggling with what to do about her husband's accident, and now this?"

My heart swelled at my father's protection of me...his little girl, his angel, his baby. But I knew that would only be giving me an "out." I couldn't do that. It was time for me to stand tall and make a decision. I knew that the family would be torn, but I had to do what I knew was right.

"Dr. Kamdar, Eric and I have discussed this in the past. We didn't honestly think it would happen to us, but I know what his wishes are. Please remove the ventilator and feeding systems. My husband would not want this," I expressed.

I heard a loud cry of disbelief, one that I knew came from Danielle. It was quickly followed by, "Oh, God...nooo...nooo," and then a hiccupping cry...that was Hope.

"You would do this, wouldn't you?" Marc accused, pointing a finger in my face. "Is this your payback for his affairs, or are you trying to get rid of my brother to be with that other man?"

My heart ripped in my chest. This was not what I wanted or needed.

"Marc! Stop it, right now!" That was Stephen Sr. "Ambiance is not doing this out of vindictiveness. You heard the doctor! We have to face the fact your brother has passed."

"No, Dad, let's face the truth! She's happy about this. Why couldn't she give him a chance?" Marc was screaming at this point and attempting to get at me, but Stephen Jr. grabbed his little brother and began pulling him from the room.

I felt Alexis' and my father's arms surround me at once, and I saw Dr. Kamdar leave the room swiftly.

I wasn't sure what happened next, but I in my mind, I went to some faraway land. People often make jokes about the old *Peanuts* cartoon, where Charlie Brown's teacher is talking to him, and she sounds like "Womp, womp, womp, womp, womp." Well, let me tell you that's not a lie. That's exactly what their voices sounded like to me, until I began to see blue butterflies, green and gold fairies, and silver fairy dust floating around.

There was something beautifully sweet and light about all those fairies and butterflies floating around. They made the atmosphere so peaceful and relaxing. They smelled like cotton candy, cinnamon, and vanilla, and their wings tinkled like wisps of hair lightly touching your nose every time they floated by. The fairies giggled at my puzzled expression as I wondered where they had come from. Something about their giggles reminded me of angels singing. I knew their voices would be what the angels sounded like when we went to Heaven. Such a beautiful and blessed sound. Such a welcoming sound and sight to behold. I would've loved to have shared this experience with everyone. But as with any thing in life, all good things come to an end. And so did my visit to fairyland as I heard Alexis calling out to me.

I turned my head left and right and couldn't determine where her voice was coming from. I could only imagine she was in a distant land, but she needed me. I could tell by the urgency that she needed my help. She was saying something about coming back to her, and I knew that I needed to. I loved Alexis; she was the only mother I had ever known and I had no plans to abandon her...not yet, anyway.

I blinked my eyes rapidly, wanting the bright lights to go away. I rolled my head to the left and saw a blue and white-striped curtain. I rolled my head to the right and saw Alexis standing by my side with a worried expression. She squeezed my right hand tightly and smiled when I looked up at her. A tear rolled down her face as she pressed her lips together in a tight line. My father stood behind her with a hand on her shoulder. He appeared to be worried about me, as well, and didn't wear a smile. Then I looked down and saw Naomi and Hope standing at the foot of the bed.

Naomi gave me a smile of reassurance and squeezed my foot, which was no longer clad in the shoes I had been wearing. I only had my black stockings on my feet. She gave me a simple wink and smile. Then I turned my eyes to my mother-in-law standing next to her. Hope's eyes were red-rimmed, and her mascara had run. She didn't wear a smile at all, but she also wasn't frowning. She was heart-broken and in pain. I could tell by the tightening around her eyes and how she was fighting back the tears.

I had no clue why I was lying in a hospital bed or what was wrong with my family. I was preparing to ask where Stephen Sr. and everyone else was. I didn't get a chance to pose my question, because my mother-in-law took the opportunity right out of my hands.

"Honey, no matter what was said, or what happens from here on out, I want you to know something," she began.

I swallowed past the dry lump I felt in my throat. My lips felt sore and chapped, but I pressed on. "What's that?" I asked, in a dry and hoarse voice.

"You did the right thing. Eric would have wanted that. And I'm proud that you stood strong to what you knew was best. He would have been, too," she stated.

In that moment, everything came flashing back to me. I recalled the decision I had had to make, along with everyone's reaction. Then I recalled the fairies, the dust, and the butterflies, and the reason they had come to visit me. I had obviously fainted from the stress and strain I had just gone through from having to confirm that we were pulling the plug on my husband. Eric Caldwell no longer existed. It was time for me to plan his funeral. I was a widower, lost and all alone. And most of all, I was unloved. And that was when I broke.

23_NAOMI_HELENA ROSE

There's only so much a woman can take. I had always been known to be that strength for my girls, and I wouldn't fail now. Paige was going through something that I couldn't quite figure out. I wanted to shake the fool out of her for the way she had behaved at her apartment. She was one of my best friends, and I loved her like a sister. But her sex addiction would be the end of her if she wasn't careful. I was furious with her. How could she make sex a priority when I was standing outside her home telling her that our best friend, our girl, our sister, had been struggling with her husband's car accident and it wasn't looking too good for him?

My daughter had been trying to free herself from me after our argument. I couldn't believe she was still mad at me and attempting to leave to go live with her father, a father she had only known for a little while. I felt so hurt and betrayed, I didn't know what to do. But I had to place my feelings on a shelf as this latest development occurred with Ambiance.

My almost nightly run to bring her dinner to the hospital had turned into a visit to offer solace in her time of grief. I had difficulty believing cocky, arrogant Eric was no longer alive. He had always been so vibrant, so full of attitude, almost larger than life. You definitely felt his presence anytime he was on the scene. And while I hadn't appreciated what he had taken my friend through, I didn't wish his life to be cut short so soon. And I definitely didn't wish the heartache and pain she was going through on anyone, let alone someone as sweet as her.

I had to get through to Paige. We were going to have to be there to support Ambiance. Eric's funeral was in three days, and Paige was nowhere to be found.

I was preparing to go back to her home when I decided to call her mother. I would let her know what was going on with Ambiance, but in all the stress and drama of the last few days, I had forgotten to call Paige's mother. She had her issues, but I knew that she cared about me and Ambiance almost as much as she cared about her own daughter.

"Hi, Helena, how are you?" I greeted Paige's mother. I hadn't talked to her in several months and felt ashamed. I usually spoke with her at least once a month, but as I calculated in my mind, I realized it had been at least four months since we had last spoken.

"Honey, I'm good! How you been, sugar?" she asked. I could hear the excitement in her voice at hearing from me.

"I've been doing well."

"What about Sasha? I bet she's gotten so big. What's she in, tenth grade now?" she asked, speech a bit slurred. I could hear her take a quick guzzle of her favorite drink…Colt 45!

"No, ma'am. Actually, she's a junior in high school."

"Oh, Lord, y'all must be getting old," Helena joked. She always teased us that her spirit was younger than ours. She said she could drink us under the table on a good day. I often thought she could drink a sailor under the table on a bad day. And although she no longer went clubbing in her older years, she was still fond of having a good time at her house or one of her friends'.

I laughed and agreed and told her about Eric's passing before I got down to the real reason for my call. "Helena, when was the last time you spoke with Paige?" I asked.

"Um, it's been a couple of weeks, now. I called her a few times this week, and I guess she's too busy to return my call." Helena sounded dejected. I felt bad for her, because although her alcoholism had caused her daughter a lot of pain, she still deserved Paige's undivided attention and love.

"Yeah, I know what you mean."

"You been calling her, too, sugar?" she asked.

"Yes, ma'am. She wouldn't return my calls so I went by earlier this week," I explained.

"What'd she say? Did you see her?"

"Yes, ma'am. She was talking crazy, as usual. You know how Paige gets." I didn't want to go into how vulgar she was acting and talking, or the fact that I had clearly caught her in the middle of sex.

"Yeah. I know. Shoulda gone up in there and whipped her butt and told her 'bout herself. Matter of fact, I think I'ma do just that. I'll go over there this evening," she declared.

"Don't worry about it, Helena. I'll go back over there. I think she was fronting for some man. I might catch her alone this evening, and things might be different. I think the only reason she said half the things she said, is because she must have been trying to prove something to whoever she had over there that day," I explained. I didn't want Helena going over there and risking the chance that Paige would hurt her feelings the way she had mine. There was a strained relationship between the two, and I didn't want to add to the strain.

"What kinda stuff was she saying?" Helena asked.

I weighed out what I would share versus what I wouldn't. I was treading on shaky grounds when dealing with those two.

"Well, she was saying how she had been so busy she hadn't had time to catch up with me. I told her about Ambiance's husband, Eric, and she didn't really seem upset about it. I told her about his accident, and at that time, he hadn't passed away. But she dismissed it like it wasn't important. So, I started lecturing her about her attitude, and she got mad. She said she didn't need us judging her," I explained.

"Doesn't need who judging her? Cuz, I ain't judging her," Helena defended.

"I know, but she was just crazy that day. As a matter of fact, she said she didn't need me or Helena Rose judg—"

"Wait, she said what?!" Helena practically shouted in my ear.

"What are you talking about?"

"She said she didn't need who doing what?"

"Me or you judging her. What's wrong, Helena?" I asked. I was clearly missing something.

"What did she call me, Naomi?"

"Helena Rose."

"Damnit! My baby girl's in trouble!" she proclaimed. I had no clue what she was talking about, and before I could ask, she began rambling on. "That was our code word when she was a lil' girl. If something happened to me or her, she was s'posed to use that name."

"What do you mean?" I asked.

"That's not my name. My whole name is Helena Yvonne. Rose was my sister's middle name, Laura Rose. Paige always seen the issues our husbands took us through in our marriages. So, I told her if she was ever in trouble or something happened to me, Helena Rose was the code word that we needed to get help. How was she acting?"

I had to rapidly think back to the day I had visited her. The truth of the matter was, I can't say that I saw anything out of the ordinary. Paige had always been a smart ass and a sex maniac. There was nothing different about that day, except that she had been kind of modest. I recalled her standing behind her door when she answered it, hiding her body and sticking her head out of the door for me to see. Paige had never shown any modesty and had no problem prancing around naked in front of me or Ambiance. But that day she wore a bra, I could tell that much, but she was hiding her body as if she didn't want to be seen. I had also been to her house on other occasions when she had a man over, and she still didn't hide her body away the way she had that day. I told all of this to Helena, now not wanting to leave out a single detail because it could be important.

"Sugar, I'm calling the police. You get on over there, and I'm heading over there, too. But don't you take yourself up to her place. Wait in that car 'til I get there. You hear?" she ordered.

The-mild mannered woman had taken over where I had left off. We had shifted gears as I went into order-taking mode, not sure what all of this meant. I went through my head, trying to remember anything that I could think of that would have put Paige in trouble. I couldn't recall her having issues with any men except for Vic, who was crazy about her. Men whose love wasn't returned had been known to lose their mind. I hoped for my friend's sake that wasn't the case.

I left my office and headed to Paige's place. I decided against calling Ambiance, because she had enough to worry about. But I did call my parents and Jaime to let them know what was going on. I wasn't sure why I called Jaime to drag him into this mess. I only knew that if something happened to me, he needed to know for our daughter's sake.

"Do you want me to meet you there?" he asked.

"No, I think we'll be fine. I just wanted you to know. God forbid anything should happen, but at least you could explain it to Sasha," I explained.

"Yeah, Naomi, about that…I'm sorry about everything that's happening. I had no intention of making things worse between you and her, or being an escape for her not to deal with her problems."

"Don't worry, Jaime. This isn't the first time she's been mad at me, and it definitely won't be the last. And I won't let her use you as an escape route. She's going to deal with her problems and not run from them."

"Is she speaking to you again?" he asked.

"No." I sighed, as I maneuvered my vehicle onto 285-West, headed to Smyrna. "She's absolutely refused to say anything to me since that day. Well, at least not just simple conversation. Sasha knows she has to answer questions when I speak to her, but other than that, she sits up in her room and sulks."

"I thought she'd be mad at me when I backed you up about her not moving in with me. So, I was surprised when she kept calling me every day after the weekend trip," Jaime stated.

I could hear both the surprise and satisfaction in his voice. He didn't want me to know that he was happy about her calling him even though she wasn't speaking to me. He tried to downplay it, but I could hear the truth. It didn't bother me, though.

"That's a good thing, Jaime. She needs to know that she can depend on you. She also has to know that we are on the same page when it comes to decisions regarding her."

I didn't want him to get caught up in trying to be her friend rather than her parent. It was a difficult situation he was in, because he didn't help raise her, but she needed to respect him as the adult in the relationship.

"Definitely. I wouldn't knowingly do anything to undermine you." He hesitated for a brief moment. "Look, she called me last night, you know."

"Trying to get you to come and pick her up again?" I asked.

"Yeah. She said that she was of age to determine which parent she wanted to live with. She said she felt she could develop a close bond with me if she spent more time with me. Then she went on to say how it was only fair, because you had put all your years in raising her and I had lived my life. Said that you deserved to live yours, as well, and it was my turn to take care of her."

There it was…Sasha had set out to do exactly what she wanted. She had played her guilt trip well, and Jaime had fallen for it hook, line, and sinker. He didn't want to admit to me that he had, but I knew he had. He was fishing for information now to see how I would react. He was hoping I would play into his hands and make the decision for him. Caught between a rock and a hard place, Jaime wasn't bold enough to tell me he wanted to take my daughter; instead, he relied on telling me the story she had weaved, hoping I would concede.

He had the wrong mama. I wasn't going to play his game, or Sasha's.

"Well, Jaime, what are you going to do?" I threw the ball back into his court. Regardless to what he decided, the decision would have to be his, because I wasn't making it for him. I wasn't going to tell him that he could have her and spend time building a bond. And I wasn't going to fight him and tell him that he couldn't have his daughter. Of course, I didn't want her to go, but they had a decision to make, and I wasn't going to make it easy for him or her.

"Well, I was thinking…I was wondering. Uh…I don't know, how do you feel? Do you think you need the time to yourself?" His voice was a little bit quivery with confusion. If I hadn't known him as a teen as well as I had, I would have missed it. But yes, he was nervous. He didn't want me to tear into him, but he wanted to make a stand for his daughter.

"This isn't about me, Jaime. This is about you and Sasha. She wants to come with you, but she also has roots in her school. You don't live in this district or even in the same town we live in. So, it's your decision. You have to consider if you're ready to take her and the impact that will have on your family and marriage. You also need to consider the impact it will have on Sasha, as well as the adjustment period that's coming with it. Don't forget to factor in what you'll do about school, because she's vested in that school. So, you have to determine if you're going to transfer her, the impact it will have on her and her academics, and if you're not, transporting her back and forth to school is a major concern. And that's just some of the factors you'll need to consider. Either way, the decision is yours. I suggest you sit down and have a conversation with Natalie before making a decision."

"Yeah, you're right," he agreed. His voice sounded a bit overwhelmed now.

"All right, I have to go, Jaime. I'm pulling up to Paige's place, now. I'll talk to you later."

"Okay. And be careful, Naomi. You've got a lot of people counting on you. And the primary one is Sasha," he warned.

"I know, I know. I'll be safe."

"Are you sure you don't want me to drive over? I can be there in about fifteen to twenty minutes," he offered.

"Nah, I'm good. But thanks for the offer."

"All right, if you change your mind, you know how to reach me," he stated.

"Okay, Jaime. Thanks. Oh, and by the way, let me know what you decide, okay?"

"About what?" he asked, sounding confused again.

"Our daughter." I clicked the phone off, not giving him a chance to respond. I believed I had been fair. Throughout this entire relationship he was building with her, I had worked hard to be fair. It had been important to me that they both felt as if they had my support as they built a relationship and a close bond. But I would not be made to feel like the villain by my daughter or her father just because I had made a mistake. As a single parent, I had made and would continue to make plenty of mistakes. They were right when they said that children don't come with handbooks. You have to learn as you go and pray that you make the right choices along the way. I didn't have a partner or spouse to bounce ideas off and hope that we got it right together. Nope, it was just me. But I was pretty sure I wasn't the only single parent who felt that way, or for that matter, even married parents made plenty of mistakes.

Pulling into Paige's complex, it didn't take me long to realize two patrol cars were already there. Her townhouse was located towards the front of her community. I quickly pulled my navy-blue Mustang into a spot three parking places down from the patrol cars. Shutting off the ignition, I grabbed my phone, keys, and purse, ignored Helena's advice, and jumped out.

I didn't bother locking it up, because Paige lived in a relatively secure, upscale community in Smyrna near the Market Village. Besides, I had the cops on my side, or at least I hoped I did. I walked the few paces to her portion of the building.

"Ma'am, can we assist you?" This came from a red-faced, red-haired police officer with his hand on his gun. Did he really think I posed a threat?

I stood at the bottom of the staircase looking up at him and his partner.

"My friend, Paige Dougherty, lives here, and her mother is the one that called you all to come out and check on her. I just visited her a few days ago, and things appeared to be normal until I had a phone conversation with her mother," I explained.

"And what's your name and business here now, ma'am?" The same officer spoke up, as his dark haired, tan, blue-eyed counterpart stood aside watching.

"I'm Naomi Blankenship, her best friend. I was coming to check on her again."

"No one's answering the door, ma'am. We've no reason to believe she might be here," the same officer explained.

"That's her red Camaro parked right there," I said, pointing to the car next to one of their patrol cars.

They both looked in the direction I pointed, and I could tell I had struck up a point of interest. "And when was the last time that you spoke to her?" The dark-haired officer finally spoke up in a deep, bass tone.

"Um, let's see, it was two days ago, around two o'clock. I stopped by to check on her and tell her about our other friend, whose husband has just passed. She blew me off in a manner that was unlike her." I knew timing was essential to filing a missing person's report. It had been over forty-eight hours.

"Did you actually see her?" This came from Officer Latkos. According to his badge, that was his name...the blue-eyed, dark-haired one.

"Yes, well, sort of. She stuck her head out the door and told me that she had company. I could only see her shoulder up to her head. She didn't invite me in, but she rushed me off rather quickly. I stopped by, because she hadn't been answering her phone in days."

"Have you called her recently?" Officer Latkos asked.

"No, I haven't tried. But she hasn't been to work, and they said she reported leaving town for a family emergency. Her mother said there's no emergency, and they don't have family out of town." I pulled her contact up in my cell phone and began calling her. Both officers stood by watching me as I attempted to reach my friend.

Once again, there was no answer. "Look, I have the key to her apartment. She gave it to me and our other friend in the event of an emergency. I can—"

"Technically, ma'am, we don't have a reason to search her house," Officer Leavenworth replied. He was the red-headed one.

"You don't, but I have permission to enter whenever I want to," I explained, as I pointed between me and them.

"No, ma'am, we can't let you do that. If there is something going on inside, you could run the risk of putting both yourself and your friend in danger. Do you honestly feel she's in jeopardy?" Officer Latkos asked.

"Well, at first I didn't, but now I'm not so sure. After speaking with her mother, I began to question everything. And it isn't like her not to answer or return our calls."

"Is there anyone who you know would want to cause her harm?" Officer Latkos was asking the questions now, and Leavenworth had begun taking notes. I could see they wanted to hear what I had to say.

"No one that I could think of." I paused, wondering if I should tell them everything. "Well, there's one guy that she dates who has a serious attachment to her. He's not happy about the fact that she's not exclusively seeing him. But there could be a number of people, because she dates quite a few different guys. I just can't think of anyone who would want to cause her harm," I explained.

"What's this gentleman's name you mentioned who is attached to her?" Officer Latkos inquired.

"Um, Vic. Victor Keenan."

"What do you know about this Victor Keenan?"

"Um, he's thirty-four, never been married, and doesn't have children. He's a systems engineer at Georgia Tech and lives in Conyers," I shared.

They whispered to one another for a moment, and then Officer Latkos jogged down the stairs to his patrol car, but not before advising me to follow along.

"Ms. Blankenship, please stay down here. I'm not sure what's going on with your friend, but we will get to the bottom of it. It would be so much easier if we could do that without putting you at risk. Can I please ask you to stay in your car and trust that you're going to do it?" Officer Leavenworth asked.

I nodded my head, because my stomach was too weak to speak. I didn't trust that I could say another word without throwing up. I had quickly become queasy and worried about the outcome and what was going on with my friend. I needed and wanted her to be okay. I had a feeling I was in for a long wait.

Paige's mom, Helena, pulled up about twenty minutes later. I dashed from my car to check on her state, because I knew that she was capable of driving while intoxicated. The last thing we needed was for her to get arrested for DUI.

"Ms. Helena, how are you?" I asked, as I grabbed her in a tight embrace. By the time she arrived, there were two other patrol cars on the scene.

"I'm fine, what's going on? Have they found out anything?" She was nervously chewing at her bottom lip, and I could tell she had been drinking more since our phone conversation. Despite the spicy fragrance she wore and the fresh scent of soap on her, she smelled like a fresh brewery as alcohol reeked from her pores.

"Yes, but let's get you settled over here with me. I don't want them to know you've been drinking and driving, because the last thing we need is to have you arrested, Ms. Helena," I explained in a loving tone.

"Oh, sugar, I just had a sip to calm my nerves. This chile got me all worked up. I've told her about living that fast lifestyle," Helena fussed, but she allowed me to lead her to my car and sit down.

Once I got her settled in my car, I proceeded to explain what I knew.

"They've confirmed that she called out of work for a week stating that she had a family emergency and would be out of town for—"

"But we ain't had no—"

"I know you told me that earlier. I let them know, and they had to confirm the accuracy of that statement. Also, they've confirmed that it isn't Victor Keenan, because he's at work right now and has been all week. They also confirmed that he was there on the day and time that I visited Paige earlier this week, so it couldn't have been him here. Her neighbors state that they haven't seen her this week, but the guy they're talking to now seems to know something." I pointed to a young, tanned, brown-haired guy who looked like a fitness buff. The police were talking to him at the moment and taking notes on what he was saying. They had been speaking to him for quite some time.

24_PAIGE_BREAKING NEWS

It took a couple of days but I knew my girl would come through for me. What I hadn't counted on was the mental state of a psychotic, sex-crazed idiot. When the police first knocked at our door, David had assumed it was Naomi again. He had unlocked the handcuffs and dragged me from the bed back to the door. Hand on the door, he reminded me that I needed to get rid of her, or that was the end of the road for both her and me. Terrified that he would hold true to his promise, I took just a moment to calm my nerves. It must have been a moment too long, because the next knock was one that resounded throughout the townhome, followed up by the announcement, "Police!"

One part of me was excited, and the other part of me was frightened out of my mind. I had no clue what would happen next. I didn't have to wait long to find out. David instantly half-dragged and half-pulled me back into the bedroom and threw me onto the bed. He didn't want to give me a chance to alert them as to what was going on behind closed doors.

He paced back and forth, alternating pointing the gun at me and turning it back on himself. He muttered threats about how he would kill both me and him before he allowed them to take him.

What seemed like hours later, but was in reality about fifteen minutes, he turned on the TV to the six o'clock news. We were the breaking story of the day. I saw the police cars outside and the cordoned-off area around my building. And then I saw a sight that encouraged me. Beyond the police barrier, I saw what appeared to be Naomi and my mother with, I couldn't believe my eyes…it was Vic and Rodney.

I couldn't see anything within the cordoned-off area. Whatever activity the police were taking was hidden from the cameras' views. I was thankful for that reprieve, because if I could see it, then I knew David could as well.

"You wanna know who the black man's number one enemies are? Huh? Huh?" His voice rose to a shout after I failed to answer immediately.

Too scared to formulate words, I shook my head in the affirmative.

"The police and the black woman! That's who! All y'all want is our demise. Y'all look down on us and then you play right into the white man's hands to help him put a foot on our neck! Black queens, my ass! More like a black mamba! Yeah, that's it. You get your deadly fangs in us and seep your venomous lies in. All the while, we're dying. You steal our hopes and our dreams. You take away our purpose and belief in ourselves. You fill up our world, suffocating the life out of us. You spit out your lies, making us believe we mean the world to you. All the while, you running around telling somebody else them same damn lies. We give you our hearts and then you rip 'em out our chest and stomp them on the ground. You crush them and grind your heel in until our hearts become like ash! Then you turn around and look down on us like we ain't shit! Every one of y'all asses need to die!"

Suddenly, he turned the gun back at me and raced towards me, causing me to cringe. Grabbing me around the neck, he pushed the gun hard underneath my jaw. I felt my top and bottom teeth clang together, and I bit my tongue again. I muffled the cry that threatened to spill forth of its own accord. Tears were burning my eyes, and my nose was stinging as well.

"Shut up, bitch! Give me one reason why you shouldn't die. Just one. And it better be good, or you might as well say goodnight!" he screamed at me.

I began to think of numerous reasons I shouldn't die. I began to reflect on what he had just spoken to me. The sad part about it is that what he said was true. I knew that I was guilty of all that. Many women were. We would stand by a man's side until he did the first thing to hurt or disappoint us, then we'd turn our backs and erect a wall to protect ourselves. And all the while, our hearts were continuing to become hardened at every mistake he made. We did it for self-preservation, but we failed to see the impact it had on the men's lives. Why? It was a vicious cycle that had been around since slavery. We were taught to break our men down and honor everything and everyone else above him. It would ruin our families for generations to come. We did it unknowingly. It was that famous syndrome that had been instilled in our ancestors, and it was no more prevalent than here in the south. What was it? The Willie Lynch mentality. Did that mean we deserved abuse or death? Hell, no!

That was why I had to fight this psycho with every breath in my body. I actually pitied him, but I loved my life more. For the first time ever, I realized not only did I want to live, but I had a reason to live. I would spend the rest of my days strengthening our young women to believe in themselves, believe in our race, and support our brothers in their hopes and dreams.

Just then, the house phone rang. David's rapid breathing and the inflating and deflating of his chest made him appear as if he were struggling to breathe, as he looked between the phone and me. The caller ID showed unknown on the screen, but we both knew the police were on the other line.

David took his time thinking it through and finally grabbed it up before it went to voicemail.

"What?" he shouted into the phone, as he punched the speakerphone button at the same time.

A deep, gravelly, yet soothing voice came over the line. "This is Sergeant Avery Whitaker of the Metropolitan Police Department Crisis Unit. I'm here to listen to you and make sure that you two remain safe," he stated, in a voice so calm I almost forgot the situation that I was in. "Mr. Wellstream, can I call you David? Or do you prefer to be called by another name?" the Sergeant asked.

"What the fuck? It don't even matter for! You don't know me, man!" David shouted into the phone, with spittle flying from his mouth.

I could only hope the man didn't try placating him, because it would only rile him up further.

"You're right, Mr. Wellstream. I don't know you, but I do want to hear about your concerns. Are you okay? Are you injured? Does anyone in there need medical assistance?" Sergeant Whitaker asked.

"Don't play me like you give a damn about me. Don't nobody give a damn about me! But I ain't hurt nobody, at least not yet. But y'all keep fucking with me, and I'ma fuck somebody up!" David screamed, walking further from the phone.

"Mr. Wellstream, right now a hostage has been taken. Nobody's been hurt. Although you're holding Miss Dougherty, all kinds of things can happen in a panic situation. Yet, you've done a good job of keeping things calm and under control so far. That means a lot, and everybody here knows that. Let's try to keep things peaceful so we can all emerge from this safely, okay?" Sergeant Whitaker requested.

"I tell you what, I'll tell you whether we keep this thing safe or not. Okay? I'm the one calling the motherfucking shots, not you! You hear me?" David asked, walking in circles, eyeing the phone in anger.

I could feel the anxiety and fury radiating from him like heat pouring from vents.

"I hear you, Mr. Wellstream. I do hear you. I want to try to do everything that I can to assist you. But I can only do that if you help me," Sergeant Whitaker explained.

"Help you? Help you? What the hell makes you think I'm gon' help you? I tell you what…figure out how you can help this bitch!" David shouted, turning the gun on me. He punched the loudspeaker button on the phone and then slammed the receiver on the hook.

"Look at this shit! You did this! Why couldn't we just live our lives together, Paige? All I ever wanted was to love you. I would've left my wife for you. But no, you couldn't stay away from the other men. Did you know I got fired a couple weeks ago? Huh? Did you even care? Yeah, that's what I thought!" he screamed, pushing the barrel of the gun against my forehead.

Hot tears were rolling down my face, and I was suffocating. It felt as if my airwaves were clogging as I hiccupped, trying to get air into my chest. I was more scared for my life than I had been at any point prior to this. Before, I felt as if I had a chance at escape by using sexual means. Now that the police were involved, David's actions were more sporadic and unpredictable. Now knowing that he had not only lost his wife, but his job as well, I realized that he felt he had nothing to live for. And if he had no reason to continue living, then he had no reason to spare my life.

"The hell you crying for?" he asked, moving the barrel from my forehead down underneath my jaw. He pressed it hard, to the point I felt my teeth clanking against one another and bit my tongue once again.

I tried to gather some compassion inside. I needed everything on my side to make him feel as if I were concerned about him. Especially if it would save my life.

"I…I…I…d-d-didn't know you l-l-l-lost your job," I stammered.

"You don't give a damn about me losing my job!" he screamed, slapping me with the back of his left hand.

I fell off of the bed. He kneeled down next to me and moved the gun along the side of my temple and down my jaw. The gun slowly made a sickening trail down my body until it rested between my thighs. Using the barrel, he forced my legs open and stuck the gun inside of my panties, pressing hard against my vulva. My stomach clenched in knots, and I felt so sick, I began vomiting all over the place.

"Damn! Look at you! What's wrong with you, girl?" he shouted at me, yanking me from the floor by my arm.

He pushed me in front of him until we reached the bathroom. "Get in the tub and wash yourself!" he shouted with a look of disgust, pointing my gun at me.

I sat down in the tub as he turned on the water, first scalding hot, and then he adjusted the temperature.

The phone began ringing again, and he looked uncertain about what to do. He had brought the cordless phone into the bathroom with us. Glancing around from side to side, he clicked it on as he leaned against the counter watching me.

This time, he didn't turn it on speakerphone. I watched him nodding his head before breaking out into maniacal laughter. Then he became silent and listened for a few moments more.

"Fuck that!" he shouted into the phone before clicking it off.

He looked back over at me as if trying to remember something. "Where was I?" he asked, as if we had been discussing the weather. "Oh, yeah, I lost my job over you," he said in a much calmer voice.

Scared to say anything to him that might rile him up once again, I looked at him with what I'm sure was a spooked look. I wondered what the police had said on the phone, but didn't dare ask him.

"All I been doing is living, sleeping, and breathing you. I couldn't focus at work, because I was wondering what you was doing and who you was doing it with. Next thing you know, I'm coming in late to work, because I'm trying to see what you're doing and where you're going. Then I stopped coming in altogether. Calling off work sick. I was sick…I couldn't eat, because I knew you was with another nigga."

He was sick, all right, but not in the way he had stated. I couldn't believe he had been stalking me all this time. I wondered how long this had been going on. I was scared at first, worrying I had spoken aloud, because he answered that exact question.

"Oh, I been doing it for about two months. When you started being too busy for me and letting me only come around once a week, I had to figure out why you was so busy. The first time I followed you and you went to some dude house out in Conyers, I left it alone, figured we'd talk about it."

He was referring to Vic. That's where he lived.

"Then, when I came to talk to you about it one night, I seen some other dude coming up in here. I was walking behind him. Had just gotten here the same time he did. I didn't think nothing about it until he reached your door first. I walked on past and pretended like I was going somewhere else. After a couple of hours, he came out and left. I had been sitting on the stairs watching. Next thing you know, I was following you around on a regular basis. I pretty much knew your schedule. Then I started missing work and getting my pay docked. Over the last couple of weeks, I couldn't take no more. I wasn't even calling out sick. That's when they fired me. I been sitting in the parking lot of your job waiting for you to leave and following you around all day long. I sit outside your apartment all night long. And you just let men use you. You got no self-respect! Let any and everything up in you, and you don't know nothing 'bout half of 'em. Trifling ass ho'!" He was staring at the floor, almost as if he were in a trance.

I was sitting in the tub, soaping my body up, thinking about everything he was saying. It was so scary that I had been followed like that and never had a clue. I was living my life in a reckless manner in more ways than one. The words he spoke, though hurtful, were so true.

I had always justified my behavior by stating that I wasn't going to let anyone hurt me. Truth? I was hurting myself worse than any man ever could.

But just as I had gotten my reality check, it was time for him to get a dose of reality, as well.

"But you were married, David. You were doing me the same way everyone else was. You didn't want me like that. Every night that you left me, you were going back home to a wife and kids. A wife, David! You're stalking me and acting like you're all about me, but you have a wife, David!" I let that sit and simmer with him for a moment.

He actually looked up at me as if he couldn't believe I had said that.

"Right now, you're acting like you're all about me, but you weren't." I rasped through my sore throat. I was emotionally and physically exhausted. I could feel that my eyes were swollen, and I knew that my nose was probably red.

He continued staring at me as if he could see right through me.

"I mean, at the end of the day, you didn't respect me like that. David, you used my body and treated it like your toy. And then, when I treated myself like that, you want to get mad? Realistically, I didn't know you felt like that about me. All I knew was at the end of every night you spent with me, you went back to that woman. I was left here alone to figure out how to live my life. David, you don't even know me like that. When you seriously think about it, what do you know about me? Think of all the things that matter to your wife, what makes her laugh and what makes her smile. What are her fears, hopes, and dreams?" I paused for a moment and saw a smile coming across his face.

"Now think about me, David. Can you answer those same questions about me? You weren't committed to me. You were committed to and in love with the idea of what I represented for you…your own personal toy, nothing more and nothing less."

Just as easily as the smile came across his face like the sun on a cloudy day, those storm clouds soon came back. I watched his features darken once more as he thought about all I had said.

I reached for a towel on the rack near the tub and wrapped it around my body. Stepping from the tub, I carefully dried myself off as I watched him. I didn't want to do anything that would appear threatening and cause him to shoot me.

He looked up at me from where he had been staring as if he had forgotten I had been there.

After I finished toweling off, I reached for my robe and began wrapping it around my body. The phone began ringing once more.

I looked at David to see what he would do, and his red-rimmed gaze met mine.

Pointing the gun at the bathroom door, he looked at me, and said, "Get outta here, Paige."

I hesitated for a brief moment, not sure what he meant.

"Go!" he shouted.

I ran to the front of the apartment like my life depended on it, because it did. I slowly opened the front door and walked out with my hands in the air.

STAY TUNED FOR THE SEQUEL: A WOMAN'S DESIGN: REDEMPTION

My head was tossed back in passion as my body shivered all the way down to my toes. What was this man doing to me? I knew when I first met him that he would have the power to do things to my body I could never imagine before being with him. His large, massive, dark hands encircled my waist and held me tight as I bucked, sliding up and down as if he were the pole and I was his own private dancer.

"Ambi, girl, work it. Work it, my mocha princess," he called out to me. When he said that, I couldn't help but look down at the point where our bodies connected. My cool, brown skin looked perfect against his dark, chocolate rippled muscles. I lowered my head as I looked into his dark eyes. They were so beautiful, and I found myself getting lost in them. I needed to taste him. I pushed plump, red lips against his full, dark-brown ones. He slowly opened his mouth and snaked his tongue inside of mine. His kisses were sweet and tangy, his breath warm and smooth.

Nick flipped me onto my back and scooted towards the edge of the bed. He lowered his head and did things to me that my husband wouldn't dare. He had me gripping the sheets tightly between my fists as I arched my back, allowing my core to meet his mouth. I felt the volcano erupting over and over into his mouth. I screamed his name out again and again. It didn't stop him from lavishing his loving kisses on my honey nectar. When he finally finished, he stood up and entered me. He pushed my hair, which I had allowed to grow long over the last four months, away from my face, spreading it on the pillow.

"Open your eyes. Look at me. I want you to know who's making you feel like this. I don't ever want you to mistake me for another, you hear me?" His slanted eyes turned into little slits.

"Yeeesss," I cried out in passion. He took one large hand and covered my breasts. And let me tell you, these girls are not small. He rubbed them back and forth in circles and then massaged one at a time. My nipples began pulling towards his mouth, begging for just one little lick. His eyes lit up, and he continued to play with them before finally giving in to my need.

Pulling his mouth back up, he once again claimed my mouth in his. His tongue searched and made love to my tongue the way it had just made love to my core. Yes! He was a man who went down, and did it well.

"Ambi…I want you to be with me. I'll do everything he hasn't done. You deserve to be treated like royalty. You're so beautiful, so fine and sexy. And you're such a strong, passionate woman. Whatever you want, or need, don't be afraid to ask me. Do you hear me?" he asked.

"Yeah, Nick. I hear you, baby." Ohhh he was making me feel so good from my head to my toes. My body would be sore, and red bruises would surely pop up in the morning. Everywhere he had kissed my light skin would show the markings of the whiskers he was growing out on his face. They felt good and rugged right now, but they were sure to punish me come the morning light. I hadn't felt this good in such a long time.

"Ambi…baby, you're involved now. Very much so," he said, looking at me with those sexy eyes. I was so tired, all I wanted was to drift to sleep in his arms.

"Ambi! Ambi!" the voice called through the darkness.

I felt a rough hand shaking me, and my eyes popped open. "Hmm?" I moaned, closing my eyes rapidly against the morning sun slanting through the curtains.

"Who the hell is, Nick?" Denver asked, frowning at me through the haze.

"Huh?" I asked, turning to bury my face in the pillow again. I wanted to go back to sleep and finish my dream.

"I said, who the hell is Nick?" Denver growled.

"I don't know. Why you asking me?" my muffled voice came through the pillow.

"Cuz. You called him baby just after you were moaning and groaning like you were having sex or something. So, you got something you want to tell me?" Denver asked, pulling the sheets from my shoulders as he disentangled his legs from mine.

Denver? Oh, yeah, did I forget to mention he was my boyfriend of six months?

Hello Reader,

If you enjoyed A Woman's Design: Afflictions, I invite you to share your review on Amazon and Goodreads, and spread the word amongst your family and friends. I appreciate your support and the time that you took to read this novel. My prayer is that you were inspired to pursue your own journey of self-discovery and know that whatever you find, there is beauty on the other side when you learn to love yourself.

If you connected with any of the characters in this book or their situations, I hope that you understand when adversity comes, if you believe in yourself and have faith, you, too, can rise above your adversity or limitations. I want you to come back for the sequel, A Woman's Design: Redemption, to learn what happens to Ambience, Naomi, and Paige.

If you took the time to write a review, please email me at chelleramseywrites@gmail.com and I will reply to your email. Once again, thank you for your time and your support.

Submit your reviews here: http://bit.ly/

Be Blessed,

Yours in Love,

Chelle Ramsey

ABOUT THE AUTHOR

CHELLE RAMSEY:

Writing has always been an outlet of expression for Chelle, as well as a way to relax and escape daily stress. Her love of reading fiction books that have the power to take you to another world, led to a desire to create that opportunity for others.

Chelle began writing stories at the age of 12 for the sole purpose of her entertainment. However, her then future husband, Marvin, would bring to her attention that she had a gift of entertaining readers with her imagination. He encouraged her to publish her works, but she was not convinced. In 2011 at the urging of her husband, she shared one of her finished works with her book club under a pseudonym. When the reviews came back and they discovered she had written it, she was further encouraged to pursue publishing her works. Finally gathering the courage to do so, she published her first book Reflections of Promises in June 2012, later to be followed by Real Secrets in December 2012.

All of her books outline how average people face struggles, but with faith and perseverance people can have hope they will rise above their limitations, and prevail.

Chelle Ramsey earned her MBA with a concentration in Human Resources Management at the University of Phoenix. A wife and mother of four, Chelle enjoys writing, reading fiction stories, hosting book club events, watching the NBA, and spending time with her family. She enjoys the works of James Patterson, Stuart Woods, Terri McMillan, Nora Roberts, and many indie authors.

For more information on other works or upcoming releases visit:

Website: www.chelleramsey.com

Email: chelleramseywrites@gmail.com

Facebook: facebook.com/AuthorChelleRamsey

Instagram: chelleramseybooks

Twitter: twitter.com/ ChellesBooks

Pinterest: https://www.pinterest.com/ChellesBooks/

Made in the USA
Columbia, SC
06 October 2017